OFF THE BEATEN PATH

A STEVE CASSIDY MYSTERY

To Steve,

"Choose your true path!"

ALSO BY JOHN SCHLARBAUM

The Doctor's Bag
A Sentimental Journey

Aging Gracefully Together
A Story of Love & Marriage

Barry Jones' Cold Dinner
A Steve Cassidy Mystery

When Angels Fail To Fly
A Steve Cassidy Mystery

A Memorable Murder
A Jennifer Malone Mystery

OFF THE BEATEN PATH

A STEVE CASSIDY MYSTERY

SCANNER PUBLISHING

WINDSOR, ONTARIO, CANADA
COPYRIGHT 2013 BY JOHN SCHLARBAUM

This novel is a work of fiction. Names, characters, places and incidents are either the product of the author's imagination or are used fictitiously. Any resemblance to actual or locales or persons, living or dead, is entirely coincidental.

Library and Archives Canada Cataloguing in Publication

Schlarbaum, John, 1966-, author
Off the beaten path / by John Schlarbaum

ISBN 978-0-9738498-6-8 (pbk.)

I. Title. II. Series: Schlarbaum, John, 1966- . Steve Cassidy mystery.

PS8637.C448O34 2013   C813'.6   C2013-904442-6

SCANNER PUBLISHING
5060 Tecumseh Road East, Suite #1106
Windsor, Ontario, Canada N8T 1C1

Cover design: Hawksworth Designs © 2013
www.hawksworthdesigns.com

Printed in Canada

MIX
Paper from
responsible sources
FSC® C107923

Acknowledgements

I would like to thank those who helped shape this novel from its lump of clay beginnings to its fully sculpted final draft. Your opinions and ideas have made this book better on each and every page.

Special thanks to the following individuals who took the time to go above and beyond what was asked of them: Dorothy Schlarbaum, Jennifer Thorne, Jennifer MacLeod, Jessica Jarvis, Tina Bezaire, Julie Deslippe, Jessica Pedlar, Kevin Jarvis, Lori Farmer and Jennifer Hawksworth.

Last but definitely not least, I would like to single out Joe Monteleone for his support and making my previous novel *A Memorable Murder* a reality.

John Schlarbaum
September, 2013

For Lori

"Where do I go? What do I do?"

Thank you for always aiming
me toward the right path.

ONE

There are few things more depressing than walking through a maze of dirty city streets at 3:00 a.m. seeking a hooker with a heart of gold.

Been there, won that stuffed teddy bear.

Yet here I am on a random Wednesday doing just that.

Before you jump to the easy conclusion that I've again fallen on hard times and am looking for love in all the wrong places, let me calm your frayed nerves: I'm working a file.

That's my story and I'm sticking to it.

Marital cases and I have a long and troubled past. They are the worst type of investigations for a number of reasons, most notably the fact that information provided by the distraught client is usually wrong. For example, the subject almost always leaves at a different time than the one given, be it from work, a buddy's house, the ex's apartment after visiting the kids and so forth. Then there's the matter of how much time these files can suck out of one's life. There's a television program that specializes in this entertaining field and it kills me when the creepy host proudly states, *"On Day 9 our investigator locates the target's vehicle parked in a visitor's spot near a friendly female acquaintance's townhouse."*

Are they serious? If I don't get results by Day 3, my head is on the chopping block.

Day 9. As if.

My current case has the added element of the potential cheater carrying on a disjointed conversation in his sleep with a

1

prostitute named Mary. Or Kerry. Or Sherri. Apparently this dolt snorted or snored at an inopportune time and the exact name couldn't be rendered. The second strange aspect of this file is the wife's claim that hubby handed over a gold heart charm hanging from a necklace. More specifically, *her* necklace.

"I'm certain he mumbled something about 'a down payment' and 'tonight at The Cougar Trap.' That can only mean that disgusting Drake Road area in the east end, right?" She paused before adding, "And believe me, I've searched everywhere and my necklace is gone!"

I examined my early thirties average everything (height, weight, looks) client and had to make a swift assessment. Should I throw her out due to such flimsy evidence or break it to her that if loverboy was making plans anywhere near The Cougar Trap, her marriage was probably already over?

Decisions, decisions, decisions.

"I'll do what I can," I stated, making sure to get her money up front, a business practice private investigators and hookers share, among other seamy traits.

The fact that my girlfriend and I were heading out on a mini-vacation in three days probably played a role in how I answered. A little extra spending cash would come in handy.

And really, how hard could it be to locate a phantom lady of the evening wearing a gold heart charm inscribed "I Luv U" and working mid-week in the roughest area of town?

Wednesday: Hump Day. Sounds about right.

***

"Hey honey, if you're lookin' for some action you came to the wrong side of the street."

"And how's that?" I asked skeptically, approaching an over-the-hill streetwalker. She was quite the vision with her garish make-up, matted mop of brown hair and Daisy Duke short shorts with fishnet stockings, topped off with a stole over her shoulders made of a mink needlessly killed circa 1972. "Let me guess - you're celibate?"

She shook her head and smiled, revealing gaps in her upper and lower rows of teeth. "Oh no, not this girl. I proudly sell-a-bit here, sell-a-bit there, sell-a-bit anywhere you'd like, sweetie," she laughed.

Given her outlandishly sad appearance, her laugh wasn't an unpleasant sound, which caught me off guard, although it really shouldn't have. After all, she was a human being with real emotions, once an innocent little girl and the glimmer of sunshine in her parents' eyes. Certain personal characteristics can't be beaten out of you, regardless of how hard someone (drunken Daddy, pimp, abusive boyfriend) tries.

"Then why am I on the wrong side of the street?"

"Because my dance card is full. I'm just waiting for a taxi to arrive."

I slowly glanced down the infamous Drake Road and noted we were the only people out at this time of night: no other pedestrians, no barflies stumbling out of the fabled Dark Stallion or Mickey's Den watering holes, and not a car in sight. It was eerily quiet, too.

"Believe it or not, I wasn't aiming to hook up, but I am looking for one of your co-workers."

"To talk or just cuddle?" She stopped and gave me a cool look. "She's not your sister, is she?"

"Not that I'm aware of, although around here I suppose anything's possible." Headlights came into view a few blocks away. "Your name wouldn't happen to be Mary or something similar sounding, would it?"

"For a price it could be," my near-toothless wonder replied.

Always the businesswoman, I thought.

"Are there any other girls in the immediate vicinity with such a pretty name?" I inquired as I lifted $20 out of my wallet. "I see you as the unofficial Den Mother down here and I want you to know your acquaintance, if she exists, is not in any trouble."

"Whenever a cop–"

"Ex-cop."

"Whatever. I'm just sayin' anytime the *likes of you* comes a-lookin', someone is in trouble." My colourful new best gal pal took the money when her taxi pulled up to the curb. "There's a fire escape at the back of The Cougar Trap that leads to a second floor apartment. You might want to start searchin' there."

I followed her gaze across the boulevard and noted the fire escape bathed in blue neon from the building's gaudy wraparound flashing sign.

"Can I use you as a reference?"

"Sure thing, babycakes. Tell the twins Truffle Divine says you're okay."

The taxi sped away before I could thank my helpful guide but not before I confirmed my client's lost necklace wasn't part of this evening's costume drama.

Knowing that being out alone in this neighbourhood was frowned upon by the police and county coroner, I began to briskly walk to my next and possibly final destination. Unlike many of my P.I. associates, I don't carry a gun, brass knuckles, nunchucks or pepper spray. I figure if I can't talk my way out of a situation and am overpowered, these same weapons could easily be used on me, which would be a real shame in my humble opinion.

"What do I have to lose except my life?" I asked myself aloud as I crossed the street.

***

I cautiously approached The Cougar Trap, a recent addition to *The Strip* that was known for its seedy nightlife, regardless of the actual time of day. Catering to a specific clientele, it's a unique enterprise that isn't a peeler bar, a restaurant or a swinger's club, yet magically combines aspects of all three.

As for its name, in the late 1960s a "cougar" was easy to spot. She was Mrs. Robinson, the horny older housewife in the classic film *The Graduate*, who seduced the son of her husband's business partner. More recently, the ultimate cougar is Stifler's divorced mom in the *American Pie* movie series. These days, the definition is a grab-bag term for any unattached woman over 30, usually with a kid or two in tow, who enjoys reliving her golden high school years in the company of younger men.

Climbing the fire escape, I noted two surveillance cameras mounted on the roof; one aimed at the stairs and the other trained on the upper back door. Recalling my science teacher's assertion that for every action there's a reaction, I flashed a big stupid grin, waved at both cameras and mouthed, "Hey dude, what's up?" As if on cue, the stair cam slowly panned upward as its lens zoomed in on my face. Finding no wall buzzer, I gently knocked on the door and waited, knowing that Spielberg and company would eventually make contact.

"What's your business, pal?" a woman asked in a loud, although friendly, tone.

I haven't been called *pal* since my father passed away during my last few months of high school. Then again, I just called her *dude*, so I guess we're even on that count.

"I'm searching for a necklace."

"Does this look like the jewelry counter at Walmart?"

"No, it doesn't," I replied nonchalantly, before quietly saying, "Mary," under my breath.

There was no immediate quip this time. Only silence for several entertaining moments, as I smiled for the cameras.

"What did you say?"

"Oh, that I agreed this didn't appear to be a Walmart location."

"After that." Getting no answer, my hidden mystery woman asked the obvious. "Did you call me Mary?"

"Maybe, I guess," I responded, playing dumb, another trick

private investigators have in common with hookers. "Is she your sister?"

"Excuse me?"

"I was thinking that maybe you were Mary's twin."

Without warning, the heavy metal door was flung open and I was warmly greeted by the barrel of a Dirty Harry-type gun targeting my forehead and then my crotch area. My police training kicked in and I calmly stood my ground, making no sudden movements. My gaze confirmed that the gun's hammer was cocked in the "let's party" position, before settling on my aggressor's beautiful eyes, which were darting around like two pinballs. Her overall features suggested a sense of impending *Game Over* doom.

"Hi, I'm Steve. What's your name?" I asked, figuring the direct approach was my best bet. While she was forming a response, it allowed my eyes to pull back a bit to get a clearer picture of what I was up against.

A crazed woman with the knowledge of firearms? A look of determination that cautioned me against pouring on the old Steve magic? A cute, blonde college student wearing a t-shirt that barely covered two enormous beach balls set upon her chest? Check, check and check.

"Wow," I managed to say, momentarily forgetting the danger I appeared to be in. "When Truffle mentioned 'the twins' I was thinking, you know, twin-twins. The ones who dress the same and cause all sorts of trouble on sitcoms." This comparison was met with a stare that conveyed, *What is wrong with you?* "Not that I think those aren't identical in their own special way, mind you," I added, not wanting her to think I was some weirdo.

"Are you done?"

Never good with rhetorical questions, I answered, "I think so."

"How do you know Truffle? Are you one of her customers?"

I saw the anger behind her eyes slowly replaced with bewilderment.

"Again, wow," I said shaking my head. "Even dressed in these old clothes, do I really strike you as the kind who'd pony-up cold hard cash for a whirl on that depressing carnival ride?"

It was now her turn to step back and take me all in, as it were. A few years past my thirtieth birthday, I attempt to keep my five-ten, one-hundred-seventy pound frame in a shape other than round. Although not vain enough to call myself handsome, I have no problem when the ladies do. I'm clean-shaven with collar-length brown hair and dark brown eyes, to which my armed appraiser continued to gravitate.

"You didn't answer my question," she stated, standing her ground.

"You see, the truth is, the lovely and I'm sure talented, Ms. Divine gave you up for $20. And before you ask, no bodily fluids were exchanged during our brief encounter." A flash of annoyance returned to my not-quite-friend's face. "If it makes you feel better, she would've taken $5 if that was all I had. Unfortunately, banking machines no longer spit those out."

Charm is a funny thing. Too much, too soon and you look like a creep. Too little, too late, you look desperate and go home by yourself. However, my slow and steady approach usually pays dividends. Behind her tough exterior and the cannon she was now gripping with both hands, I felt my first impression was correct: a young girl paying her way through school the hard way.

"Can we talk without the gun being part of our conversation? I promise this won't take long and I'll remain way over here by the railing," I offered as I took several steps back, coming to rest against the wall at the top of stairs. "Is your name really Mary?"

"It's Terri," she relented, lowering the gun to her side. "I don't know anyone here named Mary, although I only arrived in town on Monday."

"What about a guy named Ryan? Do you have one of those on your speed-dial?"

"Nope."

I reached into my pocket and retrieved a snapshot of my client's husband. "Does this face ring any bells?"

Terri looked intently at the photo and shrugged her shoulders. "He might have been in the audience for my show but in the dark they all sorta look the same. I know I didn't give him a private dance or anything like that."

This was going nowhere fast. "Do you wear any necklaces?"

"We're back to that again?" she asked exasperated. "The answer is no. I don't have your stupid necklace."

"A gold charm in the shape of a heart, maybe?"

"And we're done. Can I go back to freshening up? I have a big spender coming to pick me up in 20 minutes."

I cocked my head in response. "A date, huh? And what would his name be?"

"If his name were Brian, not Ryan, would that be of any interest?"

"Maybe. Deviants often use a new name that sounds like their own, so they don't get confused if things go sideways."

"To be honest, I have no idea what his name is. All I know is he paid the owners up front. Maybe his last name is Money. Brian Money. That would be kinda funny, right?"

"Hilarious," I stated without emotion, putting the picture away and heading down to street level. "It was a pleasure to meet the three of you, Terri. Take care of yourself and that new boyfriend of yours."

At the base of the stairs, I heard rushed footfalls coming up the alley. *Poor bastard is probably paying by the minute and is worried he's late,* I thought. I stepped around the corner and figured I'd have a little fun to end my night. "She's all primed and ready for you, sailor," I said to the startled man who was now blocking my path.

Wearing a dark overcoat with the collar up and his hands in his pockets, he reminded me of a superhero looking for a place to change into his tights and cape. Yet on closer inspection, I knew this wasn't the case. Ryan Hartford was a mild-mannered accountant, with no visible abnormal super powers.

"What did you say?" Ryan asked nervously, not knowing if he should stop to chat or keep quiet and proceed to the second floor.

Ladies and gentlemen, welcome to amateur night at The Cougar Trap.

I ignored his question and asked one of my own. "Do you know you talk in your sleep? You'd make a really poor spy."

"W-w-w-hat?"

"And you're aware that necklace you are clutching in your pocket is ultimately going to contribute to your social, personal and professional failure, right?"

"Who are you and how do you know–"

"Everything? How do I know everything, Ryan Hartford? It's a gift. It's a curse. It's who I am, I suppose." My prey appeared to weeble then wobble but refused to fall down.

"Is this a robbery? I'll give you everything I have. Money. Credit cards."

"He wants the necklace and a heart of gold," a heavenly female voice from above shouted. "Just give him the damn thing and get up here now! I don't have all night."

Oh, how he wanted to run. To the untrained eye, this had all the earmarks of a classic set-up. Lure the naïve target into a dark alley with the promise of sex and then rob him blind. Ryan's eyes were wide with fear and his face turned a ghastly shade of oatmeal.

"Take it! Here!" he cried out, removing his left hand from his pocket and tossing something shiny over my head. As I involuntarily followed its trajectory, Ryan busted a move in the opposite direction, rounding the side of the building, out of view.

"Are you kidding me?" Terri screamed down over the fire escape railing. "You're going to be sorry you did that," she continued. "That's him. That's the guy who wanted to beat me up for a lousy $20!" she lied. "Well I'm not that kind of girl, Sicko Steve!"

Within seconds, a small army of very large bouncer-types were careening down the steps, racing to see which one could land the first deadly blow to my tender solar plexus.

Note to self: Comparison shop for nunchucks at the mall.

I snagged my prized booty off the ground and hightailed it out of the area with the sole aim of not becoming another unsolved murder statistic. My would-be welcoming committee were huge, muscular men, the kind who strike fear into the hearts of unruly club patrons. They weren't, however, very scary or athletic when challenged to a sprint. As I easily outdistanced them block by block, one by one, they ran out of stamina and were left gasping for precious air in the middle of Drake Road.

I found my van still intact in the well-lit lot of an all-night pizzeria where I'd left it earlier, knowing it might be useful to have some witnesses to relate exactly how I was killed. I believe it's easier on those left behind to know how their loved one's last breath was taken, regardless how grotesque the crime scene might be.

"A dead body is always better than no body," a homicide detective once told me.

Pulling off the lot, I checked my mirrors and blind spots for any incoming winded gorillas. None had survived the mini marathon. With this all-clear sign, I draped my client's necklace over the rearview mirror and admired the attached heart of gold charm. As it gently swung to and fro, streetlights and oncoming headlights illuminated it as if it were somehow alive.

"Another job well done," I stated to my smiling doppelganger in the mirror. "Your girlfriend better appreciate your effort tonight to help make this vacation one to remember."

I was soon home, quietly slipping into bed, trying not to disturb Dawn's slumber. Consciously or unconsciously, her mind instructed her body to gradually push against mine, allowing us to form the perfect spooning position.

"Are you okay?" she whispered sleepily.

"I am now," I said. "Night, you."

"Night, you too."

TWO

A quick rule of thumb for everyone involved in a serious relationship: trouble is looming when your partner begins to introduce you as their *insignificant other*. They'll say they were just joking and you need to lighten up but without a doubt, it's one of the first fiery shots across your heart's bow.

Trust me on this. I know things.

However, there are always exceptions to the rule, with Dawn being one of them.

The best part of our evolving courtship is we can pretty much say anything to the other knowing there's never malice behind the words, even when the literal definition sounds mean spirited. Maybe it's the age difference or my insecurity. I might overstep the boundaries of acceptable humour to make Dawn laugh, although it's only because I know she's smart enough to see how desperate this older man is to keep her around. Of course, that's enduring and pathetic at the same time - two qualities often attributed to me by the fairer sex. Why she remains with me is one mystery I don't intend to investigate. She could choose from a line-up of younger, wealthier and more debonair men than yours truly, yet every night she returns to my house. A real leave-with-the-one-that-brought-you type of girl, so far. This scenario suits me just fine. I could use some positive romantic energy after a lifetime of failed dalliances that included a marriage, one-night stands and long distance relationships. Then there was that short-lived engagement to a librarian, which ended when the female associate

I was having an affair with was killed during a botched martial investigation.

Sucks to be with me, right?

Dawn entered my life after I threw myself a drunken pity party at the local Sunsetter Pub & Eatery where she works as a waitress. When it comes to women, I don't have a type, per se. If I did, Dawn's killer smile, curvy small build and curly brown hair that rests easily on her shoulders would surely be checked off a "Steve's To Do" list.

We're an unlikely pair. I'm by no means a curmudgeon when it comes to trying something new; still, I don't go out of my way to find anything new to do either. For example, I have no issue with checking out a happening bar but only to drink, not to dance, karaoke or ride a mechanical bull for several nauseating seconds; three things Dawn loves to do. The same goes for house parties, no matter who is throwing it or what the reason. Mind you, working solo day in, day out, doesn't give me the opportunity to mingle with many people, or become friends with them. Dawn is in the complete opposite situation and takes full advantage of it when the occasion arises.

Tonight's social gathering invitation indicated a starting time of 8:00 p.m., which we figured was code for 10-10:30 p.m.

"It'll be fun. You'll meet a bunch of cool people," Dawn said as she checked her hair in the hall mirror.

"Says you," I said, pulling on my jacket. "The only person I'll know there is you."

"And Doug."

"Really? Doug, The Sunsetter's master short order cook? Why didn't you mention that before?" I asked with a grin. "Maybe if we get bored, he can whip us up a burger or wings."

Dawn zipped up the side of her knee-high boots and walked past me to the front door. "If we get bored, I can assure you Doug won't be whipping you in any way. Me, on the other hand . . . "

I turned and gently pushed her up against the wall to give

her a kiss, which she generously returned. "Promise about that whipping part?"

"To clarify," she began, looking up at me, "I was talking about the white fluffy stuff you put on dessert."

"Yeah, sure. You. Me. Dessert topping. That's what I was talking about too."

"Uh-huh."

***

It was 10:15 when we arrived at a very nice two storey house, set comfortably in a section of Darrien that the mid-1980's yuppies had claimed for their own.

"Remind me again why this stockbroker invited us to his soirée?" I inquired as we walked up the driveway.

"I don't know. During the week he'd come in for lunch with a few buddies, then one day he started coming in by himself. I thought it was odd, so I asked him about it and one thing led to another."

"How exactly did one thing lead to another?"

"You know, this party invitation."

"So, he wasn't one of the lucky few you slept with before we became exclusive?"

"I like it when you show your jealous side, but sadly no," Dawn replied with a warm smile. "I don't think his wife would have gone for that."

"One look at how cute you are and she might have changed her mind or even joined in. Did you think of that?"

"I suppose I could ask her tonight."

"I suppose you could."

The door was opened by a slim woman in her late forties, who exuded the confidence and charm I assumed she'd been trained to fake from an early age. "Hello, please come in. I'm Patricia Wallace."

14

"Thank you. I'm Dawn and this is my insignificant other, Steve Cassidy."

Our hostess glanced at me with a mildly shocked expression while extending her hand, which I took. "It's very nice to meet both of you. Daniel has spoken about you often, Dawn. He's a stickler for good service and thinks you're one of the best waitresses he's ever had."

"We appreciate his business, especially after the firm let those brokers go last month," Dawn said.

"These are tough times," Mrs. Wallace replied shaking her head. "Actually, a few of those who were laid off are here tonight. You might recognize them, even without their business suits on." She paused and took in Dawn's smoking hot outfit and boots, before adding, "I'm sure they'll recognize you in any case."

Zing! Pow! Wham!

Ladies and gentlemen, please give it up for the comic stylings of Patricia Wallace!

We hung our coats in the foyer closet and were escorted into the living room to be introduced to the assembled crowd, many of whom were already showing visible signs of motor skill impairment.

"Dawn and Steve, everyone. Everyone, Dawn and Steve."

There was a smattering of slurred "Hello-Hey-Hi" greetings, possibly even some applause, before backs were again turned on us.

"With that taken care of, would you like me to open that for you, dear?" Mrs. Wallace asked, pointing to Dawn's bottle of white wine.

"Actually this is a gift for tonight's invite," Dawn replied cheerfully. "It's from a local winery. I like to support area businesses."

As a keen observer of people, I'm pretty good at determining the meaning, hidden or otherwise, behind a person's body language. The way Mrs. Wallace's nose crinkled ever so slightly, combined with the downturn, then quick phony smile upturn of her lips was bad enough, without her adding a barely noticeable stagger backwards for good measure.

Now you're just showing off, I thought defensively.

"The wine is very generous, but please let's share it."

After pouring a glass for Dawn in the kitchen, our wholly unimpressed lady of the house left her glass empty, making the excuse someone in the other room had called her name. Once out of earshot, Dawn raised her wine to my now Jack Daniels-filled tumbler and noted, "She has very good hearing or—"

"Is a first class snob," I offered, finishing her thought.

"Exactly."

We toasted each other and after downing a large amount of whiskey, I thought the evening could turn out to be an entertaining one after all.

Our first decision was which one of the stereotypical party cliques to initially crash. Maybe the rich, established crowd that included our hosts? Or what about the sad sack, newly unemployed barely graduates, discussing strategies for dealing with their current midlife crisis? As these whiners were all male, it allowed, or forced their female partners and one metrosexual male to form their own separate splinter group. We were still debating our next move when Doug sauntered away from a throng of three couples, none of which, surprisingly, looked particularly well off, distressed or neurotic.

Just what kind of party is this exactly?

Doug had been at The Sunsetter for a few years, working his way from dishwasher to cook in a relatively short time. He was in his late twenties, average looking and with a sense of humour that is an acquired taste. Always in a happy mood, Dawn enjoyed working with him and that was good enough for me.

"Hey guys," Doug said, before bending forward for an obligatory hug from Dawn. I raised my drink to my lips and held out my other hand, which he fist pumped for some reason. "You two look lost."

"That's because we don't know anyone here," Dawn replied, "aside from you and Mr. Wallace. I feel like we're crashing a wedding reception."

"I'm in the same boat. Daniel . . . ah, Mr. Wallace . . . just said 'the more the merrier' and gave me his address, although I don't think his wife is too pleased."

"Shocker," I interjected, sharing a knowing smile with Dawn. "We think she's against local businesses, which regrettably includes the good old Sunsetter. From an earlier experience, I don't think she's accustomed to socializing with the help."

"The help, huh?" Dawn said. "Look at us with a title all our own, Doug. I kinda like it, even if others here don't." She raised her glass. "To the help!"

"The help!" Doug and I joined in, much to the consternation of the nearby whiners.

"Are you excited about your murder mystery tour this weekend?" Doug asked. "I'd think as a P.I. you would be, Steve."

"I'm sure visiting a bunch of locations where murders took place will be interesting in a touristy type of way, but when I was a cop I used to arrive at murder scenes, sometimes only minutes after someone was killed. Now *that* was exciting." I got the feeling more than just Dawn and Doug heard this statement, as a few guests turned their heads in our direction. Maybe I was speaking louder than I realized. I lowered my voice a notch and added, "I don't really care what we do. It'll be a nice relaxing getaway, no matter what."

"Will you actually be entering the murder scenes to examine them?" Doug asked Dawn.

"A few maybe," she answered, looking to me for confirmation. "For the most part, I think it's like a typical bus tour with some walking involved. Instead of seeing enormous churches, skyscrapers or historic landmarks, we'll visit houses, apartments and other places where a big time murder happened."

"Like those *Homes of the Stars* tours in California that point out Jennifer Love Hewitt's mansion or George Clooney's house," Doug said.

"Exactly," I chimed in. "Except instead of learning the length of Jennifer's pool or how many rooms she has, we'll get details about where a puddle of blood was discovered on the property and how it got there." Once again my words held some kind of fascination with these partying strangers. I caught the attention of one of the job-losers glaring at me. "What are you staring at?"

A look of *Who me?* registered on his face.

"Yeah, you," I said. "Do you need medical help? We can call 911 if you want."

This raised not only the intended's ire, but also Dawn's.

"Steve, what are you doing?"

"Don't worry, Dawn, I won't cause any trouble," I assured her. "I just overheard this unemployed bonehead talking about how unfair the world is, after the same world provided him a $2000 a week job for the past three years playing the market with other people's money. He rubbed me the wrong way. Unlike us, he obviously doesn't appreciate the value of a buck."

"Are you going to fight him?" Doug asked expectantly, a glimmer of bloodsport twinkling in his eyes.

"And hurt my knuckles? I don't think so."

As my opponent half-stumbled across the room, the groups seemed to break apart to form one bigger, yet still dispersed crowd. Had I picked on their de facto leader? It wouldn't have been the first time I'd messed with the wrong person and certainly wouldn't be my last. I pegged this tough guy to be about 28, not bad looking, an inch shorter than me, clean cut, wearing his casual Friday's khaki pants, Blue River designer shirt and surrounded by an aura of entitlement. You know the type, full of themselves until someone knocks them down a peg or two.

Let me demonstrate.

"Do I know you?"

"In what sense?" I answered indifferently.

"What is that supposed to mean?"

"Didn't they teach you any sense at that preppy business school you're bragging about? What's its name again? Cylinder, Solenoid?"

"The *Solinder* Institute of Finance is not preppy!" my adversary declared loudly, which brought a stop to any other conversations in the room. We were now the main event.

"Ah, yes, Solinder. The home of flipped up collars and wing-tips worn by trust fund daddy's boys, inexplicably named Kal or Regent, who go by equally inane nicknames like The Calculator or Righteous D. Bill." I paused to allow this information to soak in. "Nah, that doesn't sound preppy-like at all, Corwin."

A look of bewilderment dawned across my interrogator's features, as his red spidery veined eyes widened substantially. You'd have thought I'd produced an elephant out of thin air and laid it at his feet. Some audience members appeared impressed, or more likely, baffled by my seemingly inside information of Corwin Stewart Donovan Mulvoy. In truth I was simply regurgitating facts he'd been randomly spewing to others over the past half hour. Luckily, being drunk only disengaged his memory recall, not mine.

"I don't know who you think you are or how you know so much about me," Corwin began his defense. "Someone said you're a cop or an investigator. Is that true?"

"If someone said it, then it must be true."

Corwin awkwardly turned to his left, almost losing his balance to pronounce, "I'd like to introduce to you Mr. Sherlock Holmes, who knows everything about everybody!" He attempted a half bow in front of me. "Good day, sir," he said, invoking a wave of subdued laughter around the room. "I beg of you, please continue to wow us with your mental . . . and I emphasize the word *mental* . . . wizardry. Tell me something about him."

A shaky finger was pointed in the direction of a nebbish male sitting on the couch. A short time earlier, he'd stood near us and I'd overheard a few arbitrary facts, which I proceeded to recite with great flare, playing to my audience of one.

"The first thing you should know about Herman is he hates to be called Herm. It sounds too much like *germ* for his liking." My target straightened up. It was, to some extent, an educated guess with a name like that. I recalled my childhood friend Wayne hated being called Wayner, because it sounded like *wiener*. "Next, if you don't know already, the striking eyewear Herman sports are cosmetic fakes to make him appear smarter. The lenses are made of plain glass with no magnification whatsoever." As Herman began to fidget, anyone not fully engrossed by my cheap parlour act before, was now. Feeling bad, I said, "The funny thing is he's very smart, graduating at the top of his class. It's all of you who aren't very bright for not recognizing this yourselves. If I had a brokerage firm, Herman, I'd hire you in a minute, with or without your glasses."

"Enough of him!" Corwin bellowed, agitated I was showing him up in front of his colleagues and friends. "What about him?" he demanded, singling out another recent unemployment statistic.

My many years working the streets, bars and in Vice sting operations had prepared me well for this task. Without having overheard this man speak a word, I had to rely on the two things I'd noted during the evening: his physical appearance and his body language, especially when in close proximity to Corwin The Great.

"I'm sorry I don't know your name," I said to my next reluctant volunteer. "I'll call you Mr. X, okay?" He nodded in the affirmative. "Okay, so . . . it's quite apparent you and Corwin frequent the same clothing stores. Those slacks and shirt hang side-by-side on the display racks at uppity boutiques. Even Mr. X's fashionable $500 Prada shoes match yours, Corwin. Did you two share a springtime retail therapy session together?" This elicited some much deserved snickering and smiles all around. "His taste in clothes and the ability to pay for them would indicate he went to an overpriced snooty business school, Solinder perhaps, to learn how to be a financial mastermind, or as you like to crow, a broker. Unfortunately, the one thing they don't teach in class is how to deal with real-life failure, like when you lose your job and are still stuck with a BMW car payment for two more years."

As I drive a nondescript family mini-van for a living, I admire the occasional Beamer or Porsche I stumble upon parked on the street. Tonight, I had seen at least seven luxury sports cars and knew Corwin and Mr. X must have keys for a couple of them.

Corwin was at a loss. I had drained his bravado in a few short minutes. I concede that with my cop training this exercise in cold-reading really wasn't fair, but I didn't start this ball rolling - he did.

"It doesn't take a genius to figure out what Scott does for a living. Most everyone here is in the stock market," Corwin proclaimed in an effort to discredit my significant brilliance. "If you're so smart, tell me something I don't know, Holmes." He dragged out the syllables for effect: *H-o-l-m-e-s.*

"Steve, let it go," Dawn said softly, gently putting a hand on my arm.

"Yeah, Steve, let it go," Corwin repeated, again dragging out more syllables: *S-t-e-v-e.*

I looked at Dawn's half-empty wine glass. "Is that the last of the bottle?"

"Yes," she answered tentatively. "Why?"

"No reason." I lifted my glass to hers and clinked the edges together. "To a wonderful party. Thank you for inviting me. Now drink up. I don't want to waste a single drop."

Reluctantly, Dawn downed the remainder of wine, as I killed off the whiskey. I turned to Doug and whispered in his ear, "Please escort Dawn to the front door and wait for my signal."

"What signal?"

"Believe me, you'll know it when you see it."

The last time I saw Doug look this confused was when he had thawed a package of hamburger and it stayed a grey colour, instead of the rosy red it should've turned. You could almost smell the wood burning as he decided if he should still use the meat for the Wednesday chili lunch special.

"Give up?" Corwin drunkenly asked.

"Not by a long shot, kid," I said, reasserting myself in the conversation and Corwin's personal space. "The question is, do you really want me to proceed?"

Corwin's face tightened and his upper lip curled into a Billy Idol sneer. "Everybody's waiting."

So they were.

"I know you asked me for only one interesting unknown fact about Scott, however, like potato chips, one is never enough." I stepped forward and began to ramp up my big finale that I knew would be a real show stopper. "What's interesting about your friend, Corwin, is how nervous he seems tonight, even before you put him in my sights. I started to think, why would a best friend be jittery in the presence of his closest compadre? You are obviously more than just business associates or classmates. You're buds who watch each other's back, which is something you can't put a price on, right?" Both Corwin and Scott were eyeing each other nervously. "You trust his stock advice, his fashion expertise. Yet, when sulking in your little Us Against Them support group earlier, I saw something in Scott's eyes you missed, which I'm thinking is exactly what Scott is betting on."

The stale living room air was still with expectation.

"Corwin, I don't know what he's talking about. He's making this shit up as he goes," Scott pleaded nervously.

Dawn and Doug had dutifully walked unnoticed to the front door, where they stood with their shoes and boots on. Doug pointed to my sneakers tucked under his arm, smiled and gave me the thumbs up. Dawn grinned and mouthed, "I like you a lot," to which I mouthed back, "I know." We shared one last moment of togetherness before Corwin broke the spell.

"I don't like where you're heading with this. There's no way Scott is into me, so you can stop going there," he warned.

I smiled and replied, "Scott and you? Please. First off, I think everyone here can tell he has better taste than that. Believe me, it wasn't only his eyes that gave his secret away. It was the way he stood in the group, the way he held his glass, the times he laughed a bit too hard and the occasions when he listened a tad too attentively." Another person in the room began to sway uncomfortably on their feet. "It was how he lightly touched the lower back of one of your group, as he made his way to the kitchen to fix two more drinks and again when delicately handing the second drink to the same party-goer. Of course, you were too busy to notice any of these romantic shenanigans going on. You can admit it, there's no shame in being the last to know. I see this type of thing all the time."

I never like to be the bearer of bad news, especially if it kills the mood of a party. In this case I had no choice, right?

"Are you saying Scott is fooling around with one of our friend's girlfriends?" Corwin asked slowly.

"I'm new to this scene and don't know everyone here, well, anyone really, but if you want to know if I believe Scott is behaving badly with that blonde in the red dress, standing beside my boy Herman, then the answer is yes."

"The blonde in the red dress," Corwin stammered incredulously, "is my girlfriend, Elizabeth."

Simultaneously exhilarated and bored, I couldn't be bothered to feign shock or outrage and shrugged my shoulders, as I moved my left foot back a step to counterbalance what I knew was coming next.

"You son of a bitch!" Corwin screamed, lowering his head and taking a run at me with all the finesse of a linebacker, which he no doubt was during his teenaged glory days.

My left leg withstood the human onslaught for a moment, before my tackler's forward motion carried both of us toward the front foyer. Corwin's downfall, literally and figuratively, was his earlier alcohol consumption. Like a drunk at a bar, he was all speed without agility, allowing me to easily grab his shirt and toss him aside to the floor. This slowed him temporarily and I soon had him bent over in a violent headlock, as I inched toward the now open front door.

"I'll start the van! Hurry up loser," Dawn taunted me from the sidewalk. "Oh, and we have to give Doug a ride home," she laughed.

I was afraid I might do the ever-flailing Corwin real harm, and pushed the bulk of his body against the doorframe for support. I looked up to see our stunned hosts cutting their way through the crowd and decided it was time to go.

"One more thing you didn't know, Corwin," I said as Team Wallace was almost upon us. "Daniel here was the one who personally recommended you be laid off, because you're such a toolbag." I dragged out the last word: t-o-o-l-b-a-g.

After this completely fabricated utterance, I heard a collective gasp from the halted tag team and many of the living room spectators. During the following five seconds of shocked silence, I dropped Corwin and hastily exited the house, slamming the door closed behind me.

The last words I heard screamed were, "You son of a bitch!" and knew that all's well that ends well.

"That was fantastic, don't you think?" I asked as I climbed into the passenger seat, out of breath. "We should do this party crashing thing every week."

"Are there any other customers likely to ask us over after this gets around, Dawn?" Doug began to laugh in the backseat.

Dawn quickly pulled away from the curb and sped down the deserted street.

"I can't take you anywhere," she said to me. "Either of you!" she added, looking up into the rearview mirror and beginning to smile ear to ear. "You owe me, Mr. Cassidy. Daniel was one of my biggest tippers and now he'll never come back."

"Never? Is that what you think?" I countered. "After meeting his wife, I'll bet you're his only daily oasis."

"Do you really think so?" she asked hopefully.

"Sure," I said, "just as soon as he's out of the hospital or jail. I'm thinking he'll be at his regular table Monday, after we return from our murderous vacation. If not, I'll find a way to make it up to you."

"Promise?"

"I promise with whipped cream and a cherry on top."

Waiting at a stop light, we heard the first emergency response sirens wailing through the cool crisp night air.

"I always get confused," Doug piped up. "Is that a police, fire or ambulance siren?"

Dawn and I glanced back and in unison said, "Yes."

As the streetscape behind us was suddenly awash in red and blue lights, I remembered we hadn't really eaten all night.

"I'm starved. Anyone up for a burger or wings?" I asked.

THREE

Arranging personal time off is a chore. When panicked clients reach out at 5:00 p.m. on Friday, they're not accustomed to hearing that I can't do surveillance on a so-called injured employee. "I overheard he's going to be playing shortstop in a baseball tournament tomorrow and Sunday! Please, I beg of you, Steve." Depending on the sport, I might work out some deal. Baseball, yes. Hockey, maybe. Soccer, probably not. As a one-man operation, there are only so many hours in a day and as it is, I work seven of them each week. If I only clocked in the standard 40 hours, my take home pay would be halved.

Dawn's restaurant schedule is infinitely more flexible. She waitresses during the day Monday-Thursday and Sunday evening. So for us to get away means finding someone to take the short Sunday dinner shift and presto, a long weekend!

The Tour of True Terror was written up in the *You're The Man, Man!* men's magazine I read during stakeouts. Like the infamous S.S. *Minnow* trip, the tour lasts three hours aboard a snazzy bus and on foot. There's even a Master of Ceremonies to guide us down the true crime memory lane of the mid-sized metropolis known as Dannenberg. A short jaunt from our own City of Darrien, it's far enough away to constitute a mini-vacation and close enough not to waste much time driving, which could be more wisely used in our hotel room.

"What's the deal with Dannenberg anyway?" Dawn asked as she replaced my Springsteen disc with her Sex At Seven CD in the van's stereo. "Is it like the murder capital of the region or just a really poor choice to call home?"

"A bit of both," I answered as the first guitar chords of Dawn's new favourite song, *The Trouble With Lies,* kicked in. "It's always been a rough industrial city, full of factories, especially during wartime, making tanks, planes and ammunition."

"There isn't much need for that today."

"Exactly, at least not on that scale. When the last two recessions hit, the first casualties were manufacturing plants. Now instead of producing cars or clothing or canned goods, Dannenberg produces the unemployed, and as witnessed with Broker Boy Corwin, anger is the number one by-product."

"Followed by crime. I gotcha." Dawn sang along to the chorus before saying, "I'm surprised there's even a tour like this. Who thinks this stuff up? A couple of drunks sitting around the bar trying to find a get-rich-quick scheme?"

"You're close. Two Dannenberg police detectives got bored and thought they could use all their experience to make a buck or two."

"Still . . . "

"It does seem a bit macabre, but it's really no different from the Criminal Hall of Fame wax museum we visited in Niagara Falls."

"I guess. That was kinda cool."

"Plus, at the end of this we won't have to exit through the gift shop," I said with a smile.

"What, no *I Almost Died on The Tour of True Terror* t-shirt or keychain or magnet?"

"Sad but true."

We checked into our hotel suite and spent the afternoon sightseeing a few of Dannenberg's attractions, albeit only through our bedroom's bay windows overlooking the city square.

"You really are fun in bed," I said with a satisfied grin, "although I need to get into better shape 'cause I feel like I'm about to have a heart attack."

"My dad used to say the same thing and then he'd pop a nitroglycerine pill." I slowly turned my head to be able to look Dawn in the face. "What?" she asked innocently, adjusting her head on the pillow.

"I need to clarify something. When I said you were a fun lover and I felt like I was about to have a heart attack, then you said, 'My dad used to say the same thing,' you were talking about having a heart attack, not making love to you, right? Because, you know, that would be a really awkward situation we'd have to further discuss."

Dawn didn't immediately react to what I hoped was a funny joke.

"Did I say dad? Sorry, I meant step-brother," she deadpanned, before we both broke out in laughter, an occurrence that almost always happens before, during, and definitely after a lovemaking session.

"Why do I keep you around?"

I smiled. "I have no idea."

We arrived 15 minutes early at the tour kiosk where the bus was parked on the street. It was more of a people-mover type vehicle, the kind used by wedding parties to get to and from the church. "Comfortable and equipped with a bar. I like it," Dawn said. "I hope the walking parts are short distances."

"From the curb to the front door of a murder scene?" I asked.

"Something like that."

"Don't worry, the walking is minimal. I walked the beat for years. I'm too old for that kind of thing now," a gruff voice declared from behind us.

We turned and were greeted by an extremely fit, silver-haired man, who was the size of a small car.

"Rodney Dutton. Are you here for our tour or to cause trouble?"

"Both, maybe," Dawn replied as she placed her tiny hand

into Rodney's huge mitt-like grip. "We tend to behave ourselves until we get bored and decide it's time everyone around us needs to lighten up."

I offered my hand to our host and calmly said, "My name is Steve Cassidy and I have no idea who this woman is or why she keeps following me around. So far, she hasn't become violent, but who knows when she might become a stop on your tour."

Rodney let go of my hand and assessed the petite firecracker in front of him. "I'm thinking along with the other passengers, we can deal with any trouble that comes our way." He paused and then asked, "Isn't that right, Miss . . . "

"Dawn."

"Miss Dawn and Mr. Cassidy, I believe we're going to have a lot of fun tonight."

We nodded in agreement with Dawn lightly hitting my chest with her hand as Rodney left us to attend to new arrivals.

"Are we even now?"

"Even how?" I replied.

"For my *insignificant other* intro at the stockbrokers' dysfunctional social gathering last night."

"That old line? Do I look like someone who holds a grudge until I see the perfect opportunity, like just now, to get my revenge?"

"You totally do."

"Then there's your answer."

"I'm sorry I called you insignificant," Dawn 'fessed up.

"Sorry you said it out loud or because it was a complete and bold-faced lie?"

"Yes."

"I knew it!"

"If you two are done, they said we can board the bus now."

Dawn and I pivoted toward this new voice that belonged to a kindly-looking woman in her early sixties who wore a wry grin. "I was young and in love once," she stated grumpily as she walked past and entered the bus.

"Ah, she thinks we're in love," Dawn said softly. "What do you think?"

"Two things," I began, having had this non-starter conversation with Dawn a few times. "One, I think l-o-v-e is a grown up term that should only be used by responsible adults, which obviously excludes us."

"And two?" Dawn asked as we made our way up the bus stairs.

"Did you catch a whiff of her coat? I firmly believe she said the same exact thing to her 17 cats before leaving the house tonight."

***

These types of tours attract a very eclectic group of people, from basic mystery fans to serious scholars of true crime, to those bored with what's playing at the multiplex to lonely widowers, and, of course, a few wanna-be killers looking for pointers. Our group consisted of four university students on a double date, two female friends in their forties, a couple in their fifties who were married (although not necessarily to each other), the cat woman I'd nicknamed Ms. Vittles, and two solo thrill seekers, both in their early thirties. The driver was a kid I assumed to be the son or nephew of tonight's guide Rodney, who now stood at the front of the bus talking into a microphone.

"The cases you're going to hear about are real. They all happened during the past 100 years. People died. Their killers were tried and sentenced for their special crime. Most went to prison for very long periods of time, while a few were executed — an eye for an eye and all that. Some escaped to kill again or vanished into thin air, their whereabouts unknown." For dramatic effect, like a campfire storyteller, Rodney let that fact hang in the air for a moment. "My business partner Lawrence Ingles and I worked together in the Homicide Unit for ten years, personally investigating a few of these files. Unlike the older cases, we can vouch 100% that the right man or woman was convicted." As if on cue, the bus began to move and we were on our way. "The first stop is several minutes away, which gives us enough time to consume a beverage from the mini-bar. What can I get you?"

"He seems like he knows what he's talking about," Dawn said in a low whisper, motioning to Rodney who was in conversation with the married-unmarried couple.

"All Homicide investigators come off like they know what they're talking about," I laughed. "It doesn't mean it's true."

"Next thing you're going to tell me is that the guys in Vice have superior intelligence."

Without hesitation I replied, "Who do you think gives the Homicide guys all their facts?"

A short time later, I raised my plastic tumbler of whiskey to Dawn's small plastic flute of wine. "To a night of murder and mayhem."

I felt a hand on my shoulder. "I couldn't have said it better myself, Steve," Rodney proclaimed to everyone present. "Please, let's raise our glasses. To murder and mayhem and not necessarily in that order. Cheers!"

***

The tour was a well-oiled machine. Rodney was the perfect host with an encyclopedia-like recall of facts and figures and an answer to every question we threw at him. I would have expected no less. Regardless of their rank or experience, cops have a gift for retaining details of any crime, petty or otherwise. Names, dates, addresses, licence plates, physical descriptions, cigarette brands smoked, the name of the family pet that happily met them at the front door. I believe the often quoted statistic that people use only 10% of their memory capabilities is a low estimation when it comes to officers. Then again, that may just be my brain pumping up its ego.

The evening's ten stops were mapped out chronologically, with the oldest murder taking place in 1898 when two brothers duelled it out over the beautiful neighbourhood harlot. The winner: the much sought-after woman, who consoled and then shacked up with the third brother. The hit parade continued with revelations of flapper-era fatalities, depression-era dirty dealings, cold war-era offings, hippie homicides, disco-era deaths, yuppies slaying preppies, and more.

"We conclude tonight's murderous adventure with a case in which I take personal pride," Rodney said with a wide smile. "This particular incident happened on my watch and was my last investigation with the department, as I took an early retirement due to a medical issue. My partner Lawrence and I were determined to get a conviction before I hung up my badge and I'm proud to say we did."

"Nothing like going out on top," one of the university students spoke up.

"You got that right," Rodney agreed as the bus stopped in front of an ancient Victorian-style house located on the river that divided the city's haves and have-nots. "This is the McDowell Mansion. That's not its official name, but one everyone around here knows it by. Built in 1902 by one of the most powerful men of his time, Theodore McDowell saw this grand dwelling as the ultimate symbol of wealth and stature. The owner of the city's only bank, he was a major financial and political player, as well as the land owner of much of the area's prime real estate parcels. Envied by the upper crust and equally despised by the working class, he was very much like the Mr. Potter character in the Christmas classic *It's A Wonderful Life*."

"So why isn't the city named McDowellville?" I asked kiddingly. "Did he have his own George Bailey to deal with back then?" I looked around and saw all except the university students smiling at the reference.

"That I don't know. I promise I'll look into it for tomorrow night's group though," Rodney acknowledged. "Keeping with the movie theme, like George Bailey, it was the stock market crash that did in Moneybags McDowell. He lost everything."

"If only he had a guardian angel like Clarence or more friends," Ms. Vittles snickered.

"I'm not sure about angels, but he did have plenty of friends. The difference was, they decided to join forces and picked over his troubled empire one business at a time, paying pennies on the dollar, bankrupting him overnight."

"And out of anger he killed one of them and you had to investigate?" a female student asked eagerly.

Expressions of *What are they teaching students in History class these days?* registered on the older riders' faces, including, thankfully, Dawn's.

"Just how old do you think I am, young lady?" Rodney replied with a nervous laugh. "In 1929, my father wouldn't have been old enough to join the police force, unless they were signing up children to fill some bizarre hiring quota."

Good-natured laughter filled the bus as the student playfully hung her head in shame. "I'm sorry," she said quietly. "That was a dumb question."

"Nonsense," Rodney said with a wave of his hand. "As my Chief used to say, 'There's no such thing as a dumb question, only dumb answers, especially when dealing with a crime.'"

"Decades later, did one of Mr. McDowell's grandchildren extract revenge in this house?" one of the solo females asked, glancing out the bus window toward the dwelling's huge porch. "Is this a museum or does a McDowell family member still live here? There are lights on in the upper rooms."

As we craned our necks to check out the second floor windows, Rodney answered, "Yes, no and yes. Yes, a murder took place here, no it is not a museum, and yes, there's one person related to the McDowell family presently residing here."

"When did this murder take place?" the other solo female friend asked. "Obviously, within the past decade."

"It will be six years next month," Rodney said reflectively. "We received a 911 call at 11:37 p.m. from a distressed female who was hiding in her bedroom closet. She said a man was downstairs, first in the kitchen smashing stuff on the floor, and then overturning furniture in the living room."

"Did she know who it was or have any idea why someone would be so angry with her?" Dawn asked, enthralled by the tale.

"Why would you say angry *with her*?" Rodney asked. "Couldn't the burglar just be trying to scare her with a lot of noise?"

Dawn thought for a moment. "Robbers don't want you to know they've broken in. They're all stealth-like. This guy made sure she knew he was in the house. Plus, breaking kitchen items, probably off the counter, is in itself like a personal psychological attack. The toaster, a blender, the coffee maker, maybe a dish or cup and saucer, are things this woman uses and will miss if they're broken."

"Wow, are you a government profiler?" Rodney inquired, genuinely impressed by Dawn's deductions, all of which I wholeheartedly agreed with and wished deep down I'd voiced.

"I'm a lowly waitress," Dawn demurred, turning to me. "I guess by living with an ex-cop and current P.I., a few investigative traits have rubbed off on me."

In almost every other situation, I have no problem with Dawn telling people what I do for a living. I'm not ashamed of my profession, although my profession may not always have the same warm gooey feelings. Tonight however, I was striving to be a regular fellow, a happy-go-lucky passenger on this magical murder mystery tour.

"I knew there was a reason I liked you from the start, Steve," Rodney declared. "You should have said something earlier.

Maybe you could have brought another perspective to some of these cases."

"I'm only along for the ride, Rodney," I admitted, "and have thoroughly enjoyed not being on the clock tonight. It wouldn't have been much of a holiday if I brought some work along with me, right?"

"I understand. Still, if you want to jump in anytime with thoughts on this last stop, don't hesitate."

"From what you've told us, this was a slam dunk. I doubt I can add anything to your finest hour. Please continue, as Dawn is tired of hearing me talk."

"I get enough of that at home," Dawn said with a grin. "I'm on vacation too."

There was a polite round of laughter from the others before Rodney continued on with his McDowell Murder Mansion speech. "Where was I?"

"A toaster was being beaten to within an inch of its life," Ms. Vittles said.

"Yes, right," Rodney began. "So, the next thing the woman on the phone cries out is, 'He's yelling something! Wait. He's coming upstairs!' Tragically, those were her final words. When we replayed the 911 call, in the background you could faintly hear the killer taunting the soon-to-be victim, 'Come out and play, Lucy. You've had your fun, now it's my turn. School's out forever.' A short time later, we heard a struggle as 24-year-old Lucy McDowell, the wife of Theodore's great grandson Eric, was dragged from her bedroom closet. By this time, we'd dispatched officers in four cruisers to the residence. They arrived within minutes of the call coming in and were still too late to save her after being stabbed once through the heart with a kitchen knife."

The bus was silent as we hung on Rodney's every word. Somehow, this crime was more real than the others he'd talked about during the night. There was an edge to his voice that gave each detail extra weight. Maybe it was the brutality of the killing or that a young woman lost her life. I examined Rodney's stone-etched face and saw an expression that wordlessly conveyed the truth of the matter at hand: this was personal.

"Was the killer in the house when the police arrived?" Mr. Married-Unmarried asked.

"I wish. It would've made this last case that much easier to close," Rodney responded. "No, the killer escaped out a back patio door, presumably as the officers arrived on scene. There were a few drops of Lucy's blood on the stairs and on the kitchen floor near the door."

"Was Lucy a teacher or an Alice Cooper fan?" I said, taking up Rodney's request to participate. "The *School's Out* reference seems pretty specific."

"As a matter of fact, she was an assistant at the nearby Dannenberg Public School's kindergarten class," Rodney answered.

"Huh," Dawn said, glancing at me with a quizzical expression.

"I'm almost afraid to ask," Rodney stated slowly.

"I guess I find it interesting she worked with little kids, instead of older students. I've always associated the song's title and the phrase *school's out* as being connected to high school or later years, not grade or pre-school. It would also date Lucy's attacker age-wise." Dawn paused, then asked, "Thoughts?"

Amazed again, Rodney said to me, "Does she help with all your files or just the tough ones you can't figure out?"

Somewhere in that question was a backhanded compliment that didn't sit well with me.

"Trust me, she will from now on," I said as I put my hand in Dawn's, now wishing to have this tour end sooner rather than later. I had no interest in getting into some stupid ex-cop pissing contest with Mr. Know-It-All here.

"What about Lucy's husband? When did he arrive?" one of the solo unattached passengers asked. "Was he ever a suspect?"

Rodney flashed a thoughtful smile. "About an hour later, he did eventually come home, freshly showered and looking like a million bucks. He valiantly tried to portray himself as a grieving spouse and actually fooled quite a few people."

"But not you," the other solo passenger said.

"Not by a long shot. Steve can back me up when I say there are people in specific situations whose actions and words don't line up." I nodded in agreement, keeping my new vow of silence. "People with a guilty conscience either act too calm or too out of control, which in most cases comes back to bite them. You can't blame them for trying. The problem is they're not trained actors. They've never done this type of deception on such a large scale. Getting caught stealing a dollar from your mother's purse isn't in the same league as being a suspect in the coldblooded murder of your sweetheart. Dear old Mom will likely forgive you, regardless of what wild excuse you spin. That's a parental job requirement. Unfortunately for Eric McDowell, I was his mom's stand-in that night, and my job requirements are a bit different."

"You said he arrived freshly showered? That was his first mistake," Dawn commented, having taken no such vow of silence.

"One of many," Rodney agreed. "Having the mistress secretary providing your alibi also didn't strengthen his case for acquittal."

I was going to jump in with a sarcastic, "Really?" when I noticed the married-unmarrieds catch each other's eye and hold their gaze longer than normal.

Busted.

"Nothing too cliché about that scenario," a male student scoffed.

This tawdry morsel of information unleashed a torrent of questions by the group:

"When did the affair begin?"

"Did Lucy know about the affair?"

"Were they getting a divorce?"

"Was the secretary arrested?"

"Did the mistress end up testifying against Eric?"

And lastly, from the other male university student came the gem, "Was the secretary hotter than Lucy?"

This abruptly ended question period, that and the fact that a distraught middle-aged woman was on the sidewalk screaming at the top of her lungs, while banging on the bus door with something metal.

"I've called the cops, Dutton! The real cops! The ones who know how to investigate a crime, unlike you and that moron Ingles!" We all slid to the right-side windows in time to see this loon using a can of spray paint to deface the large *Tour of True Terror* logo on the side panel. When the can was empty, she threw it against the bus and continued to yell at Rodney, and by extension, us. "Everyone in there should be ashamed of themselves, especially you Dutton, you money-grabbing sleazeball! How dare you bask in the glory of a case you got wrong? Eric is innocent. You knew it six years ago but railroaded him anyway!" As a police siren cut through the night air, our attacker kicked the door. "Get out of here and leave us alone!" she cried out, before stomping back to the mansion and slamming the front door behind her.

"You know the drill," Rodney said to the driver. "Go up a block and park. I'll smooth everything over and we'll get everyone back to the kiosk as soon as we can." He directed this last sentence to his stunned, yet still captive audience.

"Friend of yours?" I inquired, knowing our *blue brotherhood* connection allowed me to bust his balls without fear of any repercussions. As I expected, he laughed off my comment.

"I apologize for what happened back there," Rodney said composing himself. "Although you were never in any real danger, I'll gladly refund your money if you want. That woman is Debra Stanfield, Lucy's mother, Eric's mother-in-law. We have a troubled past that flairs up every once in awhile."

"His mother-in-law believes he's innocent? That's got to be rare," a female student commented. "Usually they hate their daughter's husband."

"I know, my mother-in-laws hated me," Mr. Married-Unmarried chimed in, breaking the tension. "Together they would've found a way to plant that bloody knife in my work locker."

"Again, I'm sorry you had to be part of this tonight," Rodney said. "I'll just be a minute with the officer and then we'll get you back to civilization safe and sound."

The moment the bus door closed behind Rodney, our group exploded in chatter, like a bunch of fifth graders whose teacher steps into the hall to speak with the principal.

"What's your take on all of this?" Dawn asked me above the din of the other participants.

I glanced out the window to watch Rodney and the officer discussing the vandalized logo. "In every trial, there's a winner and a loser," I said. "The term *sore loser* wasn't coined because some guy turned his back and said a few bad words under his breath about his opponent. Violence usually enters the equation in some form. Tonight it was a spray can and a boot."

"Didn't you find Rodney's *non-reaction* reaction odd? I thought he'd have flipped out and called the police himself," Dawn speculated. "He must have a few friends left at headquarters."

"He reminded me of an embarrassed parent whose young child throws a tantrum in the grocery store checkout line. There are only two options at your disposal: The first is to make an even bigger scene, damn the consequences. Unfortunately, shrieking at your former bundle of joy, 'Shut the hell up or else,' risks a home visit from Child Protective Services."

"I take it Rodney chose the second option, which is what?"

"Which is full denial a situation is taking place a few feet away from you. To yell at the kid only lowers you to their immature level. The other shoppers, regardless if they're parents or not, would look at you with the same scorn as they do your little brat."

"But if you ignore the screaming kid," Dawn began, realizing what I was trying to say, "they'll respect and maybe sympathize with your predicament."

"Seriously, are you taking psych classes on the side that I don't know about?" I asked in wonder.

"Maybe." Dawn playfully smiled. "I'm right though, right?"

"You are. What I saw tonight was a man genuinely mortified by this woman's physical attack and verbal accusations that he's a fraud. Plus, I don't think this is the first time this kind of incident has occurred. I'd bet dollars to donuts Rodney and his partner have an arrangement with a local auto shop to do quickie clean up jobs when needed."

"The officer is leaving without going to the house," one of the single females said in astonishment.

"That's because Rodney doesn't want any charges laid," I whispered in Dawn's ear. "In this case, bad publicity is simply bad publicity."

Rodney re-entered the bus, gave the driver a sign to start driving and addressed us for the last time.

"Most nights, I take a few more minutes at that last stop to go over the case. In a nutshell, Eric McDowell claimed he didn't kill his wife, although all the evidence pointed to him and only him. It was a circumstantial case, but one which a jury of his peers took only two hours of deliberations to find him guilty beyond a reasonable doubt." Rodney turned to look out the front window as the tour kiosk came into view. "This concludes our tour. I hope you enjoyed it and will tell your friends and family about us." He bent forward to open a cardboard box that had been sitting on the seat behind the driver. "At this point, I usually try to sell you this book that goes into more detail about the crimes we visited tonight." He held up a small paperback titled *Tour of True Terror – The Book*. "But after what we put you through, I want to give each of you a free copy as a way to again say how sorry we are."

Rodney handed out our complimentary souvenir and we soon found ourselves at the kiosk saying our goodbyes.

"We had a really good time, Rodney," Dawn said. "Steve tells me stories of his past cop life, but doesn't take me on a tour of the best crime scenes."

"Maybe he will now," Rodney responded with a smile. "Just promise me you won't take her to any spots where crazies still live."

"That would only leave a visit to the mall to recount shoplifting incidents," I said as I shook Rodney's hand. "I've had my share of Debra Stanfields in my day. I know what you're going through. Maybe one day she'll come to her senses and see the truth about her killer son-in-law."

"We can only hope."

"Thanks again," I said, taking Dawn's hand in mine as we walked to the van. "Now you have something to read."

Dawn looked at the cover. "It was written by Rodney and his business partner, so I'm thinking it should be pretty good." I opened the passenger door and as she entered Dawn asked, "You know what?"

"I do not," I admitted.

"I think this is even better than some old magnet or t-shirt anyway."

"I agree," I said, closing the door and making my way around the front of the van. "Plus," I said to myself, "it was free and free is always better than an overpriced trinket." Starting the van's engine, I asked, "Feel like getting a bite to eat?"

"I was thinking of skinny dipping at that secluded beach we saw on the tour earlier," Dawn said, never taking her eyes off the book's back cover.

"The beach where the arthritic Italian woman killed her husband the chef with a frying pan, as her busboy lover watched from the woods?"

"Yes, that one," Dawn said in a sly tone. "Surf, sand, a full moon, a forbidden love triangle and a fry pan to the skull." Dawn turned and fixed her eyes on my face. "Now *that's* amore."

"I'm not sure where you're going to hide a fry pan while skinny dipping, but I'm 100% for seeing you try."

I pulled out of the parking lot and glanced over to see Rodney and the bus driver examining the destroyed logo. As they grew smaller in my mirrors, I was relieved I'd have no further contact with this troubling situation and thought, *Good luck with that boys. You're going to need a lot of it.*

FOUR

With no schedule to speak of, Dawn and I took a leisurely approach to our Sunday morning. The previous evening's quick dip in the warm lake and subsequent beach bonfire had a very calming effect on our bodies and minds. It was just what we needed after the roadside chaos aboard the terror bus.

"I'm going to hit the gym. Meet you poolside in an hour?"

"Sounds like a plan," Dawn said while packing a small beach bag with suntan lotion, her music player and the souvenir paperback from the tour. "I'm planning to read the Eric McDowell chapter first to see what all the fuss is about. I skimmed it a bit already and it took a year to get to trial. So for this Debra woman, it's been five years proclaiming Eric's innocence. That's a long time."

"For me, the intriguing part is it's his mother-in-law doing all the screaming and spray painting."

"I've never been married, so don't know all the ins and outs of in-law relationships," Dawn smiled. "Did your former mother-in-law like you?"

I had to think back a very long time for my answer. "We were always on good terms, although if on trial for killing her daughter, she wouldn't be protesting with a sign reading FREE STEVE! Nor would I expect her to."

"Oh yeah, your personal *arrest code* for family and friends. How does that work again?" Dawn asked with a tinge of sarcasm in her voice.

"Laugh all you like at my code. I just hope you'll never have to abide by it."

"But you're not making any promises, right?"

"No promises, correct. My previous track record indicates a criminal reoccurrence may very well happen in the future."

"And that's when the code kicks in."

"Exactly." I sat on the bed and tied my shoes. "So, unless you actually witness the crime I've been charged with, no matter how heinous or trivial, when asked by the media, 'Do you think he did it?' your answer should always be what?"

Dawn sported a new serious face. "I wasn't there, but this would be totally out of character for the Steve Cassidy I know."

"Perfect," I said as I crossed the room. "There's nothing sadder than seeing loved ones claiming their child is innocent to a mob of reporters. It doesn't matter if they've confessed, their blood is mixed with the victim's, their alibi doesn't hold up, or that the accused is heard yelling, 'I'm going to shoot you with this gun and kill you dead.' These poor shell-shocked people destroy their credibility one sound bite at a time. It's depressing."

"Then you don't buy the idea parents should stand behind their children at all costs?"

"Not if Little Jimmy or Sue are outright criminals," I said. "And my code isn't about whether my friends believe I'm guilty, it's that I have no problem with them *not* defending me in public. I'm trying to save their reputation with *their* family and friends."

"You are like the bestest friend I have," Dawn laughed.

I held the door open for her as we walked into the hallway. "And don't you forget it."

***

My gym regimen consists entirely of using equipment that will do most of the work, such as a treadmill, elliptical or stationary bike. Even when I'm doing laps in the pool, the water is helping in some capacity. Through diet, some exercise and the benefits of good genes, it's not hard for me to stay in decent shape. I have nothing against the barbell and weight lifting devotees, although having biceps the same shape and feel as a small bag of potatoes is beyond my understanding. On the machines, I can also catch up on the world by watching sports, news and sometimes cooking programs, which are broadcast on the suspended television screens. Why a gym member would want to view The Chocolate Channel at 6:30 a.m. while trying to lose weight is also beyond my comprehension.

After working up a mild sweat, I found Dawn soaking in the sun on a lounger with a fruit drink in one hand and the tour book in the other. "Good workout?" I kidded her as I reclined in the chair beside her.

"Sun tanning is being considered for the next summer games, if you must know," she replied.

"In that case, I'd like to submit an application for the official Lotion Applier position. I have good hands you know."

"Oh, I know," Dawn smirked. "Even so, I'll have to equally consider all applicants before choosing you."

"Is that so?" I countered. "Would the same apply if I started to train as a pole vaulter and needed someone to help with my–"

"Vaulting techniques? Yes, definitely."

We both laughed, secure in the knowledge that over the past few months, our male and female *friends with benefits* had slowly been set aside to pursue a monogamous relationship.

Noticing Dawn was reading one of the first chapters of the book, I asked, "What's the deal with the McDowell murder anyhow? Did he do it or not?"

Dawn set her drink on the side table and sat up, flipping to the final chapter. "Rodney wasn't kidding about it being a circumstantial case," she replied. "For the detectives everything came down to Lucy's life insurance policy and Eric's cheating. Case closed."

"Was there any physical evidence Eric had stabbed Lucy?"

"None, but remember it was his house. His fingerprints and DNA were already all over the place."

"No matching shoe prints or hairs in her blood on the floor?"

"Nada."

"What about the killer's voice from the 911 call? Did they identify it as Eric's through some sort of high tech audio analysis?" I inquired, not wanting to go zero for three.

"They did run tests but the results came back inconclusive," Dawn said.

"Sounds like Eric's jury was made up of angry insurance agents and spurned spouses," I offered. "There were no other suspects?"

Dawn turned a few pages. "Not really. Rodney and his partner talked to all of Lucy's friends, co-workers and parents of the children she taught. The only problem was, they all had alibis, and no one had a motive to want her dead, especially not in such a violent way."

"The stabbing was a very personal act, along with the taunting beforehand," I agreed. "I take it Lucy was portrayed as the good wife, trusted friend, and amazing teacher of our youth, without a mean or deceptive bone in her body?"

Dawn closed the book and picked up her drink. "Pretty much."

"The question remains, why is her mother so adamant Eric was framed?"

"Maybe she has a sixth sense."

"Maybe she's the killer," I said, "or knows the real killer, but is too frightened to reveal them to the police because she likes to breathe."

"Both scenarios sound far-fetched, although I'd still love to see you prove either one," Dawn responded.

"I've seen stranger outcomes," I replied, as I removed my t-shirt and settled back into the lounger. "Do you want to grab some lunch, maybe check out those boutiques and bookstore around the corner in awhile?"

"Let's aim for noon, do some sightseeing and then get back here for more rays."

"You got it."

Dawn put on her headphones and I flipped through Rodney's book of murderous tales, enjoying the additional information he didn't have time to relate during the tour. Like when reviewing other investigators' surveillance reports, as I read I found myself thinking, *Investigated that, investigated that, dated the subject's girlfriend after I investigated that, investigated that.* A majority of the cases consisted of life's three necessary evils: money, sex and jealousy.

I set the book aside and closed my eyes, envisioning the time when Dawn's newly tanned skin would be against my own pale white skin in some way, shape or form, preferably all three. Sleep came quickly and the next thing I knew, Dawn was gently waking me, having already packed everything up.

"Hey sleepyhead, what about that lunch? I'm starving."

I slowly returned to the land of the living and stretched my arms above my head. "High noon, already?"

"Time flies when you're having fun," Dawn said with a grin.

We walked through the hotel lobby to the city's touristy shopping district, a nice section of shops, restaurants with outdoor patios and a waterfront ice cream parlour advertising its 34th year in business. Deciding a light lunch was all that was required, we settled on *Book A Lunch*, a combination independent bookstore and sandwich shop. A former residence, the living room and dining room areas had nice oak shelves featuring new books, all of which had their covers facing out for quick review. The sandwich shop was conveniently located in the kitchen on the main floor, where four bistro tables were set up for customers.

"I love this place," Dawn commented to the sole female employee. "Everything has a very warm and cozy feel to it. Have you been open long?"

"Almost a year now," came the reply. "I'm Dara, the owner of this fine establishment. I take it you are visiting our lovely waterfront this weekend."

"We are," I said, as I noticed a shelf beside the checkout counter displaying three novels written by one Dara Revin. "An author who owns her own bookstore. Is this how you cut out the middleman?"

Dara glanced at her novels and smiled. "Trust me, I'm not making my living off those self-published books, although owning the store allows me to generate a little more interest in them. Better out in the open than in my basement."

Dawn walked to the shelf and picked up the one I knew would attract her attention. *"The Beginning of Dawn.* What's this one about?" she asked our genial host.

"Dawn is a young widow trying to start life over."

"I like the tagline on the back cover," Dawn said. *"A coming-of-age story, if you believe life begins at 28.* I'm going to buy it. Would you autograph it for me?"

Like a seasoned pro, Dara replied, "When I'm asked that question at book shows my response is usually, whenever there's a signing event, I figure I should be there for it."

We all laughed as Dawn set the book on the counter and handed over a $20 bill that Dara set to one side, not ringing it through the cash register. As she inscribed the front inside cover *To Dawn – Today is just the beginning!* the bell inside the front door rang, indicating a new customer had arrived.

"Thank you so much," Dawn gushed. "I've never met a real author. Now if I like this one, which I'm sure I will, can I order your other books online?"

Dara handed Dawn a bookmark that displayed all three covers of her books. "Take one of my functional business cards, as I like to call them. My website is listed on it."

"Sweet," Dawn said, placing the bookmark in her new book.

As our attention was on the local celebrity book signing process, none of us had taken into account the other patron. Dawn and I were about to move into the kitchen to select one of the freshly made sandwiches on display, when the fourth person in the room spoke up.

"Well if it isn't one of the Tour of True Terror terrorists. Did you enjoy the show last night, Missy?"

To say we were startled by this would be an understatement.

"Excuse me?" Dawn asked, as the question was aimed squarely at her.

"Debra!" Dara broke in. "You can't come in here and abuse my customers."

"Why not?" Debra Stanfield countered. "She abused me last night when she stopped in front of Eric and Lucy's house, gawking at the place like it was a freak show exhibit, all the while listening to Rodney spreading his vicious lies."

I was baffled how Eric McDowell's mother-in-law knew Dawn had taken the previous evening's tour. I was sure neither of us had made any type of direct eye contact during her deranged ranting episode. Had she staked out the kiosk and taken pictures of each person exiting the bus for future reference? Before I could come to some logical answer, it was presented, as Ms. Stanfield pointed to the tour's souvenir book sticking out of the side pocket of Dawn's beach bag.

"Did you get to the part where Detective Dutton and Detective Ingles write that Eric was their one and only suspect? That's because they didn't investigate any other options or leads."

Having dealt with her share of angry, belligerent bar and restaurant drunks over the years, Dawn knew exactly how to handle this situation. The look she gave me was *I got this covered, big fella. No need to be my hero.*

"As a matter of fact, Steve and I—my name is Dawn by the way—did read that section and we both wondered about your son-in-law's case." That we knew who she was made Debra stop in her tracks as she approached us. "As for being terrorists, well, that's just not the case. Tourists, yes, terrorists, no," Dawn continued undeterred. "There's a daily guided tour of the city's art gallery we could've signed up for, but decided the True Terror evening sounded more interesting. Obviously, as out-of-towners we have no axe to grind with you personally. We're sorry about the death of your daughter, which is something a true terrorist wouldn't feel."

Our accuser was at a loss for words before saying, "I know. I'm sorry for my outburst. My anger is with Detective Dutton and I hate that he's making any kind of money off Eric's situation."

Seeing that she appeared to be on the verge of crying, I asked, "Dara, do you serve coffee in the kitchen as well as sandwiches and soup? I think we could all use a change of scenery and tone, maybe to sit and talk more." Dara said she'd put on a fresh pot and headed to the kitchen. "I used to be a police officer—"

"Who now works as a private investigator on different files, including cold cases," Dawn interrupted proudly.

"Yes, I've worked a few cold case files," I said. "With my background, I know how detectives think and would like to discuss the circumstances surrounding Eric's case, if you have the time. Maybe I can give you some insight into why Eric was charged and prosecuted."

"An outsider's perspective," Dawn suggested.

The anger was gone from Debra's face, replaced with an expression combining weariness and resignation. "I would like that, if it's not taking time away from you."

"We came in here for a good book and lunch," Dawn said. "I found the book, so now it's time for lunch."

Not quite friends, definitely no longer enemies, the three of us joined Dara in the kitchen where she served us lunch at a table, leaving every once in a while to attend to customers out front. We learned Debra had lived in Dannenberg her entire life, had gone to school with Retired Rodney years earlier, and had been his friend, until Lucy's death.

"When she opened this place, Dara carried Rodney's book on consignment, wanting to promote local authors and area history," Debra mentioned between spoonfuls of French onion soup. "But when I told her how the investigation was carried out, she decided not to renew the contract once the initial ten copies were sold and she's kept her promise."

"Have you convinced anyone else of Eric's innocence?" I asked, before devouring my chicken and bacon wrap. "What about the newspapers or TV stations? Any interested investigative reporters wanting to make a name for themselves?"

"Yes and no," Debra replied wiping her mouth with a napkin. "A few people were interested but soon learned how powerful Rodney and Det. Ingles still are in the community. The stories never saw the light of day. I even hired two independent investigators to look into Eric's case and their reports both came back with substandard results. I think they were approached by the current police brass not to make waves."

"Can you prove that?" Dawn asked.

"Both investigators were former city officers. I thought that would be to my advantage, as they'd know all the players involved. I think it backfired though and they were threatened that the force wouldn't be co-operative on any future files needing assistance."

I thought back to my own early days in the P.I. game and getting the same kind of runaround. My police corruption trial and subsequent firing were quite scandalous. Police services around the country knew my name and face. I was toxic to any employee brave enough to give up a new lead or assist on some case, no matter if it was a minor car accident report request, or something more serious.

"That's very possible," I agreed with her. "The conversation would go something like, 'Stop looking into this case and we'll guarantee to help you out later.' It's almost like a plea bargain."

"Can they do that, legally?" Dawn asked me.

"Like any government run organization, they have the power to slow down requests, lose requests or simply ignore them, if they believe their case was justified and they got a conviction fair and square," I said.

"No one likes to admit they got it wrong," Debra added, making eye contact with Dawn, then me.

"How do you know you're not the one who's wrong?" Dawn asked point blank.

The question temporarily stumped Debra. Either she was stunned by the very notion or still didn't have a clear answer in her head. Thus far she hadn't given us any hard facts to back her claim. I was expecting an explosion of emotions like she'd demonstrated earlier in the front room and during the tour, yet she remained calm.

"Because a mother knows," she said softly. "Are either of you parents?" We shook our heads. "When you two have children, you'll immediately feel a bond stronger than anything you've ever experienced. Kids are the ultimate game changer and not only in the way they take up your free time. They transform you as much as you try to shape them. You can't have one without the other." She paused. "Unlike Lucy, Eric wasn't my flesh and bones but he might as well have been, even with all his faults."

"Did you know they were having marital problems before Eric came home that night?" Dawn asked gently.

I almost didn't hear her answer as I tried to wrap my head around the concept of having children with Dawn.

That's never going to happen, right big fella?

"Lucy told me she had her suspicions about Eric. He was working late and being stand-offish around her. Little things she couldn't prove."

"Did she ever come right out and ask him?" I questioned.

"Not that I know of," Debra said. "She would've told me."

"Debra, is it possible she did ask him during breakfast or

over the phone the day she was killed?" Dawn asked.

"Anything is possible." Debra appeared to be worn down by our questions. Glancing at her watch, she said, "I've taken up enough of your time." She withdrew money from her purse, placed it on the table and stood. "I do appreciate our talk. After all these years, I think Eric's only hope is that the real killer is arrested, probably during a routine traffic stop, and confesses."

Even then, with Eric already convicted, the killer could delay things by saying Eric had hired him in the first place, I thought.

Dawn and I stood to say our farewells. "Do you still have those private investigator reports?" I asked, my competitive juices beginning to simmer.

"I do. I have an entire banker's box filled with trial evidence and news clippings. Everything related to the case."

"Would you mind sending me copies of the reports? Again, maybe I'll see something you haven't. You know, read between the lines using my past experience to guide me." An expression of hopefulness flashed on Debra's face. "I can't make any promises."

Without hesitation, Lucy McDowell's grieving mother asked for our home address. "I'll send them tomorrow morning."

I shook Debra's hand and Dawn gave her a warm hug.

"Hope is all I have left and you've provided me with some today," Debra said, fighting back tears. "You can't imagine how glad I am for your help." She stepped forward and gave me a hug before leaving the store, saying goodbye to Dara as she did.

Dara re-entered the kitchen with a grin on her face. "I don't know what you two said, but I haven't seen her smile like that for a very long time."

"Steve's a private investigator and offered to look over the evidence against Eric," Dawn said.

"That explains everything. Do you think you can help her?"

"I made no guarantees. Either way, good or bad, a fresh set of eyes is always a positive thing," I answered. "Plus, I have no connection to the original investigation or the police force."

We helped Dara clean off our table and left a short time later.

"I got a new book and you picked up a new file," Dawn said taking my hand as we hit the boardwalk. "We need to visit *Book A Lunch* more often."

"Wonderful. Our new vacation destination is the murder capital of the region," I said. "As for Debra, she freaks out last night and we get a free souvenir. Today she freaks out and we get a free lunch. Is it just me or do I seem to attract only crazy women these days, present company excluded, of course?"

"Of course."

"And until I see what she has stored away, I'm not counting on this being a new file, per se."

"I don't believe that for a minute. I know you," Dawn said boldly. "Once Debra said two other investigators hadn't found any new evidence, your brain started working overtime. I swear I heard the hamster wheel in your head begin to squeak into motion."

"If you must know, that hamster is always on the move," I said with a laugh, "but like me sometimes it needs to close its eyes for a while to refocus on what's important in life."

"That's what you're doing in your recliner while we're watching television most nights, refocusing?"

"That and charging my batteries to keep up with you when we go to bed."

"Ah, that is the nicest thing any old man has ever said to me," Dawn said with a funny smirk.

We walked in silent bliss through the nearby riverside park, circling back to the hotel to relax poolside. Dawn cracked open her new novel and I put on my headphones, preparing to drift back to sleep listening to a classic rock playlist.

"I'm going to take this time to refocus, okay?" I asked, as Pat Benatar began to accuse me of being a heartbreaker, dream maker and love taker.

"You do that. One topic I'm sure you're not going to focus on is having children with me." Dawn let out a mischievous laugh and looked over to me.

As she knew I would, I pointed my index fingers to both ears and with a goofy smile mouthed the words, "What? I can't hear you over the music."

In turn, she lightly hit my shoulder with her hand and blew me a kiss. "Don't worry. I'll think about it for both of us. Sweet dreams, *baby*."

Sweet dreams?

Baby?

We had yet to have any truly serious conversations about our future. This was fun, why spoil it by mixing in adult situations neither of us were prepared to contemplate?

Did Dawn grow up dreaming of having 2.3 kids, the white picket fenced yard and a husband who was home every night?

If so, would that be a relationship dealbreaker later on?

Closing my eyes, the only thing I could concentrate on was the little devil on my shoulder whispering, "You got yourself a live one here, Steve. Proceed with extreme caution."

Unfortunately for me, the words *caution* and *Dawn* do not readily go together.

FIVE

There are days when I have *zero velocity*, which is an actual scientific term. It relates to the highest position a ball thrown up in the air can achieve before beginning its descent back to earth. Neither moving upward nor heading downward. A sliver of time when the ball is frozen in space.

Looking at Debra Stanfield's box of evidence resting at the feet of a courier caused my zero velocity moment. I was temporarily stymied whether I should move forward with this investigation or decline to sign for the package, halting my involvement in its tracks.

Stop, go?

Left, right?

Over, out?

The two reports Debra had promised to send arrived a few days after Dawn and I returned from our trip. Both documents were on the thin side, although each P.I. did speak with several people the police had interviewed during the initial official investigation. The problem: no one had a clue why or who would want to kill this popular woman, aside from her homicidal husband wishing to trade up. Throughout history this storyline has been told time and again and, from all appearances, it was the only narrative that fit this tragedy.

Yet, something didn't feel right.

I'm always bothered when no hard evidence is found at a crime scene. Much was made at Eric's trial about the open patio doors the killer had purportedly gained entry and escaped through. According to Debra though, these doors were usually unlocked during the late afternoon and evening, when Lucy liked to read in the garden. In addition, the gate into the fenced backyard had a latch but no lock. Therefore, anyone strolling by could quickly enter the yard and walk into the kitchen in a matter of seconds, without detection.

The prosecutor hammered home that there was no indication anyone else had been in the house the night of the murder. The few stray fingerprints, hairs or fibers examined were all traced back to friends or family who'd recently visited the McDowells. No mystery prints were found.

This leads me to the following conclusions: Eric did it, a family member or friend did it, or the killer was very careful about not leaving anything behind. The last theory was the one I'd pursue. A person that meticulous is either a pro-for-hire or an obsessive compulsive thinker who's watched a lot of crime shows, learning how best not to be caught.

For Eric to murder his wife, and leave her in a pool of blood, only to return an hour later smelling like an Irish Spring commercial, would even stretch the imagination of Dr. Seuss. Such cases do exist, with the murderer using the *Would I be that stupid?* argument in court later on. From the few news articles I read after returning home, another popular scenario had Eric paying someone to kill Lucy. The failure with that logic is, why pay good money to do the deed, and immediately screw yourself over with a horrific alibi and squeaky clean hair?

I couldn't make the poor courier wait any longer and signed my name beside the X. "Have a great day," he said cheerfully, trotting down the walkway.

"What's left of it," I muttered, picking up the banker's box full of evidentiary goodies supplied by Eric's former lawyer's office, as attorney George Mulhall had recently passed away.

"We felt under the circumstances he was a good lawyer but

physically he was very overweight," Debra had told me over the phone.

"Did he die of a heart attack?" I'd asked her.

"Nope, hit by a bus stepping off the curb, while shoving a hot dog down his throat," she'd replied. "All that hard work at law school, making plenty of money and done in by a Greyhound."

"I hope you're referring to the bus company and not the hot dog," I'd said with a bemused laugh.

That conversation had taken place three weeks ago.

When Dawn arrived home, she saw the still unopened box inside the front door. "Did you lose the instructions on how to open that?" she asked. "Or misplace the scissors?"

"I might be losing my mind," I replied. "I'm not sure I want to get involved in this case."

"Not enough money in it for your trouble?"

I handed her the envelope that had been attached to the side of the box. "Oh, my fee is not the problem."

Dawn took out the enclosed bank draft and whistled. "Apparently. Wow, we could vacation in Italy for a month. Longer, depending on the exchange rate." She gave me a withering look. "Are you now against living like the rich? Should I be searching for a new Sugar Daddy to fulfill my needs?"

"This Sugar Daddy is still able to fill all your needs," I laughed. "I'd love to take you on a trip with all that dough but that's what's bothering me. There's too much of it being thrown my way and it makes me nervous."

"Isn't this a retainer that you bill against?"

"Usually. The thing is I'm not a greedy man," I stated proudly. "The amount I quoted Debra was five times lower than what that's made out for. There are only two reasons for such an exorbitant amount: Debra is really bad at accounting or she's treating this as a game she believes she can pay to win."

"I didn't get the impression she was a diva who thinks she can buy loyalty or use her wealth to intimidate anyone."

"It feels like a bribe."

"To do a good job? How is that a bribe?"

"Bribe might be too strong of a word," I conceded. "I guess I should find out what's in the box first and then I'll make my decision, okay?"

"Fine with me. While you do that, I'll make eggplant parmesan for dinner to keep the Italy vibe going," Dawn said walking into the kitchen.

For such a big box the contents were not all that plentiful. The most substantial item was a hefty court transcript of the ten-day trial. There was also a picture of a beaming Eric and Lucy on their wedding day. A few of the other enclosed folders that caught my eye were marked: School, Life Insurance, News Clippings, Police Reports and Julie Trenton.

I picked out the Julie Trenton file, curious what tantalizing information the police and defense team had got out of Eric's mistress, aside from the obvious. In newspaper snapshots, she was on par in the attractiveness department with Lucy, with short brunette hair, an oval face, and wide eyes that were no doubt the result of being confronted by hostile reporters on the courthouse steps. I already knew the basic plot she'd peddled under oath: Eric began working late on a new project that required her help. Then over a two-week period, one dinner break turned into innocently massaging her boss' tired shoulders, followed by a glass of wine to relax, which culminated into a full blown skin-on-skin body rubdown on the office couch.

These terrible things happen to hard working woman all the time, or so I'm led to believe.

Who am I to judge?

Had it been any other person under any other circumstance, Eric's alibi would've been solid. As it happened, watching a movie and having sex at your secretary's apartment as your wife is brutally stabbed to death, left much to be desired. In this case, being secretive backfired magnificently. Eric's cover story was he'd met a client for drinks and lost track of the time. I was wondering how he'd have explained away his damp mop top in this scenario. A strip club's on-stage shower performance gone awry? Then I read he often went to the gym after work, cleaning up there before coming home. This was the reason he first gave to police, which quickly fell apart once records revealed he hadn't attended the fitness centre in three days.

Moron.

Julie claimed they hadn't talked about any future plans. "We aren't in love," she stated emphatically. "It was just about the sex and maybe some companionship a couple nights a week. Eric wasn't going to leave Lucy."

It was reported that Julie's testimony on the stand was strong, but the female jurists couldn't get past the cheating aspect, or that Eric had recently "loaned" her $2500 to buy new clothes for work.

Moron's girlfriend.

The police probe of Julie (unlike Eric's) was superficial. In their minds she was covering for him and was a possible accomplice, an avenue Detectives Dutton and Ingles failed to go down, presumably not wanting to jeopardize their perfect conviction record. The hired investigators also barely scratched the surface of what made Julie tick. If I took the case, Eric would be my first interview, followed by a sit-down with Julie not long after. If they really didn't have any connection to Lucy's murder, I needed to be sure before pursuing other leads I might find.

As we ate at the kitchen table, Dawn and I sifted through the other folders.

"Any gut feelings, yay or nay?" I asked Dawn. On past investigations, I'd found her to be a very good judge of people and trusted her point of view. The difference this time around was she'd met the potential client, whom she thought was genuine in her beliefs.

Dawn put down her fork and pointed to an insurance policy

receipt. "I'm a bit troubled that Eric bought this two years earlier, not two months or two weeks, which would have been a dead giveaway he was planning something."

I nodded in agreement. "Go on."

"But the thing that really bothers me is the 911 phone call," Dawn continued. "No one ever found a connection between the killer's *school's out* line and Lucy. The prosecution said it was Eric's last sick joke because she was a teacher, but to me it doesn't ring true. That line meant something specific to the killer and to Lucy. When he was interrogated, Eric was so clueless he didn't know it was a song lyric. The line meant nothing to him."

"Interesting," I said stroking my hand on my chin in an exaggerated manner.

"Interesting as in, I never thought of that Dawn, you're a genius or as in, when I was speaking all you heard was Charlie Brown's teacher's voice?"

"Surprisingly both," I replied with a wide grin.

"Loser," Dawn said with an equally wide smile. "What about you, smart guy? Share your wisdom with the little people."

I picked up my empty plate and placed it in the sink. Returning to the table, I said, "What I want to share with the little people is not wisdom, but since you asked." I sat and organized the folders. "The insurance policy isn't a big concern for me. Two weeks, two years, doesn't matter. It only comes into play if it appears to be the sole motive for getting rid of Lucy. From what I can piece together, Eric isn't the vindictive kind. He didn't hate Lucy and he already had plenty of money. A divorce seems like the most natural play here."

"What about his reputation or family pride, once word got out he'd been cheating on his wife with his secretary?"

"Do you think being charged and convicted of murder helped his reputation in the community?" I asked.

"No, but I'm just saying most killers believe they can commit the perfect crime."

"In this case though, even if someone else was convicted of Lucy's murder, Eric's dirty laundry would be exposed in time, ruining his reputation in the process. A dead wife is still going to cause him problems down the line."

"Then what about Julie's influence over him?" Dawn countered. "Maybe she gave him an ultimatum."

"I've read all her interviews and get the impression she's simply an educated young woman who got caught up in an office romance that ended badly—"

"For Lucy."

"Yes, for Lucy and Julie, and possibly Eric," I said.

"You appear to be leaning toward taking this case," Dawn said as she took her plate to the sink.

I cleared the table and put all the folders back in the box. "My intuition is telling me Eric and Julie had nothing to do with Lucy's killing. They could have been leaving an out-of-town movie theatre with a hundred witnesses, instead of watching television at her place. I think that fateful night began like all their other clandestine evenings, only this time they were caught in a lie."

"Bad karma."

"Very bad karma," I agreed.

"So, if Eric wasn't involved and there are no new leads, where would you start your investigation?"

I took Dawn's hand and led her to the couch to relax after our delicious and filling meal. "The lone person left in this love triangle."

"Lucy?"

"The one and only."

"Are you saying the victim brought this upon herself?" Dawn asked slowly.

"I'm saying when you eliminate two of the three people in this equation, you're left no other option than to train your sights on the third party, regardless if they're dead or alive."

"Lucy holds the key."

"In my mind, yes."

"Her mother isn't going to like this, you know that, right?"

I took a deep breath and stared at the bank draft on the coffee table. "No, I don't think she will."

SIX

Aside from the occasional courier or school kid peddling overpriced chocolate bars to finance a field trip, it's not that common for someone to darken my porch. My clients don't know where I live and the hope is my subjects never find out. This is why I get nervous when my doorbell is rung three times in quick succession, followed by sharp raps on the door.

"Who is it?" I called out, making sure to approach from an angle to avoid being directly behind the door if my guest tried to force their way in or heaven forbid, let a bullet enter first.

"Rodney Dutton," came the curt reply.

I peered out the window and confirmed it was our once genial sightseeing guide, although that facade had fallen along the wayside upon reaching my place.

"And so it is," I said when I came face-to-face with the man. "From your expression, I'm guessing that you're not here to discuss expanding the Tour of True Terror to lovely Darrien."

"Last we met, you didn't tell me you were *that* Steve Cassidy," he stated coldly.

"I figured you'd put two and two together and were being polite not mentioning to the others a celebrity was in their midst," I responded. "Autograph seekers can be such a pain."

"Now look here–" Rodney began, taking two steps toward me, his hands outstretched aimed at my chest or possibly neck.

Instead of side stepping him and *guiding* him into my living room, I moved forward to meet his advance, colliding full force

64

with him sumo wrestler-style, staggering him backwards. "What is your problem?" I yelled. "I thought we were friends."

Having not expected such a violent reaction, Rodney re-evaluated the situation and stepped down to the walkway. "My problem is people sticking their noses in places they don't belong," he huffed, out of breath from our chest bump.

The first response that popped into my head was, *Do you mean like midgets at a nudist camp?* Figuring that wouldn't move this conversation along, I replied, "I take it you're referring to the Eric McDowell case?"

"You know damn well what I'm talking about," came the reply.

Along with my age and physical advantage, I knew the thing that was driving Rodney crazy was being forced to look up to me, like a child to an adult. When conducting an interrogation your sheer presence and attitude are your biggest advantages, not a badge or a gun. In one interview room I used to work, the Chief ordered the suspect's wooden chair legs shortened by one inch, ensuring they were always in a subservient position from the moment they sat down. Another easy technique was ordering a ball cap wearing suspect to take the cap off, getting the point across they're not sitting in their living room. For those jokers wearing a perfectly good ball cap to the side gangsta-style or backwards, thinking it made them look cool, I'd go all fashion police on them and flick it to the floor in disgust. *Hey, buddy, you are what you wear and you look really stupid wearing that cap that way,* I'd say.

"I suppose I should ask how you knew about my involvement. Debra? A snitch at Eric's lawyer's office? Or maybe good old George Mulhall sent you a message from the great beyond." Only the comment about the hot dog eating attorney had any effect on Rodney's face, which I found interesting. "You don't have to tell me. I'm sure you are still well connected with plenty of sources."

"You don't want to mess with me," Rodney said in a

threatening tone.

"For a man so highly regarded, you don't seem confident that a new investigation will confirm your findings that Eric killed his wife."

"I don't have to answer to you or anyone else," Rodney replied, angrily shaking his head. "He did the crime and is doing the time. Period. Between several media investigations and two other private investigators looking into the case, not a shred of new evidence has been uncovered to cast doubt on what I handed the prosecution." He paused to take a breath. "This isn't about my reputation, it's about stirring up old feelings in the community and giving false hope to Eric's loved ones, especially Debra."

"I totally agree," I said, noting he hadn't added Debra's surname in his statement. "My reputation always precedes me when I get involved in high profile cases, but the results are never questioned afterward. You think if I take this case, I'm out to vilify the force, which I assure you I'm not. I have no personal axe to grind here, regardless of who's paying my fee. If Eric killed his wife, so be it. I move onto my next file. If I prove he didn't do it, again, so be it. In my experience, there's nothing wrong with double checking the known facts." Rodney appeared to have regretted tracking me down. "Whenever my father and I built something together he used to say, 'Measure twice, cut once, Steven.' It's a rule I try to live by today."

"I hope his intelligence didn't skip a generation, Cassidy." Rodney turned and headed toward his car. "I'll let you get back to reviewing the McDowell case. My involvement is well documented, so I doubt you and I will be speaking anytime soon. Just know that I'll put my words, actions and reputation up against yours any day. And in Dannenberg that counts for quite a lot. I look forward to *not* hearing from you."

When Rodney entered his blue sedan, I saw he had a male passenger, probably his partner in crime Det. Ingles. I waved to both of them as the car was driven out of view. Inside, I bolted the front door shut and returned to the kitchen to paw my way through the evidence at hand.

Setting the box on the table, I recalled Rodney's outbursts, and another of my old man's nuggets of wisdom came to mind: *Sometimes the guilty yell just as loud as the innocent. Don't be fooled by either.*

"I won't, Dad. Don't worry," I said aloud.

***

Armed with the case essentials and leaving Dawn behind, the following morning I trekked to the maximum-security Sellcan Correctional Institution to meet with Eric McDowell. *Hell Can*, as the inmates call it, is located in the rolling farmland outside of Dannenberg. Cleaner and more efficient than old-style prisons, the only downside was the lousy company you kept while waiting to appear before the parole board. Only entering year five, Murderer McDowell still had almost a decade to go before getting his slim shot at freedom.

From the comfort of my interview room chair, I watched as Eric was pushed through the doorway. "You've got 15 minutes," the guard said, as he removed Eric's handcuffs, "and that's being generous."

Eric stood in place as I got up to extend my hand. "Good to meet you," I said.

Eric waited until the door was fully closed before relaxing, his shoulders slouching instinctively and facial muscles smoothing slightly. He wasn't a big man, 5'8", maybe 5'9", pushing 165 pounds, with cropped fire engine red hair and a scruffy beard and moustache. Gone was the baby-faced 29-year-old man who adorned the front pages of newspapers and led the evening newscasts. Today, I saw a man both irritated with the world, yet resigned to his fate within these thick concrete walls.

"I don't know why Debra keeps wrangling new people into my case," Eric stated, taking a seat and ignoring my hand, which I drew back. "I've told her to stop and take Lucy's life insurance money, all my money and live her life. It would be a good life. I should know, I used to be living it."

"Then your wife got herself murdered and your whole dream world with Julie Trenton collapsed," I stated matter of factly, as I slumped back into my chair. "Aside from the prison stretch, I know exactly what you're going through," I continued. "Although in my case, it was the heartbroken fiancée leaving me after the mistress was killed. Small world, huh?"

By the shocked expression on his face, I assumed the other investigators treated Eric with a higher level of reverence, promising him they were going to get his conviction overturned. He hadn't bought into that line of malarkey then, nor was he prepared to swallow it now, so why bother?

"The good life I was referring to *was* with Lucy," Eric said through clenched teeth, glancing over to where our nice guard and my potential saviour was visible through the glass wall. "Life with Julie became a nightmare."

"Hey, I didn't stop by to judge, Eric. We're about the same age and I can tell you that up until recently I was incapable of being in a monogamous relationship. The outside world sees what they want to see, which might not reflect what's really happening on the home front. That's why couples are always traumatized when the neighbourhood lovebirds break up for no apparent reason. It scares them. They start thinking, *Could this happen to us?*"

"Did I miss something?" Eric asked bluntly. "Are you a private investigator or a relationship counsellor? Because the last thing I need is a stranger giving me advice on how to save my marriage. It's a little late for that, don't you think?"

I sat up and placed my hands on the table. "It is too late to save your marriage, I agree. Though saving your sanity from a life in prison isn't out of the question. At least not yet." I checked my watch. "By my count, you have about 12 minutes left to convince me I should take your case. For the record, I think you were shafted by the system and especially Detectives Dutton and Ingles. They were retiring as a team and you happened along at the wrong time carrying a can of icing for their party cake."

"Yeah, some party," Eric said, his right hand fingers slowly turning inward to form a fist. "The last two so-called investigators said all the right things too, only to get nowhere fast. What makes you different?"

"I've got nothing to lose," I replied quickly. "Unlike those bozos, I don't live here and I've never worked on the police force or in the courts. I'm a nosey nobody, albeit with a helluva track record for solving cold cases."

Eric sighed and pointed to the prison numbers sewn on his jumpsuit. "I think you're a little mixed up, Mr. Cassidy. They issue these for closed files, not cold cases."

"Yes and no," I said. "There was a murder conviction. You're living proof of that. What I'm saying is Lucy's murderer is still out there, therefore, to me, it's an unsolved cold case. As I said before, from what I've read, I think you're innocent, which means you're one less person I'd need to investigate. Fewer suspects equal a shorter work week for me." I think Eric welcomed my straight talk. I wasn't making any ironclad guarantees, just that I wanted to look into his situation. "I'd really appreciate your help," I said.

"What do you need?"

To start I confirmed the basic timeline for the night of the murder. He and Julie had worked late on his new investment project and headed out around 9:10 p.m., which was backed up by a parking lot security camera. At her place, they watched the last half of a bad Jean-Claude Van Damme movie, had sex, showered together, and said goodbye around 12:25 a.m., when he drove home. Or, as the police would refer to it, the crime scene.

"There's no way Julie had anything to do with this?" I asked.

"She was book and bed smart, not street smart," Eric laughed. "She liked the money and the sex. She was also young and looking for fun. I was a passing fling and we both knew it. She'd have found another older man to fool around with and I was fine with that. More than likely I would have moved onto my partner's new receptionist down the hall."

Nice.

"So there was no jealousy toward Lucy whatsoever?"

"The exact opposite. Julie pitied Lucy for being stuck in a loveless marriage."

"Loveless?" I asked. "Was that her take on the marriage, or yours?"

Eric gave me a cold look and answered, "Julie thought all marriages were loveless if one partner strayed outside of it. The concept of true love eludes her. From her standpoint, she was in the perfect relationship with all the benefits and none of the commitment hassles."

"I guess she was the one living in a dream world and not you after all," I said with a quick smile. "Does she keep in touch? I'd like to talk to her."

"Sadly, we broke up the moment I was charged with murder."

"You don't say."

"I hear she's still in the city. For all I know she's the Madame of a brothel. She'd be good at that."

"I will definitely have to look her up now," I said. This line brought the first genuine smile to Eric's face and I knew he was okay with me working his case. "During this entire ordeal you have never brought up another possible suspect who might have wanted Lucy killed."

"My defense lawyer was none too pleased with that."

"George Mulhall?"

"Yes, good old George," Eric replied. "You can scratch him off your list of people to interview. He died awhile back. Stepped off a curb or tripped or something and was hit by a bus, I think."

"That's the story Debra told me."

Eric began to laugh. "He was a nice man but if he was the same size as he was during my trial, I'm pretty sure the bus was totalled."

We both chuckled at the vision of such a bus-man collision. If you can't enjoy some sick dark humour in a maximum-security prison, where can you?

"Speaking of Debra," I started lightly, "is there anything I should know about her? She apparently really believes that you're innocent."

"If you're asking if she's crazy, the answer is no," Eric said. "She's always been a great mother-in-law to me."

"Even after the affair details came out?"

"She knew Lucy and I were having our problems and she was plenty mad at me for a time. Once the trial came around though, she set everything aside and became my biggest supporter. Obviously, she still is."

"Extraordinary," I marvelled. "I'm sure deep down, you can appreciate what Debra's doing to keep the case alive. Although, picking public fights with Rodney Dutton and vandalizing his tour bus, in my opinion, isn't the way to go about it."

"Dutton deserves every bad thing coming his way," Eric shot back. "His investigation was a joke. Once he had me in his sights, it was over. He got his last big score and I got life for a murder I didn't commit."

"Where should he have looked instead?" I asked.

"I don't know. You're the ex-cop, you tell me. All I'm saying is Dutton and his cronies didn't do their job because they got the wrong man. The real killer pulled off the perfect murder." Eric's voice broke with annoyance. "And the hardest part is not knowing why Lucy's life was snuffed out. She was a big-hearted, decent woman without an enemy in the world."

"If she was a victim of a serial killer, which I think you're implying, finding those psychos first requires recognizing a pattern even exists, and that can take years." I was not telling Eric anything he hadn't already thought of during his time inside. "Maybe I'll stumble across a lead that is a lot less complicated."

"Either way," Eric replied, "I'm not getting out of here anytime soon."

That was as good a line to end our conversation as any, and I motioned to the guard to come back in.

"I'm not going to be able to run in and out of here at will to talk with you," I said, gathering up my pad of paper. "Is there anything of importance you haven't told me about the death of your wife?"

"I wish I could be more help to you, and ultimately to me. The fact remains, I have no idea what happened that night and still don't."

SEVEN

Tracking down Eric's former side squeeze Julie Trenton began with a call to his old business firm. After learning she hadn't been with the company for five years, I inquired if anyone there would know her current whereabouts.

"She's still around. I believe she's working for Dreamhouse Realty and calling herself an Executive Consultant," the helpful receptionist said with a slight laugh.

"That sounds like a very impressive position."

"So does Maintenance Service Consultant, which is what we call the guy who cleans the toilets around here," came the cheeky reply.

"Got it," I chuckled.

Eric had said Julie was smart and liked money, making the real estate field a good fit.

I found the Dreamhouse Realty office and double-checked the address. The nondescript storefront was located in a rundown strip mall that I'm certain was the hub of shopping excellence in the 1960s and 1970s, only to find itself discarded once the indoor mall opened nearby. The new big box stores in the area wouldn't have helped foot traffic either. I couldn't imagine meeting an agent at this location when it was time to buy an actual dream house. The two images didn't go together. Then again, I suspect most appointments are set up over the phone and the agent rushes to the client's present home to get down to business. The client would never have to visit this shabby little hole in the wall. Always trying to adhere to the *never judge a book by its cover* sentiment, I walked in hoping to find my next interview victim.

"Hi," the receptionist mouthed as she remained on the phone jotting notes on a pad. Her brief smile was pleasant, but she was way too skinny, her face thin with hollow cheeks. I wondered if she had an illness.

I acknowledged her with a nod and took a seat in the lobby, my eyes wandering to wall photos featuring fake smiling agents under the words Our Superstars! It was the stereotypical cross section of young, old, male, female and ethnicity. A realtor for every kind of house hunter. Missing was a glamour shot of our Ms. Trenton. The thought she might own the place briefly entered my mind, until I saw the posted business licence stating a Mel Ducharme was the proprietor. Her husband perhaps?

The wafer thin woman hung up the phone and gave me her full attention. "How can I help you today? Are you a buyer or a seller?"

"Presently, I am neither," I said, deflating her smile. "I'm looking to speak to someone I was told works here."

"One of the agents?"

"That I don't know."

"Oh."

The pouty look of growing annoyance caused this woman's facial features to align in such a way to spark a memory of recognition.

"You wouldn't happen to be Julie Trenton?" I asked.

A complex mixture of emotions greeted my question. *Of course she was,* I thought, recalling her media interviews at the courthouse during Eric's trial. Back then she was rarely smiling, having found herself entangled in a love-triangle murder case featuring her boss and his dead wife. Yet the smile would appear every once in a while for the cameras, just as it had when I strolled in the front door. Aside from her eyes and toothy grin, the rest of the once successfully assembled Sexy Julie package had completely disappeared. Booze, pills, cocaine, rock and roll or all of the above?

In spite of her suspicions, she answered, "I am. And you are?"

I stepped forward and introduced myself. "My name is Steve Cassidy. I'm a private investigator."

She examined my business card. "Is this about the accident I witnessed last month at Sandwich and Richmond?"

"It is not. I hope it wasn't too serious."

"No, a minor fender bender. One driver following too close, that kind of thing. I was walking to the mall for lunch and saw it happen." She paused and asked, "So, as my life is otherwise pretty ordinary, why would someone hire a P.I. to track me down?"

"It may be relatively normal now but six years ago it was quite exciting," I responded, not certain how Julie might take this observation. The previous flash of irritation resurfaced, although a moment later it was like an internal switch was flicked off and a kind of serenity fell over her.

Interesting, I thought. *I wonder if she remembers back that far?*

"Exciting wouldn't be the word I'd use to describe that period of my life. It wasn't normal by any means either, I grant you, not even in this city and that's saying something." Julie relaxed back into her chair, any anxiety or fear of me gone. "Is your employer writing a book about Eric's trial? If they are I'd have no problem telling everything I know for $50,000. Take it or leave it."

"I can't believe you haven't written your own memoir," I said unimpressed. "I can see the title now: *Framed By Love!* Or maybe, *Framed, My Love!* What about, *My Love Framed!* I definitely see the word 'framed' and an exclamation point screaming off the cover."

"Don't think I haven't been offered the chance to tell my story."

"I'm offering you the chance right now, so we have something in common. Well, that and Eric McDowell, though I don't know him as intimately as you once did." Julie perked up, believing I was presenting her a deal of sorts. The chance to give a more detailed account of her life with Eric than the one she'd told on the witness stand. "Your asking price is not quite what my client had in mind."

She was quickly all business, having obviously learned a few tips about the art of negotiation from the agents. "I only said $50,000 to see if you were legitimate. You didn't flinch, which tells me you're serious, unlike the other jokers who've come sniffing around."

Sniffing around? Classy.

More than ever, I was certain some type of substance abuse problem had reared its ugly head during the intervening years and consumed poor Julie whole. The winning smile was left intact, as was her ability to briefly appear articulate and refined, only to be cruelly betrayed by a short circuit in her mind that believed "sniffing around" was an appropriate thing to say.

"Have you worked here long?" I asked, ignoring her comment. Believing any information I extracted from this woman would be suspect, I decided on a scattershot approach to my questioning, hoping to get some unguarded response that might help me. "Were you fired from the firm where you and Eric worked together or just quietly asked to leave? Have you been in contact with him since the trial? Did the police offer you a deal to roll over on Eric, you know, to say the two of you weren't having sex at the time his wife Lucy was being brutally stabbed to death?"

With each inquiry the optimistic outlook for a quick cash grab faded from Julie's face, her shoulders slouching and her body deflating like a balloon with a slow leak.

"I was not fired! . . . What? . . . No, I never . . . Where did you hear . . . " she stammered, in an attempt to keep up. Then, as before, she abruptly summoned something internally and another round of spooky calm overtook her. Taking a deep breath, she said, "You're seeking quite a lot of free information there, Mr. Cassidy. I was born at night, but it wasn't last night. So I suggest you pick up the phone to find out what kind of financial arrangement can be worked out with your client."

"You want me to call Debra Stanfield right now? I will." The name evoked a slight tremor at the corner of Julie's right eye. I figured this might be her *tell*, in the same way a poker player unconsciously indicates if they're bluffing by a facial tick, hand gesture or smile.

"You're working for Debra?" came the cautious response.

"I like to think of it as working *with* Debra. Now based on your past shared experiences, is that a good thing or a bad thing?"

The stammer briefly returned. "I haven't spoken to her, well, since . . . "

"The trial?" I offered.

I knew Debra held no deep-rooted hard feelings toward Julie and her affair with Eric, no matter how wrong it looked to the outside world. "Eric and Lucy were very unhappy in their marriage at the time and no amount of counselling or helpful motherly advice could fix that," Debra had admitted to me. When asked if she believed Lucy also may have strayed from her wedding vows for the same reasons, she emphatically said, "No!" On her side was the fact the Dannenberg police, as well as the other two clown investigators, never found any evidence of such an affair, thus taking the jealous-lover-turned-killer option off the table.

"She called me the day Eric was sentenced," Julie managed to say.

"To say what?"

"To move on with my life and never look back." Julie's eyes began to water involuntarily. With her emaciated features and diminutive frame, she transformed into a scared young girl separated from her parents at a busy shopping mall. For this type of loss there were no magic breathing exercises or mental mind tricks to help reset her composure.

I'll confess I've never been comfortable in the presence of a crying woman. In most cases however, I'm the cause of the outpouring of tears. These are usually accompanied by a backlash of anger, after the distraught women discover I've cheated or lied to them. Yet, even in circumstances like the current one, I'm simply not wired to exude the level of confidence or empathy a woman like Julie desperately needs. I remained quiet, not wanting to step on this moment, and to allow this odd creature to compose herself.

"I wasn't aware you and Debra had a relationship of any kind," I began. "You obviously did move on."

Wiping tears away with a tissue she'd found in a top desk drawer, Julie appeared to be trying to decipher if I was being sincere or sarcastic. Believing me to be the former, she said, "That was the last time we spoke but it wasn't the only occasion. One day out of the blue she contacted me and asked if we could talk somewhere in person. I suspected she hated me and was so terrified I set up the meeting at my lawyer's office in a conference room with glass walls."

"That was clever thinking," I said with a laugh. "Eric said you were smart." This brought a small smile to Julie's lips. "When exactly did this meeting occur? Before, during or after the trial?"

"During. It was right after I testified." Julie's hands began to shake and she clasped them together to stop the movement. "Prior to that day, I knew the entire city, my friends and colleagues despised me, wanting nothing to do with me, as if I was some virus with no cure. I didn't think that kind of scrutiny and backstabbing could get any worse."

"Until it did, right?" I asked. "Death threats? Your car vandalized? Fingers being pointed in your direction by busybodies at the grocery store? That sort of thing?"

"How did you know that?"

"Trust me, you're not the only one present ever hit by the

slings and arrows of well intentioned, yet completely smug holier-than-thou do gooders, who really need to shut the hell up and keep their feelings to themselves." After unloading that on my emotionally unstable conversation mate, I too wished there was a mental happy place to which I could run and hide.

"Clearly we have another thing in common, aside from Eric and his mother-in-law," Julie said. "Is she writing a book?"

"Not that I'm aware of," I replied. "We bumped into each other in a bookstore where she told me her story and I told her mine. I thought I could help bring her some peace of mind."

"And get paid along the way, right? I doubt you're doing this pro bono or out of the kindness of your heart. You don't look the type," came Julie's caustic response, as her mood cycle swung back in the opposite direction.

Maybe she's bipolar, I thought. *Let's get as much information as possible and get out of here!*

"I assure you Debra will get her money's worth."

"The other investigators told her that and they found squat."

"And how would you know that?" I asked. "I'm pretty sure their findings are not part of the public record."

"I have my sources," Julie said proudly. "The reason those reports aren't public is they don't contain any new information showing someone else killed Lucy that night."

Having read both barren reports, I played dumb and innocently replied, "But there was some new information found?"

"Maybe."

There comes a point in every question-and-answer session when the bottom line is dictated by the bottom line. Although $50,000 was a bit steep to pay for information, I decided to play along with Jittery Julie's brazen little bribery game for another few minutes. I reached for my wallet, which I opened carefully, shielding the stash of cash within from prying eyes.

"Fifty bucks says there was no new information about the killing," I said, pulling out the appropriate bill.

"Really, a fifty?" Julie laughed, as I knew she would.

"How much did the other investigators offer?" I countered, taking her by surprise. "And more importantly, how much did you take?"

"More than fifty!" was the condescending remark.

"Oh, so you did pass along information to them then?" Knowing I had caught her in a compromising situation, she remained silent. "And this so-called new information would have helped to get poor Eric out of the slammer, right?" I stepped closer to Julie's desk, causing her to stiffen. "Yet, after they ran down this superior lead from one of the main players in this murder they apparently found nothing. Otherwise, don't you think they'd have put it in their reports? Well?" I asked raising my voice.

Little Girl Lost reappeared before my very eyes. *Great, now you've done it, Cassidy,* I chastised myself, as tears began to fall down Julie's cheeks.

"I gave both of them the same information but George said there was nothing in the reports about looking into it."

It was time for me to trip over my tongue. "As in George Mulhall, Eric's former lawyer?"

"They killed him you know," Julie replied, a look of paranoia now etched across her face. "They pushed him into traffic. I think it's because he started to look into my idea that Lucy was caught up in a blackmailing scheme and was murdered because of it."

"Okay, just slow down. Catch your breath and I'll catch mine. Deal?"

"Deal." Julie opened the top drawer again and pulled out a handful of tissues, which she applied to her cheeks and eyes. "George was kind of a friend of mine," she began a few moments later. "Two years ago he dropped off some legal documents for a client who had purchased a house from us. I didn't recognize him at first, but he remembered me and asked how everything was going. I lied and said I was doing great. I couldn't tell him my personal contract at the investment group wasn't renewed. It was their way of getting rid of me. They couldn't outright fire me because of the affair with Eric, since that office is practically a swinger's club, and I'd have sued them for wrongful dismissal."

"How did you get this job?" I asked.

"Through the one friend who didn't abandon me after the trial, or even when my savings ran out."

For my own curiosity I was about to ask if that was when she got mixed up in drugs or booze or the wrong crowd, but stopped myself as I already knew how the story ended. "Did George do a lot of business with this office?"

"No, that's the funny thing, he never came in again. If he was in the area he'd randomly call me up to meet for a coffee. He was a really nice man who'd always pick up the bill and asked for nothing in return."

"You two must have discussed the trial or Eric from time to time."

"We did. Not always though," Julie said calmly.

"Tell me about this blackmail plot involving Lucy," I said, silently placing two fifty dollar bills on her desk. "Consider those a tip," I added, waiting to see her response.

To her credit, she left the bills untouched and said, "Eric said he found a letter addressed to Lucy."

"When was this relative to the night Lucy died?" I interrupted.

"Two months before, maybe."

"Did he show it to you? Was it an old flame trying to reconnect?"

"He only said it read, 'Recess. 4:01 p.m.'"

Nowhere in Eric's box of evidence had there been any mention of this mystery letter. No handwritten notes on yellow legal pads from one-on-one interviews with Eric prior to the trial. No assignment forms for anyone at the law firm to follow-up this spectacular clue linking Lucy to another man or woman. No hints anywhere that there'd be a bombshell revelation that might turn the spotlight's blinding glare away from the accused.

"Did Eric ever tell the police or his lawyers about this? It seems kind of important in the big scheme of things."

Julie was ready for this question. "The letter disappeared and he never discovered any more. With no physical evidence he thought if he told anyone about it, he would only look more guilty or crazy."

"Did he at least ask Lucy about it?"

"He didn't want to rock the boat," Julie said. With a laugh she added, "He was sorta glad about it because it took the pressure off him at home sexually. He figured his long work nights at the office with me wouldn't be noticed as much, giving Lucy time to play around as well." She stopped and gave me a mischievous come-hither look. "You know what they say, 'A happy wife equals a happy life.'"

"I'm not sure that applies in this situation, but who am I to talk?" I said. I was now of the opinion this story was a complete sham, in the same vein as a panhandling junkie swearing they'll only use your street donation to buy food. "When was the last time you saw Eric? Have you two spoken or corresponded since he's been locked up?"

"The last time we were physically in the same room was the day I testified. When I got off the stand I had to walk past the defense table and I touched Eric's shoulder. That was the end of our no-strings attached/friends with benefits relationship."

"He went his way and you went yours. At least you'll always have Courtroom 8."

"You make it sound like a bad thing," Julie said. "It wasn't though. It was the exact end both of us envisioned from the start. We were each other's fling." Seeing the grin on my face, she whispered, "You know what I'm talking about, I can tell."

Dreading an offer to meet again for coffee in the near future, I prepared to leave when two thoughts collided in my head.

"When we were talking about George Mulhall, who did you

mean when you said, they killed him?" She had to think about that for a moment. I wasn't certain if she'd name names or had already forgotten that bit of conversation from five minutes ago.

"Could be anyone involved in this case."

"But for what purpose? The police got their man, he's sitting in jail and there are no appeals left for his lawyer to file. From what I've heard, he absentmindedly stepped off a curb and was hit by a bus. That happens every day."

The seriously intelligent and arresting Julie of old stared daggers at me, and in a tone similar to a veiled threat declared, "The police *didn't* get their man because Eric was with me that night. No matter how the prosecution wanted to spin his alibi to the jury and the media, Eric didn't kill his wife!"

"What about George then?"

The desk phone began to ring, giving both of us a start.

"He told me he was working on something for a new appeal and next thing you know he's dead. How convenient." She picked up the receiver and greeted the caller with, "Dreamhouse Realty, can you please hold? Thanks." She pressed a button on the phone's base and said to me, "I don't know how you found out about George's death, but you need to examine your sources a lot closer. Now I really have to get back to work. Thanks for stopping by Mr. Cassidy."

With that I was summarily dismissed and walked out into the parking lot. In her final soliloquy, Julie had inadvertently answered my second question: Are you positive Eric had nothing to do with his wife's murder?

I may not have believed her tale about Lucy's odd note, yet I wholeheartedly thought Julie was telling me the truth about Eric's innocence. After all these damaging years, she had yet to change one detail about that night.

Why would she? The truth is the truth is the truth.

Pulling out of the lot, I recalled her whimsical ability to refocus her thoughts. I wondered if it was some yoga or meditation

based mind trick. The idea you can mentally transport yourself to another time.

As I slid into the busy mall bound traffic, I began to smile when it came to me what Julie's key phrase might be:

Eric did not kill his wife.
Eric did not kill his wife.
Eric did not kill his wife.

EIGHT

"What are you going to do next?" Dawn asked over the phone. "I hope it includes returning to me in the near future."

I could picture the smile on her face and the nervous twirling of her index finger through a strand of hair above her ear. Both visions making me homesick. "If 'near future' means in a day or two, then yes, I'll be seeing you shortly."

"You need a real job," Dawn replied with a sigh.

"Any suggestions? Is there a chance Dougie will be leaving his Sunsetter gig to pursue his dream of working as Head Chef at Steak 'n Spuds anytime soon?"

"I could get him fired," Dawn responded, "claiming he sexually harassed me, not that I'd mind because he is cute in a boy band kind of way."

"You'd do that for little old me?"

"I'm not sure about the *little* part, but you've definitely nailed the *old* part," Dawn laughed. "Working at the pub and living together might not be such a good thing. I think you'd get bored with me being around 24/7, always brushing against you in the kitchen or storage room or walk-in freezer. Bending over to pick up a dropped fork or leaning across a table to wipe it down."

"Not to mention getting all soaped up to help with the dirty, dirty dishes," I added.

"Ha! So much for the long distance phone sex talk. Anyway, I don't do dishes. You're on your own there."

"Just like I am today, unfortunately."

"And tonight."

"And tonight," I said, while grinning ear to ear. "I could've probably used your womanly charm to help reign in Julie Trenton. She's a bit of a nut job and I'm not good with those. I think Julie might have warmed up to you though. Maybe next time."

"Did she give you any new information?" Dawn asked.

"Only that I need to look closer into Eric's lawyer's death."

"The daydreaming hot dog lover? What's there to investigate?"

"That's what I was thinking until Julie became serious and said I should consider my sources."

"And who are they?"

"I've discussed or mentioned Mr. Mulhall to three other people and after checking my notes I discovered their stories don't quite line up. Nothing drastically different, but the devil is in the details, right?" I replied. "First, our client Debra Stanfield gave the Reader's Digest condensed version about George plowing a footlong down his throat, stepping off a curb in mid-chew and being hit by a bus."

"When Debra mentioned that, it did sound plausible, although terribly sad," Dawn said.

"Next, when chatting with ex-detective Rodney Dutton on my porch during his failed scare tactic visit, I wondered aloud if George had told him about my investigation from the great beyond."

"He didn't laugh?"

"Just the opposite, Dawn. He looked worried, but didn't address the ghostly possibility."

"And Julie was the last person?"

"No, it was Eric at Sellcan. He said I could cross off talking with George because he, quote, 'Stepped off a curb or tripped or something and was hit by a bus, I think.'"

"Or something? Interesting," Dawn commented. "What did Julie say that's got you all wound up?"

"Wound up sounds about right," I agreed. "She believes he was working on a new clue or angle for another appeal and was killed because of it."

"Did she give any specifics?"

"Some malarkey about a letter addressed to Lucy that Eric found, but didn't bother to tell anyone about," I said.

"A love letter?"

"That's what I thought, only there's no record it existed in any legal notes or the court discovery. Like I said, Julie is a tad out there. Given another five minutes, she'd have tried to cut me in on a fantastic real estate deal involving soon to be developed swamp land in the Everglades."

"I like Florida," Dawn joked. "You can drive around aimlessly all day with your left turn signal on and no one notices. How fun is that? We could use some of my tip money to get in on the ground floor."

"You have expensive taste, lady. To afford a purchase like that, I might have to apply to Steak 'n Spuds before Doug."

"You don't have to worry about me, Steve. It's always vacation time no matter where we are, as long as we're together."

"There is that," I said. "I don't think I'll be here much longer. This case really is cold and even though the police appear to have been incompetent in some aspects, there doesn't seem to be any new avenues to pursue."

"But you still believe Eric is innocent, right?" Dawn asked hesitantly.

I thought about that. "I do."

"Then there must be new avenues to pursue."

"As always, you're correct. Thanks for the pep talk."

"Anytime."

"Okay, I guess I'm off to the *Dannenberg Echo* office to see what newspaper articles they have on the dearly departed George Mulhall. He was a well-known figure in the city, so I expect they covered his bus accident death in some detail."

"Good luck and call me later tonight."
"I will."
"Bye, you."
"Bye, you."

***

Regardless of their readership decline over the years, the local newspaper is usually my first stop to officially start gathering the true facts of any new case. Meeting with Debra, Eric, Julie and in a lesser sense, Rodney, is fine and dandy, but each has an agenda and slanted recollections to make themselves look good.

For example, Debra is not likely to divulge any information that might tarnish her daughter's reputation. Rodney (and his former partner Lawrence Ingles) simply feel they got it right the first time. They'd never admit to any details which could cast doubt on their supposition that Eric magically transported himself from Julie's arms to the murder scene and back again. As for Julie, well, at this stage she's like the vacant hole in a chocolate glazed doughnut: a necessity to have, but not really there anymore. This leaves us with Eric, whose reputation hasn't only been completely trashed, it has no chance of being rehabilitated, even if I somehow found the real killer. You would think he'd be the one person I could trust to tell me everything he knew, yet that wasn't the case. After years of dealing with hundreds of wrongly-convicted convicts, every cop develops an internal B.S. Meter. It begins taking readings from the second you find yourself in the personal space of a suspect, victim, or witness, and it's rarely wrong.

Before you get your panties or boxers in a knot and begin thinking, *But you just told Dawn you thought Eric was innocent*, let me clarify my suspicions. When I met Eric he was exactly how I'd pictured he'd be: resigned to life inside, hardened over time although still friendly, which I assumed was a pre-trial attribute, and by all appearances co-operative. The trouble is, being co-operative and being truthful is like comparing apples to oranges. The Sellcan guard listening in the hallway might have overheard our conversation and concluded Eric was an angry prisoner who firmly believed he was framed. However, if the same guard had stayed with us, I'd bet money he'd think differently. Cops, guards, lawyers, social service workers and doctors all know who's being honest and who's not:

"I got this black eye when I tripped and fell into a door."

"Yeah, I was in the area, but I didn't see anyone get robbed."

"I fractured my arm when I slipped on a toy truck my son left on the stairs."

"I broke up with her last week and haven't seen her since."

"I admit I fooled around a little but I didn't kill my wife."

"Go ahead and check my alibi, it's air tight."

Every line is uttered with a degree of certainty, pleading the listener to accept it as truth, and quickly move on to the next question. Due to time constraints at the scene of a crime or other pending issues, this often does occur. The questioner skips ahead to another angle or line of interrogation, trying to gather as much information in as little time as possible. What the person telling the half-truth fails to realize is, that in the days ahead, there'll be plenty of time to go over each answer more thoroughly, to scrutinize and compare it with other statements and data collected separately. In most cases, a second or third asking of the original question is common practice when the pieces of a puzzle don't fit.

Was there one statement Eric gave that tipped me off he wasn't being 100% truthful? No. His answers were the ones I'd expected. The thing that triggered my B.S. Meter wasn't a word, it was his eyes. You'd think being surrounded by liars, cheats, murderers and the like, Eric would've learned a thing or two about hiding his true emotions. In my assessment, he'd make a lousy poker player, even if he knew the rules and could win the occasional hand. My working theory, however, is that if forced into a winner-takes-all showdown with a truly skilled player, he'd be outbluffed and lose everything quite handily.

By the end of my investigation, when all of the psychological chips had been pushed into the pot, I fully anticipated taking on the role of the truly skilled interrogator and asking Eric one more time, "Is there anything of importance you haven't told me about the death of your wife?"

Entering the newspaper's small lobby, I hoped that day wasn't too far in the distance, although I have a spotty record about these predictions. Stepping up to the Service counter, I began to smile when I noticed an appropriately themed poster tacked to the side of a cubicle that read: "Once I thought I was wrong, but I was mistaken."

No truer words have been written.

***

Having dispensed of the work place niceties, I was advised that the Records room was located on the 3rd Floor. I decided to take the stairs for a change of pace and soon found myself standing in front of the Archivist's desk, winded.

"Is the elevator out of service? It was working a few minutes ago," inquired the matronly woman in her sixties whose nameplate read Melinda Hanson. "They keep threatening to build us a swanky new building around the corner, but I don't see it happening in my lifetime."

"I don't know if the elevator is functioning or not. I saw the stairs and thought I'd get some exercise," I explained, still trying to fill my lungs with air.

"And how'd that work out for you?"

"Not as well as expected, Melinda."

"If you need some water there's an old fashioned fountain on the wall," she said pointing across the room. "Of course it's lost favour with the younger generation in the office. They don't

90

trust any liquid that doesn't come in a sealed bottle, yet have no problem cramming their pie holes with takeout meals at lunch. I guess they haven't seen that movie about the fast food industry."

I chuckled. "I might be wrong, but I think at the end of that documentary the host advised viewers of easy ways to stay fit, like taking the stairs instead of the elevator," I said with a smile.

"Well at least you gave it a shot once. Lesson learned, right?"

"Definitely."

"Now that your breathing has stabilized, is there something I can help you with today?"

"I hope so," I said. "My name is Steve Cassidy. I'm a private investigator looking into the accidental death of a Dannenberg attorney a while back."

"Accidental as in a radio dropping into a bathtub, or by sexual misadventure involving illegal drugs and a woman who wasn't his wife?"

"Close, but no," I replied. "Accidental as in a hot dog and a–"

"George Mulhall!"

"–Greyhound bus."

We stared at each other with expectant eyes until Melinda said, "I knew there was something off about that story and now someone has hired a real life Jim Rockford to uncover the truth."

"First of all, I wasn't hired to look into Mr. Mulhall's death, although it might be connected to the file I'm working on."

"And second?" Melinda asked, completely captivated.

"To equate me to the great actor James Garner is a huge disservice to the man, who I'm fairly certain even today could climb three flights of stairs without risking a coronary."

"Plus you probably don't drive a cool gold Pontiac Firebird like he did in the mid-1970's."

"That too," I replied with a grin. "Now by chance, did you know George, personally or professionally?"

"I've probably known him for 20 years," Melinda said, her exuberance subsiding, maybe now feeling bad for that *illegal drugs* remark. "Before the paper went digital and was accessible on the web, George would come in a few times a month to do research for cases he was working on. I'd help thread the microfilm spools on the machine and let him be. He was the nicest man."

"So I've heard."

"You know, he wasn't always that big. He used to be quite fit until his wife died when they were in their thirties. Cancer, I think. He went into a deep depression and started to eat as a way to cope with his loss I suppose."

"His wife's passing really was a double tragedy."

"A few years back he told me in confidence," Melinda began, lowering her voice and leaning forward, "that although he hated being so obese, he couldn't stop craving the rich foods he'd become accustomed to eating every day. He said he was a thin man trapped in a fat man's body."

"Specializing in criminal defense cases probably didn't help his stress load either. Long hours, lack of rest, vending machine dinners at midnight."

"You sound like you know a thing or two about that kind of lifestyle."

"Ex-cop and now lowly investigator for hire," I said. "Both careers have similar work schedules, meaning there are no set schedules."

"No matter what, George never let his weight or his personal life get in the way of giving clients his full attention."

"I'm sure he didn't," I agreed. "Now, getting back to the reason I almost killed myself climbing those stairs. Being from out of town, I never met George and only recently became aware of his bizarre death."

"And you want to read all the sordid details, right?" Melinda gave me a quizzical glance. "Like I said earlier, everything you need is online. You could have just logged on with a credit card sitting in your hotel room and accessed the articles. No stairs, no muss, no fuss."

"But no Melinda either," I said with a wink. "Searching the website wouldn't have given me insight into George's personal life. That useful information can only be obtained by talking face-to-face with family members, friends, colleagues, and maybe the occasional pastor or rabbi. I'm sure the paper's site is state-of-the-art, but it can't be that good. You, on the other hand, are very good, especially for my purposes."

Melinda blushed a bit at the compliment. "And what exactly are your purposes?"

"To learn more about George's death and determine if there was something going on behind the scenes that may have got him killed as you suggested."

Melinda tapped a few keys on her keyboard and looked up at her computer screen. "You're in luck, Mr. Steve Cassidy. At this very moment, 233 people are slowing down our website's server accessing old records online, while only one person is accessing me. I am all yours. What do you need to find out?"

***

Mr. George Mulhall was known as a prominent man not only for his girth, but also for his heart and soul. His obituary revealed a long list of charities and sports teams he supported, as well as various community-based boards on which he volunteered. I wondered if the new appeal information he was allegedly gathering came from anyone involved in these outside interests; a chance encounter at the ball diamond, soup kitchen or hospital fundraising event where he was pulled aside and told, "George, I overheard something yesterday you might be interested in."

"*Died tragically* instead of *died suddenly* was a nice call by the obit writer," I said to Melinda as she continued searching for more articles. "*Caught the last bus out of town* would have sounded insensitive."

"He might have thought that was funny," Melinda laughed.

"George had a good sense of humour, although I doubt he'd find any in the hot dog story everyone keeps passing on." She stopped and sighed. "He deserves more respect in death than that."

"Him and Sonny Bono," I agreed. "Can you imagine getting Cher in her prime, becoming a beloved music star, getting elected first as a mayor, then to the House of Representatives, only to end it all by skiing into a tree in broad daylight?"

"Everything except the 'getting Cher in her prime' part, I can imagine," Melinda replied with a smile. "It just doesn't seem right in the big picture. No pun intended, George," she said looking upward. "So, what stories do you want me to search for now? Those related to George's defense tactics at Eric's trial or maybe more recent appeal themed articles?"

"I think I've already read most of the Eric ones. They were in a box I received containing everything about that trial," I added. "Right now I'd like to read any article that covered George's death. There must have been more in the paper than this obituary."

The Records room consisted of three distinct research areas: physical copies of the newspaper from the past year, microfilm spools covering from the first edition in 1903 up to four years ago, and a user-friendly row of computers to access everything digitalized since then. Melinda had returned to the physical copies section and grabbed a second paper that she placed in front of me.

"There you have it. The sum total coverage of his untimely demise."

I looked at the front page and noticed an Inside Today listing reading *Lawyer Killed By Bus - A3*. I flipped to the third page to find a picture of George behind his desk, alongside a time-lapsed action shot of a city bus flying through an intersection. *Tragedy Strikes Popular Lawyer* read the headline with *Defense Attorney for Eric McDowell* written in smaller letters below. The quarter-page story was similar to the obituary, very respectful, and conveyed a real loss for the community. Surprisingly, the only mention of food possibly playing a role in George's death was revealed in the final line: *It has been reported Mr. Mulhall purchased a hot dog from a sidewalk vendor moments before stepping off the curb and being struck.*

"That's it?" I asked astonished. "All this 'death by hot dog' talk stems from the last line of this article?"

"Did you expect Clarence to speculate on what condiments George put on his hot dog?" Melinda asked. "Before you ask, I'm referring to Clarence Manning, the reporter who wrote that piece."

I checked the byline to confirm Melinda was correct and scratched my head. "I had no real expectations I suppose, aside from thinking that fact would be played up more."

"Oh it was in the cafeteria and hallways, just not in the pages of the paper," Melinda said, mildly disgusted. "On my way to work the next day, I heard a radio host wonder if George would still be alive if he'd craved a cheeseburger instead. His sidekick then said, 'Or something from Subway,' which resulted in a listener's poll segment on the best way to die on public transit! I accept that morbid humour is our mind's defense mechanism against thinking about our own death but it shouldn't become fodder for radio and TV programs."

"Do you remember the winner?" I asked with a grin. "I'd have voted for ferries. Drowning seems more peaceful than being hit by a subway train or run over by a bus. No offence, George," I said looking to the ceiling panels in a reverent manner.

Melinda silently shook her head in disapproval, while rolling her eyes in disbelief. "George is going to haunt both of us now, you know that, right?"

"A good haunting never killed anyone. Oh wait . . . "

"Is there something else I can help you with?" Melinda asked good-naturedly, reaching for the paper in front of me.

"Not that I can think of," I replied, about to close the paper. As I glanced at the duelling A3 images again, it struck me that I'd missed a very important aspect of George's story: the bus wasn't part of the Dannenberg Transit System, a fact clearly stated in the third paragraph. *Mr. Mulhall was fatally struck by an Edenville bus in the city's downtown core*, a point I had mentally skipped over. "Why didn't you tell me George was killed in Edenville?" I asked Melinda, who was no longer attempting to pick up the section.

"Probably for the same reason you didn't tell me you were *that* Steve Cassidy," Melinda responded. "If you want to read what the *Echo* has written about you over the years, I can track down those articles as well. I guess we both assumed the other knew the facts of what was going on here today."

I slowly turned in my chair. "Sometimes my past scares people and they don't want to deal with me. But I don't think that's the case with you, Melinda."

"You're doing your job. Anyway, I've been in the newspaper business my entire adult life and believe me, you don't scare me in the least," she laughed, causing me to laugh along.

"If it's any consolation," I began, handing back the newspaper, "I'm thinking of getting new business cards printed which read, '*That* Steve Cassidy' so there are no surprises in the future."

"Instead of listing 'Private Investigator' under your name, you might consider 'Former Sonny Bono Fan'," she suggested smiling.

I stood and watched Melinda replace the newspaper on its proper shelf. "Do you know Jack Daniel of whiskey fame died from blood poisoning? The story goes that early one morning in his office he kicked the floor safe when he couldn't remember the combination. Unfortunately, he injured a toe which became infected and voilà, dead before his time."

"I have heard that one," Melinda said. "So are you saying you'd rather put 'Former Jack Daniel Fan' on your new cards?"

"But that would be a lie, Ms. Hanson," I said holding open the door as we walked to her desk. "I'm still very much a fan of J.D. or at least of his wonderfully distilled concoction. In fact, I think I'll have a glass of it over ice cubes at dinner later today."

"Well if you do, don't forget to toast the life of George Mulhall while you're at it," Melinda said, settling into her well-worn chair.

"I'll do that," I promised. I reached my hand across the desk and said, "It has been a pleasure spending time with you. I really appreciate your help."

Melinda took my hand and gave me a strong handshake back. "If you need anything else, call me ahead of time and I'll have the information waiting for you."

"Thanks again," I said as I made my way to the elevator. "One more thing. Being around the news on a daily basis, I forgot to ask if you thought Eric McDowell was guilty or not."

The question appeared to catch Melinda off guard.

"George thought he was innocent, so if it was good enough for him, I guess it should be good enough for me too, right?"

I gave her a quizzical look. "And if you'd never met George?"

Melinda adjusted the position of her keyboard on her desk and with a polite smile and in a low soft voice replied, "My daddy always told us kids that where there's smoke, there's usually fire. Therefore, I believe that if Eric McDowell didn't kill his wife, he sure as hell knows who did."

NINE

Taking the elevator down one floor to the newsroom felt like a waste, having already climbed three flights earlier. I blamed this decision on mental exhaustion caused by close proximity to Melinda for the past hour. Learning a non-Greyhound bus had killed George Mulhall wasn't earth-shattering, although it was another detail passed along to me as fact. However, discovering the accident hadn't occurred in Dannenberg put me off slightly. Maybe I was taking this conspiracy angle, one only that Crazy Julie and I saw merit in pursuing, too far. George could have had clients or court appearances to attend to in Edenville. Nothing sinister about working out of town. Look at me stomping around this city and temporarily living out of a hotel room, instead of in Darrien slipping into bed beside Dawn at night.

With that last thought in my head, I wondered if maybe George wasn't away on business that day, but for pleasure. To go 20 years without a loved one to share his hopes and dreams with was too lonely of an idea to conjure up. It's only natural he'd have a girlfriend at some point after his wife's death. I'm probably not the right person to ask about this, as I've had daily female companionship pretty much all my adult life, if you conveniently discount (as I do) the times I was imprisoned for various and sundry reasons.

I took in my new surroundings. There were probably fifteen desks for reporters, two large conference rooms, and four spacious offices for those lucky enough to be listed on the paper's masthead.

I approached a brunette in her early twenties at a nearby desk who was typing furiously, glancing at handwritten notes as she did so. With no visible nameplate, I noted the inside inscription of a birthday card pinned to her cubicle that read, "To Stacey," as well as some printed internal mail addressed to her.

"Could you help me?" I asked. "Stacey, is it?"

"One sec," she replied, holding up her index finger. "This needed to be done an hour ago."

"No problem," I said. "I've got all day."

"Must be nice to live without deadlines."

She was right about that. The majority of cases I take on have no true calendar time limit. Insurance companies usually give me a month or more to complete a two-day surveillance of their claimant. Missing persons files last right up to the moment I find someone. Same with witness statement requests. Marital cases, I guess, qualify as having a completion deadline as the suspicious spouse is expecting results the next day. As for cold case files, several years have already passed, so what's another day or two, right?

With an exaggerated hand motion, Stacey hit the Enter key and fell back into her chair. "Done!" she proclaimed happily. "Well, until the editor asks for a rewrite."

"Still, he couldn't ask for that without the original," I said. "One deadline down and possibly one to go."

"I like the way you think."

"I live by the *No Ulcer Attitude* theory," I replied, "which states it's useless to worry about situations beyond your control. There'll be time to get all bent out of shape again once that rewrite assignment is lobbed back to you grenade-style, but there's no need to sweat about it until it arrives."

"Live in the now," Stacey agreed, shaking her head in the affirmative.

"Exactly."

"So, how can I help you *now*?"

Off the Beaten Path

"I'm looking for a reporter named Clarence Manning," I
said, as I glanced around the reporter's bullpen, not sure if I was
looking for a cub reporter or a grizzled veteran. "It's regarding a
story he wrote."

Stacey swivelled in her chair and turned her attention to a small
work area in the back corner. "It doesn't look like Spanky, ah,
Clarence, is at his desk. I saw him earlier. He couldn't have gone
far. Let me check for you." She stood and walked to one of the
offices, briefly sticking her head into the doorway, as I remained
planted in my spot. When she returned she said, "Apparently he
went down to the printing floor. He should be back soon. Do you
want to wait for him?"

"I can wait."

"Ah yes, you said you had all day," Stacey laughed, as she led
me to Clarence's workstation.

"So is Spanky, I mean Clarence, a good reporter?" I asked.

Without missing a stride, Stacey replied, "Don't tell him I
mentioned that to you, please. He'd kill me. It's a stupid nickname
an editor gave him one day and it's stuck, much to his horror."

"It'll be our little secret," I promised. "If I do slip up, I can
always tell him that as a private investigator I uncovered his alias
during my research on him."

"You didn't tell me you were a private investigator."

"And you didn't tell me your name was Stacey, yet somehow
I knew even without asking anyone about you. Weird," I said as
we arrived at Clarence's desk.

A curious expression materialized on Stacey's face. "I didn't,
did I?"

"You still haven't answered my question. Is Clarence a good
reporter in your eyes?"

"So far, so good, I suppose. He's a recent journalism grad and
this is his first stop of many, if other reporters' careers are any
indication."

"I live out of town and don't get the *Echo*. Being the newbie,

100

does Clarence get all the lame local interest stories that seasoned reporters would bitch about being assigned?"

"Pretty much." Stacey's attention became fixated on something behind me. "You can ask him yourself. Here he comes." Stacey brushed past me and whispered, "Not a word about Spanky, okay?"

"No problem," I whispered back. "Oh and by the way, happy belated birthday."

Stacey turned her head and gave me another curious look as she returned to her desk. Sitting down, I saw her examine the pinned birthday card and slowly open it with her finger. She spun in her chair and gave me a big smile, accompanied with the thumbs up sign.

Like Stacey, Clarence Manning was in his mid-twenties, with a sturdy build and slicked-back 1950's-style black hair. He epitomized the earnest, green-behind-the-ears graduate determined to make the world a better place by the sheer power of his written words.

"Clarence Manning, I presume," I said, extending my hand. "My name is Steve Cassidy. I'm a private investigator and have a few questions about a story you wrote a few months back."

Clarence shook my hand with a firm grip. "A private dick, huh?"

Private dick?

So much for the professional attitude or courtesy I'd expected. Maybe he was drinking from the same water supply as whack job Julie "Sniffing Around" Trenton was these days.

"Why do they *really* call you Spanky around the office, Clarence?" I gently shot back, returning his opening volley. The question actually made him cough in surprise, as I continued to hold his hand, producing a mild expression of terror in his eyes. "I prefer the term 'investigator', but I guess 'dick' will have to do today, huh?" I released his hand from my death grip.

You have to respect your elders, son, I thought.

"I . . . hmm . . . didn't mean anything by that, sir," Clarence replied, stumbling over his words.

Sir? Nice touch.

"I've been called worse, trust me," I assured him. "I just wasn't expecting that from someone of your stature."

Visibly shaken, Clarence quickly peered toward the room Stacey had visited, where I assumed his supervisor was stationed. "Please have a seat, Mr. Cassidy," he half-mumbled, steering me to a chair.

Mr. Cassidy? I now own you, Spanky.

Clarence tidied up a few stray papers on his desk, no doubt a stalling tactic while attempting to regroup his thoughts. "What story did you have questions about?" Clarence asked as he sat down.

"The one on a local lawyer, George Mulhall, who was killed by a bus in Edenville."

"The hot dog guy."

"Yes, the hot dog guy," I sighed, wondering what glib three-word term Clarence would imagine to categorize my death. The dead dick? The Private Indeadstigator?

Clarence opened a lower desk drawer to retrieve a steno pad. "What do you want to know? I have my notes right here."

"Did you drive out to Edenville for your story or rely on police statements and phone interviews?"

"I was about to head out," he said eagerly, "only another story broke that I had to cover first. By the time I was done, there was no time to go. My editor wanted the story for the next edition, so I started working the phones."

"What about the picture of the speeding bus used for the article?" I asked. "Was that taken by an *Echo* photographer?"

"It might have been a generic stock shot." Clarence clicked on the *Echo* database and brought the story up on his computer screen. "It's an original shot credited to Robyn Hebert, one of our freelance photographers. I can give you her number."

I jotted down Robyn's name and cell number in my notebook. "Thanks. I'll contact her later," I said. "Can you tell me who you spoke with about the accident?"

"Sure." Clarence flipped through several pages filled with his own shorthand chicken scratches. "It was Henry Sand, the Edenville Police media liaison."

"He wasn't the investigating officer?"

"No, that was . . . Constable Travis Crawford. I didn't speak with him, as Mr. Sand had all the relevant information from the accident report and Crawford's notes."

If I was thinking a trip to Edenville might not be necessary, those ideas were now dashed. I could only hope that city's police force was more willing to assist inquisitive investigators than Dannenberg's had been.

"Okay, well, I guess I'm heading to Edenville in the near future," I began. "I'm not sure if this would be in your notes, but do you recall what was said about Mr. Mulhall eating the hot dog that supposedly got him killed? Or the circumstances leading up to him leaving the curb and getting hit by the bus? Did the media person tell you anything that didn't make your article?"

"It was a strange part of the story, wasn't it?" Clarence said with a smile. "Let me check." More flipping of pages commenced. "Here it is," he declared. "Bought vendor hot dog - holding it when hit - distracted in crowd at crossing. That's all I've got. I think this was information off-the-cuff, you know, details the liaison mentioned at the end of the call."

"I get that," I said, thinking things through, temporarily lost in thought. "So from the investigating officer's notes, there's no indication that the hot dog purchase or consumption had anything to do with the accident?"

"I guess," Clarence agreed. "My story doesn't say it did, if that's what you're getting at." He was becoming defensive. "I thought it was an interesting detail and included it, that's all."

With this last statement, Clarence proved for the third time since we met that he had no class. First, the "dick" mention, second "the hot dog guy" line, and lastly the "interesting detail" defense. I didn't immediately reply to him, slowly closing my notebook and putting it back in my pocket. I'd have loved the opportunity to wipe the silly smirk off his face. We both knew the only reason the hot dog was included was he thought it was funny that an overweight man died while holding his lunch in his hand. Nothing more, nothing less. Sophomoric humour at its worst, not usually tolerated by newspapers published outside the perimeters of a high school campus. Shame on the *Echo* editor who was more worried about time and space considerations than content.

"You do realize that your hot dog reference now overshadows Mr. Mulhall's fine track record as a trial lawyer, volunteer and philanthropist in the community, don't you?" I asked as I stood to leave.

"I'm sorry if that's the way you feel," Clarence said, "or if other readers interpreted it that way. At the time, there was an inference the hot dog had played a role in Mr. Mulhall's death."

"Kind of like the belief Mama Cass of The Mamas and The Papas choked to death on a ham sandwich," I stated, all buddy-buddy, wink-wink, nudge-nudge-like.

"Yes," Clarence said hesitantly, having zero clue who Mama Cass or The Mamas and The Papas were. "Like that."

I didn't extend my hand as I walked away. "Thanks for your help. I appreciate it," I said as I continued to the elevator, passing Stacey's desk and noticing there were now several reporters in the room. I pressed the wall button and stared back at Clarence, who remained beside his desk, watching to make certain I wasn't coming back to further interrogate and embarrass him. When the elevator doors opened I entered, pressed the ground floor button, and turned to see Stacey.

"Thank you," she said softly.

I started to say, "You're welcome," when I caught a glimpse

of Clarence's smarmy smile begin to creep alive at the corners of his lips. "Stacey, I'm sorry to do this, but you'll thank me later," I said, as a concerned look formed on her face. "Hey, Spanky!" I yelled out, every head snapping in my direction and then to the mortified Clarence. "Mama Cass died of a heart attack, not by choking on a ham sandwich. Look it up and check your facts, kid! You know, facts are a *real* news reporter's best friend!"

With perfect timing, the elevator doors closed as an uproarious chorus of Spanky-themed catcalls and laughter filled the bullpen, signifying my work at the *Echo* was done.

TEN

Robyn Hebert was waiting for me in her downtown apartment, hoping the paper's assignment editor would call soon. She was a pleasant-looking woman in her early thirties, with a stylish bob-style haircut that fit her face. After introducing myself, I noted her smile, which surely helped get her past police lines or behind locked doors when required.

"Would you like something to drink, Steve?" she asked, closing the door behind me. "I have water, tea, coffee."

"I'm good, thanks," I said. "This is a great loft. Lots of sunlight, open space. Are these your paintings as well?" I asked, before noticing her initials in the bottom corner of several framed prints on the walls. "Was painting or photography your first love?"

Robyn motioned toward her kitchen table. "It's a bit of a chicken and egg scenario," she replied. "Please, have a seat." As I took a spot at the table, she went to the fridge for a bottle of water and returned to sit across from me. "When I got my first camera I used to take pictures of objects, toys, people, landscapes, then rush to the drug store to get the roll developed. When I got the pictures home, I'd reproduce the images on canvas. So my artistic first love was really a 50/50 proposition, because until I was finished painting, the picture I'd shot was still incomplete, if that makes any sense."

"It makes perfect sense," I agreed. "I'm guessing songwriters feel the same way. The song isn't truly complete until both the words and music are on paper and can be played."

Robyn took a swig of water. "I never thought of it that way before. Do you have any talents, musical or artistic?"

I laughed. "I have the gift of getting into trouble, mostly," I said. "Followed closely by the talent of trying to get out of trouble." This produced an easy laugh and smile from Robyn. "As for instruments, I took piano lessons for two years when I was maybe ten. I could read music and play relatively well."

"Then what happened?"

"I was given the option to continue or not. In my youthful wisdom, I chose to concentrate on my budding hockey and baseball careers instead."

"Any regrets?"

"Only every time I walk into a room where a piano sits waiting for someone to play it," I admitted. "In all honesty, I did the same thing in my late teens after begging for a guitar so I could play Bruce Springsteen songs."

"You took lessons for another two years?"

"No, I quit after my fingertips became raw from practising." I slung my head low. "Another few weeks and calluses would've formed and I'd probably still be playing today. Sad, I know."

"I'm not sure about that," Robyn said with a smile. "Everyone has a talent. Mine is knowing how to dramatically frame an image inside my camera's viewfinder or how to mix the right combination of paint and brush stroke flair onto a piece of canvas. I have friends in bands that couldn't do either to save their sorry lives, but they can play instruments and write music to perform in front of audiences. I have other friends who are good at accounting and managing their own retail stores. I can't do any of those things."

"Focus on what you're good at and others will pick up the slack."

"That would make a good bumper sticker, don't you think?" Robyn asked.

"Or a title of a self-help book," I suggested.

"So, if by our esteemed estimation everyone has a talent, what's yours? Or, in the very least, the one you'd like to put on display today?"

"Clarence Manning at the newspaper thought I was a dick, but I straightened him out in short order," I replied.

"I heard that from our mutual friend Stacey, who asked me to say that you made her day."

"Message received," I said with a grin. "Now to answer your question, I suppose my greatest talent is looking at the same question asked of others and coming up with a different answer. Take lawyer George Mulhall's unfortunate run-in with a city bus. The general opinion is that while distracted by his hot dog lunch, he absentmindedly walked off a curb to his eternal detriment. Case closed."

Robyn reached for a manila envelope on the table and began to empty its contents. "Case not closed?" she asked, as several photographs of buses were strewn in front of us.

"That's what I'm trying to determine," I said, picking up a copy of the *Echo* picture that had accompanied Clarence's article. "I've spoken with five people who have five different versions of how this man died."

"I doubt I'll be number six, as I shot these pictures the day after he was hit," Robyn admitted. "I was out in Edenville visiting my sister when I got the call to get some shots of the intersection. That was fine with me, as I billed them for the travel time to get there and back."

I examined another shot from a different angle. "And these are all the ones you took that day?"

"Yeah, just like you asked for. I basically stood on each of the four corners and snapped various buses zooming by."

"Which one shows where the accident occurred?" I asked.

Robyn spread the pictures around and chose one. "Here. I was standing on the southwest corner and the accident happened on the northeast corner."

I examined the photo, not sure what I'd find. There's always a moment in cold case investigations when the reality of the situation hits home. It might be the first time you view the police video shot the night of the killing. Maybe it's pictures taken of the victim at the morgue. I had already viewed pictures of the McDowell crime scene, but had purposely not looked at the bloody forensic shots that included Lucy on her bedroom floor. The graphically detailed report and newspaper clipping photos of Lucy did more than enough to reinforce the importance of my work at hand. These images from Edenville, however, were my initial on-the-scene contact with George's accident.

"Anything catch your eye?" Robyn asked slowly.

"Everything looks harmless," I replied, focusing my attention on the curb and crosswalk areas. "When were these taken?"

"Lunch hour. I can't recall the actual time, maybe 12:15-ish."

"That would explain the crowd waiting for the light to change. It looks like a lot of people streaming out of these doors," I said, pointing to a revolving door and two adjacent single glass doors. "What is this place?"

"It's a mall entrance." Robyn grabbed another picture taken further back. "Yes, it's The Galleria. You can see the signage in this one."

I took the photo and immediately noticed something that had been cropped in the other image: a semi-permanent hot dog cart with stairs and a small attached eating area. *Sam's Weiner Wagon* was written on the large umbrella.

"If George is waiting for the light and is standing here, I think it's safe to say he was travelling south, thereby eliminating him coming from the south side of the street."

"Meaning what?"

"Meaning it's highly improbable George would, as reported, buy a hot dog from this vendor, and cross the street to the mall entrance side, only to turn to go back in the same direction moments later, and be hit by the bus."

"Maybe he forgot to add mustard?" Robyn speculated.

"Or maybe he never bought a hot dog in the first place," I countered.

"Could he have bought one in the mall's food court before exiting?"

That took some wind out of my sails. *Damn you logic!* I thought.

"Anything's possible," I said grudgingly. "I'll check into that when I scope out the area myself."

"This mystery wiener seems very important," Robyn said in a sly sarcastic tone. "Why are you so fixated on it?"

I glanced at the other pictures and neatly stacked them together. "I know how crazy this sounds," I said. "Getting back to our talent discussion, my brain is telling me the detail about George eating doesn't fit in this storyline. You know it's always the small details that trip up crooks, like a fingerprint they missed wiping down or a dropped book of matches from their favourite hangout. The idea George was scarfing down a hot dog is something a fiction writer might invent. It sounds good. It sounds plausible. In this instance, it might have actually happened, yet, it's too neat of an explanation."

"For you. It's too neat of an explanation *for you*."

"Yes, for me and only me at the moment."

I left with Robyn saying if I needed help getting around Edenville, I could contact her sister Joyce, who would be more than interested in helping.

"I might do that," I said, stepping into the hallway. "Thanks for your help, Robyn. I hope your next assignment comes in soon."

"Me too," Robyn said shaking my hand. "Until then, I'll just have to keep myself amused."

***

The streets of Edenville are 90 minutes west of Dannenberg.

Not very far to travel, but remote enough to cover up a crime, out of view of an *Echo* reporter or other local media. In essence, it's still a small farming community gobbled up by urban sprawl, otherwise known as the (now adjacent) City of Brighton. Due to its folksy past, large homes and spacious backyards, Edenville is referred to as "Old Brighton", a desirous destination for wealthy young families, big shot business moguls and retirees. Area farmers who had tilled and planted crops for generations were eventually squeezed out, albeit holding a real estate developer's cheque with more than a few zeros written on the amount line.

The Galleria mall was right where Robyn had told me it would be, as I stood in the same spot where she'd taken her pictures. The sidewalks were filled with people of all shapes and sizes, the streets were clogged with cars and bicycles and most importantly, the hot dog vendor was dishing out his product across the way.

My lifelong attitude about what goes into hot dogs and sausages is simple: I don't care, as long as the combined ingredients make them tasty, especially when cooked on a sidewalk barbeque and marinated in vehicle exhaust fumes.

I jaywalked to the other side of the street and approached a rotund, balding man in his late forties with a close-cropped salt and pepper beard.

"Sam, how ya doing today?" I said with a gregarious smile, which still didn't measure up to the huge grin I received in return. "I love your sign there," I continued, pointing to a framed caricature of Sam holding a hot dog in each hand under the headline, *Never trust a skinny chef!* "If I can't trust you, who can I trust?"

This over-the-top greeting and immediate familiarity with a total stranger can only be pulled off when dealing with a public figure who craves such attention. Someone like the news anchor, the mayor or the homegrown athlete, all of whom have a highly visible profile within the community. Below these so-called celebrities are the local legends, usually comprised of crazy car salesmen who star in cheap commercials, or the owner of a clothing shop where your father, his father and his father have been buying suits for decades. Finally, we lower our sights to the rung where the likes of Sam The Hot Dog Man or Lou The Newsstand Guru reside. In some ways, they're more important in the life of a hard working regular Joe or Jane because you can interact freely with them on a daily basis at the same location. Plus, they're providing a service you know you'll want at some point. Hungry for a hot dog? See Sam. Need to read the latest swimsuit/college football preview issue? See Lou.

"What are you in the mood for, my friend?" Sam asked, moving his metal tongs across the top of the grill where several items were bubbling, bursting with flavour. "My footlongs are at their peak of perfection, but the German sausages are running a close second this afternoon. Must be the gloomy weather!" he said with a hearty laugh.

Having noted his available condiments and wanting him to feel he owed me something in the near future, I declared, "I've been craving one of your world famous sausages smothered in sauerkraut all day. The juicier the better."

"One juicy sausage coming up," Sam said joyfully, taking a warm bun from a cart compartment, expertly reaching for a sausage from the back of the grill. So absorbed in showcasing the best service possible, it took him a few moments to realize he was about to disappoint me. "Did you say sauerkraut?" he asked regrettably. "As you can see," his tongs touching the top of an empty container, "I ran out a few customers ago."

"Are you kidding me?" I replied, hesitantly taking the sausage and bun from Sam and handing him a $5 bill. "You must have more in the cart somewhere."

The word "panic" wouldn't be found in Sam's vocabulary.

"I'm sorry, no. My wife makes a fresh batch every morning and when it's gone, it's gone," he explained, giving back my change to conclude our business transaction. "I have some hot sauce you might like instead and onions, maybe some relish?"

"I was really looking forward to that sauerkraut," I replied glumly, continuing to hold the sausage and bun between us, as if I might ask for a refund. "Do you know if The Galleria's food court has a hot dog place that might satisfy my craving?" I slowly turned my head in the direction of the mall entrance, Sam's gaze was following mine, a combination of dread and anger now seeping from his pores.

"No one sells hot dogs or sausages around here except me," he stated dismissively, trying to keep his emotions in check as the phrase *The customer is always right* was no doubt ping-ponging between his ears. "There are only fast food chains in there, all frozen hamburger patties and soggy limp lettuce." As I continued to play hard to get, Sam offered me the next best thing: free stuff. "Look, what if I throw in a free can of pop today and when you come back tomorrow, I'll give you a 2-for-1 sausage deal? How does that sound?"

For most impulse buyers, it sounded like a story they'd be gleefully retelling to their work colleagues. "I showed Sam who was boss today. After I was done with him, he gave me a free pop and a 2-for-1 deal tomorrow. What a loser!"

Loser - check.

Finding myself in the exact same circumstances, my highly functioning mind (if it does say so itself) kicked into overdrive and I observed a slightly different scene before me. To start, at the side of the cart I noted a case of pop containing 24 cans with a $3.99 sticker slapped on it, meaning my freebie drink cost Sam about $0.16. Next, I calculated he could cover this minuscule expense using some of the profits reaped from the 500% markup on his wholesale bought wieners and sausages. However, the real brilliance of Sam's make-good gesture was offering a 2-for-1 deal "when you come back tomorrow." Not, *if* you come back, but *when*. He practically guaranteed himself another overpriced sale the following day with wording straight out of the *Always Be*

Selling! Selling! Selling! handbook.

"Any flavour of pop I want?" I asked.

"Whatever your heart desires," Sam responded, his tongs gesturing toward cans on the table. "It's yours, free of charge."

"Okay, you have a deal," I said, much to Sam's relief. "I'll take the diet one and you'd better have that sauerkraut ready when I come back tomorrow."

"Oh, I will. Don't you worry about that."

I covered my sausage with ketchup, a splash of hot sauce, onions and shredded cheese, took my pop from Sam's outstretched hand and sat at one of the patio's bistro tables. Across the street, I noticed consumers with take-out containers exiting The Galleria and knew I needed to check the food court for any wiener-type items for sale, although that now seemed unlikely. Another investigative activity useful for passing the time was watching the arrival of buses in the area. I had believed the bus stop was located on the northeast corner of the intersection at the light. However, I soon realized the stop was actually a half-block up the street, just past the intersection. My guess was this would allow right-turning vehicles to continue moving in the curb lane, instead of halting traffic flow behind a parked bus. With these two factors in mind, I concluded that for George to be hit with any kind of deadly force, the westbound city bus had to be proceeding through the intersection on a green light at a fair clip.

As an experiment, I singled out a male senior citizen standing near the mall doors, waiting for the light to change to cross to my corner of the intersection. Even though the traffic flow wasn't heavy, cars, motorcycles, SUVs, minivans and buses rapidly cruised down the street in both directions. Like the small group of people around him, my test subject regularly looked up at the traffic light, then to his right and then his left to watch the oncoming vehicles. For him to be struck hard enough, the light would have to be green for a minimum of ten seconds, a long time to be "distracted" before stepping off the curb into eternity.

Too long in my opinion. This left only two possibilities: George purposely walked into a path of a fast moving bus (the size of a one-bedroom apartment), or he was helped off the sidewalk by some means. Although I hadn't done much background checking into George's personal life, I couldn't believe a man with his reputation would end his life by being bumped off in such a grotesque manner. What if he survived the crash, then what - laying down on railway tracks?

The recollection of Melinda's disgust with the radio hosts joking about such a situation made me pause to scold myself.

Having eliminated death by distraction (hot dog or no hot dog) and suicide, I was left with what, exactly? An unexpected crowd rush that propelled him forward, causing him to lose his balance? Or was it a push from behind by someone in the crowd? Either way, unlike my old-timer test subject, George left that corner curb and didn't make it to the other side.

"Hey, Sam," I said. "Good sausage."

"Even without the 'kraut?"

"Yes, even without it," I agreed, pausing to take a swig of my drink. "Are you here every day of the year?"

Sam pushed a few wieners around the grill using his Edward Scissorhands-like tongs. "Only weekdays during the winter, then I add Saturdays and Sundays during the summer months. I have my nephews work the weekends. They like to meet pretty girls after the bars close down," he laughed. "At Thanksgiving dinner last year, one of them said with some pride, 'Girls downtown like guys with big wieners,' and my wife nearly died of embarrassment because our priest was present!"

"But you thought it was funny, I bet," I said with a grin.

"Who do you think taught him such wisdom? My brother the accountant? I don't think so." Sam closed the lid on the barbeque and took a seat beside me.

"I'd also wager you have a thousand great stories from working down here all these years." Sam nodded his head. "I'm not sure if you were working that day, but isn't this the intersection where a lawyer got hit by a bus a few months back? I read it in the paper."

Sam's eyes widened and he involuntarily looked in amazement across the street. "I was right here when that happened! I saw the whole thing. It was crazy."

"Wow, seriously?" I said excitedly. "All I remember was the paper saying he was eating a hot dog at the time. It wasn't one of yours was it? That would be really weird."

"The newspaper is stupid," Sam scoffed, waving his tongs in the air. "I never seen that fat man before, which is kind of surprising don't you think? An eater like that not trying one of my wieners doesn't seem possible but it's true."

"So the paper was wrong?"

"I tried to tell people that but no one listens." Sam looked around the area and in a low conspiratorial whisper confessed, "I feel bad about that man and his family, I really do, but after that story ran my sales doubled over the next two weeks. Doubled! My theory is someone else was eating a hot dog on the corner and during all the commotion it fell next to the guy on the street."

There it was, the proof I was looking for, which in the big picture still didn't amount to much of anything concrete.

"That's crazy," I said astonished. "You said you saw the whole thing happen?"

Sam stood and used his ever present tongs to point across the intersection. "There was a bunch of people standing on the corner. The big man was in a light brown coat, which made him stand out even more in the crowd." I nodded in agreement. "I saw the bus coming down the street and thought nothing of it. The light was green and I knew it'd be soon slowing down through the intersection to pick up new passengers over there." The outstretched tongs were aimed at the bus area up the block. "As I was about to turn back to flip my Italian sausages, I saw the big man turn his head to the left. He saw the bus coming. I know he did."

"And he just stepped off the curb into its front grill?" I asked, barely able to breathe in anticipation.

"No, there was a commotion on the sidewalk. Two men fighting or horsing around and one of them bumped into the man, pushing him off the curb." Sam stopped and looked at me, his eyes beginning to water. "He had no chance. The bus hit him, his briefcase flew way up into the air and he was . . . gone."

This must be a bad dream, I thought, hoping Dawn would wake me up with a kiss.

"What happened to the two men?" I blurted out. "Where did they go? What did they look like?"

"Never seen again," came the sombre reply. "From way over here, they looked white and in their twenties, but I may be wrong. Anyway, it was an accident. It would've happened no matter who was standing in his spot, I'm sure of it. It is just sad, sad, sad."

Sad and maddening.

Lost in a troubling kaleidoscope of thoughts and images, I barely noticed Sam greeting his next customer with his friendly, "What are you in the mood for, my friend?" line. I pitched the remainder of my sausage, as well as the half-filled can of pop into a trash can and wandered back to The Galleria's garage.

"Two immature twenty-somethings fooling around, bump into a crowd of people," I said to myself in my van, attempting to dissect this new information. "It happens all the time. It could have happened in the food court, causing someone waiting for their fried chicken order to spill a drink or drop their purse, maybe knock a child to their knees. It happens all the time. The idiots then run up the escalator and out of the building before mall security is even notified. The perfect getaway and never to return in case they're recognized by store employees."

I drove out of the area in a state of confusion, certain only of two things: I needed to learn why George was in Edenville and find a way to steal that kiss from Dawn to make the white noise in my head go away.

117

ELEVEN

Before leaving town, I spoke on the phone with a bored Constable Travis Crawford, who was at a suspicious house fire scene, making sure no one disturbed or looted the property.

"Not the most glamorous assignment, as I recall from my police days, but not the worst either," I said. "Do they know how it started?"

"The Fire Chief says it looks suspicious. It's a dilapidated house, chopped up into low-rent units. Local hangout for dropout teenagers and older slacker types," Constable Crawford replied. "Apparently, a couch combusted into flames all by itself, you know, the one set up on the roof."

"I remember a few frat parties where the same thing occurred. Couches and roofs are never a good combination."

Crawford laughed. "I don't know why I'm here. If you combined all of the contents from every unit the value might top $200."

"Meaning a pawn shop payday of $50, if that."

"Exactly. A total waste of my time, although I'm getting some reading done and now have three confirmed coffee dates with a few of the hotter neighbourhood female gawkers."

"Fire groupies, nice," I said. "Well, I'll keep this conversation to a minimum so as not to cut you off from your fans for too long."

"Thanks."

"No problem," I said. "You see, I'm investigating the death of George Mulhall, a lawyer killed by a city bus. You were the investigating officer."

"I was. Big guy, right? Poor bastard never had a chance," Constable Crawford stated hesitantly.

"I've spoken to one of the witnesses, Sam the hot dog cart man, who said there was some type of commotion before Mr. Mulhall was killed. I haven't read your report, but was wondering if anybody else said the same thing?"

"Sammy also probably told you that everything happened real fast. That was the general consensus of the ones who stuck around," Constable Crawford said, a mild irritant in his tone. "A couple people said two Caucasian males maybe in their early twenties, made kind of a scene when they left the mall. They were goofing around and one shoved the other, who then bumped into the lawyer. When the accident occurred these boneheads fled the scene, probably thinking they'd be charged with murder or something."

"Did you look for them?" I asked eagerly. There was an uncomfortable pause, during which I wished we were speaking in person to gauge the officer's expression.

"Police resources are pretty stretched these days, Mr. Cassidy," Constable Crawford responded robotically, as if reading from a prepared script. "Even if they were tracked down or voluntarily walked into the station, it's not likely any charges would be laid. It was an accident, plain and simple."

Of his three matter-of-factly given statements, I only believed the first two. Police Service budgets were always being slashed and investigating two idiots play fighting on a sidewalk might not have resulted in any charges. As for it being an accident . . .

"Is there any conceivable way this was more than an unfortunate mishap?"

"How so?"

"Like maybe those men had something to do with Mr. Mulhall leaving that curb against his better judgement," I offered.

"They planned it that way? No, I don't think so," Constable

Crawford said firmly. "There were too many pedestrians waiting to cross the street. Your Mr. Mulhall was at the wrong place at the wrong time. It was lunch time. Had he not been standing there, someone else would've been."

Your Mr. Mulhall. Indeed, I thought.

"I'm just going through all the scenarios in my head. No worries, Constable Crawford," I said in a soothing tone. "But to be clear, you didn't investigate the identity of these two men at all, not even The Galleria camera footage?"

"No."

I commended Constable Crawford on his dating prowess and thanked him for his time, knowing he'd immediately pass along our conversation to a higher-up on the police food chain. Or maybe he'd open his book and begin reading again.

***

Reluctant to leave Edenville without turning over this latest evidentiary stone, I returned to The Galleria, locating the security office next to the Crazy Daze Dollar $tore. The space consisted of two sections: a work area with a bank of TV monitors and a holding/interrogation room, which was empty when I entered.

"Can I help you?" a husky uniformed male in his sixties asked, as he continued to fill out paperwork. "If you're looking for the Lost and Found, it's at the courtesy desk inside the north entrance."

"I'll keep that in mind next time I lose my marbles," I said with a grin.

Old enough to get my reference, the guard put down his pen and smiled. "If the ones they have in storage aren't yours, they're probably mine," he said, eyeing me head to toe.

As he stood to greet me, there was something in his manner that screamed *Former Police Officer!* Unlike the majority of my ex-colleagues, I never looked down on individuals who worked in the security industry. Although often dismissed as *rent-a-cops*, in my eyes they were doing a job they'd been hired to do, be that at a concert, an amusement park or shopping mall. I always pitied the fool who didn't take these men and women seriously and found themselves in handcuffs facing a very real criminal charge.

"Walter Lewiston, Head of Security," he said stepping toward me. "Are you with the police or a private investigator? You have that aura about you."

"Steve Cassidy," I replied extending my hand. "Ex-police, now simple P.I."

Walter shook my hand. "I hear ya. Why don't you take a load off?" he said, pointing to an empty chair next to the desk. "You probably can't tell by my big old gut, but there was a time I was fit and ran an intelligence unit with 15 officers answering to me." He swept his right hand into the air. "And look at me today. I have 25 unmotivated part-time students and lazy laid-off factory employees working under me. Most of them can barely spell their own name or correctly write up an incident report."

"I used to be in Vice and did undercover work, before the force asked me not to return," I laughed. "Oh, how the mighty have fallen."

"In my case, I wasn't asked to leave. My wife told me, 'It's either them or me. I'm tired of being a lonely cop's wife.' Faced with that ultimatum, I took an early retirement package."

"So what happened? Did you get tired of living out of suitcases while travelling first or being in the same space 24 hours a day?"

"A bit of both, I suppose," Walter admitted. "We got divorced when she ran off with a widower we'd met while vacationing down south last winter."

"Bet you didn't see that coming," I said, unable to suppress a smile.

"That and learning she'd cleaned out our retirement savings before leaving for parts unknown," he sighed, shaking his head in bewilderment. "Next thing you know, I'm applying for this security job."

"And living the high life once again," I said sarcastically.

"Do you want to know the kicker?"

"Sure I do."

"The reason we got along so well with that fella was because he'd just retired from a cop career as well. He and I spent all day swapping old war stories like we'd known each other our entire lives."

My smile turned into a hearty laugh. "I guess his stories were better than yours."

"Maybe," he said dejectedly, straightening a stack of arrest forms on the desk. "The ex is now living off two police pensions and I'm stuck here talking to you. Go figure," he said gruffly. "So how can I help you, Steve?"

I glanced over at the monitors, each showing a different mall hallway and entrance. "How long do you keep the tapes for those cameras?" I asked hopefully. "I'm looking for someone who visited the mall once."

"Just the once?" Walter asked suspiciously. "Management claims 4,000 people come and go on a daily basis and you're looking for one person, who came here once?"

"He was here with a friend, if that helps," I added with a smirk.

"Oh, well why didn't you say so," Walter said mockingly. "Do you have a specific day these two were in attendance?" he asked, walking to a bookshelf to retrieve a large fabric carrying case. "They got rid of the videotape system before I was hired. I've been told those tapes once took up every wall of the other room." He returned to the desk and unzipped the case, revealing plastic page after plastic page of shiny discs, systematically organized and labelled with a date. "This case goes back a year. Is that far enough?"

"It is," I stammered, leaning forward in my chair. "June the 23rd of this year."

"Okay, let's see here." Walter flipped through the pages. "That day sounds familiar. You're not investigating the robbery of the Kitchen Maven store or the slip and fall at Lori's Sew 'n Sew shop, are you? I think they both happened around that time." Finding the corresponding disc, Walter pulled it from its sleeve and closed the case. "There it is, never touched by human hands since the 24th of June. What are we going to be looking for and more importantly, for what time?"

The accident took place a few minutes past 12:00 p.m. "Maybe around 11:45 - 12:05," I suggested. "Are all the cameras' footage on that disc?"

"Every one of them and saved under their own file name for convenience," Walter answered, as he placed the disc in a dvd player. "Again, what are we looking for? This will go a lot faster if both of us watch the screen. Just sayin'."

The disc menu appeared on a monitor and I pointed to one of the listed chapters. "That one."

"The Main Street doors?"

"Yes," I said. "We're looking for a very large man in a light brown coat–"

"George Mulhall? The lawyer that got hit by a bus?" Walter broke in, his eyes wide and his attention fully on me. "I was working that day. What's there to investigate about that?"

What is there not to investigate about that? I wondered. "I'm not even sure Mr. Mulhall was in the mall, only that he might have been due to the proximity of where he died."

"But you said two people. Who is the other person?"

"That's where it gets complicated," I replied. "You see, witnesses outside say two men exited the mall and one of them bumped into Mr. Mulhall, subsequently sending him to his death. The investigating police officer told me they were Caucasian, maybe in their early twenties and have never been seen since, although no one has apparently been looking for them either."

"Until you," Walter said with a knowing grin. "Okay, I'm

game." The disc began to whirl inside the machine and Walter fast-forwarded through the footage. "Let's see if the lawyer exited through those doors. He shouldn't be hard to spot."

And he wasn't.

"There at 11:53, he's coming out of that store with a small plastic bag in his hand," I said pressing my finger to the screen.

"The Biz Emporium," Walter said recognizing the storefront. "It's a stationary place, office supplies, that kind of thing."

"Can you rewind a bit to see when he entered? That might give us an idea what he was doing in there." Walter dutifully went back through the footage to when The Galleria opened at 9:30, but we never saw George go into the store. "How is that possible?"

"He must've entered through their exterior Main Street door. It's the only way they can open earlier than the rest of the stores inside The Galleria."

"Do they have cameras?" I asked.

"I think so, although I believe they erase their footage once a month."

"Of course they do," I said flatly. "Okay, well let's skip back to 11:53 and see if we can track George's final moments."

I was dreading watching him walk to the food court to buy a non-Sam's hot dog. Instead, he sat on a bench and opened his briefcase to place the shopping bag inside. *Where's that briefcase now?* I thought, adding it to my growing list of things to follow up on. Closing the briefcase, George stood and walked to the Main Street exit where he disappeared into a glare of sunshine.

"Did that help?" Walter asked, knowing it probably hadn't, as he paused the image on the monitor.

"Keep playing it. Those two bumbling morons can't be far behind."

And they weren't.

From their demeanour, I could tell they weren't an experienced surveillance team. Although both wore low-slung ball caps making facial recognition impossible, some personal style and hygiene characteristics couldn't be hidden. Subject #1 was clean-shaven of average height, with collar length scruffy blonde hair. He was wearing a lumberjack-type shirt and jeans, and a pair of work boots. His buddy Subject #2 was the same basic height with possibly a shaved head, who sported noticeable dark coloured sideburns, a t-shirt with a logo that read *Unfinished Tattoos*, jeans torn open at the kneecaps and boots of the cowboy-kind. Also of note was a large tattoo peeking out from under his left sleeve.

Appearances aside, what initially struck both Walter and me was they'd also exited The Biz Emporium. They then tried to blend in with the lunch crowd when their target sat on the bench to open his briefcase. Blondie appeared to be making a cell phone call but turned away from the camera before I could confirm this. The two were again moving as George walked to the Main Street doors and exited onto the street.

What we witnessed next was chilling. The mystery men remained inside the mall entrance, apparently waiting for George to cross the street. However, Blondie soon became animated, pointing down the street. From his hand gestures and smile, you could tell he was excited about something. Next thing we knew both men bolted through the mall doors. Moments later, we saw the city bus with George and his light brown coat affixed to its front bumper whiz past the mall doors. This was immediately followed by a blur of pandemonium activity by the other sidewalk pedestrians who narrowly missed their own appointment with the Grim Reaper.

"Satisfied?" Walter asked me as he stopped the playback.

"That might not be the right word," I replied slowly. "Vindicated, however, now that's a good word."

Walter was kind enough to print off grainy pictures of my new subjects and dub a copy of the entire day's video. "For your eyes only," he'd warned me. I left Walter my business card and spoke with Jason, The Biz Emporium manager on duty, who confirmed their surveillance videos were erased on the first day of each month. "They only cover the cash registers. The aisle ones are dummy cams to deter shoplifters," I was advised. As I doubted Blondie or Curly had time to buy anything, the footage would only have confirmed George's purchase. Unsure if I could trust the police, I wasn't ready to share my new circumstantial evidence with them yet. They hadn't been interested in the culprits at the time of the bus accident, why would they be now?

I needed a break from Edenville. She'd given up plenty of her secrets and I knew she'd give up many more by the time my investigation concluded. It was time to regroup and organize my thoughts.

"Hey you," I said, leaving a message on Dawn's cell phone. "I should be home in time to take you out for a nice dinner. That is if you don't already have plans. Don't work too hard. See you soon."

TWELVE

In the beginning, one of the most challenging aspects of Dawn moving in was trying to keep my daily file progress talk to a minimum, or at the very least, not allow it to overtake every conversation. I believe my previous relationship with a librarian suffered greatly from too much P.I. chatter. That and cheating on her, a situation that ended in a very public hail of bullets, but that's another story. Fortunately for me, Dawn's appetite for any tales that occurred outside of her humdrum waitress job were viewed as nightly entertainment.

"You're like my own personal Magnum, without the awesome moustache, hairy chest or red Ferrari," she pronounced, after viewing video I shot of a dolt waterskiing when he should've been home sick in bed. "It's too bad that beach wasn't in Hawaii."

"And that you weren't applying suntan lotion to your skin in the foreground," I'd replied with a smile. "Maybe one day."

It's rare that an insurance file subject decides on an idle Tuesday morning to take a vacation, drive to the airport and catch a plane to an exotic hot spot. Even if they did, it'd be even more rare for my client to foot the bill and send me along for the ride. "Get shots of him boarding the plane now, then go back when he returns all sunburnt and wearing one of those stupid souvenir sombreros," I've been told in the past. However, that same scenario would change if it were a marital case, as money would be no object.

I had barely set my overnight bag down in the front foyer when Dawn jumped up on me, her legs straddling my waist, her arms around my neck and her lips pressed against mine.

"Hi," I managed to say. "Did you miss me?"

"Maybe a little bit," Dawn replied coyly, as she worked to undo my shirt buttons. "What about you? Did you miss me?"

"Actions speak louder than words," I replied, kicking the door closed and carrying Dawn across the room.

"I do like a man of action."

"Yeah you do."

Any well-intentioned thoughts of going out for dinner vanished in a fun-filled torrent of discarded clothing, pillows and sheets onto the bedroom floor. It's impossible to explain the connection Dawn and I have, except to say the absence of any pressure to change the other person makes her/me/us/this work. Most relationships consist of one partner boldly telling their friends, "Oh, they've just been with the wrong people in the past. Just watch me. I can change them, don't you worry."

I. Can. Change. Them.

Those four dirty words will eventually kill any good times, which is all Dawn and I ever seemed to have when we're together.

Our mutual admiration society Welcome Home party lasted into the early evening, interrupted only by a lucky pizza delivery boy met at the door by Dawn looking ravishing (and ravished) in my long sleeved shirt.

"After high school and my parents' deaths, I left Delta *to find myself* and delivered pizzas and chicken for a while," I admitted, "but don't recall ever being greeted by someone as sexy as you."

"When was that - the early 1970's?" Dawn said with a laugh, as she placed a slice in my hand. "Aside from Farrah Fawcett, who else was hot back then?"

"Nice," I replied. "I'm not that much older than you."

"A skinny small town boy lost in the big city probably wouldn't know what to do if a lonely housewife came onto him anyway."

I smiled at that. "You're probably right. Then there's your generation. With a click of a computer mouse you have access to more porn in 0.009 seconds than I could get my hands on all during my teenage years!"

"Ah, poor baby," Dawn said playfully, sliding against me, her soft warm skin on mine. "You had it so rough back then and it's so unfair today," she cooed. "Is there anything I can do to make those bad memories go away?"

"I can think of a few things," I said, setting my uneaten slice back in the pizza box, which I set on the night table out of harm's way. "But I'm open to any ideas you have to make me forget. So why don't I just shut up and listen to them now, okay?"

"Now?"

"Now's good," I replied.

"Yeah it is."

The remainder of the evening pleasantly slipped away as we were reacquainted with each other. It had been a very long separation after all and there really is no place quite like home.

***

"Why are you awake so early? It's Saturday, right? Aren't you off today or did you switch shifts with someone?" I asked groggily.

"And miss waking up with you?" Dawn called back from the kitchen.

"If you haven't noticed, you didn't exactly wake up with me because I'm doing that right now and your side of the bed is empty."

Still looking sexy as ever in my half-unbuttoned dress shirt, Dawn walked in carrying two plates of scrambled eggs, bacon and mini pancakes in one hand, cutlery and syrup in the other hand. "First of all, it's 8:39, which is not early–"

"It's earlier than 8:40," I cut her off with a smile, as I sat up to take a plate from her.

"And technically," she continued, "I did wake up with you. The fact you were still dead to the world doesn't change anything."

Like the skilled food server she was, Dawn leaned forward to kiss me, while pouring syrup on my pancakes.

"You're quite the multi-tasker this morning," I said, as she handed me a knife and fork.

"Just this morning?" she asked, settling in beside me. "Have you already forgot about last night, loverboy?"

"That's what happens when you tire out old geezers like me," I laughed. "Although I do recall a few of the finer points."

"I bet you do," she said stabbing a forkful of bacon.

I turned on the TV hoping for something interesting to jump out at us to watch over breakfast. I flipped through the computer generated cartoon programs, a commercial for a hair removal product for the entire family, then briefly stopped on the all news channel before shutting it off.

"Did anything special or cool happen while I was away?" I asked Dawn.

"Not really. Day shifts are pretty tame."

"Are you still happy you switched to days or does your heart again yearn for the occasional drunken brawl on 3-for-1 wings and karaoke weekends?"

"Sometimes," Dawn replied. "There aren't many partiers at 7:00 a.m., although we do get a few all nighters craving macaroni and cheese covered in bacon."

"My party days may be over, but that sounds appetizing all the same," I said. "What about the lunch crowd? Did the investment guy ever return after we trashed his little house gathering?" I turned to Dawn and batted my eyelashes. "Because his crazy wife said you were his favourite waitress of all time."

"I don't know about all time," Dawn responded, pretending to be bashful, "but, yes, he and three new hires arrived at noon that Monday like nothing had happened."

"Sooner or later, I'll no doubt be hired by the Mrs. to confirm his lunch dates."

We ate in blissful silence, comfortable in simply being together with no set plans for the rest of the day. In other words, the perfect start to the weekend.

***

We moved from the bedroom to the living room couch, where Dawn painted her toenails a bright orange colour, while watching a get rich quick, real estate infomercial scam. "Can I see the pictures of the two thugs who killed George?" she asked, calling my new dead client by his first name, as it felt we were now helping out a dear old friend.

I was organizing my Edenville notes and located The Galleria shots Walter had printed off, as well as the camera footage disc. "I don't think you want to watch the dvd," I said, setting the photos on a cushion beside Dawn. "It's one thing to hear about an accident and another to see it happen. Trust me."

"I do," Dawn replied as she put the final touches on her baby toenail. Closing the polish bottle and setting it on the coffee table, she picked up the sheets to examine them. "Wow, what losers," she declared. "I'd be scared standing beside them at a crosswalk too. Of course George didn't know they were around," her voice trailed off.

"Yeah, not the most trustworthy looking types, even in a nice mall," I said, locating Robyn Hebert's street scene photos in my mess of papers. "Here's the corner where the accident occurred. Those are the mall doors from which everyone exited." I held out the copies for Dawn to take, only to find her still transfixed on the mall shots. "Something wrong?"

Dawn angled an image toward me. "Did you notice the t-shirt the one on the left is wearing?"

"The bald guy, Curly?"

"Curly, really?" Dawn said shaking her head.

"I named the other one Blondie because he has–"

131

"I get it. Blondie and Curly. Fine," she replied with an eye roll. She scooched over a few inches and pointed to Curly's chest. "Unfinished Tattoos."

"Aside from the obvious, should I know what that means?"

"You really need to turn down all that classic rock you listen to. It's causing you to lose too many brain cells," she said, making her way to the entertainment unit to grab a CD, which she tossed in my general direction.

I turned the case over and saw the words *Unfinished Tattoos - Finished* staring back at me. "It's a concert t-shirt? Do I know any of their music?"

Mildly upset with me, Dawn wordlessly pressed Play on the stereo remote and a catchy tune I was familiar with began to fill the room.

> *I put her book of love*
> *Up on the fiction shelf.*
> *And thought life is too short*
> *I'm gonna live for myself.*
>
> *When all is said and done*
> *I'm going to even the score.*
> *And then go over my limit*
> *By nine or ten more.*

"Hey, I like these guys!" I acknowledged.

"I know," Dawn groaned, turning the volume down. "You say that every time I play this in the van."

I opened my arms and Dawn snuggled against me. "They don't match the musical majesty of your Sex At Seven trio, but they're passable."

"Duo, now. Gerry left the group to pursue a solo career."

"What is he thinking?" I asked. "Doesn't he know how good he has it playing with . . . "

"Byron and Will?"

"Yeah, those guys," I chuckled. "Byron on bass–"

"Drums."

"–and Will on guitar."

"Keyboards." Dawn gave me a bewildered look and we broke out in laughter. "So, anyway, getting back to Blondie's–"

"Curly's."

"Curly's t-shirt and album cover," she continued undaunted. "That disc was only released in mid-June, within a week or so of George's death."

I examined The Galleria picture again. "At the top of his shirt it says, *World Tour*. Aren't they just some local band or did they hit the big time and get signed by a record company?"

"No, they're still an indie band, but really popular. A world tour for them would be travelling 100 miles away from home. I think it's tongue in cheek."

"I wonder if they're still on tour?" I walked into my office and fired up the computer. "I bet they sell merchandise on their website. Maybe we can track Curly down through that t-shirt."

Dawn stood behind me holding the mall shot. "Or find out if they were playing near Edenville in June."

I was impressed by the *Official Unfinished Tattoos'* simple, yet user-friendly website. *Finally ... Finished is released!* the top banner ad screamed in bold letters. Underneath it read, WORLD TOUR NOW!!!

"I'm not sure three exclamation marks were needed, but to each their own," Dawn mused. "Click on Tour Schedule."

I did as I was told and discovered their global tour consisted of twelve venues with names like The Devlin Hatch, Hannah's Pleasure Box and Ed's House of Hitz. "Impressive," I stated, scrolling through the dates of past shows, all of which were SOLD OUT!!!!

"June 21st," Dawn said excitedly. "The Muck Trucker Tavern in Edenville."

"Well, well, well," I said. I clicked on the band's store link to review the t-shirts for sale. Taking the mall picture from Dawn's hands, I held it beside the monitor and compared the designs on screen. "None of these match Curly's. I'm thinking he must have bought it at the concert."

"Which means he probably lives in the area," Dawn said, concluding my next thought.

"If we do track these two down, Blondie isn't going to be pleased with this fashion faux pas." I clicked back to the Tour Schedule. "The world tour rolls into Barton tonight. Are you up for a concert road trip?"

Checking the listed venue name, Dawn said, "Hell, yeah. If we can't find some crazy fun inside The Whole Goat Bar on a Saturday night, I think our party like Mick Jagger rock star days are over."

I pulled Dawn onto my lap. "But you'll always be my groupie, right?"

"Definitely," she said. "Because you're my old man, my main squeeze, my Daddy-O."

"And you'll never go solo like uppity Gerry?"

"Nope. I know exactly what's good for me and that's you/me/ us/this. You don't have to worry about that."

THIRTEEN

After starting some laundry, Dawn and I had lunch at a favourite bistro uptown. From there we stopped in two local shops to pick up groceries and a bottle of wine. Waiting at a crosswalk, Dawn pointed to a large store window where we were framed in its reflection.

"All that's missing from that picture perfect scene is a . . . "

"Dog, perhaps?" I said gently, cutting her off with a smile.

"Sure, a dog, for starters," she somewhat agreed, returning my smirk. The traffic light changed and we made our way across the street, a block from the house. "Are you really that much against having any children of your own?"

"Is there something you want to tell me?"

"No. It's just that you're not getting any younger and men have biological clocks too, you know. Tick, tick, tick."

"That is so not true," I replied. "The only important ticking for a man is his heart or his pacemaker. Tony Randall from The Odd Couple fathered his first child when he was 77. Of course, having a wife who was 27 at the time probably helped."

Dawn stopped and stared at me with a stunned look on her face. "Wait, what? A 77-year-old dude got a 27-year-old woman pregnant? That's just gross. And they were married? Why would you tell me that?"

"You started this conversation."

"Well, I now want it stopped."

"Deal."

We continued in silence for several moments before Dawn inquired, "Who is Tony Randall? And why would he call himself and his wife 'the odd couple'? That's just strange."

I laughed out loud. "No, Jack Klugman was the other half of The Odd Couple. It was a very popular play that was turned into a TV show."

"Who's Jack Klugman then - the child bride's father?"

The terms 'Quincy M.E.' were on the tip of my tongue, but I stopped myself fearing another 1970's reference go-around about my age. "I'm sorry I brought the entire affair up and no, Jack Klugman wasn't having an affair with anyone," I said. "What was the original question again? Why do I hate kids?"

"I never said you hated them." A worried expression transformed Dawn's features. "Do you?"

"That's such a strong word," I smiled back. "The thing is, I was an only child. No brothers or sisters, therefore, no nieces or nephews. Maybe if I'd been around more children, I would appreciate their inherent charms."

"But?"

"I wasn't, so I don't," I stated, "as in I don't have any real point of reference. As I grew older, I became selfish and focused all my energies on my police career, maybe a bit too much focus in certain areas. I didn't have time for kids, nor have I ever felt I missed out on not having any. Bottom line: I went down a path that didn't include a mini-me calling me Daddy. It's all good."

"I can still call you Daddy-O though, right?" Dawn asked as we approached the porch.

"Anytime the urge overtakes you, Sunshine."

We put our groceries away and were contemplating a quiet afternoon of movie watching, when I noticed the Cassidy Investigations answering machine had a new message.

"Hi, Steve. It's Walter Lewiston from The Galleria," the message began, my heart beginning to pound harder. "I just became aware that an Edenville police officer stopped in asking for a copy of the June 23rd camera footage. Liane, my on duty desk guard, told him he'd have to speak with me on Monday morning. Unfortunately, she's still pretty wet behind the ears and he assured her a duplicate could be made at the station and the original returned by noon. She did note his badge number: 3059." There was a fatigued pause, followed by an audible sigh. "I doubt I have to tell you what happened next. Long story short, there was a freak accident with the disc hitting the floor and being stepped on by a passing Sergeant. 'Broke right in two,' I was advised by your buddy Constable Crawford on the phone. Anyhow, I thought you should know the footage in your possession is now the only one in existence, so take good care of it. If you need anything else, give me a shout."

"Your buddy, the one at the house fire?" Dawn asked.

"That's him," I replied, erasing the message and taking a spot on the couch.

"Accidental destruction of a defenceless disc aside," Dawn began, settling herself into the opposite end of the couch, "I take it you don't believe the police were following up the lead you gave them?"

"They were following it up all right," I said with a grin and a shake of my head. "But only to cover their butts now that an out of town sleuth is asking questions."

"Super sleuth," Dawn corrected me.

"Right."

"Do you think Constable Crawford is involved with Blondie or Curly?"

"When it comes to police corruption and illegal side activities by the supposed protectors against crime, anything's possible," I answered. "I'm a perfect example of that. The veteran group of officers I was part of were involved with blackmail, loan sharking. You name it, we did it."

"And did it well, if the newspaper articles I read about the trial were true." Dawn laughed. "Just who have I got myself involved with? I was always such a good girl."

"Sure, you *were*," I replied sarcastically.

"I was. I mean, am!"

"You don't have to convince me," I said. "I'm thinking though, I might need you to tap into that underutilized bad girl personality tonight at the bar."

This got Dawn's attention, as I let her tag along on the occasional surveillance stakeout. Although I've curtailed the number of marital files in recent months, when working out of town and away from possible Sunsetter customers, Dawn has played the flirty vixen to my client's cheating husband. After what happened to my last assistant/lover/mistress, I take no chances with Dawn's safety, never letting her out of my sight.

"Can I dress up in a sexy outfit?" she asked.

"What were you planning to wear before?"

"Jeans and that tight fitting Sex At Seven concert shirt."

Like most men, I too found that the sexiest outfit a woman can wear consists of jeans and a tight fitting t-shirt. I have no problem with Dawn getting all dolled up in a dress and heels, but that persona wasn't the one I saw on a daily basis. That was my jeans and t-shirt girl.

"That's sexy," I replied.

"Or I could only wear your dress shirt," she said seductively. "The delivery boy liked that outfit and I mean he *really* liked it."

"You could tell, could you?" I asked with a knowing smirk.

"It was in the way he was holding the pizza box and had trouble letting it go, if you get my meaning."

We stared longingly at each other, neither making the move we knew would happen eventually.

"I'm thinking your first idea would be more appropriate for a bar setting, especially one called The Whole Goat," I concluded. "You can wear the dress shirt when we get back, if you so desire."

"If I so desire, huh?" Dawn grinned and began moving in my

direction. Before reaching me, however, she picked The Galleria photos up off the coffee table. "Now that my wardrobe is settled, what's the plan for tonight?" she asked, nestling against my side.

"It'd be nice if George's killers were in attendance and we could follow them afterward. Although the show is only an hour away from Edenville, I doubt they have the means or desire to follow around the band like the Grateful Dead's Deadheads."

"Or Jimmy Buffet's Parrotheads," Dawn added. "I wonder what the fans of Unfinished Tattoos call themselves?"

"Tats, maybe?"

"Oh, good one," Dawn agreed. "Even if they have no name, I'll call myself the Ultimate Tat when talking with everyone there. It might become a new thing and we can take credit for it."

"We should probably copyright it first," I said. "As for talking to people, my hope is that the band or their manager can confirm if Blondie and Curly were at the June 21st show. It's a long shot, but we can't find them until we know where they're from unfortunately."

"And you can't trust the Edenville cops."

"Well, definitely not Constable Crawford. Their Major Crimes or Vice units may still be able to identify these two," I said pointing to the mall mugshots. "I'll play that card as a last resort."

Dawn set the paper down and leaned her head against my chest. "Do you really think these two are connected to Lucy's murder? From the looks of them, they'd only be in their late teens at the time and too young to carry out such a brutal premeditated killing. They don't exactly appear to be the brightest bulbs in the batch either."

Dawn wasn't putting forth any ideas I hadn't already considered. In cold case files, the new investigation is broken into two distinct sections: Then and Now. You start by looking at what happened at the time of the incident – back *then*. The idea is to review the known facts, confirm the conclusions of previous investigators and determine if something important was missed.

Once those areas have been established, you can move onto the *now* part, which includes sifting through any uninvestigated clues and revisiting witnesses armed with additional questions. When I re-interview people and uncover a vital new lead, I invariably ask why they hadn't told the police this information earlier. With a shoulder shrug and a shake of the head, the universal response is, "They didn't ask."

The final aspect of the Now investigation is to think outside of the box. Quiz witnesses (old and new) with as many questions directly related to the case as you can, solicit personal opinions of the individuals involved and most importantly ask where they believe the initial investigation was lacking. It doesn't matter that these people have no formal training and their only information comes from the media. What's imperative to keep in mind is that everyone has a theory about the case and will gladly share it, if only they're asked. Many unsolved crimes have been closed when an investigator disregards his or her common sense to play a hunch.

"The two incidents may not be related," I admitted. "The passage of time, the distance between locations and the seemingly different M.O.'s would indicate that."

"But?"

"But there is one common thread: George Mulhall, who was possibly looking into new information for another appeal."

"So says Strung Out Julie," Dawn interrupted.

"Noted," I said. "However, George was in Edenville for some purpose. On that count, I'm hoping his law office can help me out Monday morning. The whereabouts of his briefcase also troubles me. What if there were important papers in it? Are they lost now or shredded by his associates because they didn't know what they pertained to?"

"Not that I want to discourage you, but this George thread does seem a bit tenuous."

"I know. Unfortunately, I've already spoken to everyone of

significance from the first go-around, albeit not as in-depth as I'd have liked with Det. Dutton and Det. Ingles, although that's understandable due to the circumstances. So I'm left hanging by this proverbial thread, praying the case will unravel like a cheap knitted sweater and lead us back to Lucy's bedroom."

"Speaking of bedrooms, I'm going to try on a few different looks in front of the mirror," Dawn said, getting off the couch. "Care to give me your best 'what not to wear' speech?"

She grabbed my hand and led me across the living room. "I do care. I have to warn you though, I'm not sure you'll actually change into the first outfit for a while."

"I'm in no hurry," Dawn smiled. "The concert isn't for another seven hours. We've got plenty of time."

***

Our road trip was uneventful, unless you would call Dawn singing along to the Unfinished Tattoos disc at the top of her lungs, with her head playfully bopping up and down an event. It is very entertaining, either way you look at it. The Barton population sign indicated 19,937 inhabitants, though that's misleading, as the region amalgamated several counties a few years back. The number of actual Bartonites was probably closer to 10,001, give or take. Never destined to be anything more than a pleasant bedroom community, Barton had no truly bad areas to live in, except for the three-block radius around The Whole Goat Bar.

"Do you think the neighbourhood was this sad before this dive opened for business," Dawn began slowly, "or afterward?"

"I'm guessing the slide started after the first two shots were drank and a nasty knife fight between friends got out of control," I stated, pulling into one of the last parking spots. From our vantage point, we could see an old-time Winnebago motor home set back in the corner of the lot, with a banner across the side reading, ARE YOU FINISHED? WORLD TOUR!!! Lingering outside the door was a collection of female fans, each one more ridiculously dressed than the next. "We are definitely at the right bar," I laughed, pointing to the scantily clad groupies.

Dawn could only stare in awe at the group, who resembled White Snake video shoot audition rejects. "In these jeans I feel totally overdressed now," she declared.

"You kind of are with your upper thighs not exposed like that," I smiled, pointing to one girl whose denim skirt barely covered her waistline. "And don't get me started about not being able to see your boobs spilling out over a bustier," I added. "Stupid t-shirt."

"Stupid everything," Dawn concurred with a huge grin. "I guess I won't be the Ultimate Tat here tonight after all."

"That might not be such a bad thing," I said as we exited the van.

Rounding the back bumper, Dawn was called out by one of the RV hanger-ons. "Hey ditch pig, Sex At Seven sucks!"

Without missing a step, Dawn yelled back, "At least when they do, your mother isn't in the room with them!"

This produced more unintelligible and unintelligent barbs sent back in our direction.

"Wow, nicely done," I said, putting my arm around Dawn, escorting her away from the danger.

"Thank you," she said. "Actually, that could've been way worse."

"How?"

"I left the donkey out of it."

"If I had a nickel for every time the phrase, 'but I left the donkey out of it' was said in my presence, I'd be a millionaire," I laughed.

Just then a half emptied beer bottle exploded against the pavement behind us.

"Tough crowd," Dawn said as we quickened our pace toward the front door.

"I hope my tires are as tough," I replied, worried we'd be returning to a stripped-down version of my van after the show.

***

It's unclear how The Whole Goat could legally renew its business licence each year, yet here we were gladly paying a cover charge to gain entry.

"Along with condoms and knock-off colognes, I wonder if they stock syringes filled with penicillin in the washroom dispensers," I said to Dawn, raising my voice above the screaming banshee rock music blaring from a jukebox. "I'd feel safer with a shot of it right about now."

"That or a tetanus shot," Dawn called back, as she led me by the hand to a vacant stand-up drink table at the back of the room. "This works," she said, taking in our packed surroundings. "It looks like the 1980's, a badass heavy metal loving biker gang and a whorehouse exploded in here!"

"And who says you can't go home?" I replied, scanning the place for a waitress. Turning to my right, I noticed Unfinished Tattoos' unmanned soundboard, which was covered by a large Def Leppard 'Hysteria' album cover flag. "Do you feel safe enough to stand here alone while I get us some drinks?"

"I'll be okay," Dawn replied easily, "as long as the lights remain up. I'll keep my eye out for Blondie and Curly."

"Me too. I'm going to make a quick patrol of the whole bar, including the washroom and outdoor smoking area for them. Do you want your usual vanilla vodka or something more dangerous to better fit into this crowd?"

"That'll be fine, thanks."

The band was scheduled to play in 20 minutes, and I doubted they'd have an opening act. Forcing a path to the washroom hallway through a sea of leather, sadly-drawn homemade tattoos and hair of varying lengths and cleanliness, I trusted that the management spoke to the boys during their afternoon sound check. "The poster says 11:00 p.m., so don't even think about making these fans wait a minute longer. This bunch will eat you alive, literally limb by limb, if you pull that prima donna attitude here," I imagined them being warned. "Because once they're through crippling you and destroying all your equipment, they'll move on to the bar fixtures and that's when the shooting starts." Having heard the band's promise to hit the stage on time, I could see the grizzled owner stomping away with one last jab: "It's bad enough you're wearing mascara. You look like school girls and not in a good way."

I didn't find Blondie or Curly and was actually relieved. It would have been a lot of mental work to keep track of their whereabouts during and after the concert. At this point, it's not as if I was expecting someone to provide me with their full names or anything. Wouldn't that be helpful? Sure it would, but so might an address associated with a car licence plate, or a vague suggestion of where they might hang out. That type of information could be followed up and lead to more clues about their identity. As it was, I only knew they were familiar with The Galleria and possibly The Muck Trucker Tavern, both in Edenville.

FOURTEEN

I set our drinks on the table. "To save time I bought us two each."

Dawn immediately made a toast. "Long live rock and roll!" she cried out with a smile, tapping her glass against mine.

"Forget rock and roll," I said, taking a swig, "long live us."

Sucking slowly on her straw, Dawn asked, "No luck finding them?"

"Not yet." I glanced around to find the soundboard uncovered. Behind it stood a large bearded technician, who was an interesting combination of part cave man, part live-bat-biting-era Ozzy Osbourne. "I want to talk to the sound guy before they lower the lights."

"Okay. Did you grab the mall shots off the kitchen table?"

"I did."

"You're so smart," Dawn kidded me. "Now you go."

"Hugo? Who's Hugo?"

She lovingly pushed me away, as I reached into my jacket pocket to extract the folded mall camera pics.

"How's it going tonight?" I asked, slurring my speech slightly as I approached my audio/lighting target. "Are you with the band?"

"I am tonight," the big guy responded coolly, while ripping thin tape pieces off a roll and tagging them to the side of the board.

"What are those for? To hold the buttons in place during the show?" I leaned forward, much to the tech's consternation.

"Hey step back! I'm workin' here!"

I straighten up and shuffled back a step, raising my glass. "Hey man, I'm sorry. Really." For the first time we made eye contact and I think he reassessed the situation.

"Buddy, you're fine. It's just that the show starts in five minutes and someone screwed around with my levels."

I made a dramatic turn toward the front of the room and then wheeled back around. "The band is going to sound okay, right? Like on their CDs? I spent $20 to get in and another $20 on drinks."

A genuine look of sadness came over the man's face as he put on a headset. "Don't worry brother, I've got everything under control." His attention drifted to the stage as a man wearing a Killer Rock 107.4 FM t-shirt walked to a microphone and turned it on. "See, that's the local DJ, tonight's MC. The show's about to start," my new friend reassured me.

Knowing this wasn't the kind of atmosphere where a nosey P.I. would be welcomed with open arms and warm thoughts, I decided my window of opportunity with this band entourage member was closing rapidly. Using the element of surprise, coupled with his need to stay focused on stage happenings, I unfolded the pictures and held them out, making sure they blocked the view of the centre of the soundboard console. Pointing to Curly's concert t-shirt first, I asked quite forcibly, "Do you know him?"

Any recognition of Curly's ugly mug was immediately replaced by panic and anger. "Are you out of your mind?" the tech shrieked, pushing aside my hand and adjusting an audio level. Moments later, we could hear the radio station's rep pumping up the crowd.

"Hello Barton and The Whole Goat!" he yelled. "Killer Rock 107.4 FM welcomes you to tonight's epic concert featuring the one and only Unfinished Tattoos!"

I again brought my hand back in place and hollered, "I know

you know him! Look again. The one with the concert tee. I bet he's here tonight and you're covering for him!"

"You're gonna get yourself killed, mister. Now get out of my face and away from the board or you're going to be really sorry."

"He got my sister knocked up and then left her," I replied, lowering my voice slightly, hoping to trigger some empathy. The MC continued his carnival barker routine in the background, stressing that the band would be out shortly and that hot dogs were half price. "Just take one good look and then we can both enjoy the concert, all right?" I pointed to Dawn and added, "My sister still loves this jerk. C'mon man, help her out if you can."

Neanderthal Osborne's eyes briefly glazed over as they took in my beautiful girlfriend's finer assets. "I've got a show to run. Give me that," he demanded, snatching the pictures from my hand and staring intensely at them. "Man, it's your sister's lucky day." Although this sounded promising, it was said with an ominous tone warning of bad things to come. "Carl's backstage with the band."

"Doing what?" I asked, trying to downplay my internal joy at this news.

"I don't know, getting them drinks or girls." He crumpled up the pages and threw them at my chest. "I found your sister's missing love, so get lost before I call security."

I pocketed the balled paper and pushed my luck one last time. "Does he work for the band?"

From his reaction, the phrase *If looks could kill* took on a very frightening meaning, especially in this setting. "He was already here when we rolled in at noon. The band took pity and let him help hang the stage banner. Apparently, he's some bizarre super fan, but you and your sister would already know that, now wouldn't you?"

"Yeah, of course. Carl's a huge fan. So is my sister," I replied as warning bells pealed inside my head and it appeared the audio tech was now silently expressing doubt I was telling the truth.

The crowning blow to my credibility came when a smiling Dawn faced us, her Sex At Seven shirt fully visible.

"Big fan, huh?"

The following few moments are a bit muddled. Using his headset's microphone, I heard the tech say, "Send a couple of roadies back to the board. There's a narc here who needs to be taken care of."

I quickly walked to Dawn and took her hand. "We've got to get out of here," I said, pushing our way toward the front entrance. Out of the corner of my eye, I saw movement at the side of the stage as two very large, angry looking men began to part the mosh pit crowd, bodies flying in every direction. Our path was much clearer and I knew if we could get outside we'd have a good chance of evading capture. In any event, I was positive we could outrun our new enemies through the streets of Barton, just as I'd escaped the clutches of the Cougar Trap's bouncers not so long ago.

Closing in fast on the front door and looking back at the roadies, neither Dawn nor I saw the wall of slutty skanks exiting the washroom designated 'Goatess'. With our hands still clasped tightly together and adrenalin pulsing through our veins, we tried to go through and over the groupies at the same time. Measuring our success on a purely mathematical basis, we cleared four of the five women for a passing score of 80%. Unfortunately, Little Miss 20% was clothes-lined by my outstretched right arm and nearly decapitated. At least that's what it felt like as we continued undeterred racing for our lives.

"That's the bitch from the parking lot who said that thing about your mother!" we heard someone shout in our direction.

"Yeah I am," I heard Dawn say proudly as we flew past the astonished ticket taker.

Leading a track race or galloping toward the end zone for a touchdown, athletes often make two crucial mistakes before tasting victory: they slow down, believing no one is behind them, or they look to see if someone is catching up, causing them to panic and lose their winning rhythm. Steps from freedom, I committed both of these offenses, although in retrospect I'm glad I did. Otherwise I would not have witnessed the angry groupie mob help their dazed comrade to her feet and start en masse after us, with the roadies close behind. That's when the lights went out, causing the approaching stampede to come to an abrupt halt as the DJ MC demanded to know, "Are you ready to rock? Ladies and gentlemen and goats, The Unfinished Tattoos!"

Pandemonium inside the bar immediately broke out, as the band kick-started the show with flash pot explosions and the thundering drum intro to their radio-friendly signature tune, *I Just Finished.*

We glided untouched out the doors to the fresh air. "Quick, down this way," I instructed, pulling Dawn along as we raced up the deserted street, ducking into an alley. "We can't stay outside too long in this neighbourhood. It's probably more dangerous than The Whole Goat."

"Well we can't go back inside there, Steve," Dawn countered, out of breath and trying to process what had just happened.

"I know a place where we'll be safe and sound, trust me."

"I do."

I peeked around the corner of the building and saw nobody coming after us. Even the outside smokers we'd passed were nowhere to be found. "Everyone's inside enjoying the concert. Let's go down this alley and make our way back around to the parking lot. We can slip into the van unnoticed and then I'll put up the curtains so no one can see in."

"Then what?" Dawn asked as we started down a back roadway behind the downtown stores.

"We wait patiently."

"For what?"

"Not for what, for whom," I said with a smile.

"You mean those freaks who want us dead? You do realize

they can't be killed with a silver bullet or a stake through the heart? Neither of which I've seen in your van, by the way."

On the edge of the parking lot, I made sure we were safe and motioned to Dawn to make a run for the van's driver's side door. "Get in quickly and switch off the interior lights, you know, the dome and floor lights. Then climb into the back."

I handed her the keys and she hesitated for a split second. With an *I hope you know what you're doing* look on her face she sprinted to the van. I continued to monitor the lot for concert stragglers before entering the van a few minutes later.

"Are you having fun yet?" I asked Dawn, who was seated on the back bench.

"I have to say that when you promise we're going to have an interesting abnormal evening, you always come through."

"I do, don't I?" I said while adjusting the thick curtains across the rear windows and the area between the front and back seats. "There, no one can see in. It's like our own private little apartment now."

"Or small tree house," Dawn said. "So if no one is after us, why are we still smack dab in the middle of enemy territory and not going home?"

In all the heart pounding commotion of late, I realized I had yet to tell her that tonight's mission was a success or would be soon enough.

"All in due time, Dawn," I replied in a calming tone as I opened the back window curtain in order to see the bar's exits. "Once we know where Carl–"

"Carl?"

"Oh yeah, evidently Curly's real name is Carl," I replied. "So, once we find out where he lives, we'll head back to Darrien."

"If you say so," Dawn replied slowly.

As the Unfinished Tattoos' set continued in high gear, amped bass and drum beats rattling the van's windows, I retold the tale of how our hero determined the name of George's killer. "I envision that once the show's over, Carl will try and hang with his rock gods until they unceremoniously kick him out, telling him to get a life. Dejected, he'll tuck his tail between his legs and speed out of here in one of the cars and–"

"We'll follow him home, wherever that may be," Dawn interrupted, seeing the bigger picture. "And then the fair maiden and her super sleuth will live happily ever after."

I repositioned our bodies into a more comfortable position on the back bench. "Sure, that's exactly how I'd like this night to end. Let's go with that happy thought, okay?"

"Deal," Dawn agreed, as her head began to bop and her body started to rock gently back and forth against me.

Unlike super fan Dawn, who sang along with the band in a low melodic whisper, the only lyric I made out during the next 80 minutes was: *"You're not finished until you're done."*

Maybe not on par with The Beatles' best lyrics but a prophetic line nevertheless. From Carl to George and back to Lucy and Eric again, this investigation wasn't finished by a long shot.

***

"Unfinished Tattoos will be signing copies of their latest release in a few minutes," the DJ MC announced. "Thank you for supporting homegrown talent and Killer Rock 107.4 FM!"

"It won't be long," I said, stretching my cramped legs. "Now the fun part begins."

"Sure it will," Dawn replied with a smile, doing some arm stretches of her own. "We don't even know what this Carl person is wearing," she said, peering out a side window.

I cracked open the curtains of another window to see the bar's rear entrance. "No, but I doubt his look changes much day to day. We're lucky the parking lot is so well lit."

"What better way to see who's shooting at you, right?"

"Or throwing beer bottles," I added.

I estimated there were about 175 fans inside the bar, a shoulder-to-shoulder capacity crowd. The front doors soon swung open with a few rough-looking couples exiting first, probably parents needing to get home, their all night rock and roll party days over. They were followed by a small, wholesome-looking group who didn't appear to be the usual Whole Goat clientele. "I'm thinking they like the band and wanted to see them live," Dawn offered. Next were the hardcore regulars with cigarettes already dangling from their lips, coming outside to shoot the breeze and give concert reviews on the patio. I pictured Carl as a heavy smoker, although being a one-night Barton interloper I suspected wouldn't ingratiate him to these locals. His arrogant boast of, 'I'm with the band,' might not help either. Other action was taking place at the back of the bar, as the roadies began loading a trailer with cables, lights, speakers and other band gear. "I don't see Carl helping out, if that's a good sign," Dawn observed.

Various cars, pickups, vans and motorcycles were driven off the lot, yet we were still well insulated by the remaining vehicles. As usual, the tricky part would come soon enough, when I had to jump into the front seat unnoticed and casually drive past everyone without causing suspicion. For any type of surveillance, this is an on-going issue. Quiet residential streets are just as likely to have neighbours calling the police, jeopardizing the investigation. Of course, the worst is when your subject is the one making the call complaining, "There's a strange van with tinted windows in the area."

"There he is!" Dawn said in a high pitched whisper. "It looks like he's alone, wearing a black concert tee, black jeans and black ball cap. He said something to the roadies and is walking toward the huge blue boat parked next to the RV."

Boat?

"At least his clothes are colour coordinated for his big evening out," I said, shifting to catch a glimpse of our infamous mall walker. "That's no boat, that's a 1978 Plymouth Fury. My parents owned a used one once. I think I took my driver's licence test in it."

"You are old," Dawn laughed.

"I did say it was used," I replied grinning. "Still, yes, I'm old. Now write this down." I recited Carl's licence plate. "That's our insurance policy if we lose him heading back to wherever he hangs his ball cap these days." I waited until he had turned onto the main Barton drag before slipping into the front seat and starting the engine. "Anyone notice?"

"No, you're good. Everyone is too high, drunk, deaf or blind from the fog machine to care anyway." Dawn remained in the back for a few more moments, waiting for us to be a safe distance from the bar before climbing into the passenger seat. "Ah, finally something comfortable to sit on," she said, reclining and stretching her legs. "My back is going to need a massage later."

"Just your back?"

Dawn reached over and placed her hand on my leg. "We'll start with that area and go from there."

"Oh, I'll be there all right," I agreed. "Now if Buddy can get that big blue beast above the speed limit any time soon, we'll be set."

Once out of Barton, our midnight surveillance consisted mainly of highway driving at speeds only slightly higher than the posted limit. I wasn't certain if that was due to the vehicle's performance limitations or if Carl simply had no interest in bringing attention to himself. With the darkness and moderate traffic flow, we kept back several car lengths, blending in with the other glaring headlights reflecting in the Fury's mirrors. Although she had voiced her desire to be my second set of eyes, Dawn soon drifted to sleep, allowing me to turn off the Unfinished Tattoos disc and continue into the night in silence.

"Are we there yet?" my sweet and sexy passenger groggily asked an hour later.

"I think so. We're coming up to Edenville," I said. "Did you have a good nap?"

"I guess," she said, straightening up in the seat. "At any time did I yell out, 'Is this elevator moving?'"

"Not that I recall. Maybe I was asleep at the time too."

"Very funny. It was part of a weird dream," she continued. "You and me, or not you and me . . . someone and me, were trying to hide from a lunatic with a gun."

"In an elevator?"

"Yes, only it wasn't a regular one, like those in a department store or office building."

"Was it installed in that tree house you alluded to earlier? That kind of name association happens all the time in dreams."

Dawn gave me an odd look like somehow I was the one telling the crazy story. "No, it wasn't a tree house," she stated firmly. "I think it might have been a funhouse or palace because it was hidden in the hallway. The sliding doors looked exactly like the panelling."

"Like those bookcases that hide a secret room in the movies?" I offered.

"Yes, like that! Only when the guy in the elevator pushed me against the wall to kiss me, I must have backed into one of the floor buttons."

"And presto magico, you're screaming to your mystery serial kisser, 'Is this elevator moving?' Am I right?"

"It seemed so real," Dawn implored.

"Like when you were actually at the Grant Gardens Country Club during your yoga teacher's wedding reception and we snuck away for a few minutes? Was it that real?" I said, vividly recalling the memory. "That was no dream, baby. It actually happened."

Dawn's hand went up to her open mouth in astonishment. "But where did the part about a lunatic chasing me with a gun come from?" she asked.

"I think that was from a different kind of word association," I said, slowly lowering my gaze, which Dawn's eyes followed.

Unable to resist, I smiled and said, "That was no gun, Sunshine, but I will admit to chasing after you with it."

"You are such a pig," she responded, as we laughed until tears formed in our eyes.

"From what I remember before our elevator escape, that reception was the best," I said, as Edenville's city lights came into view. "Is Violet still married to her spiritual swami, Monty the factory worker?"

"Yes, they're still together and for your information he owns the factory."

"Oh yeah, it's coming back to me now. Plastics, right?"

Dawn was about to confirm this when she pointed out the front window. "Carl's getting off the highway."

With that we were slammed back into reality. In my head I heard Rod Serling warn, *"That's the signpost up ahead. Your next stop, the Twilight Zone!"* This case had a feel of just such an episode, starting out with a straightforward premise, only to take a sharp unexpected turn for both characters and viewers in the final moments. The discovery that George was murdered should have been the story's big twist, however, I now believed it was simply the cliffhanger before the first commercial break.

Don't touch that dial.

On Main Street, I was glad to see quite a few cars on the road, most likely the result of downtown bars closing for the night. As we passed The Galleria, I showed Dawn where the bus accident had taken place and Sam's hot dog cart. Her sad and muted response was, "Oh." A short time later, Carl took a right onto a side street and I cruised through the intersection, before making a quick U-turn out of his view. We waited at the light and watched as Carl pulled into an apartment building lot a few blocks away. I slowly crept the van up the street in time to see our man use a key to unlock the side door and enter. "It looks like a converted prison block," Dawn commented on the unremarkable three-storey, brick walk-up. From our vantage point, we could see all of the north side units, none of which had lights on. Even with a good chance to discover which apartment Carl lived in, the odds were against us and no lights came on in any of the units.

"He obviously lives on the south side then," I said, "which isn't a bad thing."

"How so?" Dawn asked, as I stopped in front of the building to check out the overall situation.

"Because those units face that rear alley," I pointed out, "and not the street." I focused my attention on a nearby plaza. "I can set up in that lot and never have to worry if Carl can see me from his balcony, plus I have an unobstructed view of the parking lot exit."

"Win-win," Dawn said as she jumped out of the van and gently closed her door. "Be right back," she promised through the glass.

"What are you doing?" I mouthed through my side window in a mild state of shock. Moments later I knew exactly what her plan was, and even though I could have accomplished the same thing in the morning, I liked her initiative.

Out of breath from the excitement, Dawn returned to the van and I drove out of the area. "So the Fury is parked in designated spot 304 and the name on the tenant board for that apartment is Len Duguay."

"Nice work, Nancy Drew," I said holding my right hand up for a high-five. "I wonder if Len is Blondie from The Galleria?"

"Or he's living with a senior citizen and pimps their ride when needed," Dawn replied matter of factly. "To me, that makes more sense because that car is ancient. For a tough guy like Carl there's nothing cool or scary about driving it around town, unless it's out of necessity. I'm sure a visit to the Super can clear that up."

It was my turn to look on in astonishment. "If you keep up this level of quality work, I'll be forced to hire you on a full time basis and The Sunsetter's customers will be out of luck."

"And what, take a pay cut? I don't think so," she grinned. "Plus,

I already get the full Cassidy Investigations' benefit *package*," she said, lightly setting her hand on my leg again.

"That you do," I agreed, navigating the city streets back to the highway, "and I wouldn't have it any other way."

FIFTEEN

Once home, after a brief discussion on the merits of being referred to as Nancy Drew instead of Jill Munroe, Farrah Fawcett's character from "Charlie's Angels," Dawn fell fast asleep the moment her head hit the pillow. I waited a few minutes before slipping out to the office to conduct some pre-surveillance online searches. I needed to confirm Len Duguay's identity and his possible relationship to Carl, a.k.a. Curly.

I struck out with "Carl + Duguay" and "Carl + Edenville" combinations, leaving me with the other two strong pieces of information to pursue: the apartment location and car licence plate. I began with a 411 reverse address search and discovered the building had a name: Waterfront Towers. That there are no sizable lakes, rivers or ponds within 50 miles of Edenville is bad enough, without the added delusion that three floors constitutes the height of a tower, but I digress. The real treasures on the screen were a record of the tenants, along with their unit and telephone numbers. I scrolled down to #304 and sure enough, Len Duguay was the listed renter. I printed off the page and clicked on the "More Info" button, which produced an area map with a red star pinned to the Towers' location and nothing else. Undaunted, I logged into a paid service I use periodically and entered my newfound information. This time I hit pay dirt. Len was born in 1919, his wife Lena (1935) had passed away in 1978, and Nicholas was their only child's name. A retired tool and die shop owner,

Len also had good credit.

As the printer churned these pages out, I concluded Dawn's hypothesis might be correct. Len could very well be Carl's grandfather, who would have no clue what his grandson was up to these days. Maybe in 1978 the new Fury was a gift for Lena, but when she died Len couldn't get rid of it for sentimental reasons. Armed with these investigative gems, there was no reason to pay for a licence plate search. I shut down the computer and returned to bed, setting the alarm for 6:00 a.m.

"Did you find what you were looking for?" Dawn asked drowsily, rolling over to drape her arm across my chest.

"Are you referring to the case or with you?" I whispered back.

"Yes," she said, a sleepy smile forming on her lips.

Before I could answer, I knew from her shallow breathing that she was again asleep. Although she'd never remember this conversation, I felt I owed her an honest answer. "Yes, I've found everything I was looking for," I replied quietly. "More than you'll ever know. Goodnight, you."

***

For Sunday morning surveillances, I start around 8:00 a.m., which allows me to catch subjects heading to church or going out for brunch. Area shopping malls usually have special hours, opening at 11:00, maybe at noon, which also lessens the need to set up too early. After toiling at the office or factory all week, Saturdays tend to be the real rush day for people to do grocery shopping, chauffeur the kids to the mall, do yard work or anything else on the To Do list. Sunday is meant as a day of rest, which is what I believed Carl would be doing until the afternoon, although I wasn't willing to gamble my precious time on that belief.

The Fury remained unmoved at Waterfront Towers as I set up a position at the (I kid you not) Ocean Wave Plaza, with a view of the apartment building's parking lot exit, as well as its front and side doors. Maybe Carl would get the urge for munchies and walk to the grocery store behind me. Knowing it was going to get quite warm, instead of hiding in the back where the air doesn't circulate, I moved to the passenger seat, cracked open the window and reclined into the shadows. You may be wondering why I wouldn't stay in the driver's seat. Well, it's a simple trick investigators employ, especially in residential areas, to deflect any suspicion from individuals aware of your presence. "Me? Oh, I'm waiting for a friend. He's a door-to-door salesman/the minister of a new church/a political protester collecting names on a petition. Where do you live again? I can have him drop by later."

That usually stops all civilian interrogations.

I read, listened to the radio, wrote up my Whole Goat surveillance notes, updated the file's budget expense form and spoke with Dawn after she woke up.

"Nothing happening?" she asked.

"I'm sure something is happening somewhere, just not with the Carl and Len Show yet."

"How long do you plan to stay on him today?"

"Until he comes out to play," I replied. "Unless things take a bad turn and I'm done early, I won't be home before you go to work. I'm planning on being back by the time your shift is over though. Maybe I can pick you up."

"Okay," Dawn said optimistically. "Good luck with Carl. I hope he leads you to Blondie."

"Me too. Talk to you soon."

For lunch I bought two pizza slices from the nearby Beachin' Good Eats location, my attention never straying from the apartment building across the street. By 1:00 I was getting restless, worried Carl had left before I had arrived. I began thinking of other boxes I could check off in Edenville, when low and behold the Fury was being driven out of the area by Carl.

"Let's rock and roll," I said aloud, sliding into the driver's seat, turning the key in the ignition and pulling onto the street.

When asked about the delicate art of following someone undetected, my stock answer is, "You stay as close as you can. The biggest problem is that the subject knows exactly where they're heading, which route they'll take and the level of urgency for the trip. I'm flying blind right up to the point when we arrive at their destination."

Like the night before, Carl was not a man in a hurry, taking his time, doing the speed limit and signalling his turns. You'd have thought he was a driving school instructor and not a cold blooded killer. I knew better. I knew it was all an act, but for whom?

We soon found ourselves in a rough area; rickety old homes more in need of a demolition crew than a handyman, unkempt yards and rusting vehicles permanently abandoned in the driveways. Carl parked in front of an unsound-looking house and climbed an exterior set of stairs to a second floor unit, where he was let in by a blonde male who looked very familiar to me. I scanned the upper windows and noted an Unfinished Tattoos flag hung across the frame as a curtain.

Hello Blondie, I thought.

I quickly drove past to jot down the house number and any possible car plates for future reference. Sadly, the only motorized vehicle in the dusty dirt drive was a riding lawnmower up on cinder blocks, its front wheels missing, overgrown weeds anchoring the assembly to the ground. I went further up the street and waited, hoping this stopover wouldn't last long.

From my briefcase I dug out the sheets I'd printed off, hoping to get some more relevant information on Carl while he was out and about.

I blocked my cell phone number and an elderly gentleman answered the phone.

"Hello?"

"Oh, hi," I said happily. "I would like to speak with Carl . . . " I paused. "Sorry I can't make out the last name on my list."

"Duguay? Is it Carl Duguay?" came the response.

"Yes, that could be it. The first letter was missing. Again, I'm sorry about that. Would you be Carl?"

"No, I'm his grandfather. Carl lives with me. He's not here right now and I don't know when he'll be returning. He keeps some late hours. What's this about?"

Nothing in the man's voice indicated he was worried or agitated by my call. "My name is Kevin. I'm calling on behalf of the University Press and doing a quick survey about movie watching habits. It's only three short questions, which will take half a minute or less to complete."

"Like I said, he's not home."

"That's not a problem, Mr. . . . . "

"Just call me Len."

"Okay, Len. I'm not really worried who takes the survey, so long as it's done. Do you have another 30 seconds to spare? I'm basically looking for one-word answers."

There was the slightest hesitation in his reply. "Okay, go ahead."

"Great," I said. "The first question is how many movies do you see at the movie theatre each month?"

"None. I think Carl might see one or two though."

"I'll note that. All right, question number two is, how many movies do you watch in the privacy of your own home each month?"

"I don't know, maybe five or six."

"Excellent. And number three is, if you had a choice to watch a movie in a theatre or at home, which would you prefer?" I asked.

"At my age," Len laughed, "at home. It's cheaper and the bathroom is closer!"

"That's true." I laughed along with him, before getting to the real reason of my phone call. "One last thing, Len, for statistical purposes, I take it you're retired?"

"Going on seven years. I had a tool and die shop that my son took over when I got sick."

"Oh, sorry to hear that," I said. "Is the business still operating in Edenville?"

"Yep, that fool hasn't run it into the ground yet," Len replied with a wheezing cough.

"Is Carl his son? Does he work for his dad? If so, I could put it down in the statistic area on the survey."

"Carl's his son, unfortunately he wouldn't know a tool from a die, if they fell on his head. Between court appearances and prison stints, he does go to the shop from time to time."

Interesting, I thought.

"And what's the name of the shop?" I inquired.

"To Die For Inc. on Dalhousie Street."

"Well, that's all I have today. Thank you for your time," I said, trying to conclude our chat. "You have a great day, Len."

"Anytime."

The beauty of this type of call is that it's short, covers a topic everyone can relate to and never raises suspicions. I could imagine Len telling Carl he'd missed a call about a survey saying, "Don't worry, I took it for you," and that would be the end of the conversation. Once the investigator has gained the subject's trust by establishing a non-threatening phone friendship, the "for statistics" questions are generally freely answered. Just as I now knew Carl's relationship to Len, I also confirmed a new address and business to keep in mind, and the good grandson was unemployed and known to police. During similar surveys, subjects divulge the reason they're off work, their physiotherapy appointment schedule, as well as other pertinent information I probably didn't possess two minutes earlier. Some people (usually the subject's lawyer) believe this is entrapment. I disagree. Flattening a tire or dumping a can of motor oil under a car to videotape a subject "being active" is entrapment. On the flipside, giving out personal information to a total, albeit charming, stranger over the phone is plain stupid.

Carl spent an hour inside the second floor apartment and returned to the Fury alone. He made a brief stop at a convenience store to buy smokes and went straight back to Waterfront Towers. I stuck around until 7:00 (another Beachin' pizza slice for dinner) and pulled the plug. Confirming Carl's identity made the day a success. The plan now was to use this information to my advantage during a phone call in the morning.

I drove to the house Carl had visited and discreetly checked the names on the two porch mailboxes: Lower - Helen Stone / Upper - Tom Evans. Was this the infamous Blondie? I could easily find out with a knock on his door, but that wasn't a risk worth taking yet.

I called The Sunsetter and spoke with Doug the cook. "Can you tell Dawn I'll pick her up at the end of her shift?"

"No problem, Steve-o-rama."

"Thanks," I said before adding, "Dawn says you make a mean macaroni and cheese smothered in bacon dish."

"Best in town," Doug replied. "It's my own secret concoction."

"Can you have one ready for me in about an hour?"

"You got it, Investigator Man."

Still trying to figure out which of the three ingredients (macaroni, cheese, bacon) might contain the 'secret' aspect of Doug's recipe, I continued to find my way out of the ghetto. At the first stop sign I dutifully looked right, then left, then right again, this time focusing my attention on the Edenville Police vehicle parked sideways in a driveway a few lots down.

"It's a dilapidated house, chopped up into low-rent units. Local hangout for dropout teenagers and older slacker types."

Crawford?

"Are you kidding me?" I wondered aloud, proceeding up alongside the cruiser's open driver's window, where an officer in his twenties sat playing a game on his cell phone. Noting he wasn't wearing badge #3059 on his uniform jacket, I felt safe greeting him with an energetic, "Good evening, Constable, how's it going today?"

"Pretty slow," he said, addressing and assessing me at the same time. Troublemaker or curiosity seeker? "By the way, I'm not a constable, just an auxiliary officer."

"Did you draw the short straw?" I said smiling, looking up at the soot covered broken windows and roof hole where the burning couch once sat. "I'd have thought you guys would've cleared this fire scene. It's been a few days now, right? Something more than a furniture fire gone wrong?"

"Do you live on this street? Is that why you know how long the police have been here?" he asked, his eyes never leaving my face.

"No, I'm from out of town," I replied calmly. "A friend of mine, Travis Crawford, was working this detail the morning after the fire." The officer's face immediately slackened with relief. "On the phone old Trav sounded as bored as you look," I laughed.

"Exciting it's not. That's why auxiliary officers are posted here now, to make sure there's no tampering with the evidence and all that."

"For how much longer?"

"Tomorrow. The regional fire investigator was away, but he'll be on site tomorrow and his department then takes over everything."

"And you'll go back to boring desk duty?"

The officer shook his head. "I suppose."

"He didn't say, but was there a reason Travis had to watch this place or was it just bad luck that night?"

In the same way the survey questions were a required prelude to get to the statistic ones, unbeknown to my young friend here, everything to this point had led to the climax of this discussion. I needed to know why Constable Crawford was in this neighbourhood, which Carl obviously frequented.

"That's an easy one. This is his beat . . . ah, area. The political

correctness committee won't allow the words 'police' and 'beat' in the same sentence any longer. It's so stupid."

That it was.

"Well, I have to get going," I said, putting the van in gear. "Enjoy the rest of your shift."

"I'll try," was the reply. "I'll tell Travis you stopped by."

"You do that." I gently stepped on the gas, while rolling up my window.

As I drove away, I saw the officer looking in the side mirror, no doubt memorizing my plate number. Soon enough Crawford would know I'd dropped by, which was exactly what I was counting on.

***

"So you really think that's Blondie?" Dawn asked, reaching across the table to stab a forkful of my macaroni, cheese and bacon dinner. "Tom Evans in the second floor apartment?"

"I'm fairly certain," I offered. "I'm hoping Walter from The Galleria has retained a few friends on the force who can help me with that in the morning."

"What about Constable Crawford? Any plans for him?"

"Don't you worry your little kitten head about him," I said with a smile. "I'm pretty sure we'll be meeting face to face in the near future."

"It's statements like that which trouble my kitten head," Dawn said with a sigh. "You should know that by now."

I took one final bite of Doug's scrumptious meal and set the plate aside. "I believe Crawford might only be an underling, not the kingpin or true boss of Carl and Blondie. My gut tells me he's not the idea man but a good foot soldier who relays orders down the line."

"Is that what you were during your wayward criminal cop days? A good soldier following orders?"

I pulled out a $20 to cover our meals (Dawn had opted for a grilled chicken wrap) and set it on the table. "No, I was an idea man. Unfortunately, most of them didn't work out, which is why I'm having dinner with you tonight, instead of sailing the Mediterranean on a luxury yacht."

Dawn took my hand as we walked to the door. "See, then everything worked out. This is where you were destined to be, with me."

And Doug apparently.

"Did you like it?" Doug asked me through the small pick-up window separating the kitchen and dining area.

"It was surprisingly good," I replied, which elicited a huge grin on Doug's face. "Give my compliments to the chef."

"Excellent!"

"Okay, Doug," Dawn broke in. "I'll see you in the morning at 7:00."

"All righty. You two have a great night."

I held the door open for Dawn and we walked out into the warm night air. "Is he always that happy?"

Dawn squeezed my hand. "He gets to see me again in the morning. What's there not to be happy about?" she laughed.

SIXTEEN

Of all the mysterious puzzle pieces yet to be hunted down, George's briefcase was my new top priority. I'd learned from Hot Dog Sam that it had flown into the air at the moment of the impact with the bus, but then what? Did the first emergency responders load it into the ambulance, or had Constable Crawford snatched it up? I knew the fleeing duo of Carl and Blondie hadn't taken it, but should they have as part of their arrangement with the person who hired them?

I got up early with Dawn and had breakfast at The Sunsetter. "Is everything to your liking, Mr. Cassidy?" she teased lightly kissing me on the cheek, which produced rabid requests for the same service from her other male regulars. "Those are only given to my best tippers," Dawn countered with a smile. "And Mr. Cassidy here is one of the biggest." The dining area roared with laughter, with one female customer warning Dawn, "From experience, I know a girl can't live by the tip alone!" which set the whole place off again.

Having refilled everyone's coffee cups, Dawn took a seat in my booth. "This is why I enjoy the morning shift," she said grinning. "These customers are like family. They come in before work to feel like they're part of something fun."

"Until their boss sucks all the fun out of them the moment they punch their time card and have to return to the real world," I added.

"Until then, yes." Dawn gave me an odd look. "Do they even

still have time cards or is that a nostalgic memory you have from the olden days?"

"They still have them, smarty pants," I replied, "especially in factories. Remember that surveillance we did for the soap plant?" Dawn nodded in agreement. "That was to nail lazy SOBs who were home goofing off and had their co-workers clocking them in and out each shift to split the extra pay."

Doug rang the order bell and called out, "Two eggs, sunny side up, bacon, home fries and wheat toast! Perfection on a plate!"

"That's my cue," Dawn said, sliding out of the booth. "I wish I was goofing off with you at home right now," she said playfully.

"That'd be much more fun than driving to Dannenberg by myself," I replied. "I'm going to miss you bopping along to the songs on the radio."

I headed out a few minutes later, making sure everyone knew how big of a tipper I really was. "I dare you to top that," I said, winking at Dawn. "This lovely young woman has to support her deadbeat boyfriend, who's still trying to figure out what he wants to be when he grows up."

"When? Don't you mean if?" an old-timer cackled at a side table, eliciting another round of sustained hilarity.

Dawn joined me at the front door. "One of these days Mr. Cassidy is going to surprise us all," she announced loudly. "Isn't that right?"

"I duly swear, Miss Dawn, that one day I'll definitely surprise you all, right after I surprise myself and that might take awhile."

"Don't worry, we'll be here waiting," Dawn said, moving to the register to cash out a customer. "Just don't keep us in suspense too long okay?"

"Deal."

***

Entering the glass doors of the law firm that George had

founded, it was nice to see his name remained in the Mulhall, Pedlar & Hawksworth title.

"Welcome to Mulhall, Pedlar & Hawksworth. How are you today?" the sleek receptionist in an immaculate business suit asked, stepping back to her desk.

"I'm doing great, thank you," I replied. "My name is Steve Cassidy and I am looking into the death of Mr. Mulhall. I think we talked earlier."

"Yes, of course, Mr. Cassidy. I spoke with our managing partner, Jane Calloway, about this matter. She has been awaiting your arrival. Please take a seat and I'll tell her you're here."

Watching this polished professional at work, I could easily imagine Julie Trenton in this same role six years earlier: young, attractive and eager to not only climb the corporate ladder but to please her boss in any way she saw fit. Life would have definitely been good, if only Eric's wife hadn't been murdered in cold blood.

So close.

"Ms. Calloway will see you now, Mr. Cassidy. Follow me."

I was led to an executive office down the hall, where Jane Calloway was standing in the doorway. "Thank you, Nora," she said to my tour guide, who turned with a smile and walked away. "Mr. Cassidy, it's very nice to meet you. Please come in."

I shook her extended hand, which took mine with a very strong grip. "I appreciate you taking the time on such short notice," I said, as we proceeded to a conference table where two piles of court documents were neatly stacked. Taking a seat, I glanced around the large room and noted how organized everything was, from the desktop to the bookshelves and filing cabinets. This didn't surprise me, as it perfectly reflected Ms. Calloway's personal style and the aura about her. In her early fifties, she was tall, with a refined motherly figure, and dark hair with touches of grey showing through. If there was a dress style the equivalent of a "power suit", the black and white number she was wearing would be it. Everything about her looked intimidating until she flashed her warm smile and all apprehension melted away. It was no wonder why George had promoted her to this position and why I was going to find myself very distracted from the matter at hand.

In the past, I had only dated women roughly the same age as me. There is an instant familiarity due to shared experiences from TV shows, music, news events and fads that help to quickly break the ice. When those relationships fizzled out, I began to consider exploring the "older woman" route. I envisioned myself easily falling into some sexy Cougar's love trap, putting all the pressure on her to keep up with the younger generation. I knew I'd never be able to sustain a partnership with a younger woman. Twenty-somethings scared me, until Dawn calmly flitted into my life and remained without a care in the world.

I'm all for sticking around until her infatuation begins to wane, at which time I hope we would part amicably. She'd go her way, while I'd go mine, possibly in the direction of a woman like the one standing before me now.

"Would you like a coffee or tea?" Jane offered.

"No, I'm good," I said, as she sat in the chair to my left. "I'm very sorry for your loss, Ms.–"

"Please, call me Jane."

"Jane it is."

"I appreciate that, Steve. George's sudden death was a huge loss for this firm, as well as the community, no pun intended, although he'd have inserted one there with a laugh."

"Had you worked for him long?"

"Over 20 years," she said humbly. "I was a late academic bloomer, deciding to be a lawyer in my late twenties. George hired me after I graduated."

"I didn't have the pleasure of meeting the man, but from all accounts he was very well liked and respected," I said.

"His accident shook everyone, although as with the medical field, in this business we know all too well that good people die unexpectedly with no rhyme or reason." There was the slightest crack in her voice and a flash of ongoing sorrow in her eyes, yet Jane remained focused on the purpose of my visit. "I must say your call caught me off guard, as I wasn't aware any type of investigation was going on. Are you working on behalf of the Edenville Transit Commission for insurance purposes?"

It was apparent she believed her boss' death was nothing more than a freak accident.

"Actually, I'm looking into the incident as part of another file," I replied slowly. "The Eric McDowell case, which George worked on several years back." This news caused Jane's eyes to widen.

"I was 2nd Chair on that trial," Jane said, a trace of excitement in her voice. "What would that case have to do with George's death?"

"Maybe nothing at all," I admitted. "I must say, I don't recall your name in the trial transcript."

"It's under Jane Campion, my married name at the time. I have since divorced and gone back to my maiden name."

"Okay, I do recall that version," I said, envisioning the defense team listings. "I was hired by Lucy McDowell's mother, Debra Stanfield, to take a fresh look at the case against Eric. She sent me the transcript and other pertinent documents of the trial."

Jane was noticeably affected by this statement and leaned back into her chair. "I can't say I'm stunned by this news. Debra always maintained Eric couldn't have killed Lucy, which we were very appreciative of at the time. Unfortunately, she couldn't provide any meaningful information to help us get an acquittal." She paused, as if debating something in her mind.

"I've spoken with all the principals of the case - Eric, Debra, Det. Dutton and Julie Trenton. It was Julie who told me that she thought George was working on a new appeal angle."

"But how would she know such a thing?" Jane asked incredulously.

"She said George was a friend and that they'd go for a coffee every so often, nothing else. Their paths crossed when he dropped off some housing documents at the Dreamhouse Realty office some time ago."

An expression of recognition came over Jane's features. "Yes, I do remember him saying he'd seen her there. I wasn't aware he'd kept in touch."

Her statement and far off stare indicated she took George's slight personally. "My read on it was that he felt sorry for her and when in the area they met for a half hour or so. Like you said, George was a big-hearted man and to see how far Julie had faired since her court appearance had an effect on him."

"Yes, I could see that," Jane responded. "He had mentioned she'd hit a rough patch once Eric was convicted. I was the one who actually handled Julie for her court appearance. Like Debra, she never wavered from her belief that Eric had nothing to do with Lucy's murder."

"And she still does," I said proudly. "With nothing new to follow up on, I started looking into George's activities in Edenville, which has brought me to you today."

With a touch of apprehension, Jane asked, "Am I to believe that you think George's death was not an accident as reported?"

Any lawyer will tell you that they try to never ask a question that they don't know the answer to, which was not the case here. Jane (and the rest of the world) had never questioned the accident story, had grieved over George's loss and had then attempted to move forward without him. Now I show up, presenting a premise that would shatter those beliefs and possibly reset the entire process back to square one. With an ordinary civilian, I might sugarcoat my findings or ease into them, but with a lawyer who defends people known to be guilty, that delaying tactic was not required.

"It's my belief that George was targeted for murder or great harm, and was intentionally pushed into that Edenville city bus. What I don't know is why and if it had anything to do with the

McDowell case." The expression on Jane's face was no doubt the same one that formed the moment she was first informed George was dead. The all-business mask crumbled, tears welled up in her eyes and she took several quick, deep intakes of air. "I'm sorry to be the bearer of such bad news," I offered, again at a loss of what to say to a crying woman. "Do you know if George was working on a new appeal and if so, any of the details?"

"He was," Jane said as she stood, covering her mouth with her hand. "Could you please give me a minute?"

"Of course," I said, standing as she walked to a small washroom on the opposite side of the room, gently closing its door behind her. Regrettably, the sounds of her crying and sniffling carried through the thin walls. I wandered over to the floor-to-ceiling window to take in a spectacular view of Dannenberg and the surrounding area dotted with farmlands, tiny towns, highways and county roads. I heard the washroom door click open, turned, and from this new angle of Jane's desk I saw a picture of George in a tuxedo and sporting a huge smile.

"I apologize," Jane said, passing the coffeemaker and reaching out to an extended bookshelf to pour herself a splash of scotch into a crystal tumbler. "I know it's only 9:30 in the morning, but would you like something strong to start your day off right?"

"A shot of whiskey on the rocks, if it's no trouble."

She brought both drinks to the table and made a toast. "To George."

"To George," I said, raising my glass to touch hers before we each took a deserved swallow of excellent liquor and sat back down.

"George received a call a week or more before his . . . accident," Jane began, putting her glass aside, her nerves settling down. "He told me he was going to meet a mystery man in Edenville who claimed he'd found some kind of diary that might help Eric."

"A diary? This is the first time I've heard of that," I said perplexed. "Did the caller ever identify himself or say whose diary it was? Eric's, Lucy's, Julie's perhaps?"

"No, to all of the above," Jane answered with a frown. "Evidently the caller was always jumpy and kept cancelling scheduled meetings with George. They then came to an arrangement where George would pick up excerpts from the diary to prove it was the real deal."

"Did this guy want to be paid for his trouble?"

"There was never a price attached, although George figured it'd only be a matter of time."

"Like after reading the diary pages?" I guessed. "At the end of the day, would George have paid?"

There was a long pause before Jane replied, "Only if he knew it was certifiably authentic through handwriting analysis, that sort of thing."

"Was that why George was in Edenville, to pick up the diary pages?"

"Yes, but I don't know if he did before . . . "

"He had a chance to," I said soothingly, completing her sentence. "This brings me to one of the real reasons I'm here. Was George's briefcase returned to the firm?"

"It was, but there were no diary pages in it. I cleaned it out myself, although I'll confess, I was in such a state of shock that until this conversation I haven't thought about those pages or why George was out of town."

"It also doesn't sound like the mystery caller has made any further attempts to get hold of George since June, which is yet another reason your mind would've dismissed any connection between the two events."

"Do you think the caller killed George?" Jane asked with a sense of alarm. "I told him to get the police involved and he refused, saying the police didn't do their job the first time and he had little faith they'd do it now."

"After a few run-ins with Det. Dutton, I can understand his thinking," I concurred. "To answer your question, I don't know if the caller was one of the men I believe caused George's death."

"Men, as in plural?" Jane faltered.

I reached across the table and placed my hand on top of Jane's. "Please relax, you're not in any danger, nor are any of the firm's employees. As I said earlier, I'm not clear why George was targeted. It may have nothing to do with this diary business. I used to work in law enforcement and know for a fact that weirdos call in tips, claiming all sorts of things that never pan out. The anonymous caller and his 'diary drop' scenario could've been a wild goose chase, signifying nothing."

"I can't believe I never made a connection between George's trip and his death," Jane said, taking back her hand. "I never thought he might have died *because* he was in Edenville that day."

"There was no basis to think of foul play," I said in a comforting tone. "It was a tragic accident that could've happened to anyone standing on that corner that day. You didn't think otherwise because there was no reason to."

"Until now."

"Well, yes, until now," I agreed. "Do you still have the briefcase or was it given back to George's family?"

"I was . . . " Jane began, then corrected herself, "I mean, George had no family to speak of. His wife passed away years ago and they had no children."

"Is the case here at the firm?" I asked, nonchalantly looking around the office.

Without a word, Jane walked to her desk and from underneath it retrieved the case, opening it on our table moments later. "I only removed documents pertaining to on-going firm cases, figuring I'd look through any other personal items later when I was feeling stronger."

"Are you feeling stronger right now?"

"I believe I am," she replied. "What are we looking for exactly?"

I examined the case's interior and withdrew a legal pad, a

short stack of documents, two opened letter envelopes and several receipts. "Anything that gets us closer to finding out if George had possession of the diary pages or where he was heading to pick them up."

"But I already told you, the pages weren't in the case when it was returned."

"Another scenario is that the pages were taken out before the case was returned to you," I countered cagily, unwilling to reveal the Constable Crawford/Carl/Blondie conspiracy triangle theory. "I haven't told you everything I know, Jane, but trust me that it's not relevant until we find a direct connection to the diary and my Edenville suspects."

Jane took a deep cleansing breath. "Okay, I'll trust you. For now."

"Thank you."

***

The two envelopes containing correspondence regarding cable TV upgrades and a Book Of The Month offer were hastily disregarded. As his long-time employee, I gave Jane the legal pad containing pages of George's handwritten notes to decipher. "These are his preliminary observations for a wrongful death suit, which was settled out of court months ago," Jane advised, placing the pad on top of the envelopes. I next set aside receipts that related to any Edenville business transactions. Sorting through them, I discovered one from The Biz Emporium that took my breath away.

"Look here," I said, handing the slip to Jane. "On the mall's video surveillance, I saw George exit this office supply store carrying a small plastic bag."

Jane glanced up from the receipt. "This is for 25 photocopies."

"The diary," we said in unison.

"He did pick it up and must have made a copy," I continued.

"But where would he have picked it up from?" Jane asked, the receipt now quivering in her hand.

"Can I use your computer?" I asked rhetorically, getting up and sliding into her desk chair. "I think we can track his movements that morning through the remaining receipts."

Jane stepped in behind me, as I called up a map search site to input the business addresses of a parking garage, a café, a Big & Tall clothing store, a drug mart and The Galleria. One by one the results placed a colourful dot on the map of Edenville's downtown core. Clumped tightly together, the dots indicating George was on foot after parking his vehicle.

"Whatever happened to George's car?" I asked, never really thinking about how he had travelled to Edenville.

"It's in our parking garage," Jane answered. "It's leased by the firm. Like the briefcase, I was the one who went through it when an associate drove it back, and there were no legal or personal papers in it."

"Okay, that's good," I assured her, as I examined the map before us. "All these businesses are within one block of the parking garage." Using the various cash register timestamps, I was able to put George's stops in order. "So, he drops off the car, goes to the café for a coffee, next to the clothing store to get a new tie, followed by buying gum at the drug store. Then there's a blank period of 34 minutes before purchasing his photocopies, which probably would've taken 5-10 minutes to do."

"Leaving a 25-30 minute gap," Jane said. "You've been down there, right? Did you notice a post office or courier station where a package could be picked up?"

I mentally returned to the view from Sam's Weiner Wagon, but couldn't picture any such places. "No, although the drop could've been taped under a park bench or in a garbage can. You said the caller was pretty nervous."

"That's true," Jane agreed. "Then why the time delay between purchasing a pack of gum and getting the diary?"

The image of Carl and Blondie blending into the mall crowd came to mind and of Blondie possibly using his cell phone. "George was putting in time," I said confidently. "He was waiting for a call from the diary guy about where the package would be left." I pointed to the map. "George's sole mission that morning was to get hold of the diary. There's no other reason he would drive all the way out there. Once in the city, the next logical step would be to meet the mystery caller or snag the diary from its hiding spot and drive back to the office. But he didn't do that. He meandered downtown, sipping a coffee, buying a tie of all things and some gum. All the while waiting, waiting and waiting."

"Then he gets the call, picks up the diary and photocopies it for safe keeping."

"Was George's cell phone also in the firm's name?" I asked, as a light bulb lit up in my head. "Accounting would have his monthly bills, listing his incoming and outgoing calls, right?"

Jane was reaching for the phone before I'd completed my question. "Mark, I need George's cell phone bills for the past five months A.S.A.P. Thanks." Jane returned to the conference table and downed the rest of her scotch.

While we waited for Mark to appear, I went over the possible chain of events after George was hit by the bus. From The Galleria footage, it was obvious that panic on the street had ensued until the ambulance and police arrived. The paramedics would've immediately worked on George, while the first officer on scene attempted to restore calm. The medics would be too busy to notice a battered briefcase. However, clearing debris and securing the victim's personal possessions (i.e. purse, shoe, laptop case etc.) would have been Constable Crawford's job before taking witness statements. I envisioned him grabbing the briefcase handle and setting it down in a secured area or his cruiser, realizing George wouldn't be asking for it back.

Mark was as proficient in manner and appearance as Jane and Nora. "As you requested, Jane," he said, handing her the bills.

"Is that number still active?" I asked Mark, who was giving me a strange look, I assume because I remained seated in Jane's chair.

As Jane spread the bills on the desk ignoring him, Mark answered apprehensively, "Yes, *George's* phone number remains operational."

"Meaning the firm has retained the actual number or that calls can still be placed and received?" I asked.

Getting no direction from Jane, Mark sucked it up like a buttercup and was suddenly appreciatively more co-operative. "The firm has kept the number and calls still come in from time to time. There have been no outgoing calls since June 23rd."

I was waiting for Mark to state the reason for that date, but then realized he must have processed what was going on and knew any additional talking was unnecessary.

You are a good egg, Marky Mark, I thought.

"Here it is," Jane said, putting the June call summary in front of me. "George got a call at 11:11 a.m. That fits our timeline."

I looked at the number and realized something odd. "The prefix isn't for Edenville."

Jane rechecked the listing. "Mark, what city or town has the 987 prefix?"

"Garland," he replied instantly.

"Where's that?" I asked.

"About ten miles outside of Edenville. Almost a ghost town with maybe 500 people," came his machine-like response.

I took out my cell phone, blocked my number and dialed the number. With pen in hand, I was poised to write down any name or voicemail message I might get.

"The number you have reached is no longer in service. Please check the number and try your call again. This is a recording."

"Unreal," I said, ending the call.

"It appears this was the same person who initially contacted

George," Jane said, highlighting another incoming call a few weeks earlier. "And then no more after the 23rd." The second mention of this specific date and the reason all communications had stopped, caused Jane to step away and look out the window, her back to Mark and me.

"If that's everything, Jane," Mark said.

"Yes, thank you. I'll get those back to you this afternoon," Jane replied, allowing Mark to leave the office and start spreading gossip throughout the accounting department cubicles.

"All is not lost," I said, accessing a telephone directory website where I entered our mystery number in the Reverse Phone prompt. "Does Malcolm Wright of 231 King Street in Garland ring any bells for you?"

Jane turned and stared blankly at me. "Is that the man who killed George?" she barely managed to ask.

I finished writing down this new information and stood. "I don't know but I'm going to find out for you." I motioned her away from the window and back to her desk, where she collapsed into her chair, visibly exhausted. "Please don't tell anyone about this for a couple days, while I try to track this person down. He may be a kook looking for attention and have nothing related to the McDowell trial." I glanced at the image of George on the desk. "I'm sure he's still smiling down on you every day and sending you his love, Jane."

"I believe that too," she said, tears forming in her eyes.

"I'll be in touch," I said.

I closed the office door behind me, hoping it was more soundproof than the washroom one had been. "Give her strength, George," I whispered, as I passed a tasteful oil portrait of the man in the hallway. "She needs it right about now and so do I."

SEVENTEEN

"Hi Walter, Steve Cassidy here. How is life at the mall this morning?"

"It was moving along fine until a 16-year-old master thief got caught leaving the game store with a video cartridge shoved down his pants," Walter laughed. "Of course, I'm the only one who can legally extract the stupid thing without his civil liberties being violated."

"Damn kids."

"You got that right. This little peckerhead was acting tough and refused to take the game out of his briefs," Walter continued joyfully. "He says, 'I bet you get off reaching into boys' underwear,' to which I replied, 'Oh, I'm not even going to attempt to get it now. I'll wait until your mom is in the room because that really does get me off.' Three seconds later, the video is sitting on the table."

"And the tears? When did they start? Five seconds later?" I asked.

"Yeah, that's about right."

"I had a few of those during my rookie years on the force," I began. "The best was a pre-teen princess who swore at me up and down, like she was the leader of a prison gang. I told her I'd let her cool down while I did paperwork in the next room. She was too young or stupid to figure out the wall mirrors were two-way and didn't see her frantic parents enter the security office. I calmly told them about the shoplifting incident and that their lovely daughter would be banned from the mall for a year, which they took in stride. They were upset about her behaviour, as she was such a mild mannered good girl. I stared at them and glanced into the other room. 'She's mild mannered?' I asked. Now they were glaring at me like I'd called their child a crack whore. 'I beg to differ. Wait here until I mention you,' I said to the mother, 'then come storming in,' and I entered the holding room again." I began to smile as I recalled what happened next. "So, I walk in and ask this little angel, 'Do you have anything to say for yourself?' and this demon child goes all Linda Blair-The Exorcist, spewing everything except pea soup at me. When she was done, I go, 'Do you kiss your mother with that mouth?' and before she could take another breath, the door explodes open and the mother proceeds to scare both of us straight! If I hadn't known what was coming, I'd have probably peed my pants too."

"Too?"

"Yeah, thankfully, I left that clean up job for the security officer on duty," I replied. "As you would know in your current position, he wasn't too pleased with me but c'est la vie."

"If you tried that with me, I'd probably write you a Trespass Notice," Walter said, chuckling at the story. "My kid has at least stopped bawling. I expect his mother to show in ten minutes."

"Okay, I won't keep you that long," I promised. "The reason I'm calling is I was hoping you still had a friend or two in the department who could provide me with some much-needed information."

"Is this about the bus-riding lawyer or some hot blonde you saw in a convertible and you need me to run her plate?" Walter asked.

"Unfortunately, this is still about the lawyer, although one of the people I need info on is blonde. Do you remember the two thugs from the mall footage? I've put names to their cap-covered faces," I said.

"No kidding," Walter said. "Sure, I have friends on the force. What do you need, Steve?"

I asked him to run arrest records for our loser thugs Carl Duguay and Tom Evans, as well as George's mystery caller, Malcolm Wright. "How long before you'll have anything?"

"Call me back in 15 minutes."

"That soon?" I said. "I'm heading to Edenville now, why don't I take you out for lunch at noon?"

"Sounds good to me. Stop by the office, I'll be here."

***

With the saying, *Don't judge a man until you've walked a mile in his shoes,* bouncing inside my head, I tried to do precisely that when I arrived in Edenville. The first step of my journey was to park in the same garage George had on that June morning. Next, on foot I followed his receipt breadcrumbs to the café, the clothing store and drug mart, ever on the lookout for a good location where the diary may have been dropped. As I'd mentioned to Jane, in this open atmosphere the package could've been placed anywhere and not necessarily hidden. The intriguing part was it appeared that the mystery caller had reservations about giving up his prized possession, making George wait for instructions. Had the giver been watching the recipient as he ambled from one shopping stop to another? I sat in a parkette located down from The Galleria, which had a view of the entire downtown core. From my bench I could see the exterior entrance of The Biz Emporium and knew I was close to where the eventual exchange occurred. I even got down on one knee to examine the boards under my bench, looking for a stray piece of tape, with no luck.

I entered the office supply store through its street entrance as George had, again checking the domed dummy cameras covering each aisle, above the Copy Centre and over the cash register area.

"Is there anything I can help you find this morning?"

I turned and recognized the manager I'd spoken with previously. "Jason, how are sales today?"

He was nonplussed by my greeting, as his large nametag clearly stated JASON - MANAGER in bold letters. Slowly, however, it dawned on him that I was more than a friendly customer. "Steve, right?"

Good memory, Jason. You're a rock star.

"It is," I replied.

"Are you still working on that bus accident investigation?" he asked eagerly. "Or do you need computer paper to print off your notes?"

"I'm still looking into that case," I said, "although today I haven't quite found what I was looking for yet. The day is young though, right?"

Jason checked his watch. "Not even noon. Plenty of time left." He noticed my attention was on the camera ceiling mounts above the photocopiers.

"I know I asked you this last time," I said, walking over to one of the machines, "but are you certain those cameras don't work?"

Jason glanced above us and then to a young brunette at the end of a nearby aisle. "Gillian, in the seven years you've worked here, have those cameras ever been hooked up to a recorder?"

The girl raised her face upward. "Never. They're dummy cameras," came her answer without thinking about it. "They're wired to the store's power supply, so that the little red light remains on all the time."

"Thank you, Gillian," Jason said in a pleasing voice with a smile. Turning back to me, everything about him changed and in a peeved tone he nearly spat, "Are you satisfied now?" and walked away without waiting for an answer.

Slightly stunned, I was momentarily left speechless.

"Don't take it personally, he's like that with everyone," Gillian said, making her way behind the sales counter. "He can be a bit of a diva, but you get used to it." She again looked above where I was standing. "What's the deal with the camera questions? Are you a security expert or something? Did corporate send you in here to spy on us, like those secret shoppers?"

I grinned. "As a private investigator, I actually have been hired to be a secret shopper a few times."

Gillian's eyes lit up. "A real life P.I.? Cool."

"It can be, although most of the time I'm sitting in a van for hours on end waiting for someone to leave or something to occur that's out of place."

"You're not in your stakeout van right now, so what are you waiting for here in aisle 14?" She looked quickly around the store. "Is whatever it is, going to happen here? Can I watch?"

"Sadly, unless Jason returns with a #2 pencil to stab me in the back, my visit won't result in anything interesting happening to either of us, although I've been wrong before."

A bit deflated, Gillian asked, "So, how do our fake cameras come into play? I'm still confused by that part."

"It's quite simple really," I said, reaching my hands out to showcase the copier in front of me. "Let's say a friend of mine came into the store to use this machine because he needed a second set of important documents. He stood right here and photocopied each page one at a time." I pointed to the camera dome directly overhead. "Now, if that camera had recorded my friend's activities, I was hoping that maybe I could view the footage and see what was on those pages."

"So, your friend did make copies?" Gillian asked with a perplexed expression.

"He did."

"And then lost them somehow?"

"It would seem that way," I answered. "Both the originals and the copies have apparently been misplaced."

"That sucks."

"It totally does," I said slowly. "I have a meeting with mall security in a few minutes, so I'll let you get back to work."

"Thanks, I guess," Gillian said. "I hope this wasn't the highlight of my shift," she said with a nice smile. "Do you have a business card that says you're a P.I.?"

I retrieved a card from my wallet and handed it to her. "If you ever need a licensed stalker to investigate someone, keep me in mind, okay?"

"Don't worry, I will."

***

As I exited into the mall, I noticed Gillian continued to hold my card like it was a Willy Wonka golden ticket. I think the public's fascination with private investigators is universal, more due to the rarity of meeting one than the actual work it entails. P.I.'s are great in books and films but in real life one of their main goals is to remain anonymous and out of sight. For the majority of cases I work, surveillance and inquiries are done quietly, resulting in a formal report that's generally read by one person before being filed away forever in a drawer. Even in higher profile cold case files, 95% of the information I unearth never sees the light of day, with the remaining 5% devoted solely to the outcome (i.e. person found, property located).

"I won't be offended if you don't want to eat in the food court," I told Walter, as I entered the security office. "I'm not sure how the Chinese place makes a perfectly good white chicken orange, but I'd just as soon not find out today."

"If you feel that way about orange chicken, then you really don't want to know where those chicken balls come from," Walter said, as he tucked an envelope into his jacket. "I know a place where we can talk and eat in private, plus it's cheap. Follow me."

We made idle chitchat about my day's findings as we exited The Galleria, walking two blocks south to a street I thought would be scary to cross after dark.

"Here it is," Walter said, stopping at The Garden of Edenville Cooking School and holding the door for me. "Student chefs learning their craft, one delicious dish at a time."

Aside from the drab and peeling marquee sign, there was nothing to indicate this place was open to the public. Before the door closed behind us, over my shoulder Walter was calling out, "Table for two today, Wanda. This is my friend Steve."

In the foyer, a stern looking woman in her sixties briefly smiled at me and curtly ordered, "This way." The room she led us to was as bland as the building's exterior. It had six square tables set up haphazardly with only a salt and pepper shaker and rolled-in-a-napkin utensils adorning their tops. No fancy tablecloth, no flowers, zero welcoming ambiance. Our host entered the kitchen and soon returned with two glasses of water. "Let me know when you're ready to order, Walter," she instructed before walking out of the room.

I looked down at the empty tabletop. "She forgot the menus," I said. "How are we supposed to order or know what the specials are today?"

"There are no menus, at least not the regular kind. There's today's menu," Walter replied, pointing to a blackboard on the wall. "They never teach the same thing twice. That means they offer something different every Monday, which is the only day they're open for lunch. The morning class ends at 11:50 and whatever they've whipped up is sold for a $5 donation. It's the best food around, bar none."

"Interesting concept," I said. "Is the class that ends at 11:50 for advanced students or beginners?"

"Strictly the senior class," Walter said. "If I wanted to eat something made by an amateur, I'd bring a peanut butter and jam sandwich from home." He took a sip from his glass. "One more thing. This is the only drink available, otherwise the school would have to apply for a restaurant licence and they don't need that hassle. Is this to your liking?"

"It's very impressive, although I'm a bit worried that we're the only ones here," I said looking around the empty room.

"They started this a few weeks ago and don't really advertise,"

Walter explained. "More for us, right? I guarantee it'll be the best money you'll spend this decade."

With no appetizers and a limited number of choices (all of which were still steaming hot, waiting to be set onto a plate), our meals arrived in no time. Walter ordered the red curry chicken served with Thai jasmine rice, while I opted for the Vienna-style breaded pork schnitzel with a twist of lemon.

"I can't believe people are going to be spending their hard earned dollars on one of Sam's grilled hot dogs, when they could be in here with us," I said, taking the last forkful of delicious schnitzel. "I may have to schedule a trip here every Monday."

"Make sure to call me first, so I can get us this Presidential table," Walter said, finishing the last of his rice.

An office group had joined us, with our host moving the remaining tables to allow them to sit together. This left Walter and I alone in the corner, which suited us for the next part of our lunch.

"Here's your dessert," Walter said, sliding his envelope across to me. "I figured out which ones were from the mall footage, but haven't a clue about the third guy you asked about."

As I took out a number of faxed police record reports, I asked, "The third guy?"

"Malcolm Wright. He sticks out as the one that doesn't belong, even with his criminal past." Walter leaned forward. "I'm right about Carl and Tom, aren't I?"

"You are," I said in a low tone. "All three of them have one thing in common: George Mulhall. I want to know why and how that happened. I was hoping these would help me out."

Walter excused himself to go to the washroom and I concentrated on the raw data in my hands. I discovered that Carl Duguay and Tom Evans might as well be identical twins, each trying to one-up the other. If Carl stole a Grand Am, Tom would steal a Grand Prix. If Carl was busted for dealing baggies of marijuana to high schoolers, Tom was being arrested for selling dime bags of cocaine at the university. Regardless of their entry-level criminal activities, nothing indicated to me that a jump to 'hired killers' was imminent. Baffled, I set aside their stack of convictions and perused Malcolm Wright's short history of crime, which included a shoplifting charge and an assault conviction. The first thing that struck me as odd was that he was three years younger than Carl and Tom, meaning it was doubtful they socialized in the same circles. Another obstacle for such a friendship to blossom was that Malcolm lived in Garland, not Edenville. His listed address corresponded with the King Street one I'd got through George's cell phone records.

"See what I mean," Walter said, sitting back down at the table and tapping the page in my hand. "That Malcolm Wright kid doesn't belong. He's younger, lives way out in the sticks and has the same criminal record as my grandmother. If they're The Three Musketeers, then I'm Batman and you're Robin."

"Why am I Robin?" I protested with a smile.

"Well, I'm sure as shooting too old to be Robin and besides you've got to admit you'd look better in green tights."

"You've got me there," I replied. "Yeah, no one wants to see you running around in tights. Even the thought is repulsive."

We carried on this mutual comedic banter, combing over the reports one last time.

Frustrated, I began to say, "Aside from Carl and Tom being friends, there's got to be something else in common—" when Walter cut me off.

"Give me Malcolm Wright's assault page," he demanded, as he began to compare all of the pages on the tabletop. "I think I found your link, Steve, although I really wish I hadn't because this is going to cause all sorts of trouble."

Silently, Walter moved his index finger across the same box on all three reports: Arresting Officer: Const. Crawford #3059

I kicked myself for not seeing this sooner. *Travis strikes again and again and again*, I thought angrily. *Why doesn't this shock me?*

EIGHTEEN

"How do your contacts feel about giving up information on a fellow officer?" I asked in disbelief. "Have you ever heard about this guy? Has he been in the news or charged for Police Act violations? Anything?"

Walter continued to look through the reports. "I can make a few more discreet inquiries. If he's a bad apple, my former colleagues won't have a problem giving up information. I'll make a couple calls when I get back to The Galleria."

"That would be great," I said sincerely.

"What's your next plan of action?" Walter asked as we exited the cooking school.

"I suppose I'll have to visit Garland at some point to check out Malcolm's address," I replied. "First, I need to track down that bag of photocopies."

"And how do you expect to do that? I would think that evidence is long gone."

I shrugged my shoulders. "I know, but as much as I'd like to read those diary pages, I'm more interested in the chain of custody. Malcolm apparently had it and gave it to George."

"So who took it out of George's briefcase?"

"Since I can't discuss the matter with Constable Crawford, I'll have to rely on the paramedics' memory, as to where the case was before and after they arrived on scene."

Walter smiled in agreement. "If they didn't take it, that'd leave Crawford with plenty of time to paw through it. It's worth a shot."

OFF THE BEATEN PATH

I accompanied Walter to the security office, where he made a call to the ambulance dispatcher. "I'm in contact with them once a day on behalf of some out of breath senior or a 5-year-old who's swallowed the toy from their unhappy meal," he informed me, punching in the numbers. "Hi Tina, it's Walter at The Galleria . . . No, everyone here's fine . . . I'm looking for the names of the paramedics who attended that man-bus fatality in June . . . Why? Well, the man's family sent an investigator here to give your people a thank you note or gift card or something." Walter gave me a wink, as he jotted down two names on a pad. "Are they both working today by chance? . . . Just Josh? . . . Okay, yeah, give me his cell number and I'll pass it along to the P.I." Another few seconds of friendly talk and Walter hung up. "There you go," he said, ripping the page off the pad. "Josh is a good guy and he's working until 7:00 p.m. His partner Danielle started a vacation this morning in the Cayman Islands. If it were me, I'd talk my client into buying a ticket to paradise so I could talk to her as soon as possible."

"With the astronomical retainer my client sent me, I could actually do that," I chuckled. "My girlfriend and you would get along splendidly," I added. "Okay, I'm heading out. Maybe Josh is between calls."

"Good luck with that. I'll call my buddies and get the lowdown on Crawford."

"Again, I'm very appreciative for the help."

"No problem and thanks for lunch."

"You're welcome," I said opening the door. "I'm sure we'll be eating with Wanda and her culinary crew again in the near future."

***

Josh gave me directions to the fire and ambulance station in the west end. "You know the drill, though. I can't guarantee I'll be

here when you arrive," he warned. "When duty calls, I gotta run."
I assured him I was well aware how emergency services operated
and drove to the parking garage exit. Handing the booth collector
my money, the office conversation about my retainer crept back
into my thoughts. At the time, Dawn had convinced me there
was nothing sinister about Debra's higher than usual cheque. In
light of all I now knew about the case, it appeared Dawn had
been correct. Still, the whole post-conviction story had yet to be
written. Malcolm was connected to George, who was connected
to Eric, who was connected to Lucy, who was connected to Debra,
who was connected to Rodney (albeit via a spray can).

Talk about your six degrees of separation.

The station was a new, modern looking structure, with two
large fire truck doors on the left side and two smaller ambulance
doors on the right. I noted that both ambulance bays were
occupied. With the nice weather, all the doors were open and
several sets of eyes watched me approach the building on foot.

"Are you Steve?" a fit male in his late twenties asked, as he
walked out of the ambulance side to greet me. Seeing my smile,
he said, "I figured with those tinted van windows."

"Tools of the trade, Josh. Thanks for taking the time to meet
me," I replied as we shook hands.

"My uncle was a slick private investigator and I helped him
on a few files during high school. Unfortunately, I was driving a
white Cavalier with no tinted windows, which didn't help with
discretion. I remember it ending badly."

"Because you were burned by the subject?" I asked with a grin.

"Not exactly," Josh replied. "In order to see my guy's driveway
I had no choice but to park near a grade school."

"Oh geez," I began. "Did you get busted by a parent, teacher,
neighbour or cop?"

"The school principal," Josh answered, shaking his head. "He
approached the car in my blind spot. I jumped when he knocked
on the window and he asked, 'Can I help you?' I was scared out of

my mind and thought a little joke might help defuse the situation, so I replied, 'Do you have any duct tape and rope?'"

"And how did that go over?" I asked, unable to hold back my own laughter.

"He dragged me out of the car and started pummelling me. Then the police arrived and next thing I know I have two guns aimed at my head and an officer screaming, 'Don't make me use this, kid!'"

"FYI: murderers and pedophiles vie for any officer's top *justifiable shooting* spot. What happened then?"

"I was handcuffed and put in a cruiser, while my car was searched. Luckily, my uncle heard about it on his police scanner and straightened everything out," Josh said. "That was my last day as an investigator, although my uncle still likes to tell the story at every family gathering."

"No doubt."

"So the dispatcher said you wanted to drop something off for Danielle and me?" Josh said as we entered a lounge area and sat down. "From that lawyer's family?"

"Walter from The Galleria overstated my purpose a bit," I replied sheepishly. "However, in a roundabout way I am working on behalf of George Mulhall's estate and law firm. I have a question you might be able to answer in regards to the accident scene that day."

"I've attended a lot of incidents since then," Josh said slowly, "but I'll do my best."

"Great. It's about George's briefcase," I started. "I know he had it at the time of his death and after–"

"Was it never returned?" Josh cut in with a puzzled expression. "Travis, I mean Constable Crawford, said he'd take care of that."

Bingo.

"No, it was returned. It's all good," I quickly responded, not needing Josh to start his own investigation by calling Crawford as soon as I left. "The law firm just wanted me to find out if the case opened upon impact, as they're looking for a divorce case file that's gone missing. They thought maybe George had it and the documents were lost in the street. That's all. Nothing serious."

Josh was relieved. "No, the case didn't open or anything. We were the first at the scene and Danielle picked it up. She set it down beside us as we worked on the guy, even though it was obvious he was dead. We went through the motions, but he was long gone."

This was the first time I'd heard George had died instantly from his injuries and it hit me hard. "As for the briefcase, did the officer take it with him?" I managed to ask. "Is there a policy concerning personal items when two agencies arrive together?"

"Not a written one. In this instance, either one could've taken it to Met along with the body. Once signed over, it's the hospital's responsibility to contact the family and return any belongings."

Yet another modification was needed to my belief that Crawford intentionally retrieved the briefcase. From the sounds of it, the paramedics could have just as easily thrown the case in the ambulance and out of view. "So the officer took the briefcase then?" I asked rhetorically. "Did you see it at the hospital afterward?"

"Yes," Josh answered automatically. "I remember it was sitting on the end of the gurney we transferred the lawyer onto."

"Was it still there when the officer left?"

"I don't know because we were dispatched to another call. Constable Crawford had to complete some paperwork, which I doubt took him very long."

I thanked Josh and gave him a business card. "If your slick uncle needs any help, have him give me a call."

"I'll do that."

I gave Josh a brief wave as I drove away, a group of firefighters and paramedics forming a semi-circle around him, wondering who had stopped in for a chat. The sight produced a mild sensation of guilt in my chest. Once, I, too, was one of those smart and courageous young men and I'd thrown it all away. At the time, there were plenty of good reasons: sex, drugs, the rock and roll lifestyle, notoriety and power. In retrospect, if I had stayed clear of trouble I'd have moved up the ranks and would be commanding my own platoon of officers now. The one lesson I had successfully learned from those dark days was that it's hard to concentrate on your future if you're always looking back at your past.

Growing up, my mom and dad had often preached the same sentiment: "It's not where you come from, it's where you're heading that counts," they'd say after I brought home a so-so report card or found myself in a seemingly dire youthful situation. In my final year of high school, both left me to fend for myself. My dad had a massive heart attack in his factory office and was dead before his knees hit the linoleum. A few weeks later, my mom went into the hospital for some tests and was diagnosed with a rare, aggressive form of leukemia. Within a month, she was also gone. One of her biggest regrets was not being able to return home to say farewell to all the comforts and objects that had brought her happiness throughout the years. In her last days, we were talking about a television program we'd watched in a common room down the hall. She'd been uncomfortable in her wheelchair but, as was her custom, didn't complain. I remember helping her into bed and pulling the blankets up to her neck. Trying to invoke a pleasant memory, I said, "I bet you miss your lumpy old recliner these days. I know it misses you and Dad." In response, she gently placed her frail hand on mine and whispered, "I miss everything," before closing her eyes to sleep.

Those three words have haunted me ever since.

Being 18 with no siblings or close relatives, I finished out the school year and walked away from the only life I'd ever known. I envisioned a carefree existence without the need of adult supervision. Unfortunately, without any grounded adult influence, I ended up leading a careless existence instead.

After my humiliating exit from the police force, I briefly took up the offer of a motivational therapist I'd been introduced to during the corruption trial. "Once this circus has left town, set up an appointment and I'll try to get you back on track," he said, pointing to the court hallway full of reporters. Although not the kind to express my feelings, especially to another man, one day I found myself in his waiting room flipping through magazines. When I glanced up to check the time on the wall clock, I noticed a colourful plaque hanging beside it, which featured a statement that profoundly changed my way of thinking forever. In simple script, it read: *If you give up on yourself, you are also giving up on those who believe in you.*

My parents had always believed in me and in a way, I was thankful they hadn't been around to have that belief tested. In their place, over the years, others had stepped forward and put their trust in me, only to experience the devastating sting of my failure to live up to their expectations, however low they may have been set.

As the Edenville Metropolitan Hospital came into view, I knew that these days only two people truly believed in me; one was a pretty waitress back home and the other was a dead man I'd never met. I had no plans of letting either of them down today, or any day soon.

***

"Can I help you?" the male senior citizen volunteer at the Info Desk asked. "Are you here to visit a patient?"

"Not exactly," I replied. "The person I'm inquiring about passed away in June."

"Visiting them would be out of the question, wouldn't it?"

"That it would," I said, returning the man's wry smile. "Could you tell me where the morgue is? I'm hoping to speak with someone there."

"Just as long as the person you want to speak with is still alive. Go to the basement and turn right."

"Thank you."

"Tell 'em Mick wanted to escort you but was afraid they'd keep him there!"

The old guy was still cracking himself up as the elevator doors closed. I was soon following a black line on the floor and thinking about my Vice days, when the morgue was a weekly stop to learn about new bodies. I'd also try to identify gang-bangers, who learned crime doesn't always pay in the way they'd dreamed it would.

"Something I can do for you or are you lost?" a male voice asked from behind me. "The cafeteria is one floor up."

I turned and was met by a man in his fifties wearing a lab coat, whose appearance epitomized the stereotypical nerd. "I'm not lost and being down here won't help my appetite. My name is Steve Cassidy. I'm a private investigator."

"Good to meet you, Steve," he said, not offering his hand to shake, which I assumed was more for my benefit than his. "I'm Rick Olsen. What brings you down to my department today?" He gestured me into his office. "Is this official business?"

I took a seat in an ancient metal chair from the 1960's. "I suppose," I said. "I'm looking into the death of a man struck by a bus a few months back."

"Oh, I was working that shift. His name was . . . George . . . give me a second . . . Mulhall, if memory serves. Big man with a tan coat?"

"That's him."

"Statistics show taking the transit is one of the safest modes of transportation but not like that. I felt sorry for him. An awful way to go."

Morbid humour (at least I thought this was Rick's attempt at morbid humour) is often the only way emergency personnel and people in this line of work stay sane. "I heard from the paramedic that George didn't suffer."

Rick swiveled slightly in his chair. "The impact crushed his rib cage, which in turn punctured his lungs and heart. There would have been a moment of realization and then bam, lights out."

"I guess that's something his loved ones can take comfort in," I said, thinking of Jane Calloway. "I'm not looking for answers about George's last moments per se, only of the time he spent here in the hospital." I paused, then added, "More specifically, the time his briefcase was in your custody."

"What are you saying?" Rick replied, looking befuddled. "Wasn't the case returned to Mr. Mulhall's family? If so, there's an official form for lost items that needs to be submitted."

"No, it was returned in good condition to his law firm," I stated, much to my host's relief. "So you do remember seeing it?"

"Of course. It was on the gurney and remained there until my assistant locked it up in our storage room."

"Prior to that, was it left out in the open? Could someone have taken items out of the briefcase without your knowledge?"

Rick tensed, like a cat with an arched back. "Are you accusing this department of pilfering something from that case, Mr. Cassidy?"

"Not at all. I'm simply trying to follow the chain of custody between the time of the accident and when the case was shipped back to Dannenberg."

"Go on."

I sat up straighter in my chair. "I know the first responders brought it here and placed it on the gurney, as you've mentioned."

"Where it stayed untouched until Henrietta took it to be locked up," Rick cut in sternly.

"One of the paramedics told me that after they left, Constable Crawford stayed behind."

"Yes, to complete the transfer forms for the body and, by extension, the briefcase. Nothing unusual took place, I can guarantee you that. After the ambulance team departed, the officer might have stuck around another ten minutes, no more."

This news didn't sit well with me, although the alternative of bringing Rick into my conspiracy cabal was even more disturbing. "Could I speak with Henrietta? I want my report to indicate I spoke with everyone here."

"Sure you can," Rick brightened up. "She was finishing an autopsy when you arrived. Let's see if she can talk now."

I suppose working with dead people allows you to become a more happy-go-lucky individual. On a daily basis, you're faced with the cold stiff fact that being alive is a privilege, not a right. On the other hand, cops usually become jaded and cynical about everything because they only deal with the ugly side of life, shift in, shift out.

"Here we are," Rick said as we entered an examination room, complete with a body on the steel table covered with a sheet. "Henrietta, this is private investigator Steve Cassidy. He'd like to ask you a few questions about the large man who was hit by the bus."

Rick's assistant was a pudgy, studious looking woman in her mid-twenties, with glasses and black hair pulled up in a bun.

"Okay," Henrietta said apprehensively, signing the bottom of a form that she handed to Rick. "Nelson is done."

"Great. I'll look this over," Rick replied. "I am going for my break, if you have no further questions for me, Mr. Cassidy."

"We're good," I said, thereby allowing him to leave the room.

"Let's go to my office," Henrietta said, closely following her boss. "Being around dead bodies makes some people uncomfortable."

"I used to be a cop. I've seen it all and then some."

"It's the 'then some' part that still freaks me out. Mr. Nelson there was a heavy smoker and keeled over during a backyard barbecue party holding a spare rib in his hand. *That* I can handle no problem."

"And George Mulhall? I suspect his autopsy was pretty

straightforward," I said.

"Actually, it was," Henrietta replied. "His ribcage had been crushed and he died of massive internal hemorrhaging caused by the impact with the bus. The end. Is that what you're here about?"

"I know this'll sound odd. I'm not so much looking into George's death, as to what happened to his briefcase afterwards. From what I've been told, it accompanied him here and then you locked it up in the morgue's storage room. Is that correct?"

"It is." I could tell by her body language she wasn't pleased with where this conversation might go. "I know for a fact it was shipped back to some law office because I was the one who sent it there."

"The case arrived in one piece," I said. "I'm not accusing you or Rick of doing anything wrong, I want to get that straight. My issue is the briefcase's whereabouts from the time it arrived to the time you locked it away."

"I don't understand. It was at the foot of the gurney the entire time."

"I was told Constable Crawford was the last outside person to have access to it, after the paramedics left to attend another call. Is that right?"

Henrietta appeared to be internally activating her thinking cap. "If you're categorizing Rick and me as inside people, then yeah, that sounds right."

I took a deep breath and for the whole enchilada asked, "Did he open the briefcase or was he alone with it at that time?"

"Like to find some identification? That type of thing?"

"Exactly."

"Then no, not at that time," came the quick forthcoming answer.

I detected something slightly off in the way her voice trailed at the end of her sentence. "You're sure about that?"

"Well, I do remember him leaving."

"And then?"

"And then returning an hour or so later," Henrietta said in a burst of words. She was on her feet and out the door before I could respond.

He came back!

"What's wrong?" I asked, following Henrietta down the hall to where an empty gurney was parked against the wall.

"Mr. Mulhall was right here when the officer returned. It must have been around this time of day because Rick was on his break, like he is now."

"And where were you?"

"I was in the middle of an autopsy. I saw him through the door's window and called out, 'Did you forget something?' and he replied, 'I think I dropped my lucky pen in here earlier.' I had no interest in searching for some stupid pen, so I said, 'Okay, look around. I hope you find it,' and that was that. He wasn't present when I was done and I never thought of telling Rick about it. I'm sorry. I forgot all about it."

"There's nothing to be sorry about, Henrietta. You did great remembering now. That's what's important."

I thanked Henrietta for her assistance and retreated to my van, attempting to formulate my next move.

You're going down, Crawford, I thought as I started the engine. *Lucky pen, my ass.*

NINETEEN

"That's crazy," Dawn said after I filled her in over the phone on the file's latest twists and turns. "This Crawford guy is totally busted."

"As much as we believe that, all I have is a bunch of circumstantial evidence and a boat load of conjecture."

"That got Eric convicted of murder, don't forget."

"True," I said, seeing her point, "but that was an entire police department and prosecutor forcibly fitting square pegs into round holes, not just one person spouting a crazy theory."

"I don't think you're crazy."

"I said the theory was crazy, not me."

"Oh, that's different."

I could picture the smile on her face, as she curled a strand of hair behind her ear, an unconscious act that drove me nuts (along with her tip-toed kisses). "The part that's bothering me about this briefcase theft is the timing. I don't get why it took Crawford a few hours to determine that Carl and Tom didn't have the diary. Once clear of George's accident, wouldn't they have called him? You know, 'Hey man, the lawyer's dead but we forgot about the diary.' It doesn't make sense." I was expecting a swift response, which didn't come. "What are you thinking? What do you see that I don't?"

"What if your earlier idea was right and Crawford really wasn't the big cheese of this operation?" she asked hesitantly.

"But he is the one who recruited these two," I interrupted.

"On whose orders though? What if Crawford gets a call from someone he trusts looking for two goons to do a job. Crawford knows a couple guys and puts them in touch with his friend. Are you following me?" she asked.

"So far, I guess."

"Now what if the person Carl and Tom called after the accident was Crawford's friend? Then the angry friend contacts Crawford to say his boys royally screwed up and it's his responsibility to make it right."

"And return to the hospital to get the diary," I said, finishing her thought.

"I'm thinking Crawford purposely stayed out of the loop so that later he'd have - what do they call it – plausible deniability?" Dawn replied.

"Look at you giving me yet another person to track down." My idea of adding Rick from the morgue to my expanding cast now didn't sound so wild. "Even if you're right, who would this mystery man be and what's his agenda?"

"Maybe his agenda is to keep Eric behind bars and hide the identity of Lucy's true murderer." Dawn said. "As for his identity, my first guess would be someone on the force whom Crawford respects. Someone who might approve of Carl and Tom, due to their criminal records. They, on the other hand, would have to trust this individual. I'm thinking he's some higher-up on the Edenville cop food chain."

I mulled this over. Dawn's approach to this problem was similar to mine, great minds thinking alike and all that. "I only have one problem with your reasoning. I don't see a local copper caring about Eric's conviction or Lucy's death six years ago. Everything happened in Dannenberg, not out in Edenville or Garland, which is where I'm heading now. Do you see what I mean?"

"Why can't these things be simple and wrapped up in 60 minutes?" Dawn replied in frustration.

"Because I'm not Hercule Poirot and you're not Miss Marple, which is a good thing."

"I bet Agatha Christie could figure this out."

"We'll figure it out. In time," I replied. "Okay, enough of my shop talk. Let's discuss your shop talk. Anything interesting happen during your shift?"

"Not really. Same bacon, different pile. Although Doug is in trouble with his girlfriend."

"What did he do now?" I asked, accelerating down the highway ramp and merging into the steady mid-afternoon traffic. "Wasn't he already in the doghouse for buying a shirt for her birthday? She didn't like the print or something, right?"

"He bought it at the +Plus Size store and completely humiliated her by saying, 'My big birthday girl deserves only the best,'" Dawn said in a mock exasperated tone, and I couldn't help but laugh. "Stop that now! It wasn't funny."

"Was it the right size?"

"I think so," Dawn responded.

"Then what's the problem? She's oversensitive about her weight, and although he shouldn't have said that, he did nothing wrong. I'll tell him that next time I'm at The Sunsetter."

"You men are all alike."

"So what's her issue with him now? Did he buy her a treadmill and a grapefruit?"

"Worse. He said he wanted to sleep with her sister."

"You're making that up," I accused her, trying not to swerve off the road as I began to laugh harder. "No man is that stupid, even if it's true. Is the sister hotter than his girlfriend?"

"She's a year older and maybe 20 pounds lighter, but still not all that different."

"And why did the Dougster confess to this?"

"He says it started off innocently. They were watching a movie in which the girlfriend asks her boyfriend which female celebrity he'd like to sleep with if she gave him a One Night Only pass."

"Jennifer Aniston?" I broke in.

"That's your dream date, not Doug's," Dawn said.

"Oh, right."

"Since you've gone down that road, which lucky celebrity did I choose?"

"Brad Pitt," I answered immediately, as we'd already had this conversation during our time together.

"You are correct, sir," Dawn replied, no doubt happy I'd remembered this fun couple fact. "Anyway, what is the fundamental idea behind such a question?"

"It's hypothetical, because you're never going to meet or have a fling with that person in a thousand lifetimes."

"Right. Unfortunately, Doug didn't hear the part about the female having to be a celebrity. So go on and finish my story," Dawn said, encouraging me.

"Are you kidding me? Doug answered that his dream sex partner was his girlfriend's sister? What's wrong with him? I mean really. You work with him, you should know this stuff." I wiped the tears of laughter from my eyes with my sleeve and added, "Although it could have been worse."

"How so?"

"He could have said you."

"I would quit my job," Dawn said quickly. "Seriously, he's such an idiot. I wouldn't sleep with him in a million years, let alone a thousand lifetimes."

"Brad wouldn't like that. If his people talked with Doug's people, you'd be going to bed alone."

"Like that would ever happen," Dawn laughed. "To think that, you must be woozy from all your investigative work today."

"I could very well be woozified, if there's such a word," I admitted.

"Let's get back to important topics, such as what time you'll be back to me?" Dawn asked hopefully, as earlier I'd mentioned I might stay over if I got a hot lead.

"I'll be heading home after I speak with Malcolm The Diary Hoarder in Garland," I replied with a sigh. A disturbing thought sprang into my head. "What if he's the mystery man? He has an arrest connection with Crawford and he knew George."

"You've got to find that diary, Steve," Dawn implored. "It holds the key to George's death."

"Easier said than done, although I'm working on it."

Oh, how I'm working on it.

***

Marky Mark from the law office wasn't exaggerating about the size of Garland. It was one of those communities that map people debate whether to include in this year's printouts. Town? Village? Hamlet? Settlement? The one advantage for me was that everyone would know everyone else's business, relatives, jobs, cars, wealth, pets, loves, enemies and criminal records. Finding 231 King Street took no time, as there were only six paved streets, seven if you included the long winding laneway stretching into a wooded area behind the Sanchez Variety store.

As with much of this case, what I found was not what I expected. The once proud brick bungalow had been reduced to a burned out shell, with dark ashy stains rising above each window opening. I did not however, see any smoldering couches. "Maybe Malcolm is an arsonist as well," I said aloud to the For Sale sign on the lawn. There were two cars in the driveway next door and I walked to the front door to ring the bell. I heard movement from within and the door was opened by a clean cut male in his twenties. I noticed that a baseball game was paused on the big screen television in the corner of the living room.

"Hey, how's it going?" I asked in a friendly way. "I'm hoping you might be able to help me out."

"I will if I can. Are you interested in buying the property next door?"

"Not exactly. I came to visit someone and obviously he's moved," I laughed. "When did the fire occur? It looks fairly recent."

"Are you a cop or a social worker?" came the terse response.

"Why would you ask that?"

"Because those were the only two types of people who ever stopped by *to visit* that place."

"I used to be a police officer, but never got into social work," I admitted. "I work as a private investigator these days. My name is Steve Cassidy and what would your name be?"

"It's Ben."

"It's good to meet you, Ben," I said offering my hand. "I take it you weren't a fan of your neighbours."

Ben gave me a quick strong-gripped handshake and took the business card I'd withdrawn from my wallet. "Before I answer that truthfully, did you actually know someone there, like one of them was a brother or is that just a smooth line you use?"

I grinned. "A little of both, I suppose. I do want to speak with a man who used to reside there. He's not a relative or anything like that. He's not even in trouble, at least with me." This fact appeared to ease Ben's misgivings. "When you said 'one of them' would I be correct in thinking this was a half-way house or something similar?"

"It was a home for borderline delinquents, the last stop before getting sent to a juvenile detention centre or prison," Ben answered, a high level of disdain in his voice. "I probably know the guy you're looking for though."

In order to look less interested in this information than I was, I removed my notebook and flipped through a few pages. "Here it is. His name is Malcolm Wright." I focused on Ben's face for any noticeable negative reaction.

"Funny," Ben started with a slight smile, "I think Malcolm was the only good one passing through. He stayed out of trouble for the most part and took on a big brother-type role."

"That's encouraging to know. What happened after the fire? Were all the tenants placed in other facilities?" I paused as I glanced across the yard, a sick sinking feeling coming over me. "No one died in the fire, did they? You know, like Malcolm."

"Everyone survived. No one was home and Malcolm had moved out."

"Did the fire department determine the cause of the blaze?"

"It was arson."

"Did a former resident come back to get some kind of revenge?"

"Maybe," Ben replied noncommittally. "A witness said she saw two guys scoping the house out but couldn't give the police any type of description, aside from 'tattooed thugs.'"

I swallowed hard and (I think) retained a cool expression at this news. "This witness, is she from town?" I asked slowly.

"Old Mrs. Perry. She lives in that blue sided house," Ben said, stepping onto the porch and pointing down the street. "She also believes in aliens and that her third husband has been reincarnated as her Shih Tzu puppy Milo."

"Was the husband's name also Milo?"

"Randolph."

"You gotta love old people, right?" I joked. "So, getting back to Malcolm, do you know where he's living?" My pen was now poised above the notebook page, looking very official.

Ben hesitated. "You promise he's not in any trouble?" he asked. "Because it's been a rough few months for him and I don't want to be the one getting in the way of his recovery."

Rough few months?

His recovery?

"I swear. I just need him to clear up a few things about a case I'm working on. He's not in any trouble, although it sounds like he might have found some recently."

"Do you think your case and his beating might be related?"

I liked this kid. He was looking out for his friend. "Ben," I began sincerely, "anything is possible, but up until this moment

I had no idea about Malcolm's medical problems, although I was aware of an assault charge against him." I realized that I'd been so focused on the arrest report's revelation that Constable Crawford was the attending officer, I completely forgot to read the date of the incident. "I'm going to take a wild stab and say the fight took place in June sometime, right around the time of the fire next door. Would I be close?"

"The fire happened the day after," Ben replied, astounded by my guess. "I visited Malcolm in the hospital. He said at first, he thought he was being mugged and fought back. Then when a cruiser pulled up he figured he was saved, until the cop arrested him as the other two ran away." Ben's face registered a panicky look. "Two thugs in an alley. Two thugs setting the fire. You're looking for those guys, aren't you?"

"In a roundabout way. I'm hoping Malcolm can fill in some blanks about their identity and why they'd come after him in the first place. Plus there's a matter of a diary. As I mentioned before, Malcolm needn't fear me, I'm on his side."

"Okay, hold on," Ben said, vanishing down the hallway. I heard a whispered conversation and wondered if Malcolm was now residing here. Soon Ben returned to the foyer clutching his cell phone. "If you're serious, Malcolm will meet you tonight in Edenville. I gave him your name and number."

"Where and when?"

"All he said was downtown at 6:00. Sit on a park bench near some hot dog cart and he'd call you with the details."

"That sounds easy enough," I said calmly, jotting down the info. "I appreciate the help, Ben. I hope your next neighbours are, well, more neighbourly."

I drove the van around the block and parked in front of the Lazy Man's Bar for a few minutes. I figured if Ben had decided to follow me, it would appear I'd stopped at the local watering hole for a beer. When I thought the coast was clear I returned to King Street on foot, taking the scenic route to Mrs. Perry's house.

The side entrance doorbell produced a buzzer-like sound and the crazed howls of a dog that had lost its furry mind. I could see the little black mophead in the hallway, glancing backwards waiting for its master to appear. Within moments I saw a spry woman in her eighties walking toward me, all the time yelling at the dog, "Stop your barking!" With no curtains on the window, we made eye contact quickly and I noticed no trepidation as she opened the door.

"Good day, young man," she greeted me cheerfully. "How are you today?"

"I'm doing fantastic, ma'am. How is your day going so far?" I replied, equalling her sunny disposition.

"I feel like I could dance for the Bolshoi Ballet, except I'm not Russian, which I think is a prerequisite, like the Pope being Catholic."

"I never thought about that, although it does sound reasonable," I replied.

"Maybe in my next incarnation I'll be able to swing that," she said with a smile, as she looked at the now quieted dog at her feet. "Isn't that right, Milo?"

I was a tad freaked out when the dog cocked its head and nodded slightly, as if agreeing with her.

Get in and get out, my mind instructed me.

"Ma'am, I'm with the county arson department. I heard you saw someone hanging around the house up the street before it was set on fire. Is that correct? Is my information accurate?"

Mrs. Perry's eyes lit up like I was E.T. asking for a bag of Reese's Pieces. "There were two of them!" she cried out. "No one else saw them. I swear they started that fire."

"And you got a good look at them?"

"I didn't see their faces because they were wearing ball caps and my eyes aren't the greatest at my age."

"What about their body shapes? Tall, short, thin, fat?"

She peered down the street as if replaying that day in her head.

"Both were kind of tall, slim. They walked with their shoulders hunched forward and their eyes down, sneaky-like. I knew they were up to no good, but with that place they could have been new wards of Children's Services."

"Are these the men you saw?" I asked abruptly, holding up the pictures of Carl and Tom from The Galleria's surveillance footage.

Grabbing the pictures from my hand, Mrs. Perry crouched to the floor and put the paper in front of her dog's face. "Oh my word, Milo, it's them! It's really them!"

The dog did appear to examine the sheet before barking his approval, first in his crazy owner's direction and then mine, which again was disconcerting.

I reached down and gently took the sheet back, putting it in my jacket. "You have been a great help, ma'am."

"Have they been arrested?" Mrs. Perry asked as she stood.

"Not yet, although with your positive identification we're now one step closer," I said, turning to leave. "Thank you for your help. I must be getting back to the station."

I could tell she wasn't satisfied with my hasty departure. "Would you like a tea or coffee? I can answer any other questions you might have about that day."

I stepped out onto the cement steps and closed the screen door behind me, not wanting to let the dog escape. As Mrs. Perry continued to pepper me with questions and suggestions for lunch, the dog got up on its back legs and peered out the bottom half of the door.

"What is your name? I didn't catch your name!" Mrs. Perry asked.

With a smile and a friendly wave, I glanced back at her and then down at the dog. "My name is Randolph Cassidy. Have a great day."

At the mention of that name, Mrs. Perry's face went slack, while Milo's eyes widened in surprise, as if to say, *You're good,*

Mr. Cassidy. I await your return to talk some more, maybe without the old lady present, eh?

Maybe, pooch, I thought, as I continued down the sidewalk. *I'd love to hear your thoughts on the hereafter and aliens.*

Back on the road, I once again updated Dawn.

"Can you really believe an elderly woman with a four-legged husband?" she asked. "Is her identification of George's killers even legal?"

"You weren't there," I replied. "Trust me, I was going by the dog's verification, not hers. He'd charm the pants off any jury."

"It sounds like he's as smart as you, only with more fur."

"I don't know about that. He's definitely not as smart as you, though."

"Please, no one is as smart as me," Dawn laughed. "Do you know I was reading *Seventeen* magazine when I was only twelve? I know stuff, mister and don't you forget it."

"What fun would there be forgetting you?"

"There is that," Dawn replied. "Just don't forget about me during your meeting with this Malcolm character. Did you get the impression he's dangerous? We know he'll fight if backed into a corner."

"Don't worry, I won't be backing him into anything, except hopefully the truth about this diary," I said, trying to calm Dawn's nerves. "From what Ben said, I get the feeling Malcolm is more scared than anything, especially after his run-in with our loser thugs and the law. I'm grateful he's willing to meet me."

"He also agreed to meet George, don't you forget."

"I haven't, Dawn," I replied soothingly. "I'll be careful and be home to tuck you into bed."

"Promise?"

"I promise on the past lives of Mrs. Perry's dog."

TWENTY

Surveillance is quite a different experience when you're on the other end of the lens. I'm usually the one secretly documenting a subject's movements; the way they walk, with whom they speak and where they go. While 007 James Bond may be 'Licensed To Kill', I'm definitely 'Licensed To Stalk'. For the majority of my cases, I'm invisible to these unsuspecting people. They won't know I was hanging out with them until weeks later, when their insurance company rep, boss or spouse's divorce lawyer calls to set up a meeting. Yet here I was, planted on a park bench near Sam's Weiner Wagon waiting to be summoned by the Mysterious Malcolm, who was nowhere to be seen (at least from my vantage point). Earlier in the day, I had imagined walking in George's shoes. Now I felt like they'd been forcibly strapped to my feet.

Twenty-five minutes later, I was tired of waiting and began walking toward The Galleria, possibly to check-in with Walter at the security office. I didn't get five steps before my cell phone rang.

"Where are you going?" an anxious male voice asked.

"To meet you, Malcolm, if you show me where you're hiding." I stopped and turned leisurely to look over the immediate area. "Come out, come out wherever you are."

"You're pretty arrogant for someone who wants something I have," Malcolm shot back.

"And you're pretty selfish keeping that diary all to yourself," I said in a slow drawl for emphasis.

"But how–"

"It's my job and I'm very good at my job." I made a sweeping gesture with my free hand. "If you want to dance, let's dance. If not, I have dinner plans with a sexy brunette back in Darrien. It's your call."

I tried not to show any anxiety, even though I was sweating behind my eyes, if such a thing is possible. This person was the biggest lead I'd found, still I wasn't about to be toyed with by a stranger on a phone. I also knew Malcolm desperately needed a big ear to talk to about this diary business, now that his previous contact was dead. His conscience had implored him to tell his story months earlier and by agreeing to meet with me, it looked as though those ethical scruples continued to gnaw at Malcolm's insides. In that scenario, I had all the time in the world to wait him out.

"To your left, half a block up. A friend of mine owns The Handleman Pub. Tell the bartender who you are and he'll take you to a booth in the back," Malcolm instructed me. "And don't make any phone calls before you get there. If I lose sight of you for more than five seconds, the meeting is off. You got that?"

"Half block, Handleman Pub, bartender, booth, no calls, five seconds," I repeated. "How long are you going to be? Should I order a garlic bread appetizer, maybe a few drinks?"

"I'm not impressed by the tough guy routine, Mr. Cassidy. I checked you out online and know about your sordid past, or should I say pasts?"

"All I can say," I began, carefully walking across the street, "is don't believe everything you read online or in the newspapers. If you did, you'd still believe George Mulhall died because he was eating a hot dog." I terminated the call and continued on my way, making sure to stay in the open. *Sticks and stones, Buddy.* My goal was to meet with Malcolm and I had arranged that. I didn't have to like him, and he sure as shooting (as Walter would say), didn't have to like me.

OFF THE BEATEN PATH

***

The Handleman Pub was busy with an informally-attired crowd milling about the bar. The open garage-door style entrance, gave it an indoor/outdoor patio-feel. For Malcolm's benefit, before entering I tapped my index finger against my chest twice and gestured that I was going inside.

"Barkeep, a Jack Daniels on the rocks please," I ordered, stepping up to the bar with a huge grin. "By the way, this'll be on Malcolm's running tab, but don't tell him until we're through with our business, okay? He stiffed me with the bill last time we went out to the club to pick up babes."

The bartender only smiled. "Sure thing," he said and dutifully fixed my drink, which he placed atop a cardboard coaster advertising an upcoming Speed Dating event. "The booth up the stairs is reserved for you."

I followed the outstretched finger to the rear of the dining section, where one large booth was set up on a three-step stage riser. It seemed out of place, until I concluded this was once a gentlemen's club and it was the former V.I.P. lounge for private dances. "Ah, good times," I said to myself as I slid into the bench, keeping my eyes on the front entrance. I noticed two waitresses conversing while looking in my direction, although neither approached to take an order. Whomever Malcolm's friend was, he ran a tight ship.

The moment he stepped through the doorway, I knew my host had arrived. Malcolm Wright was a tall black man with an athletic build, no older than 22. He walked with a heads-up confidence that only experience can teach you. I was relieved he was alone, even though I knew a meat cleaver-clutching chef could be ready to pounce on the other side of the nearby kitchen door. He wasn't the weakling I was led to believe he was by his former neighbour. Malcolm gave a nod to the bartender and came to a stop at the top of the riser's stairs. It was only when highlighted by the glare of the ceiling lights that I saw his face had been battered and bruised at some point.

"Mr. Cassidy, I'll be up front. I'm not here to play games. I don't have the time or the patience," he declared. "Ben said you might know who beat me up and left me for dead."

"Don't forget, the next day they also burned your old house down," I said, taking a sip from my glass. "And they killed our mutual friend because you gave him a diary or something. Believe me, Malcolm, I'm not here to listen to bullshit either. Sit down and talk or leave me to my whiskey." If he didn't know I meant business before, he did now. "Honestly, relax. I won't bite." I could see he was more than a little confused as to how to proceed. Maybe he was plain scared that his honourable actions had set a world of hurt into motion and wasn't willing to continue that trend. "We'll be two guys killing time, you at that end, me at this end, with the bartender watching your back, along with every other employee," I said, noting a few more staff members eyeing our table.

"I read that you used to be a corrupt cop. How do I know you aren't part of this?" Malcolm asked, remaining on his unsteady feet.

"If you think I've partnered with Constable Crawford, you're way off base. I want to nail that scumbag as much as you do. The difference is I'd fully expect, and maybe even welcome, a trumped up assault charge in doing so." I let that sink in before adding, "And what do you mean by 'part of this'? What is *this* exactly?"

Malcolm uneasily took a seat in the booth. Either I had persuaded him with my good-guy swagger or he simply felt beaten down (no pun intended), and needed to get this dark secret off his chest. With no buses or police cruisers scheduled to pull up any time soon, he began to spill his tale of discovery, civic duty and betrayal, which ultimately circled back to Lucy McDowell's long-ago murder.

You remember Lucy, right? This is a story about her murder.

217

"During some renovations at the house in Garland around the first of June, I found it in one of the bedrooms," Malcolm started with a rush. "When I pulled up the old carpet, I saw a loose floorboard and wiggled it open. Underneath I found a notebook and a woman's ring."

"The notebook is the diary?" I asked, trying to balance my breathing.

"How do you know that?"

"As much as I want to hear this story, let me first fill you in a bit." In very general terms, I told Malcolm about investigating the bus accident and learning about George's phone calls concerning new evidence, maybe a diary. "Once I got to Edenville, other pieces started to slip into place, until I was certain George had once had the diary you phoned about in his possession. What I don't know is how it's related to a murder that happened six years ago in another city."

"After reading the notebook, I believed, and still do, that a former resident at the home had something to do with that woman's death. Lucy, right? Lucy McDowell?"

Malcolm's eyes were pleading with me to take him seriously.

"I'm a bit confused," I said, sitting taller in my seat. "You said you found this in June of this year, correct?"

"Yes. At the house."

"Ben told me the house was for juveniles, not adults. If the notebook entries are already six years old, how could a prepubescent boy be part of a premeditated slaying of a schoolteacher?"

"No, you're missing the point," Malcolm said, waving his hand. "The home was for teenagers but there were adults running it, sometimes former residents, like me. That's why I was still there helping with the renovations. I stayed on after my time was up, to be a mentor to the younger kids."

"Got it. Okay, so do you know who wrote the diary? And how do the entries tie into Lucy's death?"

"His name was Joseph Waddell, but everyone called him Joey Wad for short. He was helping to run the place when I arrived at 16. He was never a warm person, but tried to help us out when he could. He'd tell us stories about how his mother died when he was two, that it was the reason he rebelled and got into so much trouble."

"How old was he at that time?" I struggled to say, my mind whirling with questions.

"Twenty-two, maybe With his moustache he looked a few years older."

"What made you connect him to Lucy?"

Malcolm gave me a curious look. "He knew her."

"Knew her how?" I could feel my right leg begin to shake nervously under the table.

"You know, *knew her*. They were fooling around."

"Before or after she was married?" The idea of a jealous ex-boyfriend killing his beloved in an if-I-can't-have-you-then-no-one-will scenario was always a possible outcome, even if it hadn't produced any leads during previous investigations. I now had a man with a criminal past moving to the top of my suspect list.

"During. He plotted the whole thing out."

"The murder?"

"The hooking up part," Malcolm replied. "He might have written down a plan to kill her, but it wasn't in this notebook."

"Do you remember specific details? I assume you read everything more than once." I was a bad combination of exasperation and exhilaration. Lucy cheating with a grown-up delinquent nicknamed Joey Wad made no sense. There is 'slumming it' and then there is *slumming it*. She was a pretty and successful woman living the good life. "Were the pages dated? Could these fantasy fondling dates have taken place way before Lucy was killed?"

"The entries about her started about a month before . . . well, you know."

"Are there any entries after that?"

"No. They end two days before she, ah, passed away. That's what got me thinking he did it."

"Can we rewind?" I asked, attempting to keep the facts clear inside my now cluttered cranium. "Tell me about the dating part. Where did they meet? How did they meet? How many times did they meet?" I was in a state of disbelief, yet still not trusting what I was hearing. I knew about Malcolm's adult criminal record, but what type of troublemaker was he before he turned 18? He must have been quite the hellion to be sent to the Last Resort on King Street out in the country.

"I don't really recall," he replied apprehensively. "By the time I got to the part about him wanting to 'make her pay,' I knew I had to contact the convicted guy's lawyer. I honestly read that section once."

I'm a firm believer that when a person begins a sentence with, 'I honestly,' they aren't being completely honest. In this instance, Malcolm wanted to gloss over all the juicy information he'd learned from the repeated readings of those sections. It's only human nature. He may have clued into the relevance of Mr. Wad's words and immediately sought outside help, but there's no way he then sealed that notebook inside a freezer bag and locked it away.

"Why George and not the police?" I asked.

Malcolm appeared to dislike my question, as though I was accusing him of wrongdoing, and a harder-edged persona emerged. "The cops and I don't play nice," he said without remorse. "It was that simple. On the other hand, I know a little about defense lawyers. They get screwed by the system right along with their clients and there's not a damn thing they can do once the verdict comes down. I searched for Mr. Mulhall's name and called him up."

"Look," I began, wanting to get this conversation back on track, "you did the right thing. I would've probably done the same thing, especially in this case. What I don't get is why you strung George along, cancelling meetings with him until what turned out to be his last day on planet Earth?"

"'Cause I got scared!" Malcolm cried out. "What if the cops came after me next? To them, I'd be the enemy. Someone who needed to be taught a lesson." Malcolm fought back the angry tears threatening to slither down his cheeks.

"Is that what happened with Constable Crawford during the alley fight? Did he threaten you?"

"He didn't have to. His posse did that before he arrived." Malcolm clenched his teeth as he recalled the night of his beating. "In my head, see, I was still on the fence about handing over the diary and then out of the blue I get mugged by two white trash hoodlums. After the ninth punch to my ribs, they started yelling at me, wanting to know where the diary was at. I was like, 'What are you talking about?' between face and body blows, but they knew I knew. I tried to play stupid and fight back, but it was no use. When I fell on my knees one of them kicked me so hard in the stomach I thought I was going to spit out my spleen. I rolled onto my side and my face was resting against the curb. That's when the guy with cowboy boots lifted his foot above my head and said, "It's now or never, bro. Tell us where the diary is and we'll let you live." The words barely escaped Malcolm's pursed and trembling lips. "I was just trying to help that Eric dude out . . . "

"I know you were," I cut in sympathetically.

". . . but he wasn't worth dying for. I told them it was still hidden in the floor at the house and they left. Next thing I know a cruiser pulls up and Crawford calls for an ambulance. He had me handcuffed to the gurney to make sure I couldn't escape! I had an oxygen mask on and was bleeding from a half dozen deep cuts at the time. It wasn't like I was going to run away."

I allowed for some much-needed silence to help quiet our nerves before motioning to the very attentive bartender to mix up two stiff drinks, which were promptly dropped off at our table. "When did this happen?" I asked, taking a long swig of my drink, again upset with myself for not noting the date on the arrest record earlier.

"June 21st," Malcolm replied, taking a big gulp from his glass. "The house fire was the following day. I'm guessing they didn't even look for the diary and decided to just burn the whole place down to destroy the evidence."

"Hold on," I said in mid-sip. "The day after the fire was June 23rd, when George was killed. Were you out of the hospital by then?" I asked, remembering how Ben said he'd visited Malcolm after the fight.

"I got out that morning," Malcolm said in a low tone, fidgeting with his glass on the tabletop.

"If the diary was burned in the house fire, what did you give to George? I know you gave him something because he made 25 photocopies of it a few minutes later."

Malcolm looked to the ceiling and took a deep breath. "The diary wasn't at the house. Those morons burnt it down for no reason." A satisfied smile appeared when that fact was uttered. "I took it when I moved out."

"Then what was in the package George got?"

"A few pages, to show him I had the real thing."

"Why not give him the entire thing?" The awkward stillness that now enveloped us told me everything I needed to know. "You were going to shake him down for money, weren't you?" I asked angrily.

The words stung but couldn't break Malcolm's resolve to be the hero in this situation. "After the beatdown I took, I deserved something," he replied, his words cutting through the stale bar air. "The plan was for him to read the pages and call to set up a money-for-diary exchange."

"Unfortunately that call never came, did it?"

"Yeah, it never did."

"So where's the diary now, Malcolm?" I asked, staggered by

this news.

"I finished the job Crawford's goons couldn't complete and burned it in my kitchen sink. Ashes to ashes, dust to dust. I didn't want anything more to do with it."

I threw back the remainder of whiskey, gave my head a shake to combat the alcohol's effects and to erase most of this conversation. "That's too bad because I have a client who'd have easily paid ten times what you were asking George to pony up," I said as I got out of the booth. "At least this meeting wasn't a total waste. You got to tell your whopper of a story with its big twist ending and I now have the name of Lucy's killer. Winner winner, chicken dinner," I concluded, throwing a $20 bill on the table and taking a step toward the stairs.

"About that," Malcolm said in a sickening sarcastic tone, as he leaned back against the booth's weathered leather upholstery. "Joey Wad stopped writing in his notebook because he was found dead two days after Lucy's murder." He paused to enjoy the stunned expression on my face. "So finding him won't be as hard as you thought, will it now?"

TWENTY ONE

Malcolm's smug expression needed to be wiped off his face, although after the beating he'd already taken I doubted I could do any real harm to him or his ego. As angry as I was at this strange turn of events, vital new clues had been doled out: Lucy was having an affair with someone known as Joey Wad, as implausible as that sounded. I called Walter to make sure he was still working and met him a few minutes later.

"Joey Wad? Doesn't ring any bells," he said after I had recounted the pub meeting. "Then again, Garland is outside of Edenville's jurisdiction. I'll make another call while you read this." He handed me a printout with a handwritten note at the bottom. "Sorry my penmanship isn't the best."

I took the paper and discovered it was Constable Travis Crawford's personnel record, and I wasn't about to inquire how it had been procured. He was 27, had only been on the force three years and graduated in the lower half of his class at the Police College. *Nothing special there*, I thought. He was doing regular beat cop duties with no indication of Vice or Street Crimes or undercover work. In the Discipline section there were also no entries, meaning he'd kept out of departmental trouble to this point. Of course, his clean record meant nothing, as prior to my corruption trial, on paper I was a prime candidate for promotion as well. I read to the end of the page and saw Walter's scribble: *Uncle/relative connection???*

"Joseph Bartholomew Waddell, 22, was beaten to death two

days after Lucy McDowell's killing," Walter said, spinning around in his chair.

"Where?"

"Twenty minutes outside of Dannenberg. Some tourist found him slumped over inside a washroom stall at a highway rest stop." The fax machine in the corner came to life. "This might help." Walter retrieved a police report from the tray that he read in silence. "The most interesting thing here is that no vehicle was found abandoned in the parking lot afterwards," he finally said. "He got there somehow with someone."

I took the report to dissect the information and reached the same conclusion. "Unfortunately, Crawford's name isn't on this, since it happened before his time as a copper."

"True," Walter agreed. "At least you now have this Joey B. Wad character in the vicinity of Dannenberg at the time of the murder. That's gotta count for something, right?"

"Yes and no," I replied, walking to the paper shredder to unceremoniously feed the police report into it. "It definitely shifts my focus back there, instead of around here. What's frustrating is that with all the leads I've accumulated, I still have no solid evidence George was murdered in order to get those diary pages."

"Good investigative work is about always moving forward. Eventually the lawyer, Crawford, his thugs, Malcolm and that diary will circle into view. When they do, you'll be ready for it," Walter said, trying to ease my racing mind.

"Yeah, you're right," I said reluctantly. I glanced down at Crawford's employment record again. "What's this notation about an uncle or relative connection?"

"I don't know if it's important, but my guy said there was a rumour some strings were pulled to get Travis hired, possibly a family member in law enforcement or local government. He didn't know."

I checked the listed Emergency Contact: Mena Crawford - Mother. I memorized the name and shredded the page, not wanting to be caught with such sensitive information. "I'll keep that in mind, although I'm not sure the relevance of it."

"Yet."

"Yes, yet."

I thanked Walter for his extraordinary help and promised I'd call with updates, as well as return for another $5 lunch in the near future. I called Dawn to tell her to eat without me and that I'd be back to her in an hour. "Plan accordingly," I said, disconnecting the call as I rolled out of the parking garage for the second time today. I was almost at the highway ramp when I heard a police siren blaring and saw a cruiser racing up the street in my mirror. I dutifully slowed and pulled over to allow the officer to pass, only to learn he was parking behind me.

Crawford. This should be entertaining, I mused, quickly grabbing the handheld recorder from my equipment bag, pressing Record and placing it above the sun visor, out of view. I watched as my sworn enemy strutted to the open driver's side window. He was a big fella with a torso and arms that wouldn't look out of place at a body building competition. Clutching my driver's licence, vehicle registration and insurance card in one hand, I noted the badge number was 3059 and happily asked, "Is there a problem, Officer? I know I wasn't speeding and as you can see, I'm wearing my seatbelt." I pulled on the seatbelt for added effect.

On an intimidation scale, I'd give Constable Crawford high marks. He was good at what he did, which was to harass people. "Licence and . . . "

"Here you go," I cut him off, handing over my documents. "I've included my insurance as well." It wouldn't have shocked me if he'd ripped them up or pocketed them for later disposal, you know, along with my dead beaten body. I pictured a fight scene where I was tied to a chair begging, "Please, anything but the face! I want my loved ones to always remember me for being this handsome!"

Crawford didn't glance down, continuing to stare at me with

a determined expression. "The problem, Mr. Cassidy, is that you weren't travelling fast enough."

"Do I at least get points for heading out of town?" I replied, never breaking eye contact.

"You're a long way from home. I can't figure out why you're in Edenville at all. Darrien is a much better place to spend time, not skulking around our malls, hospitals or cooking schools."

"Don't forget the newspaper or fine eateries, such as The Handleman Pub. Hell, for that matter, let's include Sam's Weiner Wagon too."

Crawford handed back my information. "Although we try our best to protect our citizens and tourists, there is that rare occasion when bad things happen to good people, Mr. Cassidy. I'd hate to think that something like that might happen to you on your next visit to our community."

His tone was threatening but steady. He wasn't going to lay a finger on me in broad daylight, wanting only to put the scare in me. *Nice try, pal,* I thought. *A+ for Effort.* His bad cop act reminded me of something Malcolm said about his beating: 'They knew I knew.' That idea had frightened him, but it didn't frighten me.

"So what would you suggest I do, Constable Crawford, badge number 3059, just never return? That would definitely cut down on any chance of being harmed." He smiled slightly and remained silent. "Or another plan would be to hire a couple of goons to protect me, you know, as bodyguards when I come back to finish what I started." He was no longer smiling. "Do you know of anyone locally who does that type of thing? I recall hearing about a two-man crew named "Carl and Tom, Inc.," or some funny name like that. Oh wait, maybe I'm confusing them with a radio morning show ad I saw plastered across the front of a city bus downtown earlier near The Galleria entrance. Do those names mean anything to you?"

As I spoke, Crawford's face gradually turned a few shades of red and his body language did all his talking.

"Is there anything else? Am I free to proceed to the highway exit up the road?" I inquired, pointing up the street, believing our charade playing time was up. "I promise that the next time I'm in town, you'll be the first person I call."

Crawford leaned forward and said in a very menacing manner, "Just remember, your first call may be your last."

"Wow, another handy piece of wisdom to keep in mind," I yelled out, as Crawford walked back to the cruiser. With the knowledge that my message had been received loud and clear and with a friendly police escort, I was soon on the highway heading back to Darrien.

Home Sweet Home.

***

Dawn was on the couch, immersed in Clive Barker's *Weaveworld* novel, a favourite of mine that I'd introduced to her a week earlier.

"It's about this bored insurance agent who comes into contact with the magical world of the Fugue," I'd said at that time. "It's inhabited by people called the Seerkind, who've woven themselves into an ordinary rug to escape being hunted down by humans." This abbreviated explanation was greeted by Dawn's warm, yet blank stare.

"Did you read this during your wild drug-taking police days and you now can't separate the two experiences in your mind?" she'd asked with a smile.

"No, I think it was before I got hired as an officer, while drifting from job to job, delivering pizzas and building bicycles."

"I so don't see you as being a fantasy genre guy."

"It might be the only fantasy book I've ever read. I picked it off a clearance table and thought it sounded different and got completely sucked into it that night."

Dawn had continued to eye me doubtfully. "It's not my kind

of book, but you've got me intrigued."

I now dropped my case on the coffee table and fell into the cushions beside Dawn. "Hey stranger," she said. "Rough day at the office?"

"The only way it could've been bumpier is if my van were strapped atop a Boblo Island rollercoaster. Every new revelation was like a corkscrew turn or freefall dive. My heart was still in my throat just thinking about everything on the drive back here."

Dawn set *Weaveworld* down and snuggled against me. "You're home now and nothing else can be done on the case tonight. So, using your own *No Ulcer Attitude* rules, you can't worry about it until tomorrow, and you know what they say about tomorrow."

"The sun will come out?"

"That was Little Orphan Annie, you moron, not They!" Dawn chided me as she began to laugh. "No, that tomorrow never comes. Therefore, it's just you and me for the duration." As was her tendency, she leaned her back against my chest and turned her face upwards to mine. "That sounds fun, right?"

"It certainly does," I replied.

We watched a few television shows in our sitting-upright-spooning-position (as Dawn liked to call it) and retired to the bedroom around 10:30. "Are you enjoying the book?" I asked as I brushed my teeth. "I saw you're more than halfway through it already."

"You didn't tell me there was a love story component. Do Calhoun and Susanna survive and find true happiness?"

"Maybe," I offered, entering the room and slipping under the bed sheets. "Truthfully, I don't remember. I was too wrapped up in the concept the Seerkind didn't know what their enemy creature looked like, because no one had ever survived its attack to pass along the information."

"Talk about your cold case file. Not knowing whom or what you're looking for at all times. Sounds familiar, doesn't it?"

"What happened to the *No Ulcer Attitude* rule you quoted

earlier?" I mildly protested.

"We're discussing the book, not your case," Dawn replied with an easy grin. "Anyway, I'm sure by the end of both stories everyone'll know what the monster looks like."

"The Seerkind at least had a name for theirs," I said, turning off the night table light. "I only have *Lucy's killer,* which doesn't exactly have the same great literary ring as *The Scourge.*"

Dawn slid up against me. "I believe you and Mr. Barker will not let me down. If Broadway Annie is indeed correct about the sun, the morning will bring a whole new chapter waiting to be written, rollercoaster rides and all."

I smiled in the dark and held Dawn a little closer. "The only chapter I'm interested in," I whispered, "is the one that concludes with the phrase, The End. I'm hoping Eric McDowell can help me with the wording tomorrow if, of course, it ever arrives."

***

I contacted the Sellcan Correctional Institution to set up an appointment with Eric and learned my request first had to go through his new lawyer, Jane Calloway.

Yet another twist, great, I thought.

"Good morning, Jane. I was planning on calling you later today about my Edenville adventures, but was just informed I needed to get your permission to speak with Eric McDowell," I said, figuring I'd make a pre-emptive strike. "I guess I can do both now."

"Oh, sorry about that," Jane replied. "After your visit here, I went to see Eric to update him. George had kept him in the dark about the diary, not wanting to get his hopes up until something concrete had been established."

I guess I could buy that explanation.

"And while there you changed Eric's legal contact info?"

"Exactly. I believe a new policy about calling an inmate's

lawyer before any meeting was recently implemented."

Since I last spoke with Eric a few weeks ago?

I suppose anything was possible, although a simple, 'I checked the box regarding contact requirements,' would've made more sense. Maybe I was being paranoid after the Constable Crawford business. Jane had been on Eric's defense team and more than likely helped with his other appeals. "How did he take the news?" I asked.

"The same way most convicts do, with a shrug of the shoulders and a, 'Wake me up when it's over,' attitude," Jane said. "He says he has never heard of Constable Crawford, Malcolm Wright or been to the Town of Garland."

This certainly is bad news, I concluded. "There was no hesitation or response when you mentioned those names?"

"None. I could've randomly picked two names and a village out of a phonebook and got nothing. He is as baffled as we are."

"This saves me a trip to Sellcan today," I responded. I took the opportunity to fill Jane in on my pub meeting with Malcolm and roadside get-together with Crawford.

"You said Malcolm found a ring along with the diary? Did he show it to you?"

Malcolm's mention of a ring was a detail I knew must be factual, otherwise why bring it up? Had our meeting gone better, I'm sure I would have asked to see it. If I could determine it was Lucy's, it would confirm Joey Wad knew her. "I didn't see it, no. Was any of Lucy's jewelry missing after her death?"

"I could ask Eric," Jane said, "although I seriously doubt he'd know. He was arrested shortly after returning home and was never allowed upstairs."

"Then scratch that idea. Ultimately, I'll have to make up with Malcolm to see that ring."

"Unless he threw it away when he destroyed the diary."

"Or pawned it," I suggested. "Once George was dead, I think he became frustrated or scared and figured his payoff days were over, therefore the diary was worthless. The ring, on the other hand, so to speak, might have been worth a few bucks. I got the impression that for all his Mr. Big Stuff swagger, a little money could still help out."

"Maybe Lucy's mother would know about a missing ring. Have you talked to Debra lately?" Jane asked.

"Not recently," I answered. "Enclosed with my cheque she wrote a short note. Basically, Eric and her are singing from the same 'call when you have something' hymnal."

"I think that time has arrived."

"Me too."

As we were saying our goodbyes, Jane received a call from Sellcan. "I'll say you cancelled," she joked.

With my morning free, I called Debra to bring her up to speed.

After a few basic salutations, she anxiously asked, "What is this about a diary? Is it Lucy's? Did you find it yet?"

News certainly gets around fast with this bunch, I thought to my dismay. "Who told you about that?"

"Eric. His new, well, old lawyer Jane Calloway told him what George Mulhall was doing before he died."

"I wasn't aware Lucy had a diary or that it was missing," I said. "When exactly did you become aware it was gone?" Having received a boxful of reports, news clippings and handwritten notes from Debra early on, I was taken aback by this omission. What other small details was I not privy to know?

"Shortly after the funeral, I guess," Debra answered hesitantly. "Eric was in jail, Lucy was gone and I stayed at their place arranging for professionals to come clean up the blood. I used the house as a kind of war room, coordinating phone calls and meetings with Eric and his lawyers. It was during the downtime that I attempted to straighten up Lucy's personal items, like her clothes, her bureau, that kind of thing. I was really just trying to keep my mind and hands active, but after a few days I couldn't pretend anymore and returned to my apartment, only going back there to pick up the mail."

"And the diary?"

"Oh yes, sorry. You see, since I bought her one for her thirteenth birthday, Lucy always had a diary," Debra stated. "When I was tidying up, I found a stack of them hidden in a cedar chest. Maybe not hidden, but under some blankets," she corrected herself. "Either way, I doubt Eric would look in there, so they were safe."

"I'm guessing the most recent diary was nowhere to be found?"

"I looked everywhere, in every nook and cranny. I even asked Eric and he said he knew she wrote a journal, but never knew where she kept it and didn't really care about it."

"I doubt that," I said with some certainty, "especially when he was cheating on her. To know her inner thoughts and any suspicions of him she had would be a goldmine. If it were me, I'd also be looking for any confirmation that she was having an affair."

"But she wasn't," Debra cut me off. "There has never been a shred of proof Lucy was fooling around, aside from my own intuition, which thankfully turned out to be wrong."

I saw that one coming.

"Do the names Joseph Waddell or Joey Wad mean anything to you, Debra?"

There was a pause before she replied, "No, I've never heard either of those names. Should I have?" she asked, a worried tone creeping into her voice.

"I have reason to believe this man was seeing Lucy romantically in the weeks leading up to her death."

"Where is he now?"

"He was from a village called Garland and unfortunately, he's dead also. He was beaten to death at a rest stop outside of Dannenberg, two days after Lucy was killed."

"I don't know . . . how did . . . could he be . . . are you sure?"

I could hear Debra choking back tears and felt terrible that I'd passed along this news over the phone. "The only thing I'm sure about is that it was his diary or notebook George Mulhall obtained, not Lucy's."

"*His* diary? If George had it, why can't you read it?" There was a twinge of accusation in the question.

"Like Lucy's, it's gone," I said sharply, not appreciating the insinuation that I wasn't doing my job. "Right now I believe if we find either diary, Eric might very well be set free but that doesn't look as if it's going to happen."

"Are you giving up? Will you at the very least tell the police about this Waddell person before you quit on me, so maybe they can look into his past?"

"Police don't investigate dead suspects. It's a waste of their time," I replied. "That's the difference between us: I will. As for giving up, I'll conclude my investigation when I'm satisfied I've done everything in my power to solve it. That time isn't now, unless as the client, you want me to stop. I'll type up my findings and you can add it to your pile of other reports to collect dust."

"I want you to keep looking," came Debra's response, after an extended silence while she weighed her options. "I need to know who killed my daughter and why. It's not right for a parent to have to bury their only child, any child." Debra began to sob. "I really do appreciate everything you're doing, Steve. Please believe me. I have to go now."

She hung up, leaving me staring at my phone.

I'm not in the habit of getting into arguments with women, as I'm usually the one who feels the worst afterwards. This was no exception.

I plopped myself down in my recliner and switched on the television to distract my thoughts. When a commercial came on for a jewelry store, I fell deeper into depression for not asking Debra about Lucy's ring collection. What was it with missing diaries that made me forget to ask about this mystery ring? Since both Malcolm and Debra were mad at me, I'd have to wait a bit to approach them, which seemed like a giant waste of time.

I turned off the television, fully reclined in my chair and closed my eyes to contemplate life as I knew it. I began to use a visualization technique my therapist had taught me, hoping I could get rid of some of the clutter between my ears. To start, I pictured myself holding a rake in the front yard of my childhood home, surrounded by fallen maple leaves. Each leaf represented a fact or clue in my investigation. With each swing of the rake, I moved these onto a curbside pile that I'd burn later (which was allowed when I was a kid). Soon the grass was once again visible and the job was almost done, except for a few stray leaves scattered about the lawn. These symbolized what I felt were the last loose ends of the case: Did I feel this Joey Wad stranger had killed Lucy? Yes. Did I think Eric had hired Joey to kill Lucy? No. Did I believe there was a connection between Joey's special hidden ring and Lucy's death? Yes.

In my mind's eye I saw myself asking the right questions of the right people and finding the answers to all of these questions. This would result in a solved case and a spotless front yard.

I can do this. This is not over. I will find Lucy's killer, I cheered myself on.

Feeling refreshed, I was about to open my eyes when the rumbling of a transport outside smacked my imagination awake one last time. I was still in the yard with no leaves in sight, but the passing truck sounded like a crack of thunder, which caused me to look up at the imaginary sky, through the bare branches of the maple tree.

Almost bare branches.

High above me one solitary leaf clung for dear life. As the thunder continued to roar, the wind whipped up, scattering my neat pile of leaves across the street, sidewalk, lawn and toes of my cool Adidas sneakers. "No, no, no!" I began to scream. "I was finished. This case was solved!"

The anger in my words carried them upwards until they struck the last leaf with full force, snapping it free and forcing it to float

downward. When it was within reach, I grasped for it, wanting to crush it into oblivion for ruining my happy file ending, yet when I opened my hand I knew how wrong I'd been about everything.

Written in tiny letters around the jagged, weather-beaten edges of the leaf were four simple words: Who killed Joey Wad?

I woke with a start, briefly confused where I was or how much time had passed since I'd dozed off. I glanced out the kitchen window and saw that my trees were still in full bloom with all their leaves intact. As my laboured breathing slowly returned to normal, I was aware that regardless if this vision were a meaningless dream, a subconscious reaction to Debra's comments or a full-blown bad visualization trip, one thing was clear: this case wasn't over and in fact, was just beginning.

Again.

TWENTY TWO

I decided to review the previous police and P.I. reports to find the names of Lucy's co-workers. I called Dannenberg Public School and learned all three were still employed and working today. I spoke with one of them, Principal Edwards, and asked if I could stop by during their lunch period. "I'm new to the Lucy McDowell case. I only have a few follow-up questions regarding your police statements six years ago, to update the file's notes."

"I don't know what more we can say about Lucy," Principal Edwards responded. "She's still very much missed around here."

"Yes, it was a real tragedy," I agreed. "I'll see you in a few hours. Thanks for making the time."

I stopped by The Sunsetter to visit The Dawn and Doug Show. Sitting in my usual spot, Dawn delivered bacon and a freshly cooked egg on a breakfast plate. "Are we all out of Sugar Crisp at home?" she asked with a smile.

"That and Honeycomb," I laughed. "I'd grab some Count Chocula too, but I don't know if it's still being made."

"Ask Doug, he eats all that stuff. Froot Loops, Alpha-Bits, you name it."

"That explains a lot," I said. I saw Doug at the kitchen pick-up window. "Hey, Doug, do they still make those monster cereals, you know, Boo Berry, Franken Berry?"

Doug's eyes lit up. "They do. Why, do you need some? I know a guy at the grocery store who 'accidently' drops the boxes and dents the cardboard. When that happens he tells me when they're going to be put on the clearance shelf at 50% off, baby."

Both Dawn and I looked at Doug in that special way when you feel sorry for someone, yet are wildly entertained by their stories. "Good to know," I said. "By the way, how's the girlfriend situation these days?"

The happy child-like expression disappeared from Doug's face. "I can't talk about it yet, Stevie. Maybe in a few days," and he walked back to the grill with his head hung low.

"Touchy subject this morning, Steve-a-reno," Dawn said, sliding into the booth and stealing a strip of bacon. "April dumped him last night."

"She smartened up or did he comment that her mother looked hot in yoga pants?"

"You're close," she replied as I rolled my eyes. "While they were making out on the couch he called her May."

"April, May, what's the big deal? So he got the month mixed up."

"April's sister's name is May."

I almost choked on my toast. "C'mon, who uses a calendar to name their kids? That's insane. I bet the hot yoga pants wearing mother has a normal name."

"Her name is June."

"Stop it! I can't take anymore," I began to convulse with laughter. "You're killing me here."

"Do you feel the same way about my name? I was named Dawn because I was born as the sun was rising."

"Dawn is a fine name," I started, taking a swig of water. "However, if your siblings were named Dusk, Twilight and High Noon, I'd have a problem."

"But you'd still date me, right?" she asked. "A rose by another name, like Shakespeare wrote."

"Maybe. Well, probably. Okay, yes," I confessed. "I do remember dating a stripper named Sunrise or Sunny once, but that was different."

"I bet it was," Dawn said with a smirk. "Now look at you, all domesticated. A kept man."

I reached for her hand across the table. "But a happily kept man."

"I hope that wasn't your idea of a gratuity," she said as she took my nearly empty plate. "Tips like those don't buy many boxes of sugary breakfast goodness these days."

"Don't worry," I said, as I followed her to the cash register, "I'll continue to take good care of you." Through the pick-up window, Doug was moping over an omelette. "Doug, forget those fickle month women. Maybe start looking for a weekly catch, like a Wednesday from the Addams Family."

"Do you really think so?" he asked hopefully.

"I do," I assured him. I gave Dawn a $10 bill and said, "Keep the change."

"Ooh, ahh, big tipper time here at The Sunsetter," she smiled as she pocketed the difference. "So you're off to Dannenberg to coax Lucy's teacher friends into telling you about her affair with Joey Wad? Speaking of stupid names."

"That's the plan. I'm hoping to use my charm to lower their guard."

"And when that fails miserably?"

"I'll beg, like usual."

"Yeah you will." Dawn escorted me to the front door and gave me a tip-toed kiss. "Okay, you go, Hugo."

"I promise to be back for dinner tonight."

"You'd better be," Dawn said, holding the door open, "because we're eating whatever take-out food you bring home."

"Gotcha."

***

Stepping into Lucy's old stomping grounds, my first impression was how small everything was, from the dollhouse-sized desks and chairs to the row of jackets and tiny shoes that lined the hallway walls. I felt like a modern-day giant and wondered how long it took new teachers to lose that sensation.

"Hello, I'm here to speak with Principal Edwards," I told the office receptionist.

"Mr. Cassidy?" a female voice from behind me asked. As I turned, she added, "He's mine, Alicia," speaking to the receptionist, who carried on typing as if I'd never spoken to her. "Mr. Cassidy, I'm Principal Karen Edwards. It's very nice to meet you." I shook her hand. "Did you have any trouble finding us? This subdivision is a bit of a labyrinth with its cul-de-sacs and crescents."

"No trouble at all."

"Glad to hear that. I've set aside a room for privacy up the hall. Wendy and Zoe are waiting for us."

Principal Edwards was in her early fifties and projected an 'in charge' aura by the way she spoke, walked and generally carried herself. One quality she appeared to be lacking was the ability to frighten her young charges in the same way the principals did when I was growing up (and causing trouble).

Entering Room 222, I was introduced to Wendy Nilsson and Zoe Jefferson, who were both fresh-faced and, most importantly, carbon copies of Lucy McDowell. I immediately knew I needed to speak to them outside the presence of their principal. With that in mind, I quickly told everyone the purpose of my visit and started my questioning with Principal Edwards. "Were you a teacher or in charge of the school when Lucy worked here?"

"I transferred in from another school in the district," came the answer. "The school opened that September, so we were all kind of new at the time," Principal Edwards said, smiling at the others, who returned the gesture.

"Did you have a lot of contact with Lucy on a daily basis? Were you friends or trying to first form a good working relationship?"

Principal Edwards shifted slightly on her heels. "Probably

the latter. This was my first school and I was attempting to keep a high level of professionalism to gain the staff's respect." She again glanced over at her colleagues. "I think I've loosened up a bit since then."

"Definitely," Wendy said, as Zoe agreed with a nod of her head and a smile.

"That's what I thought your relationship had been, Principal Edwards. You see, I'm looking for a little more personal information, which I believe you two could help me with today," I said indicating the younger teachers. "I wouldn't want to keep you any longer from your duties."

Principal Edwards was smart enough to get my coded message and gracefully bowed out of the conversation. "If you need anything else, Mr. Cassidy, I will do what I can." She again offered her hand, which I took.

"I appreciate that very much," I replied. When their boss had closed the door, I focused my attention on the remaining women. "I'm well aware that in the past you both co-operated with the police, as well as two other private investigators. I've read your statements. Unfortunately, I know there's something missing, which is why I'm here today."

"Missing? I truthfully answered any question asked of me," Zoe protested.

"Me too," Wendy echoed.

"I'm not accusing either of you of lying, unless you believe omission is a form of lying," I countered. "In your statements you clearly said that Lucy had confided that her marriage was going through a rough patch and she thought her husband was seeing another woman, although details were sketchy."

"That's the truth," Wendy spoke up. "How can that be considered an omission of any kind?"

"As it turned out, Lucy was right. Eric was having an affair with his secretary," Zoe added.

I could tell I wasn't going to get anywhere unless I confronted them with the one piece of information nobody had uncovered until I arrived on the scene. "Protecting Lucy's dignity and reputation is very admirable. However, I'm trying to find her real killer—"

"Eric murdered her," Wendy interrupted, "and was convicted."

"Like I said, I'm looking for the *real* killer," I continued undaunted. "I believe he started seeing Lucy a few weeks before her death and went by the name Joseph or Joey. Early to mid-twenties and sporting a moustache that made him look older. Now for the love of all things Lucy, could you please help me with a little more information on him?" Wendy and Zoe appeared stricken with fear. "You tell me, I tell no one where I got the information. I'm a vault. Plus, Lucy's lover is dead. So how 'bout it, ladies?"

The only comparison I can make regarding what happened next is that of children being caught red-handed and then being asked to explain themselves. Both teachers spoke at once, a rapid torrent of apologies for not telling anyone what they knew, therefore, keeping their shared knowledge a secret.

"I told Lucy it was a bad idea," Zoe began.

"She didn't even really know the guy," Wendy continued. "He just popped up out of nowhere and suddenly they were meeting for a coffee, then dinner."

"She was angry with Eric's affair and figured this was payback, right, Wendy?"

"Yeah, she was tired of being sad and she said Joey made her happy."

"Did you ever speak with this Joey individual?" I asked, happy to have confirmed a fact no one else had been able to do. I recalled Julie's insistence that Eric had found a note with the words, 'Recess – 4:01 p.m.' on it and then there was the 911 call with the 'school's out' reference. "Did they meet here, maybe in the parking lot?"

"I saw him a few times on the street, standing by his red car waiting for Lucy to meet him after class. We're usually out of here around 4:00," Zoe replied.

"But neither of us talked to him," Wendy added.

"Red car? Do you remember if it was a two door or four door?"

"Two door, a little sporty thing. I don't know the make or model, sorry," Zoe said.

"What about his background? Did Lucy know what he did for a living or any other personal information?"

"He said he was a social worker trying to help troubled teens," Wendy said.

"That was appealing to Lucy. Someone who was selfless, unlike her husband," Zoe interjected. "Plus, they had both lost a parent when they were young."

This was the first time I'd thought about Debra being the only parent on record in regards to Lucy. "Lost, as in dead or divorced?"

"I don't think Lucy knew who her father was and Joey's mother died when he was really young or so he claimed."

At least Joey's story was consistent with what Malcolm had told me. "What about notes or love letters? Did Lucy receive any from Joey?" I asked.

"She said he'd leave little notes under her car's windshield and, of course, there was her diary," Wendy replied. "I'm sure it will contain some details that'll help you."

"I think that diary went missing after her death, unless she was hiding it here at school," I said.

Wendy and Zoe looked at each other and for a fleeting moment I saw them pulling the diary out of one of their desk drawers. 'Fleeting' was the operative word here.

"She never brought it to school, as far as I know," Zoe replied. "It's missing?"

"Who would take it?" Wendy's voice drained away, realizing Lucy's killer may very well have walked out of the house with it.

"I just know she wrote a diary and that she hid it from Eric, for obvious reasons."

"Do you really think Joey is the murderer or is he like Kennedy's mystery sniper on the grassy knoll?" Zoe asked in a heartfelt tone. "I think he was into Lucy and she liked him too."

"I agree," Wendy said, equally sincere. "I'm not saying they were in love or anything, but Lucy was in a much better place when he was around. I can't imagine he'd turn on her so violently in such a short time. Why would he do that?"

The same question was asked about Eric McDowell and his jury answered it with a resounding 'Because he could' verdict, which I no longer believed. I didn't like the path my mind was leading me down. If Lucy's death wasn't part of a jealous lover's spat, resulting in a bizarre tragic accident, it left only one possibility. "He was targeting her," I answered, to Wendy and Zoe's shock. "He deliberately got close to gain Lucy's confidence and then, as you mentioned, Wendy, turned on her for reasons only he knew."

"He was stalking her?" Zoe asked slowly.

"Out in the open?" Wendy followed up.

"I used to be a police officer and this type of crime, where the victim knows her assailant, is more common than is reported in the news. Most times the end result is an assault, not a death, and a protection order is issued by the court. Unfortunately, there are details in this case that indicate that Lucy wasn't aware her boy toy was a psychopath, playing her all along." Tears began to well up in their eyes and I knew I should make a rapid exit. "Lucy had no choice but to be the innocent victim," I said in a comforting voice. "She was in the wrong place with the wrong person at the wrong time of her life, that's all."

"Do you think Eric put Joey up to this?" Zoe asked through gulps of air as she started to hyperventilate, Wendy putting an arm around her for support.

"If what you told me today is true, I don't believe so," I

answered honestly, not feeling the need to share the details of the existence of Casanova Joey's hidden diary. "As callous as this might sound, this isn't about Lucy's death anymore, it's about Joey's two days later. Solving that case might just help me set an innocent man free."

TWENTY THREE

Outside the school, I sat in my van attempting to rest my weary head and its mile-a-minute-whirling-dervish brain, to no avail. How had a simple romantic weekend away with Dawn led me here? With Joey Wad, I was now working on my third unsolved murder of this case. *No wonder Debra's retainer for my services had been so large*, I thought. I toyed with the idea Joey and Lucy were somehow related; him without a mother, her without a father, both in their twenties, but didn't get very far, remembering they might have slept together. I know that could have happened with Lucy in the dark about her new friend's past, which isn't uncommon at the start of a relationship. If Joey had been stalking her, he'd have a clear advantage of knowing things about Lucy, like where she shopped, her favourite restaurants, her work schedule and maybe even when Eric would be home.

I needed to dig deeper into his past.

"Hey, Melinda, how is *The Dannenberg Echo* treating you today?"

"Well, well, well, if it isn't my favourite troublemaker, Mr. Cassidy," she replied with a chuckle. "Did you know that 'Spanky' Manning is no longer with the paper? Having been mercilessly teased by his co-workers, he jumped to the competition, although *The Sun Times* isn't much competition when it comes right down to it."

"Was it something I said?" I asked innocently. "It's not like I gave him that nickname."

"You may not have given it to him but it's sure immortalized with him now."

"I do what I can," I replied. "Serves him right for calling me a private dick."

"I hadn't heard that part of the story."

"Feel free to spread it around the newsroom."

"Oh, I will."

"Now, the reason I'm calling is to see if you have any information on a person who died six years ago, half way between Edenville and Dannenberg."

"Was this one eating a hamburger or walking and chewing gum at the time of his demise? I hope public transportation wasn't involved. I hate to think about all those bus passengers who saw poor George hit that day. How is that investigation going? Did you find out what really happened?"

As much as I knew Melinda was asking as a concerned friend, she worked in the newspaper business and couldn't be fully trusted with sensitive information at this time.

"Not yet," I lied. "The gentleman whose background I'm looking into may have some connection to George's accident and the McDowell murder, although it's doubtful."

"I don't believe that for a moment, but I'll play along," Melinda said. "As long as I get a mention in your memoirs, I'll be happy. So what's the name?"

"Joseph Bartholomew Waddell, also known as Joey Wad."

Melinda typed the names on her keyboard. "Three names usually means serial killer territory, although in this case, Joey Wad sounds like he's a gangster for some lame crime syndicate."

"Or lead singer in a creepy boy band," I added, waiting for the search results.

"And we have a winner," Melinda said with an upturn in the pitch of her voice. "It looks like he made one enemy too many."

"At the highway rest stop?"

"Now the 'resting' stop, you bet."

"I read one account of a tourist finding him in a washroom stall, but no car was found in the parking lot," I said. "Do you have any personal information in the article or an obituary? I don't think he was all that popular in life, let alone death."

"Let me look," Melinda responded, her fingers again working fast. "He had a short obit, which might help."

"He was buried around here? What was the funeral home?"

"Died suddenly . . . Kane Funeral Home in Edenville . . . internment in Sunrest Revival Cemetery, also in Edenville."

"Relatives?"

"None living, apparently. Preceded by his mother Sarah Rymal."

No siblings or close relatives might explain a life of crime and foster homes. "Can you cross-reference his mother for me? I think she passed away when he was very young."

"I knew you were holding out on me," Melinda said, as keys tapped away under her fingertips. "Wow, you weren't kidding. She also died suddenly when he was only two years old."

"Are there any details on how she died?" I asked expectantly.

"And your luck runs out," Melinda replied. "Not entirely, but for the time being. I have a reference number for an article, but those editions haven't been digitized yet. I'd have to track it down in the microfiche section. Unfortunately, I can't do it until tomorrow at the earliest. Would that be okay? I'm swamped researching stuff on our beleaguered mayor and his past troubles."

"Is he the one who used campaign funds to pay for his son's wedding reception?"

"And for the bachelor party hooker, allegedly."

I laughed. "Who knew that kind of thing was illegal? Anyway, that story is more important than one that occurred two decades ago. You have my number. Call if you come up with something juicy. Maybe I'll uncover a few live leads at the funeral home."

"Or more dead ends. I'll get back to you as soon as I can," Melinda promised.

***

The cross county trip to Edenville gave me time to plot my next moves. Finding the connection between Joey and Lucy was paramount and I wondered if Malcolm's floorboard ring was the missing link. I swallowed my pride and made the call, only to get his voicemail. "Hi, Malcolm, Steve Cassidy here. I was hoping you might show me that found ring, that's if you still have it. I'm heading into the city now. Give me a shout. Thanks." Hitting the End button, I thought I sounded pleasant and non-threatening enough to warrant a second chance.

As I'd mentally swung the spotlight onto the role Joey Wad might have played in Lucy's death, the spectre of Constable Crawford and his merry henchmen faded into the darkness. Although I knew they were responsible for George's death, from a legal standpoint everything I'd learned was as flimsy as a sapling during a hurricane. I had to continue to believe that the diary, or diaries, would ultimately tie the whole lot of them together.

"Any new news that's good news?" I asked Walter over the phone.

"The only good news I've received lately is I don't have to paw through the crap of a thief who swallowed two diamond earrings and fled the store. Metro coppers get that dirty job," Walter laughed. "Maybe your pal Crawford will get that assignment."

"Yeah, I wish," I said. "His high ranking connection wouldn't allow that to happen though. Still no name of who pulled those strings?"

"I'm working on it, don't you worry. My two sources are away on a training course and I didn't think it was a rush job."

"It's not. We're good," I stated. "I've got a lead on Joey Wad and his mother, not that I think she's relevant to my case, but you never know. When I'm done maybe I'll swing by and we can grab a bite in the food court."

"Thanks for the warning," Walter said. "I'll pop a few antacids just in case."

"Save some for me," I replied before hanging up.

To my astonishment, the Kane Funeral Home was no rinky-dink operation, with the main building the size of a museum - one of those mammoth, majestic structures from another century, no doubt owned by the area's wealthiest family. To give you a further appreciation of its mass and stature, the imposing McDowell Mansion where Lucy was murdered would make a nice poolside cabana.

Upon entry, I found myself in a huge marble-floored foyer and was met by a fashionably dressed man in his early fifties.

"Welcome to Kane Funeral Home," he greeted me with a winning smile.

"Thank you. It is a good day so far," I replied. "This is an amazing place you have here."

"It certainly is," he replied, as we both took in and appreciated the room's beauty. "We've been here seven years now, moving from our former location in the east end."

"I've been in the east end and I'm guessing it wasn't as upscale as this one," I responded, wondering how a low-life like Joey Wad could've afforded a funeral in this palace.

"It was a very nice building, but not as elegant as these premises to be sure. Regardless of the home's setting, we are still a family-run operation and I'm certain we will be able to assist you today."

Assist me. Smooth.

"That's my hope also. You see, I'm a private investigator looking into the death of a man a few years back and this funeral home was listed in his obituary. I'd like to speak with someone who might help with some blanks I've been unable to fill, in regards to that time."

"That would be Vince Kane," came the quick reply. "I'll inform him you're here. Your name, sir?"

"Steve Cassidy."

As Jeeves walked behind the reception desk, I strolled over to a large framed picture of the house and read the attached plaque. To paraphrase the stiffly-worded decree, sure enough, this used to be the prime residence of the city's founders, a clan named Eden. When the last of the elders passed away, seeing an opportunity for a massive financial windfall, the grandchildren promptly sold their heirlooms lock, stock and barrel to the Kanes, who relocated their funeral business to the property. I gave the Kanes credit for keeping the dignity and sense of history intact. I often wonder what the minister of a closed church thinks as he passes his former house of worship that has been converted into a podiatrist's office. I imagine the conversation going something like, "Lord, that's just not right but it's Your plan, so I'll just have to live with it."

"Mr. Cassidy?" I turned to greet another impeccably attired man in his mid-forties. "I'm Vince Kane. It's a pleasure to meet you," he said as he extended his hand, which I shook.

"Thank you for taking the time, I appreciate it."

"Of course, anything I can do to help. Now I hear you're interested in one of our clients."

"Yes, his name was Joseph Bartholomew Waddell. He passed away six years ago."

A concerned expression came over Vince's face. "To be honest, that was before my time here. I only moved back to Edenville a few years ago. Thank goodness for computer records. Let's go to my office and I'll see what I can find out."

The office appeared to have been assembled by a furniture store's display team to showcase their in-stock workspace products, bookshelves, desks, cabinets and chairs. Don't get me wrong, every item in the spacious room was high quality and impressive-looking, but was also sterile and didn't have that 'lived in' feel. Vince slid easily behind the desk and began entering Joey's full name into his laptop. "This is interesting," he commented when the results came back.

This can't be good, I thought. "Interesting how?"

He turned the screen to show me the client's intake information. "You see here," he began pointing to a box in the upper right corner, "FIC."

Forget It Cassidy?

"Yes, what does it mean?"

"That's an accounting code. FIC stands for Free Internal Charge. I've never seen anything like that before. We usually use it for incidentals, like boxes of tissues or coffee in the waiting area. Items we don't charge for providing."

I could have got into a discussion about hidden fees, but held my tongue. "Are there any relatives listed or someone who signed off on everything?" I asked, quickly scanning the screen for something to catch my eye. Unfortunately, Vince spun the laptop around, believing Show & Tell time was over.

"This is odd," he said as his eyes raced from side to side. "My father signed off on this."

"Would he be in today?" I asked calmly, my head back in spin-cycle mode.

"If he's not on the golf course, he should be."

Vince made a quick phone call, informing the person on the other end of the line of my visit, and we were soon heading to a second-floor office, a former bedroom the size of a small ballroom.

"Dad, this is Steve Cassidy."

Vince's father turned out to be a personable silver and grey-haired fox in his seventies, who exuded class, wealth and power from the moment he stepped around his stately mahogany desk. "Mr. Cassidy, I'm David Kane, at your service." His hands were big with a strong grip. "Please have a seat. Would you like something to drink?"

"No, thank you."

"Was there anything else, Vince?" David asked, addressing his son with a cold, yet amicable look that I'm certain wasn't so warm when they were alone.

"No, sir," Vince said with a slight nod. "It was good meeting you, Mr. Cassidy."

"Same here," I replied as he walked out of the room, gently closing the door. "How many family members do you have working under this enormous roof?"

"At last count nine," he said with a grin, as he settled into his chair. "So what's this all about? Are you trying to solve that poor boy's murder?" He leaned forward. "Off the record, the police did a sad job the first time around. I have several old friends on the force and they just swept this case under the rug for some reason. A disturbed young man with no family is on the same level as a dead prostitute or drug dealer. No one is going to miss them, so why spend valuable detective time on their crime?"

David Kane was exactly the type of man I was looking for in regards to Constable Crawford's boss and benefactor: well-known and liked as a successful businessman, probably involved in local charities and civic groups or boards. A virtual 'untouchable' with a stellar reputation in the community with powerful friends in high places. However, his last two sentences conveyed a genuine distrust for the police. I liked him immediately.

"As a former police officer, I agree with everything you've said, Mr. Kane. It's sad, but true. Poor and troubled victims don't get the respect they deserve. Meanwhile, some blonde-haired, blue-eyed co-ed from a rich family goes missing and every available law enforcement officer is ordered to drop everything and concentrate on finding her."

"Exactly," Kane declared. "I knew Joseph Waddell through a halfway house he helped run out in Garland. A family friend's boy had lost his way and was sent there as a last kick at the can to shape up. For emotional support, I went with this boy's devastated mother to visit him a few times."

"Joseph must've made quite the impression for you to pay for his funeral out of pocket."

The expression on my host's face briefly registered disgust, until he realized I wasn't accusing him of any wrongdoing. "I barely spoke to the man, but when I heard how he died and that he had no family, something inside me wanted to help. Since I started working for my father five decades ago, practically every day I've encountered grieving people whose sole goal is to send their loved one onto the great beyond with class and respect. I saw no reason why Joseph shouldn't have the same chance."

Except that maybe he was a ruthless cold-blooded killer, I thought. There was no way I was going to share this view with Good Deed David, though. "Were there many people in attendance at the funeral?"

Kane leaned back in his chair. "Technically, there was no funeral, only a brief memorial service. I recall a handful of friends attended it, maybe from the halfway house. It wasn't advertised to the public, as we didn't know what type of crowd it might attract, due to the violent nature of the crime. We did issue a short news release the next day, to comfort those who might have felt Joseph had been forgotten and was buried anonymously in one of the city sites."

"I see your point," I said. "The last thing you'd want is the actual killer present at the service. That wouldn't be the respectful send-off you had planned for Joseph." My sarcastic tone may have slipped out during this exchange. All I could think was that this upstanding citizen had done something quite admirable in secret, yet found the need to gain positive press for his funeral home by crowing about it the next day.

"No, it wouldn't," came the curt reply. "Is there anything more I can assist you with, Mr. Cassidy? We're very busy with four funerals and visitations going on today."

"It sounds like everyone's dying to get in here," I said with a friendly smile and in a light joking tone, as I stood to leave. "I bet you've heard all the bad puns, haven't you?"

David came around the desk. "All of them and more," he said cordially, offering his hand to shake. If I'd ruffled his feathers in any way, he gave no sign of it.

"I can find my way back to the front lobby," I said. "Thank you for the information. It gives me a better understanding of Joseph's situation."

"Glad we could be of assistance."

I found the stairs and was preparing to say my goodbyes to Jeeves at the front door, when I passed Vince's open office door. "Vince, thanks for your help."

"Was my dad able to straighten out the FIC code?"

"He did. From the sounds of it, he acted in the same way a lawyer occasionally takes on a legal case pro-bono. A kind of 'pay it forward' initiative." A strained look came over Vince's features. "Does that surprise you?"

"No, of course not," he replied unconvincingly.

"You should ask him about it. Maybe you'll see another side of the old man," I suggested.

"Maybe."

"Okay, I'm out of here. Thanks again."

"You're welcome."

Jeeves wasn't at his post when I exited. As I walked quickly to the van, a light rain began to fall. Pulling out of the parking spot, I saw Vince running toward me under a large black umbrella. I rolled down my window and asked, "Did I forget something?"

"It's hard to forget something you didn't know existed," Vince said, catching his breath.

"I don't follow."

"I found this in storage and thought it might help with your investigation," he replied, taking a small book from inside his jacket and handing it to me. I noted he made sure no one in the area could see the exchange. "It's the guest book from Joseph Waddell's memorial service. Usually it's given to the family afterwards as a keepsake. It only contains a few names. Still, it's better than nothing, right?"

I quickly glanced down at the book and set it on the floor out of view. "I will definitely look at it once I'm back home or away from here, if that's alright."

"That would be fine," came Vince's response. "I have to get back. Don't worry about returning the book either."

"Okay, thanks again," I said. "Vince, why did you come back to the family business? I get the feeling it wasn't by choice."

Vince stopped walking and turned to face me. "I used to work in the computer industry, but lost everything when the dotcom bubble burst. I had no other option than to return to the fold."

"Trust me, I've been there," I said. "Do you really think being a private investigator is my first love? One day we'll both return to our former glory." As I rolled up my window, I gave Vince a quick peace sign wave and yelled through the now heavy downpour, "And if you don't believe me, do an internet search using the keywords 'Steve Cassidy'. I think you'll be quite shocked to learn just how far I've come. I know I am."

.

TWENTY FOUR

I was too nervous to open the guest book and drove to The Galleria to meet with Walter in the security office.

"You're like Indiana Jones finding The Ark of the Covenant," he laughed as I placed the book in front of him. "I hope we don't melt like those Nazis when it's opened up. That might spoil my big date with the owner of the Tea Room Café tonight."

"Nice. Did you ask her out or did you force her to make the first move?"

"I think she likes men in uniform and when I walked in her heart began to flutter something awful."

"That's your story?"

"For the moment."

"And it should be, it's a good one," I said sarcastically. "Now let's see who showed up for Joey Wad's memorial service."

"I never pictured you as the panicky type, Cassidy," Walter replied as he turned to the first page that listed Joey's personal information, followed by the one page of signatures and comments. "Five names, that's all."

I walked to the desk and peered over Walter's shoulder. "The first two don't count. David Kane owns the funeral home and Reverend Bates was probably doing Kane a favour being there."

"Okay, what about Ian Renfro, do you have any psychic impressions about him?" Walter asked of the third signature.

"Nada."

"Bruce Myers?"

257

"Nope."

"Rachel McKellen? 'Say Hi to your Mom for me.' That begs the question, how does she know Joey's mother who died 20 years earlier?"

"Let's find out. Do an internet search on them and maybe something useful will come up," I instructed.

"Your wish is my command," Walter said, entering Ian Renfro's name. "Executive Director of Youth Outreach Services of Greater Edenville."

"That's some title. They probably run the Garland halfway house. His attendance would make sense," I said.

"Died three years ago," Walter groaned after scrolling down Renfro's bio page.

"Strike one. What about Bruce Myers?"

Several keystrokes and mouse clicks later, Walter said, "If this is the same guy, you've just swung at strike two. Convicted of burglary and aggravated assault and sitting in Sellcan with your wrongly convicted buddy Eric McDowell."

"Small world," I said despondently. "His attendance may have been because they were friends."

"Or partners in crime. Maybe there was a double-cross and Bruce was making sure Joey was really dead."

"That's another possibility. I'll call Sellcan later to confirm it's the right guy," I said. "Okay, bottom of the 9th, two outs and Rachel McKellen steps up to the plate."

As Walter entered her name, he said, "A swing and a . . . "

If not a single, then a solid double. No death or crime blotter notices flashed up immediately, although several listings did appear. "I wish we knew her age, to help narrow the search."

"Why don't we add more search variables, like 'Garland', 'Edenville' and 'Dannenberg'?" Walter asked as he punched in the new items. "See, now you only have three to track down," he said pointing to the screen.

"If she's from one of those places."

"I'll print off the full list just in case."

With the list in my hand, I suggested lunch at The Handleman. "Maybe Malcolm is there during the day."

My encore appearance was much less dramatic and we were seated far away from the infamous stripper stage booth. The servers were different, although I did see one familiar face. "I'll be right back," I told Walter as I wandered to the bar.

"What can I get for you?" the barkeep asked.

"Malcolm Wright's head on a stick," I replied with a smile. "Otherwise, the usual is fine, plus a diet something for my friend over there."

The barkeep slowly realized who I was and said, "Jack Daniels, right?"

"Good memory."

"Part of the job," he said. "As for Malcolm, I'm not sure when he'll be back. I can pass along the 'head on a stick' message if you want," he laughed, pushing two glasses across to me.

"No, I want to give him that one in person," I said, taking a short sip from my drink. "Do you know if he has caller I.D. on his phone? I think he's avoiding me."

"He might."

"Can I use the bar phone to find out?" I asked nicely, gesturing to the handset at the end of the counter. "It's a local call and you can tell him I grabbed it when you were in the kitchen." I took out a $20 bill and placed it on the counter. "This is for the drinks and fantastic service."

He eyed the cash a second before pocketing it and handing me the phone. "I'll be in the kitchen. Make it quick."

"Yes, sir."

Believing he was being contacted by a friend, as expected, Malcolm picked up on the second ring and sounded chipper. "Darcy, how's it hanging?"

"Hi, Malcolm, quick question."

"What do you want? I got your message and was thinking of

calling you back."

"Well, you can continue to consider doing that, after you tell me how Bruce Myers knew Joey Wad."

"They were roommates at the house. You're going to have to make an appointment to talk to Myers because—"

"He's in Sellcan for burglary and assault. I know," I cut in. "Okay, thanks for the info and sorry to disturb you. I'll wait for your return call in regards to my earlier message. We should really get together. Oh, did I tell you my client authorized some type of payment to see that ring? Gotta go. Talkatcha soon."

It gave me great satisfaction to hang up on the twerp, knowing he was now in a state of confusion. I grabbed our drinks and went back to the table.

"I ordered you a bacon cheeseburger. I hope you don't mind," Walter stated. "What did the bartender have to say that was so interesting?"

"We were just catching up."

"You don't hand me $20 every time we catch up," Walter said with a laugh.

"I don't like men in uniform, it's that simple," I said as my cell phone began to vibrate. "What a shock, it's Malcolm. By the way, our Bruce Myers was Joey's bunk mate back in the day."

"Impressive work."

I pressed Send and said, "Long time no hear, friend. What's shakin' your tree this afternoon?"

"I don't know who you think you're dealing with, but I don't appreciate your tone," Malcolm snapped at me.

"And you need to respect your elders, Malcolm," I countered. "Why are you so angry anyway? You were the one who terminated our budding friendship. I'm the one trying to rekindle it."

"You started a fire all right."

I waited several seconds, hoping the dead air would calm him down. "Are you done?"

"Not until you tell me about the money for the ring."

"So you have the ring? You didn't melt it down when you burned the diary?" I asked.

"Yeah, I still got it and for the right price it's yours," he offered.

"$100."

"Are you kidding me? That better be your lowball opening offer because I could get double that at the Gold Exchange place downtown."

"Okay, then do that. Sorry we couldn't do business, Malcolm. You have a great day."

"That's it?" he stopped me. "You're not even going to try and bargain with me? I thought you said your client was loaded."

"For the diary my client was hemorrhaging money. The ring, well that's different." This time it was Malcolm who initiated a lengthy pause. "Are you still there, Mr. Wheeler Dealer?"

"I'm here."

"And?" I prodded.

"$250," Malcolm relented.

There was a hesitation in his voice that struck me as odd. It reminded me of someone coming clean about a crime, only to then 'fess up to another previously unknown one. "I admit I killed that woman last night, as well as three other women in 1979 when I was a long-haul trucker."

"Deal," I said slowly. "Where do you want to meet - The Handleman again, since I'm already here?"

"I'll be there in 20 minutes."

"Perfect," I replied. I let a beat pass before adding, "And if you have anything else you'd consider selling, bring it along. I feel like Monty Hall today. See ya." For the second time I got a childish rush hanging up on Malcolm. "Wanna meet Malcolm?" I asked Walter.

"Like I have a choice with our food ordered," he said, taking a swallow of his drink. "What was that nonsense about buying anything else he might have to sell? I didn't get the sense you were talking about stereo speakers. If you want those, there's this

guy in a white van who'll give you a much better deal than old Malcolm. He conducts business on the roof level of The Galleria parking garage. I can hook you up."

"As appealing as that sounds, I have a hunch Malcolm is going to bring me an item more valuable than the ring, the funeral home guest book and The Ark of the Covenant combined."

"What's more valuable or elusive than the Ark?" Walter asked, perplexed by my riddle.

"The key that opens it, Walter."

"Which is what exactly?"

Before I could tell Walter of my suspicions that Malcolm still had the diary, hence, *the key* to solving this case, our waitress arrived with our food. "I don't want to spoil the surprise or get your hopes up. Your Tea Room doll wouldn't appreciate you suffering cardiac arrest before she can close the deal herself."

"Fine, be like that. If this bacon double cheeseburger doesn't kill me, nothing will."

"In just a few minutes all your questions will be answered."

"My wife's divorce lawyer said the same thing," Walter said, "and that didn't hurt at all."

***

"I'm not certain who is playing whom at this point, Malcolm, but I've been waiting for an hour. Time's up. I'm leaving. Call if the urge hits you," I said into my cell phone. "Oh, and if you haven't tried it already, the cheesecake is very good here. Cassidy out!"

We left the pub and headed back to The Galleria.

"I didn't tell you about the young whippersnapper I had to let go this morning," Walter said.

"When you say 'let go' you mean fired, right? Otherwise this conversation has taken a very awkward turn."

"Yes, fired," Walter confirmed.

"What was his offense?" I asked. "Did he complain about your overuse of Old Spice aftershave?"

"I could handle that," Walter said with a smirk. "No, his shift started at 8:30 and I caught him surfing porn sites on the office computer when I arrived at 10:00."

"Those damn kids get into everything these days," I laughed. "Was he in the act of *doing something* or just jumping from site to site?"

"He was printing pictures using my ink!" Walter was smiling from ear to ear as he retold the story. "I walked in and he kind of froze when I said, 'Hey, Jimmy.' Suddenly he clicked the mouse a few times, then shut down the tower and the printer. I was like, 'What the hell?' and made him turn the computer back on."

"He erased the History, right?"

"So he thought," Walter answered with a cocky grin. "He knows I'm technologically obtuse and believed he'd outsmarted me, which in truth, he had. I warned him about the company's policy on computer usage, blah, blah, blah, and sent him out into the mall to patrol."

"You obviously showed him who the boss was by scolding him and sending him out for a walk."

"Would you please let me finish the story?" Walter implored. "So, after he left I searched online for ways to undo what he did. I knew he hadn't permanently deleted the History file from the hard drive, which is a novice criminal's mistake. I was about to call our I.T. guy at corporate, but decided to make a copy of one of the search results first. When the page didn't start to print, I figured the kid had screwed up the whole system, until I noticed the printer's power was off. And wouldn't you know it, when I powered it back up it began to print a lovely picture of two well-endowed women who were more than just office co-workers."

"Busted," I proclaimed. "You're smarter than you look, Old Timer."

"I called I.T. for an explanation and the tech said that the machine's internal memory first stores any page or image sent to it and then prints it off. Jimmy stopped the process, so as soon as I brought it back online, all systems were a go. One nudie shot later and I had one less guard to deal with on a daily basis."

"Technology is a wondrous thing, isn't it?" I stated.

"It is, but computers, printers, cell phones and the rest of it are still programmed by humans, meaning any problem usually has a solution."

"I wish cold case files could be solved with a call to tech support." I checked my watch. "I'm going to get going."

"What about your three Rachel McKellens? You can call them from here, if you like. I have to make a round of the stores and let the still employed guard go for lunch."

I picked the list out of my jacket pocket. "Might as well, thanks."

After showing me how the phone system worked for outgoing calls, Walter grabbed a clipboard and was out the door.

"Hello, is this Rachel McKellen?" I asked an elderly woman.

"I am."

"I'm hoping you can help me. I'm looking for a woman with the same name who knew a Joseph Bartholomew Waddell and attended a memorial service for him six years ago. Would that have been you?"

"I'm sorry, that name doesn't sound familiar. I live in a retirement home and sadly attend many memorial services, just not that one."

One down!

"Who wants to know?" a gruff man asked during my second attempt.

"I'm a private investigator working for a law firm that's trying to locate a woman in regards to an inheritance sum she might be eligible to receive."

"How much?"

Money talks.

"A sizeable amount. Is Rachel home now?" In the background, I heard whispering and then footsteps.

"This is Rachel McKellen," a soft, bird-like voice floated down the phone line.

"Hi, Rachel. To verify you're the person I'm seeking, could you tell me if you knew anyone by the name of Joseph Bartholomew Waddell?" I asked.

There was a pregnant pause that gave me hope until Rachel replied, "Yes, I believe that was the name of my father's long lost brother. Uncle Joe, we used to call him."

Nice try, sista.

I wasn't optimistic that area girl #3 from Edenville would be any different from the others or the other 19 women on my expanded list.

"Yes, this is Rachel McKellen. How can I help you?"

A promising beginning, I thought.

There was a maturity to the voice that caught my attention. Not too old, not too young. "My name is Steve Cassidy and I'm trying to locate a woman from this region who might have known a man by the name of Joseph Bartholomew Waddell. Later in life, he also went by Joey or the nickname Joey Wad. Do any of these names mean anything to you?"

"What is this concerning?"

I was thankful she hadn't dismissed my question entirely. "I'm a private investigator looking into the final days of Mr. Waddell's life. He passed away six years ago."

"And how do I . . . I mean, how does the Rachel McKellen you're trying to find fit into your investigation? Is she in trouble?"

The Freudian 'I/Rachel' slip and the slight stuttering of words confirmed I'd located my mystery memorial attendee.

"Rachel," I began very carefully, "how did you know Joey's mother, Sarah Rymal? Was she a friend of yours?"

"Why are you opening up old wounds?" Rachel asked between a fit of sobs. "Sarah and Joey only had each other in life and now that they're reunited in death, can't we just leave them in peace? Nothing we say or do is ever going to bring them back. Nothing!"

Surprisingly, Rachel didn't hang up, as I'd expected she would. I could hear her continue to cry softly and imagined her slumped against the wall or holding onto the back of a chair for support. "I know nothing about Sarah's death, except that Joey was very young at the time."

"H-h-he was two when it happened," Rachel stammered.

I cursed the idiotic Dannenberg mayor for taking up so much of Melinda's time at the paper. "It sounds to me as if her death was sudden. Was she involved in an accident of some kind?"

"After a house party in Edenville, they were taking a shortcut down a gravel road, trying to get back to their college dorms before curfew."

"Were you in the car?"

"No, my boyfriend drove us separately, but we both tried to stop the three of them from driving back. Everyone was wasted and there was plenty of room for all of us to stay overnight."

"Would Sarah and her friends have been expelled for not returning that night?" I asked, recalling many such nights when I was in the throes of alcohol and drug addiction. Getting home to my own bed was always my first priority, regardless of the irresponsible circumstances that task would entail.

"I doubt it. We were an elite campus clique that got away with anything this side of murder. Until that night. Everything changed after the accident," she said, sounding out of breath.

"Did the car roll into a ditch or a pond?"

"She was killed due to the recklessness of the driver who thought he could sit on the top of the convertible's seat like a monkey and steer with his feet. *That* is what and who killed Sarah." Rachel broke down and was unable to speak for several moments. It was as if I was telling her this bad news for the first time and she was going into shock. Between heaving sobs, she began to mumble, "She had an innocent little boy waiting. He was so innocent. So, so innocent. They killed him when they killed her."

I let her babble for some time, waiting for an appropriate space to fill. "Rachel, I'm terribly sorry for having you relive this tragic event. That wasn't my intention with this call. I saw your name in the funeral home's guest book and hoped you might give me some background information on Joey. It's obvious you cared for his mother and kept in touch with him over the years."

"Again, how does anything I say today help either one of them, Mr. Cassidy? Both died horrible deaths and have found peace together after all those years apart," Rachel said.

When I was an interrogator the most important lesson I learned was when your suspect became defiant, the best way to get results was to steamroll your questions through their anger. The same technique also worked well on civilians. "Did Joey not stay with family after the accident?"

"Sarah had no family. WE were her family!" Rachel cried out. "Her loser husband skipped town and the rest of us were immature college students. No one was prepared to take on the responsibilities of raising a child."

"So he was put in foster care." I uttered this as a statement of fact, not as a response. "He never got out of foster care, did he?"

"No," came the depressing reply. "The system just took and took from him, year after year. He was in trouble with the law from the age of nine and never looked back. Still, no matter where he was living, I'd see him every few weeks. After awhile though, he pushed me away like everyone else who was trying to help."

"Were you in contact with him at the end of his life, when he was working as a mentor at the halfway house in Garland?"

"He called me one night out of the blue saying he had a plan to get his life back on track. I told him that was wonderful news and wanted to hear more about it," Rachel said, a glimmer of hope returning to her voice.

"Did you find out where this epiphany had come from?"

"He said from a book a counselor had left behind. The guiding message was 'rectifying your past to move into the future.' When I asked how he planned to do that, he yelled at me, 'I'm going to make my mother proud. It's time someone paid for her death.' I was stunned. When I went to see him the next day to talk about it, he slipped out the back door and didn't return. I left an hour later."

As fascinating as all of this new information was, I was still blind to how Joey's revenge plan had ensnared Lucy McDowell.

"What about the others in the car that night? Did they survive the crash?" I asked, trying to remain focused on the time period that Joey had set his psycho mind to avenge.

Rachel steadied her emotions and now spoke like a woman who could grieve no more. "They survived. My mother said it was a bona fide miracle, but everyone else knew the truth. They were so far gone their bodies and minds didn't have time to react or to tense. They were like rag dolls thrown into a cornfield. A few cuts, bumps and bruises."

"But not Sarah?"

"Not Sarah. Somehow, by fate or the grace of God, she found the one stand-alone tree on the side of the road. The next tree was more than a mile away." Rachel paused and then said, "While I didn't embrace my mother's miracle idea, my father said something at the time I've never forgotten."

"And what was that?" I asked.

"At dinner, he said, 'Life is a game of inches,' and shovelled another spoonful of mashed potatoes into his mouth, never to speak of the accident again."

"Was the driver charged with anything? Reckless driving? Driving under the influence? Speeding?"

"I guess you didn't hear me earlier," Rachel said, her tone lowering an octave. "We were the popular kids, the cream of the crop, the chosen ones with our upper crust pedigree. To charge anyone would be seen as a failure of our parents. That just wouldn't do."

"No charges, no fines, no penalties."

"And no closure for the two year old boy who lost his mother, then lost his way for the next 20 years," Rachel said with an air of resignation.

A troubled man-child goes on a killing spree. That was hardly news these days, no matter what his twisted reasons.

Killers kill, it was as simple as that.

End of story.

End of investigation.

Let's move on.

Why Lucy?

Why George?

Why Joey?

"I'm grateful for your help," I said in my most sincere and consoling tone. "I'm sorry for opening up old emotional wounds."

"Apology accepted, although my crying wasn't entirely your fault," Rachel replied. "It wasn't only Joey's passing I was thinking about during our conversation. I was also reliving another heartbreaking funeral I attended a few days before his memorial service."

"Oh?"

"It was for the daughter of one of my college friends I've kept in touch with on and off over the years. She was one of the survivors of the crash that took Sarah's life. She lives in Dannenberg now."

"Really?" There are very few times in my life when I have been rendered speechless. This was one of those times. My mind was too busy processing a million pieces of information I'd collected over the past few weeks to speak proper multi-word sentences. "Her name?"

"Debra Stanfield."

"And the driver?"

Why (or how) I even asked this question is beyond

comprehension, as I knew the answer well before Rachel stated it for the record.

"Rodney Dutton. He went into law enforcement. You don't know him, do you?"

TWENTY FIVE

"Yo, Cassidy, buck up," Walter said re-entering the office, a coffee cup and muffin in hand. "You have that same shell-shocked stare first time fathers do after leaving the delivery room. A 'what just happened in there?' look. You okay?"

I had no inkling how long I'd zoned out after hastily concluding my conversation with Rachel. I remember saying I'd keep in touch, placing the phone in its stand and being oddly fascinated by the printer. Maybe I was subconsciously willing it to start spitting out pictures of naked women to divert my thoughts from what I'd been told about Debra and Rodney.

Hey look, a distraction!

I clearly recalled Debra telling us that she and Rodney had gone to school together and were friends up until Lucy's death. I never imagined they shared so much emotional history prior to that night. The death of their friend under such bizarre circumstances would've surely brought them closer together.

Had they been college, maybe even high school, sweethearts?

"While you were out mall walking and buying that bran muffin, this case blew up in my face," I grimly told Walter.

"That sounds painful," he remarked, collapsing into the spare office chair. "Do tell."

I updated him as best I could. He nodded and asked basic follow-up questions, as if he were interviewing an accident victim. I was mentally drained by the end of my tale. "What do you think?"

"Well, you've always been puzzled by both Rodney and Debra's reaction to re-opening the investigation," Walter began, peeling away the muffin wrapper. "Sometime during the past two and a half decades, their friendship obviously turned adversarial."

"I thought that was due to Lucy's death, but maybe it was Sarah's on that country road," I said.

"Are you going to get them together and talk about all of this, or take them aside separately to gauge their individual expressions? For what it's worth, if it were my call I'd speak to each of them alone first."

"I'll have to figure that out," I said. "I was actually leaning in the opposite direction, getting them in a room and seeing how they react. This news should be devastating for both of them, to learn that their youthful misadventure caused Lucy's death all these years later." I stood and offered Walter his chair. Reaching for the phone number list on the desk, I was drawn to the printer again, which Walter noticed.

"If you really want to see that picture, it's in the filing cabinet as evidence."

"Thanks, but no thanks," I replied weakly. "There's an idea rolling around in my head that has something to do with the printer. Unfortunately, it's lost in all the confusion this new case angle has taken."

"Don't worry, it'll come to you," Walter reassured me. "It always does."

"I'm going to give Malcolm one last shout out and then go home. My girlfriend is great with these types of puzzles. I'm sure the new pieces will intrigue her."

"My wife hated me bringing work home. She never wanted to discuss any case, no matter how trivial. It was very odd," Walter reflected. "Your girl on the other hand, sounds like a peach. I'd keep a hold of her, if I were you."

"I'll tell her that. I'm certain she'll agree with your assessment," I said with a laugh as I shook Walter's hand. "Now if I can only get out of the city without Crawford pulling me over."

***

I left another friendly message for Malcolm, saying all was forgiven and that I was still interested in buying the ring. "Don't be a stranger or stranger than you already are. I mean it, call me."

The Galleria was busy, mostly with students milling around the food court and clothing stores. I watched one group of teens talking by the Main Street exit and wondered if I had been that short during my pre-high school days. Waiting for the parking garage elevator, I looked at several wall advertisements for upcoming movies, sales events and one recruitment poster featuring a diverse group of energetic looking models wearing police uniforms. *Have you thought about a career in Law Enforcement?* the tagline read, which sparked a memory from my conversation with Rachel.

Rodney Dutton. He went into law enforcement.

I sprinted back to the security office and startled Walter with my entrance. "I've got it."

"Is there a pill you can take or are we talking about two different things?"

"Different things," I said, pulling out my notebook. "I think I know who Constable Crawford's mentor might be."

"Do I get three guesses or a clue?" Walter asked bemused.

"I think it's Rodney Dutton," I exclaimed. "Is that a big enough clue for you?"

Walter remained silent as he reviewed what we knew about the two men. "It's a fine thought, I grant you that. Highly decorated detective Dutton helps his nephew, maybe even his grandson, get on the Edenville Police."

"And a few years later, he asks Crawford to return the favour by setting him up with Carl and Tom to rough up George," I said, finishing Walter's sentence.

"I could get my sources on the phone right now and pull them out of class," Walter said. "I'll say it's a family emergency."

I held open the page on which I'd written down information from Travis Crawford's police personnel record that Walter had obtained. "I have a better idea, although it still involves family." Walter let me sit in his desk chair as I did a telephone search on the computer. "Bingo," I said, memorizing the needed number. Although most police officers have unlisted numbers, their civilian parents usually don't.

"Hello, Crawford residence," a woman answered.

"Good day. Is this Mena Crawford, Constable Travis Crawford's mother?" I asked.

"It is," came the suspicious reply.

"Ma'am, I'm with the Edenville Chamber of Commerce and we're planning an event to salute our fine men and women in uniform. This will include fire fighters, first responders, paramedics and of course, the police department."

"Well that sounds like a great idea," Mrs. Crawford said. "What does this have to do with Travis though?"

"That's the reason for my call today. As part of the program we'll be singling out one member from each branch and Travis has been chosen to receive this honour for his outstanding record on fighting crime." I heard a quick intake of air. "How does that make you feel as his mother?"

"I don't know what to say," she gushed with pride. "I can't wait to tell him the good news."

"Unfortunately, you can't tell him just yet."

"But why not?"

"The Chamber wants this award to come as a complete surprise to each person," I said. "However, we'd like to have a few relatives attend this function. Think of it as a surprise party for each deserving recipient."

"If they knew, it wouldn't be a surprise. I understand."

"Great. Now I'm calling you because each family will be allowed six special guests. You know, people who mean a lot to the individual we'll be honouring," I continued, as Walter watched me with a huge smile on his face. "A co-worker here mentioned that Travis has an uncle or grandfather in law enforcement whom he looks up to very much. I wouldn't want that person to be left off the list." There was a slight gap of dead air in which I thought I may have overplayed my hand.

"Are you talking about Rodney Dutton, Travis' godfather? He retired from the Dannenberg Police homicide department a few years ago."

"Rodney Dutton, yes, I believe that was the gentleman," I said, giving Walter the thumbs up.

"When will this be held?" Mrs. Crawford asked. "I go to Florida for the winter months, but wouldn't miss this for the world."

"I don't have a firm date yet, possibly at our Christmas meeting, although I'm thinking it'll be put off until next Spring. So there'll be no need to change your travel plans, Mrs. Crawford."

"That's wonderful," she replied. "Is it okay if I tell Rodney and other members of the family?"

"As nothing has been finalized, I think it's best not to say a word to anyone for the moment. I know how hard that's going to be for such a proud mother but it really is important to keep this our little secret. It should only be for another few weeks until I have a firm date, I promise."

"I guess I can hold out for another few weeks," she said. "Thank you for calling to tell me about this, Mr. . . . . "

"Stevens," I replied, "Cassidy Stevens."

"Well, Mr. Stevens, I hope you have a great day."

"After speaking with you, it just got a whole lot better."

I placed the phone on the desk and Walter began to clap. "The award for Best Phone Manipulator goes to Cassidy Stevens!"

"The one and only," I replied, standing up, feeling as if a great weight had been lifted from my shoulders.

"Now what?"

"I need a nap."

"Naps are good," Walter concurred. "When you wake up and

are ready to brainstorm how to take our group of evil geniuses down, give me a call."

"I'll do that."

Both of us were riding an emotional high and if we'd been legitimate partners in the detective unit, I'm certain we'd have given each other a manly congratulatory hug, like the players who win the Stanley Cup or World Series. Working as an unofficial team, it appeared we'd solved the mystery of who had killed Lucy McDowell.

There was a long way to go before Eric was breathing fresh air again, but it was a start.

***

I called Dawn from the parking garage and filled her in. "We're going to celebrate tonight!" I declared. "Be ready in an hour, okay?"

"I'll be here waiting."

I slipped out of Edenville unnoticed and was enthusiastically greeted at the door by Dawn. I put my equipment case on the floor and asked, "Where should we go for dinner? Do you feel like steak, lobster or both?"

She took my hand and led me into the kitchen where a red and white checkered cloth covered the table and a bottle of white wine was set in an ice bucket. "When you called I was making my famous pasta primavera, using fresh local vegetables, of course, and figured eating in would be much more enjoyable than going out to some overpriced restaurant. I hope that's okay."

I looked at her in amazement. "Seriously, why are you with me?" I asked as I sat in the chair Dawn had pulled out for me.

"That's one mystery you're never going to solve. Stop trying."

Possibly not the best listener in school or on the police force, I'd learned to appreciate that good things came my way when I listened to Dawn. The pasta dish and wine were fabulous and soon we moved to the living room couch to relax before dessert. Although clearly very happy for me, throughout our dinner conversation Dawn hadn't quite sounded as excited as I thought she'd be. "What's wrong?" I asked as she stretched out beside me, her head on my legs, her face looking upward into mine. "The case is solved."

"Lucy and George's cases are solved and I couldn't be happier, really. You've worked really hard on this file and got results no one else was able to get," she replied.

"But?"

"But it's not over-over until you find out who killed Joey Wad."

It's not as if I'd mentally swept Joey's death under the rug, although the idea was an appealing one. "What if Joey was killed for a completely unrelated reason? Maybe he was hitchhiking and something went sideways with the driver or other passengers and he was beaten to death in the washroom. Or one of his criminal buddies from the halfway house got into a fight with him over a deal that went bad?" I could tell by Dawn's frown that she wasn't interested in my very realistic (or so I thought) reasons.

"Or someone found out he was Lucy's killer and went all biblical eye-for-an-eye on him," she said, raising her eyebrows for effect.

"C'mon, until today no one had put the whole picture together," I said defending my superior investigative methods. "It's much more likely Joey died from a random act of violence, than someone figuring out his mother died 20 years earlier and he wanted to get revenge on those he felt were responsible. It's so twisted, I'm having a hard time believing it happened and I'm the one who confirmed it did."

Dawn sat up and moved to the corner of the couch. At first, I thought she was angry with me, which wasn't the case. "I get that. What I'm saying is, that whoever beat Joey to death didn't necessarily have to know his entire screwed up history, only that he killed Lucy and nothing more."

"Like if I see a guy covered in blood running away from a body in an alley, I *know* he's the killer . . . "

"Precisely."

" . . . without knowing *why* he killed."

"See, my example works."

"It does," I said, getting off the couch to pace the room. "What you're implying is that a mysterious vigilante somehow solved Lucy's murder, tracked Joey down and killed him, correct?"

"Sure," Dawn replied slowly. "The question is who would be in a position to connect Lucy to Joey? The only people to admit they knew what he looked like were those teachers, Wendy and Zoe, and I doubt they formed a tag team to beat him to a pulp. When you take them out of the equation, who do we have left?" Getting no immediate response from me, Dawn said, "I suppose almost anyone could have solved the case under the right circumstances."

"Like what right circumstances?" I asked, half lost in my own conflicted thoughts.

Dawn picked up a small pillow and hugged it against her stomach. "What about at a bar? Joey has one too many and confesses to a total stranger, who then decides to take matters into his own hands, literally." Dawn stopped and looked toward me. "I guess you're right, there really are too many possibilities to investigate. Maybe the eye-for-an-eye thing really was justice served in this case, because we're never going to find out how Joey was exposed in the first place."

"The diary," I said, my voice faltering. "The diary makes sense."

"The one hidden in the halfway house floor? Do you think another boarder read it and killed Joey after Lucy was murdered?"

"Not Joey Wad's diary, Lucy's diary!" Goosebumps appeared on my arms and a shiver rolled down my spine. "Debra told me it's been missing since the night of the murder." I took a deep breath as another tumbler crashed into place. "What if Joey didn't take it with him when he escaped into the night? I've been assuming the killer grabbed it because it contained information about his identity, which it did. Lucy had been writing in her diaries since she was 13. She'd have written everything in it, like Joey's name, background, his family and his job."

"Then when the person who found it realized they had all the pertinent information they needed to find Joey, they snuck it out of the house," Dawn speculated, as she also got off the couch to aimlessly pace with me. "But why not hand it over to the police who were right there?"

"Maybe the police already had it. Maybe one specific officer held onto it for safekeeping. Maybe the very same high-ranking detective went out to avenge his college sweetheart's sorrow at losing her only daughter to a madman."

"What if Debra found the diary and gave it to Rodney?" Dawn asked. A shocked expression came over her strained features. "Steve, what if they were in it together, plotting to hunt down and kill Joey on their own?"

Frustrated, I began furiously running my fingers through my hair. "That's ludicrous, isn't it? Rodney could have easily solved the case and still gone out the local hero. Which brings us all the way back to the beginning of this insane saga. Why send an innocent man to jail if you knew who the real killer was?"

"They needed a scapegoat and Eric McDowell fit the bill perfectly," Dawn offered as we both sat back down on the couch, mentally exhausted. "Maybe they became so focused on tracking down Joey, they didn't notice that Lucy's lying, cheating bastard husband had a real shot at being convicted. Once Joey was dead, they could've decided it was too risky to present another suspect, possibly implicating themselves in his death."

"Man, my brain hurts," I said. "Yours?"

"The same. I don't think the wine is helping either," Dawn said, a tiny smile parting her lips.

We rested our aching heads on the back couch cushion and

closed our eyes, deep in contemplation for several minutes. At one point, Dawn placed her hand in mine and gave it a squeeze, reminding me that life was pretty good, regardless how this case would ultimately turn out. I had once told a newspaper reporter that I only collected the data, wrote up my report and added, 'What the lawyers or private clients do with my findings is up to them.'

"You said we had to go back to the beginning of this insane saga," Dawn said. "By that you meant Eric's wrongful conviction, right?"

"Correct," I replied, my eyes still comfortably closed. "That's where everything begins and ends."

Dawn slightly tightened her grip as she said, "But the true beginning started 20 years ago when a little boy was orphaned and grew up plotting revenge against his mother's so-called killers."

"Yes, that's all true, at least from what I've been able to cobble together," I replied, an uneasy pain starting to form in my chest.

"So why only Lucy?" Dawn wondered aloud. "Killing her takes care of Joey's revenge plan against Debra. A 'you-took-away-someone-I-loved-so-I-am-going-to-take-away-someone-you-love' scenario, which he appeared to have pulled off brilliantly. Lucy's dead and Debra grieves." Dawn paused to take in a few cleansing yoga-inspired breaths, which she was apt to practise when under a great deal of stress. It was her internal reset button.

I didn't dare move or open my eyes. I merely braced myself for whatever Dawn was building to in her own sweet loving way. *Keep your hands inside the car and remain seated at all times.*

"With Debra's life now ruined, Joey's next logical step would be to move onto Rodney, to take away someone he loved and destroy his life. Yet that didn't happen."

"That's because he was killed before he could carry it out," I whispered, trying not to sound condescending.

"That's where I think you're wrong," Dawn countered. "Malcolm read Joey's notebook and from what you told me, he said Joey had targeted Lucy in order to get retribution on those people he believed had killed his mother. He was planning a singular act of vengeance to take care of those responsible. Am I right about that?"

"Basically," I mumbled. "A single act to end the madness in his head. So what?"

Dawn sat up and turned her body toward mine, the movement causing my eyelids to open involuntarily to see what she was doing. With her free hand, she reached down to cover our clasped hands and then looked at me with the serenity usually reserved for monks and angels.

"For that scenario to work, Steve," she began slowly, "one fact, which Joey must have learned at some point, has to be present."

"Which would be?"

"Rodney was Lucy's father."

TWENTY SIX

Neither of us slept very well and we were both groggy when I dropped Dawn off at The Sunsetter for her morning shift.

"I want to be the first to know every new detail," Dawn playfully ordered as she exited the van.

"You will, dear," I replied submissively with a bow of my head. "Say hi to Dopey Doug for me."

"I will. Drive safe and watch your back in Dannenberg," she advised. "Do you know how you're going to confront Rodney and Debra yet?"

"I'm swinging by the *Echo* to have Melinda pull the articles about Sarah's accident and its aftermath. I want to know exactly what happened before seeing either of them."

The trick was how to get them together without involving a bus and a can of spray paint. To reveal Lucy's true killer and then to also expose Rodney as a killer to a group of paying tourists sounded wonderful, but too many things could go wrong. I wasn't interested in anyone else being placed in harm's way, especially me. Fortunately, I had a trump card I could play that would get their attention simultaneously: Sarah Rymal, dead college friend.

On the way to the *Echo's* Records room the elevator doors opened to let off riders on the newsroom floor. "It's nice to see you're still working here, Stacey," I called out. "Unlike some other people we know."

The startled copywriter looked up from her desk and flashed a smile. "Hey, I have to thank you," she said as the doors closed.

"I'll be down in a bit. Wait for me," I said. "Nice girl that Stacey, right?" I randomly asked the other three passengers, who were no doubt happy to see me get off on the next floor. "If it isn't my favourite archivist," I said as I walked toward Melinda's desk. "Have you toppled the corrupt mayor in today's edition?"

"Not yet, Cassidy, but if we uncover one more 'massage expense' he'll be done," Melinda replied. "I got your message this morning and printed off the articles you requested. Sorry about yesterday."

"It's all good," I said. "I didn't expect you to do all this for me. I really appreciate it though." I took the four copies from her. "Since we last talked, I learned more about the accident and the occupants of the car. Is there anything else of interest here I should concentrate on? I guess there was a bit of a scandal when no charges were laid against the driver."

"Rodney Dutton? Yeah, he and his lawyer father spun their story so many different ways you could have made ten quilts out of it," she laughed. "The surviving female was never in danger of being charged, except maybe with stupidity for dating that jerk."

They were more than just friends, I thought. Lucy was born a year after the accident, so the timeline worked out nicely. During their grieving period, Debra must have become pregnant and for some reason Rodney didn't marry her. That in itself would've caused the animosity they now shared. Not knowing any of the details, Dawn had also speculated that when Debra found out she was pregnant, they were no longer a couple and she chose not to tell Rodney. "I wouldn't want to be attached to a man I no longer loved for the next 20 years," she'd stated.

I sat at a nearby research table and read each article. Aside from Debra and Rodney's relationship status at the time of the crash, there wasn't much I didn't already know. It had been one stupid night that had changed their lives forever.

"Thank you for your help with this, Melinda," I said, preparing to leave. "I'm heading down to the newsroom to find a reporter who might want a scoop. I would have tapped Spanky for the job but . . . "

"But indeed," Melinda said. "You should try his replacement. She's eager to prove herself to the old cronies, plus from what I've heard, she's a big fan of yours."

"Stacey the copywriter?"

"Yep. She's our new Metro Beat reporter and doing a bang up job so far."

"No wonder she said she wanted to thank me," I smiled, heading to the elevator. "I thought it was for getting rid of Spanky for her."

"Oh, it is," Melinda confirmed. "If you need anything else, you know where to find me."

***

I was sitting in Stacey's desk chair when she returned from the photocopy room.

"I like your shiny new nameplate: Stacey Giles - Metro Beat. It has a nice ring to it," I said as I stood to allow her to sit down.

"Like I said before the elevator doors so rudely interrupted us, I want to thank you for the promotion," she said with a humble smile. "Technically, I should've got the job before but Spanky had one day of seniority over me and the union's a stickler for those things."

"I'm glad I could help you and the rest of the reporters out," I replied.

"What brings you back to the good old *Echo*?"

"I need a detached, unbiased evaluator of facts to help me catch a killer or two. Would you be up for the job or do I have to speak to your assignment editor?"

"You're kidding me, right? Did someone put you up to this?" came the cautious response. Realizing there'd be no further follow-up to my question, such as balloons or a camera crew, she said, "No, I don't have to get clearance to do a story within the Dannenberg region."

"Are you sure? I don't want to see you following Spanky to the other paper."

A worried look crossed her face, although only for a couple seconds. "Forget about the catching killers part. Give me a ten word description of what you're doing and I'll pitch it to my editor."

"Ten words, huh?" I looked off into space as if thinking intently. "What about this: Private Investigator looking into a local cold case mystery."

"That's only nine words."

"Oh, then why don't you add 'renowned' at the start of the sentence and you'll be fine," I said with a smile.

"Funny."

"I know."

"Give me five minutes."

Four minutes later, we were heading out of the building.

***

"I need a public setting and a photographer," I said handing Stacey the accident articles as we entered my van. "Do you think Robyn would be available to take some covert shots?"

"Let's find out," she said, pulling out her cell phone and calling our mutual friend. "Hey, Robyn, Stacey here. Do you remember that investigator looking into the bus accident?" . . . "Yeah, that's the one. Well, I'm in his van right now and we're heading to a stakeout, I think, and he's requested a shutterbug to take some pictures." Robyn turned to me. "She wants to know why a P.I. can't take his own pictures."

"Tell her because it's kind of hard taking covert photos when I'm wired to a recorder and talking with my subjects face to face."

"Did you hear that, Robyn?" . . . "Okay, she heard that. When and where do you want her?"

"Have her get ready and we'll call back in a few minutes," I said.

Stacey relayed my message and hung up the phone. "I'm thinking The Navy Yard Park is as good as any to conduct your meeting. It's wide open, not too busy and with plenty of spots for Robyn to set up without bringing attention to herself."

"Near the bookstore and ice cream parlour. I know the area," I said, recalling the post mystery bus tour excursion. "And the parking is good, too."

"Why's that important?"

"Because I like to have a back-up audio system, in case my body microphone and recorder fail me. I figured you could aim a directional microphone out the van's window to tape my conversation. That way you can listen as everything goes down."

"This is the coolest day of my journalistic life," Stacey said, looking like I'd offered her a backstage pass to meet Bon Jovi. "If there's trouble, do you have a 'safe word' or whatever they call it, so I can call the cops?"

"Harder."

"That's not a very good safe word."

I began to laugh. "It is if you're with the right person. Trust me."

After much discussion, the new safe word was changed to 'Chewbacca,' Han Solo's hairy sidekick from the *Star Wars* movies, as it was a name that didn't pop up in everyday conversation and wouldn't be mistaken once uttered. I found an excellent parking spot under a tree, not far from the stand-alone gazebo, which would be perfect for what I had in mind.

I dug out a file folder from my equipment bag and handed Stacey an overview of the case I'd written up the previous night with Dawn. "Here's some background information for your article, if we get that far. I'm going to call my subjects and set up the meeting. While I'm doing that, call Robyn and tell her about the gazebo."

"Okay," she replied, beginning to scan the notes.

I proceeded to a park bench, made myself comfortable and dialed Rodney's number.

"Tour of True Terror, this is Rodney. How can I help you?"

"Rodney Dutton, I don't know if you remember me. My name is Steve Cassidy and I'm looking into the murder conviction of Eric McDowell, a case I know you remain deeply involved in."

"Stop wasting everyone's time," he spat, his sunny, friendly tone gone.

"If someone doesn't agree with your view are they wasting everyone's time as well? What about poor George Mulhall? Was he wasting time trying to find evidence that would set his client free?"

"He was wasting his own time, *that* I know," a more confident and smug Rodney replied. "He was running down an idiotic dream out there in Edenville. Unfortunately, the bus ran him down first."

I didn't hear an actual laugh, snicker or titter from Rodney, but I knew he was smiling so wide his mouth would hurt in the morning. What the ignorant fool hadn't realized was he'd just established that he knew why George was in Edenville. I was always perplexed about how Rodney had found out about George's diary quest. "And how would you know that, Rodney?" I asked.

"Because he called me, bragging about this great lead that was going to change everything! He couldn't help himself with stuff like that. Sadly, over the past six years, none of his evidence materialized."

"And what was he tracking down this time? The murder weapon?" I asked, needing to have Rodney state something definitive about the diary.

"Some stupid diary or notebook," came the response. *Thank you.*

"Of the killer?"

"Who knows," Rodney said dismissively, believing he was in total control of the conversation. "Maybe it was the written thoughts of a drycleaner remembering getting blood stains out of a pair of pants the night after Lucy died."

The callousness and outright lies of these statements was hard to take. The man was in complete denial of his sordid part in George's death three months ago, and possibly of Joey Wad's six years earlier. He had retired with a sense of invincibility and it had only grown over time. Now it was my turn to be cruel and insensitive.

"Or the ramblings of Sarah Rymal's troubled son. You remember her, right?" The silence on the other end of the line assured me Rodney was no longer smiling. This, of course, caused me to grin joyfully.

"You don't know what you're talking about, Cassidy," Rodney said in a jagged voice. "And how dare you bring up Sarah's name. You're the worst kind of investigator there is and your reputation proves me out."

"Luckily for me, these days my reputation is that I unmask killers long after they thought they got away with their perfect crime, Rodney."

"If that's the case, you needn't look any further than Sellcan Correctional," Rodney replied, his angry voice rising with each word. "Eric McDowell killed his wife. He was convicted of that crime and no one, especially the likes of you, is ever going to change that."

I felt it was time to unleash my best 1-2 punch combination.

"That's not what your godson Travis implied the last time we spoke on the side of a road." I waited a long beat before adding, "Nor what Joseph Waddell's diary clearly indicates took place that night. If you want to discuss this matter further, meet me at the Navy Yard Park gazebo at 11:00 a.m. Don't even think of bringing company, as the gazebo will be crowded enough."

"What's that supposed to mean?" Rodney asked, fear and suspicion in his voice.

"It means, tick tock. You have an hour to appear. See you soon."

***

I looked up and noticed Stacey watching me from the van. She gave me the okay sign and I gave her the hand sign for five minutes, as I dialed my next number.

"Hi Debra, Steve Cassidy here. How are you doing today?"

"Steve, I'm doing fine," she replied. "Do you have news or just checking up on me?"

"A bit of both," I answered cheerfully. "I was wondering if you could meet me at the Navy Yard Park gazebo at 11:00 to talk? It's a beautiful day and I thought afterward we could grab something at the *Book A Lunch* store again."

"Oh, well, I guess I can. I didn't have any lunch plans and it is a nice day to walk by the water."

"Fantastic," I replied. "I'll see you soon."

I returned to the van feeling bad about lying to Debra. Going mano-a-mano with Rodney had been fun, but I just couldn't believe Debra had any role in Joey Wad's death, or George's tragic transit mishap. However, years of experience had tempered my resolve not to let emotions get in the way of the facts. Debra had clearly misled me about her relationship with Rodney. If I was wrong about Lucy being their daughter, everything regarding the diary's contents would be moot.

"Call Robyn again," I said to Stacey. "As you heard, the meeting is at 11:00 and she needs to focus on the man and woman I'll be speaking to. Tell her to take plenty of pictures when they arrive, because I don't think they'll be sticking around long."

By 10:50, I was ready to rock and roll and made my way down the path to the gazebo, where I stood awaiting my prey. I glanced around the park in search of 'men in black' types, snipers (not of the photographic kind) and anyone with young children out for a stroll.

As I'd expected, Rodney was the first to arrive, making a beeline to me. "I spoke with Travis and he said he doesn't know what you're talking about," he proclaimed in a self-assured tone. "That diary never existed, George found that out. At least he died trying. What are you willing to do for it?"

"For your non-existent diary, nothing, I suppose," I answered, "but for the actual diary, well, that's another story."

"Rodney, what are you doing here?"

I was so focused on Rodney's stern face, I hadn't seen Debra approaching.

Rodney also did a double take. "Debra?"

"Now that we've all been reacquainted, I want to tell you why I've brought us together today," I said, not intending on losing the shock momentum.

"You really are out of your mind," Rodney responded, pushing me in the chest and taking a step toward the stairs. "Get out of here before he fills your head with lies, Debra." He stopped and turned to look at her. For the first time, I saw genuine alarm on his face. "We have our differences, Debra, but this man is a disgraced police officer with a slimy track record. I assume he's already spent most of your money by now." He gave me a withering glance. "There's nothing new he can tell us about Lucy's murder. Eric McDowell killed her. End of story. Lucy is never coming back. I beg of you, please, just let your daughter rest in peace."

"Don't you mean *our* daughter?" I cut in. This declaration was either going to be the high point of my investigation or the absolute lowest of the low. By Debra's traumatized expression and Rodney's gaping mouth, I was certain I was about to burst into flames, and rightfully so.

"How did you know?" Debra began, before Rodney stepped

forward and glared at her.

"She means, how dare you make such an accusation?" Rodney demanded.

"An accusation? Is that what you call your dead love child, Rodney?" I countered as Debra broke into tears and had to steady herself against the railing.

As with our confrontation at my house, Rodney attempted to punch me in the face with a left hook but lost his balance as I counteracted his movements, guiding him past my side and against the opposite railing.

"I never told a soul," Debra cried, her tear-stained face looking squarely in Rodney's direction. "No one, I swear."

"You damn well did at some point, Debra!" Rodney yelled at her. "I've lived with that secret since the day you told me you were pregnant and tried to ruin my life."

"Lucy was your baby and you knew it," Debra shouted. "I didn't try to ruin your life, I was trying to bring a new one into the world with your help. I still don't think that was so wrong, regardless what your father thought back then. I ruined your life? You really are delusional!"

"I did what I thought was right at the time. We were young. I had plans. You had plans. We could have *taken care of* the pregnancy."

With these wonderfully inspired arguments, it was clear this was a battle Rodney was never going to win, place or show. His insensitive outbursts cut through Debra like a sword.

"How dare you speak of her as if she never existed," she shot back, her entire frame now shaking uncontrollably. "And to think I loved you once. I wish I had left with the money your parents offered me and never looked back."

This time it was Rodney who was floored.

"They did what?" he blubbered.

"They were going to give me $10,000 to get out of Dannenberg, so their precious son could establish himself as an officer or lawyer," Debra replied. "But I said, 'He still loves me, I know he does.' Oh, were we ever young and stupid back then."

"I never knew about that, I swear."

"I don't care, Rodney. After you abandoned us, Lucy and I did just fine on our own." Debra tried to calm down. "And then you came riding back into our lives 20 years later, casting yourself as some electrifying white knight to save the day, only to fail miserably when you arrested Eric." She stopped and pointed a finger at him. "You knew he was innocent. We didn't need you to screw up our lives again!" Debra surprised me by brushing past and getting to the pathway before Rodney spoke up.

"I didn't fail, you miserable, crazy old bag. I had that man who murdered *our* daughter killed! I did what I could to make it right. Feel free to thank me anytime!"

Even though he was directing this appeal to Debra, I figured 'anytime' meant 'now', and I silently thought, *Thank you, Rodney . . . again.*

Debra came to an abrupt halt and spun on her heels. "You did what?" Her pleading, saucer-wide eyes gravitated to me. "Is Eric dead? Is that the news you wanted to tell me today, Steve?"

I raced down the steps in time to catch her petite frame as she fainted straight away. Rodney was a step behind me and helped lay her down on the grass.

"She has a bad heart. Call an ambulance!" he began to scream at me and anyone else within hearing distance. He took her hand and started to cry. "You can't die without knowing the truth. Eric is alive, Debra, you've got to believe me. Please wake up. He didn't kill Lucy, Sarah's son did, as revenge for what we did that night in college. Eric's innocent. He's alive and innocent. I didn't have him killed, I swear on my life."

I quickly glanced to the van, where Stacey sported a huge smile. To our left, Robyn was out of hiding and rapidly snapping pictures, as a number of park visitors jogged to our spot.

One last nail is needed to close this coffin for good, I thought.

"Your partner Lawrence Ingles is going down for Joey Wad's murder, you know that, right? I'll make sure of it. He'll lose everything," I said to the weeping ex-detective.

The tears temporarily stopped flowing down his cheeks, as if I had slapped him hard across the face. "Lawrence had nothing to do with that! It was Travis who beat that kid up, not my partner!" From his crouched position, Rodney leapt forward at my knees, tackling me backwards against the iron handrail and then to the ground. "You leave Lawrence and his family out of this! He knew nothing about it!" he screamed repeatedly, his spittle flying in my face. He landed one nice jab to my right cheek before the crowd of helpers pulled him off my chest.

In my semi-conscious state, I began calling out, "Chewbacca! Chewbacca! Chewbacca, already! Stacey, call 911!"

Rodney had been subdued beside the gazebo by two muscular men, although the fight had left him.

It was finally over.

Almost.

In all the commotion, I hadn't noticed that Debra was sitting upright with her legs crossed in a yoga lotus position. She was calm and no longer appeared to be breathing heavily or in any physical distress whatsoever.

With a satisfying smile, she looked at me and said, "It's interesting Rodney remembered I have a bad heart, but forgot I majored in the performing arts when I returned to college after Lucy was born," she said. "I knew one day it would come in handy and today was that day."

EPILOGUE

Cases as complicated as this never end smoothly, no matter how much audio tape is recorded or physical evidence is gathered. I felt I'd laid out a very reasonable explanation for Lucy, Joey and George's untimely deaths for the police detectives and county prosecutor. There was, of course, a considerable push-back against the alleged facts by Rodney's defense team. "Mr. Dutton was afraid for his life and felt threatened by Private Investigator Steve Cassidy, a known disgraced former police officer. Our client cannot be held responsible for the so-called confession he uttered while under duress."

After a week-long series of superbly written articles by Stacey, accompanied by Robyn's pictures, the public response was leaning heavily in favour of my version of events, which was the only compliment I was expecting to get.

On the day after the memorable Navy Yard Park takedown, I received a call from Walter to congratulate me, as well as pass along some disturbing news.

"The Handleman's bartender stopped in this morning. I guess he recognized my uniform when we were there for lunch. Anyway, he told me Malcolm was found in his apartment barely alive and is in the hospital, but it's touch and go."

"What happened?" I asked, shaken by this development.

"He was beaten with a lead pipe and baseball bat," Walter replied. "Two thugs, one who likes to wear cowboy boots. Sound familiar?"

"This was about the diary. They must have figured out it

wasn't burned in the house fire," I stated as my stomach began to turn. "Please tell me Crawford wasn't the investigating officer."

"As luck would have it . . . "

"You've got to be kidding me! How many lives does that man have left?"

It turned out the answer was one.

As a result of Rodney's gazebo confession that his godson had beaten and killed Joey Wad prior to joining the Edenville Police, an internal investigation was quietly started. When super-thugs Carl and Tom were caught breaking into a television store, they revealed themselves to be smarter than they looked and immediately asked to speak to a rep from the prosecutor's office. Later that afternoon, Constable Travis Crawford was arrested for his part in the murder of George Mulhall, with more assault-related charges pending further investigation. Joey Wad's murder investigation was also re-opened.

The mystery of the missing diaries was solved in two very different ways. During questioning by a current Dannenberg Police Detective, former partner Lawrence Ingles recalled Rodney showing him Lucy's diary on the night of her killing. "After reading it he told me, 'Nothing in there except a bunch of girl stuff,' and that was the end of it. I assumed he signed it into the evidence room."

He hadn't.

Joey Wad's diary, or at least parts of it, were discovered in a very unusual place.

"Hi, is this Steve Cassidy, the private investigator?" a nervous young woman asked over the phone. "You gave my friend Gillian one of your business cards the last time you were in the store."

It took me a second to recognize the name. "The Biz Emporium in The Galleria?"

"Yes," she said with relief. "My name is Chelsey and I run the Copy Centre. I was off the day you were in asking about the cameras in the ceiling."

"I thought one of them might have recorded what my friend was copying a few months earlier," I said, having no idea where this conversation was heading. "Are you calling about that or is there something you need me to investigate?"

"No, it's about your friend's copies. Do you still need them? You see, I can print them off for you, but it has to be done today. They're replacing the machine for a newer model in the morning."

"And how's that possible?" I asked, flabbergasted at the thought of being able to read Joey's diary entries.

"Oh, because the photocopier is digital and stores every image it scans onto a hard drive," came Chelsey's reply. "Yesterday I was talking with a repairman who happened to mention that and I thought of you. He showed me where the USB port is and everything. If you want, I can download the files. I'll put the copies in an envelope and keep them here until you pick them up, if that's okay?" Getting no immediate response, she asked, "Mr. Cassidy, are you still there?"

I was lost in a daze, realizing now why I'd been staring at the porn printing printer in the security office.

"The tech said that the machine's internal memory stores any page or image sent to it and then prints it off."

To save time, Walter supervised the printing of the diary files and I had him email them to me.

"I can see why George thought the diary was so important for Eric's appeal," Dawn said as we read the pages together at the kitchen table. "This Joey Wad guy was seriously angry at Debra and Rodney for killing his mom and ruining his childhood."

"Childhood and beyond," I said, reading a section about how Joey would leave little messages on Lucy's car windshield at her school, as part of his plan to get her to lower her guard.

"I think you need to read this one," Dawn said as she handed me a page. "This answers how Joey learned that Debra and Rodney were Lucy's parents."

Both had adamantly denied telling anyone of their secret creation, although Rodney's parents obviously knew, but probably didn't advertise the fact to their snooty friends.

> Rachel McKellen stopped by again. She made us dinner and said I should get out more. "Your mother used to like playing tennis," she said. That made me mad. I asked, "Why don't you have any kids of your own to bother?" and she said, "After what happened to Sarah, I didn't want to risk leaving a child behind if I died suddenly." She said she once talked about it to the girl who was in the car that night and found out the girl and the driver were going to have a baby. That made me even more mad. They got to have this happy family life together when I got nothing. It's not fair! I want to take away their baby like they took away my mom!!!!

After handing these pages over to the police, a few days later I gave them the entire notebook courtesy of Malcolm, who was recovering from his injuries at home. A short note inside the mailed package indicated he was sorry for lying about burning Joey's diary and wished he'd never found it. Taped to the front of the notebook was the mystery ring. "I was going to bring it to The Handleman that day, when Constable Crawford and his boys delayed me. I don't know if it belongs to Lucy, but I have no use for either of these items. No payment required."

I met Debra for our belated *Book A Lunch* get together and slid the ring across the table.

"This was found alongside Joey Waddell's diary. Could it be Lucy's? If so, you should have it."

A strange expression came over Debra's face as she examined the ring. "It's not hers," she finally said, "but it was Sarah Rymal's. She used to wear it all the time in college." Debra pushed the ring back to me. "I loved Sarah dearly, but I don't want to keep that because it helped fuel the rage within her son over the years to kill my Lucy."

I said I understood and placed it back in my pocket. Not sure what to do with the orphaned ring, Dawn suggested I contact Rachel McKellen. "I think she'd really appreciate having something that Sarah owned from the good old days."

And she did.

***

"I got a message from Debra today," I said as I carried Dawn's suitcase to the van. "In light of the new diary revelations and Travis' unexpected confession to killing Joey Wad on Rodney's orders, she expects Eric's conviction to be set aside soon."

"All because of you," Dawn said, stopping in the driveway to give me a congratulatory kiss.

"And this trip is all because of her," I said. "Refusing to take back any of the leftover retainer money is getting us to Italy for the next two weeks."

"Not just Italy, Tuscany!" Dawn called out jubilantly. "I can't wait to get there. You/me/us/this, sipping espresso from tiny cups at a street café, eating tiramisu for dessert. Then there are those cooking classes we're doing together! It's going to be the greatest trip you've ever taken."

"If it's with you, I know it won't be dull," I replied. "Do you have everything?"

"I think so."

I locked the front door of the house and got into the van. "For this getaway can we just have fun and not get involved in a local mystery?" I asked, putting on my seatbelt.

"I'll be on my best behaviour the entire trip," Dawn replied with a devilish smile.

"That doesn't sound like much fun."

"For you maybe."

On the way to the airport, we passed The Sunsetter and I inquired, "What's the story with Doug's love life these days?"

"He's such an idiot," Dawn scoffed. "He's going around telling everyone that he was the one who broke up with April."

"What's wrong with that?"

"Really?"

"Sure. When you break up with me, I'm going to claim it was my idea."

Dawn started to laugh. "Like anyone would believe that. You totally adore me and would so miss me if I was gone."

"That is true," I confessed.

She pondered this idea for a moment. "Yeah, I'm definitely going to be the one who ends this craziness sometime in the future."

Turning onto the highway, I looked into Dawn's beautiful, smiling face and said, "I know. But don't worry, I can wait."

The End

Praise for the
STEVE CASSIDY MYSTERY Series

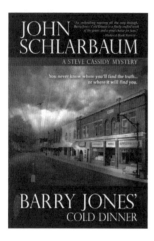

"An enthralling mystery all the way through. *Barry Jones' Cold Dinner* is a finely crafted work of the genre and a great choice for fans."
– THE MIDWEST BOOK REVIEW –

"*Barry Jones' Cold Dinner* has sturdy traditional crime bones. Schlarbaum isn't lacking in wit or an attractive protagonist."
– SUN MEDIA –

After kissing his wife and boys goodbye, Barry Jones departed his small town and headed to work in the city. He never arrived. Now seven years later, his wife wants the courts to declare her husband dead once and for all. Enter P.I. Steve Cassidy.

"Schlarbaum masterfully creates a mystery where the only thing more intriguing than the plot is the development of Steve Cassidy's character."
- ALAN COOMBS, ASTRAL MEDIA RADIO –

"An entertaining mystery which draws on the elements of humour, romance, and hard-boiled investigation, *When Angels Fail to Fly* is a mystery that'll keep readers reading."
– THE MIDWEST BOOK REVIEW –

When strange events happen to Steve Cassidy's loved ones, the police, the press and his friends start questioning his every move. To complicate his life further, a cryptic telephone call begins a new investigation into the bizarre death of a woman keeping a secret.

For more info, videos and to order: www.scannerpublishing.com

Praise for
A MEMORABLE MURDER
A JENNIFER MALONE MYSTERY

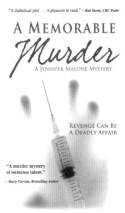

"This is a murder mystery of immense talent. Once you finish with this book, you will want to read everything else by this writer."
~ **MARTY GERVAIS,**
Bestselling author of *The Rumrunners*

"A diabolical plot, well drawn characters and written in a quick and quick witted narrative."
~ **BOB STEELE - CBC Radio**

The characters are a perfect marriage of dark humour, and likability making this a pleasure to read". ~ **ALAN COOMBS - Astral Radio - CJBK London**

Schlarbaum has crafted a richly layered mystery with lots of unexpected twists and turns."
~ **ANNETTE HAMM, anchor and former crime reporter - CHCH TV**

On a cool October morning, viewers are transfixed to their television sets for details of a gangland-style murder carried out during the live broadcast of *The Nation Today*. Upon identifying the dead man as Robert Barker, CEO of the country's largest pharmaceutical company, the police quickly discover clues indicating the killer is none other than his wife, Lynn, who has mysteriously disappeared.

While authorities attempt to locate Mrs. Barker, intrepid newspaper reporter Jennifer Malone uncovers information the shooting is related to a new memory wonder drug. Yet, the harder she digs, the more twists and turns she unearths. As her leads turn into revelations, Jennifer learns Lynn Barker is the only person who has the answers connected to the shooting. Unfortunately, she is nowhere to be found.

A Memorable Murder is a story of greed, revenge, political cover-up, and a country's insatiable appetite for tabloid worthy news stories.

For more info, videos and to order: www.scannerpublishing.com

Praise for
JOHN SCHLARBAUM'S
Inspirational Books

The Doctor's Bag: A Sentimental Journey is the heartwarming tale of the life of Thomas Sterling and his son Robert. Readers will become enthralled with *The Doctor's Bag* as the intimate story between father and son unfolds, giving new meaning to the actual doctor's bag itself. As the doctor's bag acts as the metaphor between healing and pain from year to year, *The Doctor's Bag* leaves the reader with an enlightening message of life, love and hope. *The Doctor's Bag* is strongly recommended to the general reader and those searching for a gentle, touching, and life changing read.

Aging Gracefully Together: A Story of Love and Marriage is an intimate auto-biographical account of one couple's undying love from the time of their engagement through their fifty years of domestic partnership. Captivating readers from first page to last, the story of Henry and Tina Cole's hopes, dreams, joys, heartaches, struggles and triumphs is an inspiring story of love and marriage. *Aging Gracefully Together* showcases a thoughtful and caring relationship and is very highly recommended reading - especially for those who are themselves about to embark upon a lifetime matrimonial journey together.

– THE MIDWEST BOOK REVIEW –

For more info, videos and to order: www.scannerpublishing.com

About The Author
JOHN SCHLARBAUM

John Schlarbaum was raised in the town of West Lorne, Ontario. He began his professional writing career working as a Writer and Field Director for several nationally syndicated television programs. He continues to work as a Private Investigator and is writing a murder mystery play, as well as his next novel.

NOW AND THEN